PRAISE FOR THE BESTSELLING

WINNER OF THE LEEDS BOOK AWARD 14-16 CATEGORY

"Heart-stopping romance." *Mizz*

"Wonderful, original." *The Sun*

"Packed with suspense and drama." *The Daily Mail*

"Fantastic...beautifully written." *Dark-Readers*

"Intricate plot twists, lots of action and adventure,
a great road trip and a swoon-worthy romance...will leave
you breathless." *Daisy Chain Book Reviews*

"Stunning...an awesome read."
Book Angel Booktopia for *Chicklish*

"Beautifully crafted, intense and creative paranormal romance...
Weatherly's writing is like a dream." *Painting with Words*

"This book blew me away. It's fresh, imaginative,
hugely entertaining and highly addictive." *Empire of Books*

"Incredibly hard to put down... If you only read one young
adult angel book, make sure it's *Angel*." *Jess Hearts Books*

"It's a sin to miss a book this good!" *Girls Without a Bookshelf*

L.A. WEATHERLY was born in Little Rock, Arkansas, USA. She now lives with her husband and their cat, Bernard, in Hampshire, England, where she spends her days – and nights! – writing.

L.A. Weatherly is the author of over thirty books, which have been published in over ten different languages.

www.leeweatherly.com
www.angelfever.com

ANGEL FIRE

ANGEL FIRE

L.A. WEATHERLY

USBORNE

To the memory of my mother,
Billie Cruce Seligman.
Mom, I wish you could have read this book.

First published in the UK in 2011 by Usborne Publishing Ltd., Usborne House, 83-85 Saffron Hill, London EC1N 8RT, England. www.usborne.com

Copyright © L.A. Weatherly, 2011

The right of L.A. Weatherly to be identified as the author of this work has been asserted by her in accordance with the Copyright, Designs and Patents Act, 1988.

Cover photograph of boy by Pawel Piatek.

Cover photograph of girl © Pawel Piatek/Trevillion Images

The name Usborne and the devices ♀ ⊕ are Trade Marks of Usborne Publishing Ltd.

A CIP catalogue record for this book is available from the British Library.

ISBN 9781409522010

PROLOGUE

IT TOOK THE WOMAN A long time to leave her house.

Across the street, Seb stood propped against a run-down grocery store, hidden in the dawn shadows as he watched the woman's front door. His high-cheekboned face had a light stubble on its jaw; his lean body was as simultaneously relaxed and alert as a cat's. He was sure this was the right place. It looked exactly like what he'd seen: a golden-yellow house on the main street, with a panelled wooden door, and a small wrought-iron balcony filled with flowering plants – a jumble of red and yellow. With his hands in his jeans pockets, Seb counted the front door's panels: ten. Then he counted the flowerpots: seventeen.

Come on, chiquita, *you're going to be late for work,* he thought.

The door opened at last and a small, round woman wearing a business suit came out. Fussily delving in her handbag for keys, she finally found them and locked the door behind her, then teetered to her car on plump feet that looked pinched in their high-heeled shoes. By the time she reached the car, she'd somehow lost her keys in her handbag again and had to stand on the sidewalk searching for almost a minute, shaking her head in irritation. Seb held back a smile. Yes, this all seemed very like her.

The moment the woman's car disappeared around the corner, Seb grabbed a battered knapsack that sat at his feet and slung it over his shoulder. He'd already checked out how to get to the back of the house; now he took a quick second to send his other self flying, making sure the way was clear. It was. He crossed the road, strolling through the early-morning silence. A tall wooden fence bordered the house on one side; Seb jumped to grasp the top of it, vaulting over easily. The back of the house was just like he'd seen, too – a tidy concrete courtyard, again filled lushly with potted plants. A faded deckchair stood folded near the sliding patio door.

The window with the broken lock that had been worrying the woman was up on the second floor. It took only seconds for Seb to scale the trellis and slide it open. He dropped silently into her bedroom – pale green, lots of ruffles. There was a smell of perfume, as if dousing herself had been the last thing she'd done before leaving.

And now she'd be gone for hours. Her job was so far away that she didn't have time to come home for lunch; it had been one of many niggling concerns on her mind the day before. The woman's thoughts had been like leaves in a whirlwind: none weighty in themselves, but the overall effect had left Seb with a headache from trying to focus on them. Psychic readings weren't always an easy way to pick up a few pesos, especially when all he wanted was to get them over with quickly, so he could buy something to eat and get back to the only thing that mattered to him. Even so, he hoped what he'd told the woman had helped. She definitely needed to relax more – though he was glad she hadn't decided to start doing it today.

Leaving the scented bedroom, Seb started searching, his steps echoing on the tiled floors. Though he rarely broke into houses any more, there'd been a time when he'd done it all too often, with much worse motives than now. Gently, he pushed open doors, peered into rooms. His face creased into a frown. She would *have* one, wouldn't she? He hadn't seen for sure; he'd just assumed. Then on the ground floor, he found it: a computer sitting on a desk in the corner.

Perfect. Seb swung himself into the chair and hit the *on* button. The local school with its computers the public could use was closed today, and he hadn't been able to get a bed at the hostel for the last few nights, where he might have borrowed someone's laptop. He entered a few words into the search engine, typing slowly. A list of options came up; he found the one he was looking for and selected it.

Diaz Orphanage, said the website's home page: *A haven for children.* Seb's lip curled. He'd seen many orphanages over the years; few could be described as "havens". But he'd only found out about this one yesterday, and he needed to check it – who knew, it might turn out to be the place where he'd finally find what he was looking for. His heart beat faster at the thought, though he was only all too aware by now how unlikely it was. Taking a piece of paper from the woman's desk, he carefully wrote down the address and stuck it in his knapsack; it was around a hundred miles to the east, in the foothills of the Sierra Madre.

Then, on impulse, he brought up a map of Mexico, gazing at its familiar shape and mentally tracing the lines he'd travelled up and down it for years now. He'd started in Mexico City and since then had rarely spent more than a few weeks in one place. Currently he was in Presora, not far from Hermosillo, with its white beaches and throngs of tourists. Presora was quieter, though; a smaller town that had still taken him days to search, checking out every person he passed on the street, entering every building he was able to, sending his other self into the ones he couldn't.

There'd been nothing. Nothing at all. It wasn't really surprising – in his whole life, Seb had never seen even a hint of what he hoped so much to find. But he had to keep trying. It was all he could do.

Enough of this; he'd gotten what he came for. He turned off the computer and stood up, swinging his bag over his shoulder – and then his glance fell on the woman's bookcase, and he was lost. He drifted over to it, squatting on his haunches as he gazed hungrily. A lot of the paperbacks didn't even look as if they'd been opened, and for a heartbeat Seb was tempted – he'd almost finished his current book, and didn't know when he'd next find a used bookstore to trade it for another one. He touched the cover of a thick historical novel. It would keep him going for a week.

But no. He hadn't broken in here to steal, even if in the past he wouldn't have thought twice. With a sigh, Seb straightened up.

As he started for the stairs he saw a hallway beside the kitchen, with a shower room visible. He hesitated, then went and looked inside. The white-tiled room was almost bare: just a hand towel and a bar of dusty-looking soap, as if the shower in here was rarely used. Which was probably true – the woman lived alone; the pristine pink bathroom he'd seen upstairs was the one with all her potions and powders in it. A mischievous smile began to tug at Seb's face. Okay, *this* he couldn't resist – he hadn't been able to get really clean in days. His clothes were cleaner than he was; it had been easier to find a laundromat in this town than a bed at the hostel.

He entered the small room, locking the door behind him. There was a tube of shower gel in his knapsack; he dug it out, then stripped off and took a long shower, relishing both the hot water and the privacy. Even after so many years, it still felt as if he could never take either for granted. His body was firm and toned; as he bathed, scars he barely noticed any more gleamed from his wet skin – some white with age, others newer, puckering redly. He hated not feeling clean almost more than anything; it felt wonderful to wash away the grime of the last few days.

Afterwards, Seb dried off as best he could with the hand towel and glanced in the mirror, scraping his wet hair back. It curled when he wore it too short, irritating him, and so he kept it slightly long, shoved away from his face. A loose curl or two always fell over his forehead anyway, just to torment him.

His jeans and T-shirt clung to him when he got dressed again, but the heat of the day would soon finish drying him off. He glanced around the shower room to make sure he'd left it the way he'd found it; then he jogged back up the stairs, eager to get going towards the Sierra Madre and the address in his knapsack. In the green and frilly bedroom, Seb paused at the window, glancing around him.

"*Gracias*," he murmured to the absent woman with a smile, and then nimbly swung himself out.

Hitch-hiking to the orphanage took a while; it sometimes did. Towards evening, a trucker was giving Seb a lift the final stretch of the way, talking non-stop about his girlfriend. Smoking a cigarette the man had given him, Seb sat leaning back against the vinyl seat of the cab with one sneakered foot resting on the dash, only half-listening as he savoured the familiar taste. He didn't often have the money these days to waste on cigarettes.

"And so I told her, *chiquita*, I'm not having this – I told you twice already. You have to *listen* to me when I talk to you. Take in what I'm actually saying, you know what I mean?" The trucker glanced at Seb for confirmation; he had a broad face, with heavy eyebrows.

"Yeah, you're right, man," said Seb, blowing out a

stream of smoke. "Good for you." He'd far rather be reading than listening to this crap; unfortunately there was a sort of etiquette involved with hitch-hiking. Making conversation was the price of the ride.

"But she never listens to me, does she? No, off in her own world, that one. Hopeless. Beautiful, but..." The man went on, talking and talking.

Seb watched him idly, noting the angry red lines that had appeared in his aura, like lightning flashes. When he'd first gotten into the cab, he'd shifted the colours of his own aura so that they matched the trucker's blue and yellow hues. He knew the man wouldn't be able to see them or tell; it was just a habit left over from childhood, when blending his aura in with those around him had made him feel safer. More hidden.

But the more Seb listened to this jerk, the more he really didn't want to share his aura. He shifted back to his natural colours as he got an image of the man standing in a kitchen shouting; a dark-haired woman looking frightened. Not exactly a surprise. The trucker didn't feel like he'd be a danger to Seb, though; he seemed strictly the type to bully those who were weaker. Seb knew he'd probably have sensed it if he had anything to worry about – and there was always the switchblade he carried in his pocket in case there was trouble. You didn't travel alone in Mexico without a weapon, unless you were terminally stupid.

"Now, take you for instance," the truck driver went on. "How old are you – seventeen, eighteen?"

"Seventeen," said Seb, blowing out another stream of smoke. He'd be eighteen in less than a month; he didn't bother volunteering that.

"Yeah, and I bet you don't have any trouble getting the girls, do you?" The man gave a guffawing laugh; his aura chuckled along with him, flickering orange. "You look like a rock star, with that face and stubble – like all the girls would have you up on their walls. But take my advice, *amigo*, never let them…"

Mentally rolling his eyes, Seb tuned out, wishing he could snap on the radio at least. People often commented on his looks, but looks couldn't get him the one thing he wanted.

"So where are you from?" asked the man finally, stubbing out his cigarette in the overflowing ashtray. "Sonora? Sinaloa?"

"*El DF*," said Seb. The *Distrito Federal*; Mexico City. It was almost dark now; the traffic heading towards them was a series of lights swooping out of the gloom. "My mother was from Sonora."

"Thought so," said the man, glancing at him again. "French, I bet. Or Italian."

Seb couldn't resist. "Italian," he said, keeping a straight face. "Venice, originally. My great-grandfather was a gondolier – then he immigrated here and there weren't any canals, so he became a *ranchero*."

The truck driver's eyes widened. "Really?"

"Yeah, sure," said Seb, leaning forward to tap the ash off his cigarette. "Over ten thousand head of cattle. But I think his heart was always with the canals, you know?" He could have gone on in this vein for some time, except the guy was such an idiot that it was too easy to be much fun.

The truck driver went back to the endless subject of his girlfriend, outlining her many failings and the ways in which she was going to have to improve. A few more flashes of the woman being bullied came to Seb as he droned on, so that by the time they reached Seb's destination and pulled over to the side of the road, he could have happily choked the guy. Instead, he filched the pack of cigarettes and lighter from the trucker's jacket pocket as they shook hands. He hadn't picked a pocket since he was a kid on the Mexico City streets, but it gave him a certain satisfaction – though really, he should let the *cabrón* keep smoking, since it was bad for your health.

As the truck pulled away, Seb gave himself a quick shake, freeing himself of the unpleasant energy like a dog shaking itself dry of water. He was almost in the Sierra Madre now, standing on a hill in the gathering dark with the shadowy hulk of mountains rising up from the horizon.

He focused briefly to make sure there weren't any angels nearby, then sent his other self searching. As he soared he found the orphanage easily; it was about half a mile down the road, a sprawling building with a barren-looking playground. He pulled on a sweater from his knapsack and started walking, letting his other self keep flying as he did. The feeling of stretching his wings was nice; it had been a few days since he'd flown any distance.

Thinking of what he'd told the truck driver, Seb smiled slightly as he walked. Actually, where his mother had been from was almost the only thing Seb knew about her – she was dead now; the last time he'd seen her was when he was five years old. From the few memories he had, he knew that he looked a lot like her. Light chestnut-brown hair with a curl to it; high cheekbones and hazel eyes; a mouth that women sometimes called "beautiful", which made him inwardly roll his eyes even more. It was a distinctly northern face; Sonora was a state where European immigrants had mixed for generations. On the streets, *gringo* tourists were always assuming Seb was one of them and asking for directions in English – clueless to the fact that millions of Mexicans didn't look like the ones in westerns on TV.

As for his father, who knew? But Seb figured he couldn't have been unattractive. None of them were.

As he crested the hill, the orphanage came into view,

and he stood staring down at it for a moment, his grip tight on the strap of his knapsack. Now that he was here, he was almost afraid to look – the continuous hope, and then the inevitable let-down, was becoming so much harder to bear. Yet he had to go through with it. The last hour of his life stuck listening to that *cabrón* in the truck would have been completely wasted if he didn't do what he'd come for. And besides, this might be the place. This really might be the place where he finally found her.

Despite himself, Seb felt a stab of anticipation so sharp it was almost painful – the hope that he couldn't ever totally quench. He left the road and lay down flat in the grass on his stomach, with the orphanage in view below. Concentrating solely on his other self, he closed his eyes.

He glided down the valley towards the run-down building, his wide wings glinting in the dusk. With barely a ripple, he passed through a wall of the orphanage and flew inside. As usual, his muscles tensed to be entering one of these places. Unwanted, the memory of the room came, with its total darkness that had pressed down on his five-year-old self like a weight. But the room had turned out to be a blessing in disguise – because it was there that he'd first realized what he really was. It was the only thing that had kept him from going insane in that place.

No one saw Seb's other self as he glided noiselessly from room to room. He saw immediately that this orphanage was one of the few that weren't too bad – it was clean, if depressingly bare. And the auras of the children and teenagers looked healthy enough, once he found them all sitting in a dining room eating their dinners with the staff; they showed signs of boredom, rather than abuse. Circling overhead, Seb scanned them, noting all the colours. A dull blue, a flicker of lively pink, a gentle green. None had even a hint of silver, but that didn't necessarily mean anything; he'd been shifting his own aura since he was a child. As he focused on each one, he opened his senses, checking out the feel of the energy – *listening* almost. His whole being craned with anticipation as he touched each person's energy with his own. They were all completely human.

He checked again, just to make sure, but his heart had gone out of it. Then he forced himself to explore the other rooms, though he knew already that he wouldn't find anyone else in them, and he didn't.

She wasn't here, either.

The disappointment tightened his throat like someone was standing on it. Opening his eyes, Seb brought his other self out of the orphanage and lay motionless, still gazing down at the stark building below.

She. He snorted slightly. He didn't even know if there *were* any others of his kind, much less what sex they might be. Yet somehow he'd always known it was a girl around his own age he was looking for. He could feel her so strongly.

Even though he had no idea of her name or what she looked like, he knew *her*. For as long as he could remember, Seb had had a sense of the girl's spirit; who she was. He thought he could almost hear her laugh sometimes; catch glimpses of her smile. Not being able to actually see her, or touch her, was a constant ache inside of him.

Roughly, Seb pushed his hair back with both hands. Why wasn't he used to the disappointment of not finding her by now? How many cities had he searched? How many orphanages and schools; how many miles spent walking how many streets? Suddenly he felt tired – so tired. Somehow this latest failure felt like the last straw.

It's never going to happen, thought Seb. *I've only imagined her all these years, because I wanted so much for it to be true.*

Rolling over onto his back, he watched his angel self as it soared in the night sky, snowy wings outspread. For once, the sensation of flight didn't soothe him. He'd been searching for his half-angel girl for so long – first, for years on the streets of Mexico City after he'd run away from the orphanage, checking out every aura he passed. Then, when he was eleven, he'd been thrown into a young offenders' facility; he'd broken out at thirteen and soon after had started his quest in earnest, travelling up and down the country, searching every town, every city and village. *Everywhere*, for almost five years now, without encountering a single other aura like his own. Without once catching even a hint of her energy, except in his thoughts.

Above, Seb felt a cool wind whispering past his wings; the evening was quiet and peaceful. *Enough,* he told himself. The thought seemed to float into his mind of its own accord, but the moment it did he knew that it was true.

He couldn't do this any more; couldn't take the never-ending disappointment. If he'd never seen another like himself in all these years, in a country as populated as Mexico, then it was time he finally faced the truth – there were no others. No half-angel girl was going to miraculously appear to ease his loneliness, no matter how strongly he thought he sensed her. She didn't exist. She'd only been a figment of his imagination all this time; a beautiful phantom. By some bitter joke of nature he was alone – the only one of his kind – and it was time to just accept that and try to get on with the rest of his life, whatever that might bring.

The decision felt right. It also felt like something had just been ripped out of his chest, leaving a jagged hole that would never be filled. Seb lay on the soft grass, gazing upwards as his angel self flew, so effortlessly agile against the stars. And he knew that what he'd been thinking wasn't quite true – as long as he had this other part of himself, he would never be completely alone.

It only felt that way.

CHAPTER *One*

THE SCISSORS WERE COLD AGAINST my neck.

I stood in the bathroom of our motel room with my eyes shut, trying not to notice how much I hated the sound of each metallic *snip*, or the odd, awful feeling of lightness that was slowly spreading its way across my head. Even though I knew how much we needed to do this – of course I did; it had been my idea in the first place – that didn't mean I had to enjoy it. Alex wasn't enjoying it much, either. In fact, he probably hated this part most of all. But when I'd brought up the idea earlier that afternoon, he admitted he'd been thinking the same thing – and now the scissors didn't hesitate as he worked them. If I hadn't suggested this, he would have.

It was weird, though…both of us so eager to do something that neither of us actually wanted.

I heard Alex put the scissors down on the bathroom counter. "Okay, I think I'm done." He sounded uncertain. Dreading what I was about to see, I opened my eyes and stared at myself in the mirror.

My once-long hair was now short. Very short. I don't even know how to describe it. Sort of a pixie cut, maybe, if the pixies had gone berserk with the scissors. And more than that, it was no longer blonde – it was a deep reddish-gold that made me think of autumn and bonfires. I'd thought it might go better with my skin tone than brown, but now… I swallowed. In the mirror, my green eyes were wide and unsure.

I looked nothing like myself.

Alex was staring, too. "Wow," he said. "That…makes a big difference."

I wanted to blurt out, *You still think I'm beautiful, right?* I bit the words back. "Still being beautiful" was not the point – not that I'd ever really thought I was, anyway; it was Alex who thought that. But the important thing now was just staying alive. In the bedroom, I could still hear the newscast that had been playing non-stop ever since we'd turned on the TV: "*Police are searching urgently for the pair for questioning... Again, if you see them, do not approach them yourself, but call our special hotline... They are suspected to be armed and dangerous..."*

I knew without looking that they were showing my sophomore school photo again – and that it was probably on every Church of Angels website in the world by now. So to be honest, changing my most noticeable feature hadn't exactly been a tough decision. At least no one knew what Alex looked like. There was a police sketch, but it was laughably wrong: the security guard who'd been at the cathedral had remembered him as being about ten years older and fifty pounds heavier than he really was, bulging with muscle like a football player.

I couldn't take my eyes off the girl in the mirror. It was like a stranger had stolen my face. I reached for the red eyebrow pencil I'd asked Alex to buy and traced it over my eyebrows. The effect was much more dramatic than I would have expected. Before, I barely even noticed my eyebrows when I looked at myself. Now they seemed to jump right out at me.

This was me, now.

Feeling oddly shaken, I put down the pencil and ran my fingers through what was left of my hair. Half of it spiked up, the other half flopped down. Someone, somewhere, might pay good money for a haircut like this – like the type of runway model who'd wear a garbage-bag dress held together with safety pins, maybe.

"I'm glad you don't want to be a hairdresser," I said to Alex. "Because I don't think your work is very mainstream."

He smiled and touched the back of my neck; it felt weirdly vulnerable to have the skin there so exposed. "No one will recognize you, that's what's important," he said. "Christ, *I* almost wouldn't recognize you."

"Oh," I said. I didn't mean to sound quite so forlorn, but the thought of Alex not recognizing me was just... wrong.

Catching my look, he wrapped his arms around me from behind and drew me close against his chest. The top of my head came up just past his chin. "Hey," he said, his eyes meeting mine in the mirror. "We'll both get used to it. And you're still gorgeous; you know that, right? It's just different, that's all."

I let out a breath, relieved he hadn't stopped thinking that. Maybe it was petty, with everything else that was happening in the world – but so much had changed already, without changing how Alex viewed me, too. I wanted that to stay the same, for ever. "Thanks," I said.

He propped his chin on top of my head, looking amused. "Well, it's sort of a no-brainer. You'd be gorgeous if you shaved *all* your hair off."

I laughed. "Let's not test that one, okay? I think this

is radical enough for one day." I rested back against his chest, taking in his tousled dark hair and blue-grey eyes in the mirror. "Gorgeous" was actually the word I'd use to describe Alex, not me. It still gave me a tingle like Christmas morning sometimes, to realize this boy I was so much in love with felt the same way about me.

Meanwhile, my hair had not stopped being very short. Or very red. I kept getting mini jolts of surprise every time I saw myself, like my mind hadn't caught up with what had happened yet.

"I wish there was some kind of dye we could use on your aura, too," said Alex after a pause.

I nodded, rubbing his toned forearms. "I know. We'll just have to be really careful."

My aura – the energy force that surrounds every living thing – was silver and lavender; a distinct mix of angel and human. Any angel who spotted it would know instantly who I was: the only half-angel in the world, the one who'd tried to destroy them all. It was a risk that couldn't be avoided, though, unless we planned to go live in a cave somewhere.

"Anyway, hopefully people won't be trying to shoot me quite as often now," I said.

"That's the idea," he agreed. "Because, you know… I kind of want you to stick around for a while." His eyes flickered with memory, and I knew what he was thinking without trying, because I was thinking about the same thing. The worst day of both our lives: when he'd held me in his arms, just a day ago, and thought I had died. My arms tightened over his. The truth was, I *had* died. If Alex hadn't been there to bring me back, I wouldn't be here now.

"That's what I have in mind," I said softly. The crystal teardrop pendant he'd given me sparkled in the light. "Sticking around with you for a very, very long while."

"Deal," said Alex.

His head lowered in the mirror, and I shivered as his warm lips brushed my neck. Then he glanced up, listening, as a new voice came from the TV: a woman caller with a Southern twang to her voice. "She must be sick, that's all. But just because she's mentally ill doesn't mean she's not dangerous. Why, you can tell from that photo – there's just a deranged *look* in her eyes..."

Actually, my eyes looked more worried than anything else, just then. Alex and I went back into the bedroom, where the two news commentators on the screen were nodding gravely, agreeing that, yes, I must be deranged to have attempted an "act of terrorism" against the Church of Angels – which was what the media was calling my attempt to seal the gate between the angels' world and our own.

I sank onto the bed. The Church claimed I'd been trying to set off a bomb in the cathedral; that I hated the angels so much I'd planned to blow the whole place up, regardless of the thousands of worshippers there to witness the arrival of the Second Wave. Me, a deranged bomber. It would have been funny if Alex and I weren't in so much danger.

An image of the cathedral in Denver from the previous day appeared: its broad white dome and massive columns; its parking lot, choked with cars and people. And its high silver doors, standing open as countless angels streamed out. I'd seen the footage several times now; I still couldn't take my eyes off it. I watched in morbid fascination as the angels' wings flashed gold in the sunset, pouring out from the cathedral in an endless river of light and grace. In their ethereal form, angels weren't normally visible except to the humans they were feeding from, but they'd made an exception as the Second Wave invaded our world. They'd wanted to hear people's cheers, Nate had told us. The cattle, cheering their slaughterers.

The Second Wave and me were the big news of the day. Everyone on the planet seemed to be debating what this meant: whether the angel footage had been faked or not, what it meant for our world if it hadn't been. The news programme showed the same clips over and over, with the headline *Angelic Arrival* scrolling past at the bottom of the screen. Then, when they got tired of that, the commentators took more phone calls, from all across the country: people who'd seen the angels arriving; people who wished they'd seen the angels arriving; people who thought they'd seen *me*; people who wished they could see me so they could give me what I "deserved".

I sat watching tensely, still hardly able to believe that just six weeks ago, my life had been relatively normal – or at least as normal as possible, when you're psychic and like to fix cars. And then I'd done a reading for Beth Hartley, a girl in my high school back in Pawntucket, New York. I'd seen her joining the Church, becoming sick and listless. I'd tried to stop her, but hadn't been able to – and in the meantime, an angel named Paschar had foreseen that I was the one who'd destroy them all.

I sighed as I watched the angels flying across the screen. God, I wished he'd been right. I thought of my mother, sitting lost in her dreams, her mind forever destroyed by what Raziel – I hated calling the angel my *father*; he didn't deserve the word – had done to her. She wasn't the only one. Millions of people had been hurt just as badly by the angels. Millions more were probably being hurt by them right that second, while all the callers on TV exulted about angelic love.

Angelic love. The words left a bitter taste when you knew the angels were really here to feed off human energy, as if our world was their own private fish farm. And thanks to something called angel burn, they were seen as creatures of beauty and kindness, even as their victims' life energy crumpled under their touch. The result might be a mental illness like my mother had, or MS, or cancer, or almost any other debilitating disease you could name. Because when an angel fed from you, there were only two certainties: one, you'd be damaged for ever in some terrible, irrevocable way…and two, you'd worship the angels until the day you died.

I glanced at Alex sitting beside me, taking in the firm lines of his face; the dark eyelashes that framed his eyes; the mouth that begged to have my finger on it, tracing its outline. By the time Alex was barely sixteen, his entire family had been destroyed by angels. Now dozens more of his friends had been killed by them too.

The black *AK* tattoo on his left bicep didn't stand for "Alex Kylar" – it stood for Angel Killer.

Alex was the only AK left. The only person in the world who knew how to fight them. The thought of anything happening to him was like razors slicing my heart – and our plan to recruit and train new AKs wouldn't exactly keep us out of the line of fire. Part of me really did want us to go live in a cave – or up on a Tibetan mountaintop, or out in the middle of a swamp somewhere – *anyplace* that was remote and safe, so we could just be together without worrying, for ever.

But we didn't have a choice, and we both knew it. No

matter how we felt about each other, we had to do something about what was happening.

I leaned against Alex; he put his arm around me and drew me close. His jaw had tensed – the special number to call if you'd seen me was flashing on the screen again. "God, I'm tempted to just stay here for a few more days," he muttered. "No one would expect you to be holed up so close to Denver. We should wait until things have calmed down a little, so that—"

"Alex, wait," I broke in. Urgency had swept through me; suddenly I felt sick with tension. *The front desk,* I thought.

I could see it in my mind: the slightly battered counter where Alex and I had checked in the night before, both of us so tired we were reeling. It had been covered by a sheet of glass, with a motel map on display underneath it. There'd been an old-fashioned bell too, the kind with a little button on top for guests to ring for attention. The inane details beat through my head, feeling dark and ominous. I had to go there. *Now.*

Concern came over Alex's face. "Willow? What is it?"

"I'm fine, I just…need to go check something," I got out.

I could see him start to protest at the thought of me leaving the motel room; then he realized what I meant. "Yeah, okay," he said. "Be careful."

I nodded. And taking a deep breath, I went within, reaching for my angel.

She was there, waiting – a radiant winged version of myself; the halo-less angel who was part of me. Her wings were folded gracefully behind her back, and I saw that *her* hair was short too now, framing her serene face. My shoulders relaxed a little. Just being near her was a caress.

With a mental flick, I shifted my consciousness to hers and lifted out of my human form. My angel wings stretched wide; I passed through the motel roof with a shimmer, soaring up into the Colorado late afternoon. *Flying.* Even at a time like this, it gave me a stir of pleasure. I was still getting to know my angel self; for most of my life, I hadn't even known she was there.

The chill of November stroked my wings as I flew to the reception building. Another brief ripple as I glided through the wall – and then I saw the clerk from the night before, talking on the phone with one elbow propped on the front desk. He was staring at a TV that was on in the corner of the lobby.

On the screen, my school photo smiled back at him.

"Well, I couldn't say for certain, but…yeah, I'm pretty damn sure," he said. "They got in about ten last night, looking dead to the world; then this morning they asked the manager to have the room for another night. They're still in there now. Been there all day, as far as I know."

Fear clutched my throat. At least he didn't realize Alex had left for a while, to go buy the hair dye and scissors. I swooped down and landed; under my ethereal feet the carpet felt strange, insubstantial. Back in the motel room my human form still sat on the bed, with Alex's fingers linked tightly through mine.

"They're supposed to come down and pay for the extra night soon; you want I should hold them for you? Oh, okay…yeah, I see…"

Behind the desk, another clerk stood waiting with wide eyes. When the man hung up the phone, she said, "Well?"

"She said not to go near them; they're sending someone right out. There's a squad car coming now – it's just a few blocks away." He shook his head. "Man, wouldn't it be wild if it *was* them? Dangerous fugitives, holed up in a sleepy little place like Trinidad—"

I didn't hear the rest; I was already speeding back to our room in a flurry of wings. I found my human self again; merged. My eyes flew open. "The desk clerk from last night – he's recognized us," I burst out. "The police are on their way."

Alex swore as he lunged off the bed. "Okay, forget staying – we've got to get out of here, *now*." He undid his jeans to strap on his holster and pistol under his waistband; when they were securely hidden, he ducked into the bathroom and grabbed up the eye pencil and hair dye stuff, shoving it all in the shopping bag it had come in, along with the long strands of my hair that had fallen to the floor. He swiped a motel washcloth over all the surfaces, removing any sign of the dye, and stuffed that in the bag too.

Trying to stay calm, I fumbled for the black pumps that were the only shoes I had now. Then I heard what was being said on TV, and glanced up. My hands slowed and stilled.

"...a dramatic new development which has just been released from law enforcement officials in Pawntucket, New York. This was the scene last night on Nesbit Street, at the former home of suspected terrorist Willow Fields..."

Aunt Jo's house appeared on the screen. I heard a ragged gasp; realized from someplace far away it had come from me. I sat frozen, my mind unable to process what I was seeing.

The house where I had lived since I was nine years old was in flames.

There was no doubt, even with the trembling footage that looked like someone had taken it on their cellphone – it was Aunt Jo's run-down Victorian home, crackling and crumbling to the ground. Even the garden ornaments in the front yard were ablaze. I could just make out one of the gnomes, standing enveloped in flames like a weird fire spirit.

The picture changed to blackened ruins, with firemen picking through them. The entire second storey of the house was gone, with only dark, skeletal fingers sticking up here and there. I stared at a smudged piece of lavender wall. My bedroom.

"...cause unknown, though local police suspect vigilantes from the Church of Angels might be behind the blaze. Early reports indicate there were no survivors. The bodies of two women have been found in the ruins, thought to be Miranda and Joanna Fields, the mother and aunt of Willow Fields..."

On the TV screen were two body bags on stretchers, being carried out from the house's charred remains.

CHAPTER *Two*

I STARTED TO SHAKE AS the world thudded in my ears.
On the screen one of the firemen slipped on the rubble;
I stared wordlessly as the too-human-shaped bag shifted
on the stretcher.

"Willow!" Alex was crouching in front of me, his voice
almost harsh as he gripped my shoulders. "I'm sorry, but
if we don't get the hell out of here, it'll be us next.
Come *on!*"

Somehow I managed to nod. I couldn't breathe; my
entire body felt crushed by the weight of what I'd just seen.
Mom. *Mom.* I got up and took the small photo of myself

with the willow tree from where I'd placed it on the bedside table, shoving it numbly in my jeans pocket. It was all I had left from my old life now. Alex kept the TV on as he edged the door open, peering out. "It's clear," he whispered, half-turning and holding out his hand to me. "Don't look like we're in a hurry. But be ready to run."

No survivors, no survivors. The words beat through my skull as we walked to the parking lot, holding hands. The only people in sight were a couple unloading their things from a car; neither of them looked at us. As we reached the motorcycle, Alex handed me the helmet and shoved the plastic bag in the storage compartment. My fingers felt thick and clumsy as I worked the helmet's straps.

A police car was just coming down the street as we roared off in the other direction. I hardly noticed. I clung tightly to Alex; over and over, I kept seeing the two body bags. Had Mom come out of her dream world before it happened? Had she known what was going on? Oh please, no. The thought of her being scared and trapped, unable to get away, hurt so much I thought it might kill me. I huddled against Alex's back as the cold mountain air rushed past, keeping my eyes closed and trying not to throw up.

I'm not sure how much time passed; it could have been minutes or hours. But sometime later, once we'd crossed the state line into New Mexico, Alex turned off the highway and into a small town. When we came to a service station, he pulled in and parked the bike out of sight behind it. My legs felt stiff and unreal as I climbed off, as if I were a zombie just crawled from the grave.

Alex's face was tight with sympathy as he put his arm around my shoulders. "Come on, we've got to talk," he said. He steered me into the restroom.

Talk. The word seemed alien; I found myself turning it over for different possible meanings. I stood hugging myself as he locked the door behind us. Somewhere deep within, I could feel the tears waiting like a tidal wave. If I gave into them, they'd sweep me away, drown me for ever.

Alex's hair was ruffled from the wind as he turned to me; his hands gripped mine, feeling warm and strong. "Willow, listen," he said urgently. "The more I think about it, the more this doesn't make sense. I mean, yeah, the Church of Angels might want your mother dead, but why would they target your aunt, too? Everyone in Pawntucket knew that the two of you didn't get along, right?"

I shook my head, too shell-shocked to get where he was going with this. He was right, though. It was a small town, and Aunt Jo wasn't the type to keep her complaints to herself. Everybody had known how put-upon she felt having to support the two of us, even with the money I sometimes brought in from my psychic readings.

"Plus, your aunt believed what the Church said about you running off with a secret boyfriend, so why have her killed?" Alex went on. "It helps their story if she's around. And if the target was your mother, it would make more sense to just stick her in a home somewhere and then quietly get rid of her. You don't do away with people by burning their house down – there's too many ways it could go wrong."

A headache spiked my temples; I could hardly take in the meaning of his words. "Alex, what are you saying?"

He hesitated, his hands still holding mine. Finally he said, "This may sound weird, but can you try to sense your mother?"

The realization thundered through me. "You...you don't think they're really dead."

I could see the conflict in his eyes: his reluctance to get my hopes up versus whatever he was thinking. "I don't know," he said. "But this doesn't feel right. The house burning down that way just seems too convenient, somehow. Almost like something you'd do for show."

I swallowed hard, barely daring to hope. "It could have been a – an unruly mob, though. People *do* burn places down sometimes. And people die because of it."

"Yeah, they do. Look, I could be totally wrong. But just try it, okay? Try to sense them."

I almost didn't want to try; didn't want to allow myself

en this small amount of hope, only to be disappointed.
I took a deep, shuddering breath, attempting to clear my
mind enough to focus.

Mom.

I envisioned her soft blonde hair, so like my own
natural shade; her green eyes that used to sparkle with
recognition when they saw me. The smell of her, which
wasn't shampoo and wasn't body lotion but a mixture of
both, plus something else that was just *her,* my mother – a
smell that when I was little I wanted to curl up in for ever.
Even later, when she'd stopped responding to anyone at all,
I'd still sit close to her sometimes as she sat lost in her
dreams, breathing in that scent and wishing for things to
be different.

It didn't take long for Mom to be firmly in my head; she
was never far from my thoughts. I stretched my mind out,
drifting, searching. Was she out there, anywhere? Please?

Endless minutes went past. I stood against the cool
porcelain sink with my eyes closed, trying not to force
things, despite the thudding of my heart – the tiny agony
of hope that had sprung up within me. Don't push, just
relax…drift… *Mom, are you there?*

Nothing. Darkness. My throat tightened as the hope
flickered and died.

And then, somewhere in the emptiness, I thought I
caught something – the faintest hint of a presence. I reached

out, exploring it cautiously…and in a rush, a wild jumble of sensation swept over me. Mom's smell; her voice; her *essence*.

She was content. She was safe.

"Alex, she's alive, she's okay!" I cried. "I can feel her!" I flung myself at him, hugging him hard; he caught me up, laughing, and lifted me briefly off the floor. At first I thought I was laughing too, but then I realized the tears had come after all – that now, when everything was all right, something in me had snapped like a frayed rubber band and I was crying as if I'd never be able to stop.

Alex's arms tightened around me. "It's okay," he whispered, his lips moving in my hair as he rocked me. "Shh, it's all right, everything's okay…"

I tried to answer and couldn't. I'd thought she was dead. Oh god, I had really thought my mother was dead. Distantly, I felt Alex pick me up and sink to the cracked tiled floor, his arms still firm around me. He didn't say anything else; just held me close and let me cry, stroking my back and occasionally kissing the top of my head.

Finally something resembling calm started to return. I pulled away, swiping at my damp cheeks. "How did you know?" I asked shakily. "How?"

He brushed a strand of hair from my temple. I could see the depth of his relief. "I didn't – I just really, really hoped I was right. Is your Aunt Jo okay, too?"

Shame scorched me like a flame-thrower; I'd forgotten all about her. But when I checked, she was fine. Actually, better than fine – she seemed happier than I'd ever sensed her. I let out a breath. Aunt Jo and I had lived in the same run-down, full-of-clutter house for years without becoming close – in fact, there'd been times when I hated her – but knowing she was all right made me go limp all over again.

I felt battered as we stood up, as if I'd been pummelled by a hundred fists. I reached into the cubicle for some toilet paper to mop my face. "So was the fire just a cover, then? Someone must *really* want the world to believe that Mom and Aunt Jo are dead."

Alex nodded, resting a firm-looking shoulder against the wall. "I think it might have been the CIA."

I looked up from wiping my eyes. "You mean Sophie?"

"Yeah, maybe. Nate told you that another department was sheltering Project Angel, now that it's been infiltrated. She could have gotten their help to set the fire and get your mother and aunt out of there – keep them both safe, so the angels can't use them to get to you."

I fell silent as I threw the damp tissue into the overflowing trash can. Project Angel had been the covert CIA department Alex had worked for; after it had been taken over by the angels, Sophie and Nate had been its only two agents left. Now Nate – a renegade angel who'd tried to help humanity – was dead, and though I assumed Sophie was still alive, I had no idea where. She'd left me at the Church of Angels cathedral with no way to contact her, believing I was going to die just like Nate.

And yeah, maybe I'd agreed to that plan, but it was still kind of hard for me to like Sophie after that. If Alex was right though, and she'd really taken Mom into protection, then she was officially my new favourite person.

A chilling thought came. "Wait a minute – if Mom and Aunt Jo are okay, who were in the body bags?"

Alex shrugged. "Two women of about the right age? It wouldn't be hard for the CIA to find a couple of unclaimed bodies; the morgues in New York City must be full of them."

In a flash I saw again the body bag on the stretcher, slipping as the fireman stumbled. Oh my god. Who had been in it?

"Or maybe the bags had living people in them, just to make them look right for the cameras," added Alex. "It depends on who was at the scene; whether they were CIA or not."

"I like that version better," I said softly.

"Okay. We'll go with that one, then." He wrapped his arms around me and I closed my eyes, just drinking in the solid warmth of him. There were no words to explain what I felt for Alex; for how grateful I was that, even with everything that had happened, we somehow still had each other.

Finally I cleared my throat, fingering the damp patch on the collar of his T-shirt. "I got you all wet."

"Don't worry, I'm waterproof." He squeezed my hand. "Come on, we'd better get going. We've still got all of New Mexico to get across."

"No, wait," I said. "There's something I want to do first." And rising up on my tiptoes, I twined my arms around his neck and pressed close against him, kissing him deeply.

I felt his heartbeat leap against mine, and caught my breath as his hands slipped into the back pockets of my jeans, pulling me closer still. The soft-rough heat of his mouth; the feel of his hair as I stroked my fingers through it…I never wanted this to end. But finally, softly, we drew apart.

"Wow," murmured Alex. He nuzzled at my neck. "What was that for?"

"Well, *A*, because I wanted to, and *B*…" I stopped. "*B*, to say thank you. I don't know if it would even have occurred to me to search psychically for Mom, after what I saw on TV. I would have spent the rest of my life just… thinking she was gone." My chest clenched; I couldn't say any more.

Alex rested his hand on my cheek. His eyes looked darker than usual – a stormy grey that melted me. "We're a team," he said quietly. "Always, remember?" Then he grinned. "Hey, do I get to say 'You're welcome' now?"

I managed a casual shrug as my pulse skipped. "You know, I think you should. It's good to be polite."

He put his arms around me. "Polite's my middle name."

"I thought it was James."

"Yeah, 'Polite James'. My parents had weird taste in names." He lowered his head to mine again, then both of us jumped as the doorknob rattled.

"Hey," came a man's voice. "Is anyone in there?"

I stifled my laughter against Alex's chest. "Be out in a minute," he called.

"What's he going to think when we both come out?" I whispered.

"Well, the truth, obviously. Two wild teenagers, making out in a bathroom." He gave me a quick kiss, and we pulled apart.

I went over to the sink and hastily splashed cool water on my face. In the mirror, my short hair was like an explosion from the wind and the crying. And it still looked very red. I held back a sigh as I tried to smooth it down, wishing I'd asked Alex to buy a hairbrush.

"You know what, I think that colour makes your eyes look greener," said Alex suddenly.

I looked up in surprise. "Really?"

He nodded, studying me. "It really does. They look a lot more…vivid now, or something." He touched a spiky lock of my hair, his finger stroking gently through it. "You look beautiful, Willow."

He meant it; I could tell. I smiled. "So, you think you can get used to me as a redhead?"

"Hmm, tough call. Yeah, I think I can deal with it." Alex dropped a kiss on my nose, then closed his eyes. I felt the slight shift as he lifted his consciousness up through his chakra points, until it was hovering somewhere over his crown.

"Okay, the parking lot's clear of angels, at least," he said after a second. "What about you, do you sense anything?"

I'd already been checking, relaxing my mind and imagining the service-station forecourt. No particular feelings came. "I think we're all right."

We left the bathroom holding hands. My cheeks were burning.

"Sorry," said Alex to the man waiting outside. He didn't sound sorry; I could tell he was trying not to laugh. The man shook his head and didn't answer, disappearing inside and banging the door.

"He thinks I'm a floozie," I said as we started back to the bike. It was almost dark now; the town's street lamps were casting soft pools of light up and down the main road. Happiness that Mom was alive still pulsed through me, making my steps light and springy.

"Definitely," said Alex. "But he thinks *I'm* lucky." He started to say something else and stopped, looking across the street.

Following his gaze, I saw a run-down shopping strip with a Goodwill charity store on the corner. The lights were on, and I knew that Alex was thinking of going in, if it was safe. Neither of us had any clothes, apart from what we had on – and hardly anything else, for that matter.

I let my thoughts drift towards the store, scanning it. "It's okay," I said. "It feels almost empty."

He nodded, eyes narrowed in thought. "Maybe we should risk it," he said. "If they have some second-hand camping gear, we could avoid motels until we find someplace safe in Mexico to hole up. Plus we could maybe get another helmet, so that both our faces are hidden."

"Oh," I said.

Alex glanced down at me. "What?"

"Nothing. I just thought you were thinking about clothes."

His dark eyebrows arched in amusement as we continued to the bike. "We're on the run, and you think I'm worrying about clothes?"

"Alex, I've worn this same outfit for three days now; it's getting *foul*. And, you know – as long as we're in there anyway…"

"This is a girl thing, isn't it?"

"It's possibly a girl thing," I admitted.

The Goodwill store was huge, but it was so near closing time that we were the only ones in there. The old woman behind the counter was reading a romance novel; she didn't even look up as we came in. We both got some clothes, and Alex found another helmet for the bike, plus two old sleeping bags and a two-man tent. Then, as we were carrying our stuff to the checkout counter, I saw them: an almost-new pair of grape-juice-purple Converse sneakers, just my size.

"Alex, look, look!" I darted over and tried them on; they fitted perfectly. *And* they were only four dollars. "Okay, these are definitely mine." I put back the pair of old running shoes I'd been going to buy.

Alex grinned. "Hey, excellent." Then he took in my face and started to laugh. "Is this another girl thing? I've never seen someone look so happy over a pair of shoes before."

He was right; I couldn't stop smiling. Maybe it was stupid, but it felt like I'd gotten back a little piece of myself that I'd lost.

We'd parked around the side of the building, in the shadows. When we got back to the bike, Alex pulled off the blue T-shirt he'd been wearing for the past few days and reached for the bag with our clothes. Warmth stirred through me as I watched the muscles of his chest and arms move. We'd been together for over a month, but it felt like longer – I couldn't imagine my life without Alex now.

"It's not really fair, you know," I said, leaning against the bike. "I can't just start changing my clothes out here the way you can."

The *AK* tattoo on Alex's bicep flexed as he pulled a long-sleeved white thermal shirt over his head; he put on a faded red plaid shirt over it, leaving it hanging open. He raised an eyebrow at me as he rolled up the sleeves a few turns. "Go for it. I don't mind."

I laughed. "No, I bet you don't. Nice try." I put our clothes bag in the motorcycle's storage compartment, shoving it down so the lid would close. "How much money do we have left?" I asked. Everything had been really cheap, but we'd still spent almost a hundred dollars.

Alex squatted down to fasten the tent under the rear of the seat. "Let's just say I'm really glad we don't have to spend money on motels any more."

I bit my lip. That bad. Part of the reason we were going to Mexico – apart from practically the entire United States being on the lookout for us now – was that it was cheaper. "We should try and save money on food too," I said as Alex strapped the sleeping bags to the bike. "If we go to grocery stores instead of fast-food places from now on, we can—" I broke off, breathing in sharply.

A flock of gleaming white angels had just glided out from over the top of the strip mall – fifteen or twenty of them. They flew across the street from us at an angle, their great wings stroking the air.

Seeing my face, Alex rose hastily; I sensed his energy shifting. His expression hardened as he spotted the angels. "Get back," he said, not taking his eyes off them. We pressed against the side of the building, Alex shielding me with his body, trying to hide my aura with his own. He drew his gun out from under his waistband. I heard a faint *click* as he took the safety off.

The angels continued on their way without noticing us, achingly glorious against the mundane buildings and run-down houses. I stared at them from under Alex's arm, my emotions in a tumult. That deadly beauty was half me. I wasn't a predator like they were, but half of me was angel all the same. As the flock grew more distant, they winked in and out of the street lights like stars, finally fading from view.

I felt Alex check out the area around us, and then relax. "It's okay; it's clear now."

We stepped out of the shadows and glanced at each other. My legs felt like cotton. If the angels had seen us, we'd be dead right now. Especially me, after what I had done – and if they still thought I was the one who could destroy them all. I knew Alex was thinking the same thing, but neither of us said it.

"That was a really large flock," I said at last.

"Yeah. I've never seen one that size before." He put his gun away, revealing a ribbon of toned, flat stomach. "I guess they're from the Second Wave – maybe heading down to Albuquerque to live."

I swallowed. It was already starting, then. The Second Wave of angels, settling into our world alongside the first. Silently, Alex crouched to finish strapping our stuff to the bike; when he straightened again he wrapped his arms around me, holding me close for a long moment. "Are you ready?" he asked.

I nodded; suddenly I could hardly wait to get away from this place. "Yeah. Let's go."

We drove for hours, heading south on minor roads, stopping only once to grab food from a tiny convenience store in the hills north of Alamogordo. The land turned to desert, vast and empty, with the stars shimmering overhead. Once, as we skirted a town, I saw another angel in flight, its pure white figure clear against the night sky. As I watched, it wheeled sharply on one wing and plummeted, deadly as an arrow. I turned my head away as we sped on, hating what I knew was happening at that very moment.

We started climbing back into mountains; the cold

wind whipped at my face and arms. I shivered, pressing against Alex's back, and was glad when he finally pulled off the road. It felt late, after midnight.

"I thought New Mexico was supposed to be hot," I said as we got off the bike. He'd taken us down a dirt road that led deep into the woods; we were at the bottom of a narrow canyon. Moonlight cast a faint, silvery light – I could see my breath in the air.

"Not up here," said Alex as he unstrapped the tent. This was his home state, and he seemed to know it inside and out. I fumbled coldly in the storage compartment for the sweater I'd bought, pulling it on over the one I was already wearing – and remembered how Alex hadn't even needed a map back in September, when he'd guided us over a hundred miles of New Mexico back roads.

"But we're not too far from the border now, and then it'll be desert again," he went on. He tossed the rolled-up tent onto the frosty ground, and started undoing the sleeping bags. "I just thought we could get a couple of hours' sleep up here where we're hidden, then cross before dawn when there's a little more light – I don't remember exactly where the crossing-place is; I might miss it in the dark."

Needless to say, we weren't going into Mexico the legal way. Pushing aside my apprehension about what the next few hours might bring, I helped Alex put up the tent.

"I've never gone camping before," I commented as I unwound a guy rope.

Alex was wrestling one of the tent pegs into the hard ground; he glanced at me in amazement, his face looking sculpted in the moonlight. "Never? Really?"

"No, Mom never took me, and Aunt Jo…" I shrugged. I had told Alex what Aunt Jo was like; I didn't have to explain.

He smiled, knowing what I meant. "Well, we're sort of roughing it," he said, moving on to the next rope. "You can get, like, fridges and stoves and stuff, but that's never really seemed like camping to me."

"Not that any of that would fit on the bike anyway," I added.

Alex shook his head, making a *tsk*-ing noise. "What, so you wouldn't carry a fridge on your lap if we got one? That's a serious lack of dedication."

"Yeah, I know. Sorry."

Crawling inside, we got the sleeping bags zipped together. The ground felt freezing through the nylon floor of the tent. "I don't need a fridge, but a *heater* would be nice," I said. My teeth were practically chattering.

Alex grabbed our things from the bike and brought them inside; then he fastened the tent closed, securing us in. "Come here, babe, I'll keep you warm."

I smiled; whenever he called me that, I wanted to melt.

He drew me to him, and we snuggled together in the softness of the sleeping bags. We were both fully dressed, apart from having kicked our shoes off – it was way too cold to contemplate taking anything else off.

"Promise me it's warmer in Mexico," I said, nestling against him. Slowly, I was starting to feel less like an ice cube – and even better, safe, at least for the moment.

"I promise," murmured Alex. He was lying on his back with his arms around me; one hand had slipped under my T-shirt and was lazily stroking my spine. I could sense how tired he was, now that we'd finally stopped moving. So was I. It felt like a million years had passed since I'd crouched in the Church of Angels cathedral in Denver, trying to stop the Second Wave from arriving. And it hadn't even been two days.

"Alex?" I whispered.

"Hmm?"

"What are we going to do when we get to Mexico? Do you have any idea where we're going?" I knew he'd been to Mexico dozens of times; from the sounds of it, he and the other AKs had crossed the border often.

His hand stopped trailing up and down my spine. For a minute I thought he'd fallen asleep; then his voice spoke in the darkness. "I thought we'd go to the Sierra Madre," he said. "There should be someplace safe there where we can hole up and start trying to recruit other AKs."

As he said the words, I got a flash of his thoughts: a dense, wild mountain range, full of plummeting canyons and almost unpassable roads. You could hide up there for years and never be found. It was the best possible place to do what we needed to do and still keep me safe; he was sure of it. Even so, I caught a sense of cold dread running beneath the images.

"Alex? What's wrong?"

"Nothing," he said.

I hesitated, wondering whether to push it. "No, there is. I mean, if you don't want to tell me, it's all right, but I can feel it."

There was a long pause; outside the tent, the wind stirred through the bare bones of the trees. Finally Alex gave a soft laugh. "Okay, I'm still getting used to this psychic girlfriend thing," he said. "I'm fine, I just…" He sighed. And suddenly I knew, the thought dropping into my head as if it were my own.

"You're worried about being in charge," I said in surprise. I rose up, trying to see his face in the darkness. "That's it, isn't it?"

The dread flickered again like the tongue of a snake, then faded as if he were making a conscious effort to control it. "It's nothing," he said gruffly. "I just saw enough about what it's like to be a leader when my dad was in charge. I'd rather work on my own, or as part of a team under someone I trust. But, you know…" His chest shifted under me as he shrugged. "That's not the way it is; we've got to train new AKs and I'm the only one who knows how. So I'll deal with it."

It didn't really feel like he was telling me everything, but I let it go – he obviously didn't want to talk about it. And even though I was psychic, I'd never thought it was okay to go probing around if someone didn't want me to. I closed Alex's thoughts away from mine, so that I wouldn't pick up anything by mistake. We were so close that this happened more and more now when I wasn't even thinking about it.

"You'll be great," I murmured. I kissed his smooth neck. "And I'll help all I can. Psychic consultant, remember?"

I could almost hear his smile. "Don't forget mechanic, too. If the Shadow's anything like the Mustang…"

The Honda Shadow parked outside our tent was over twenty years old; I knew Alex was suspicious of it. "Hey, you leave the Mustang alone," I said. "It was a complete classic. And Shadows aren't bad either, you know – for a cheap bike, they're pretty classic themselves."

"Why did I know you were going to say that?" The sleeping bags gave a soft rustle as he rolled towards me. It felt much warmer in the tent now; almost cosy.

"I don't know, maybe because…" My voice trailed off.

Alex had taken my hand and was kissing my fingers, one by one. His lips seemed electric, zinging at my nerve endings as if I were an exposed wire. I felt myself go weak as he bit gently at my little finger; then his warm mouth slid down to my palm, pressing against it, and I shivered.

"Let's stop talking for a while, okay?" he whispered.

That night I had a dream.

I was standing at the top of a high tower, gazing out at what had to be the largest city in the world. It was endless, like something from a science-fiction film. Low mountains crouched on the horizon in every direction; the city crept over them and kept right on going, fading into hazy infinity. Somehow I knew this was in Mexico – and that it was where Alex and I were meant to be. My heart tightened with urgency as I stared at the sea of buildings. We had to come here. We *had* to.

In the middle of the city lay a broad stone space: an immense square, with a cathedral at one end and a long, official-looking building stretching down the side. There was a stage set up near the cathedral, and rock music playing – it thumped through me as thousands danced. Dozens of angels glided over the square, too, like hawks hunting over a field. I took a panicked step backwards. They'd see my aura; they'd know what I was—

The world whirled and shifted; the crowd scene disappeared. Now twelve angels hovered over the city, brighter than any I'd ever seen – like twelve blazing suns that poured light over the concrete buildings below. An ancient, ruthless power connected the twelve; I shuddered as I felt it. The angels started to glow even brighter still, burning my eyes until I had to duck my head away. As I did, they vanished in an explosion that was sensation rather than sound – a shock wave that howled past, knocking me off my feet.

Seamlessly, I was in my angel form, flying from the tower as the screams of a million angels tore through me. But my wings were too heavy. I couldn't stay aloft; I was falling – I had to hold on tighter, fly harder—

I landed with a bump. Silence, so still and perfect, like cut glass. I was in a park, in my human form again. Soft green grass; palm trees mixed with poplars and cypresses. The twelve angels were gone…but I wasn't alone.

A boy stood watching me. He was a little older than me, about the same height as Alex, with brown hair that fell in loose curls. A glint of stubble; high cheekbones and strong features – a beautiful face that I knew had been through great pain, yet it held such humour and tenderness that it twisted my heart.

We stared at each other. I had no idea who the boy was, but the thought of ever being without him filled me with despair. The unexpected feeling robbed the breath from my throat, so that at first I couldn't speak.

"Who are you?" I whispered at last.

In answer, the boy stretched out his hand. "Come, *querida*," he said softly.

His eyes were urging me to say yes, and part of me wanted to link my fingers through his so badly that it hurt. *No, I'm in love with Alex*, I thought. And then: *But, oh my god, to not be with you – how could I possibly bear it?*

I woke up with a start. It was still night-time; I was in the tent, safe in the sleeping bag with Alex asleep beside me. What had all *that* been about? Heart thudding, I pressed against Alex's bare chest. He shifted in his sleep and pulled me closer; I hugged him hard, feeling almost guilty. Even in a dream, how could I have ever felt that way about someone else?

Especially now. My cheeks heated slightly; I smiled to myself as Alex's breath stirred my hair. We'd been taking things slowly since we first got together, and then earlier tonight…well, basically we'd both been kicking ourselves that Alex hadn't made another purchase along with the hair dye and scissors at the drugstore. We'd managed to hold back, though, and meanwhile it had still been just – incredible, and wonderful. I kissed his shoulder, feeling the warm weight of his bare leg looped over mine.

Okay, forget the part about the boy, I told myself. *That was just the dream disintegrating into weirdness.* But the rest of it… I frowned as I went over the images: the endless city; its huge square pulsing with music and people. Then the twelve fiery angels exploding – the heaviness of my wings, the millions of angels screaming. Remembering it all, urgency tugged at me even stronger than before – along with a cold dread that coiled in my stomach.

The dream was a premonition, I was sure of it. Wherever this city was, Alex and I had to go there.

CHAPTER *Three*

THE ANGEL DRIFTED IN AND out of consciousness, memory mixing with the now.

He was lying in bed in his chambers; the covers were soft. Sometimes there was the hum of the central heating as it came on, then the faint click as it went off again. Over and over Raziel saw the assassin: the dark-haired youth who stood pointing a gun at him, his arm around the half-angel abomination. The girl's face was pale, her green eyes wide.

The knowledge that he was the thing's father had rocked him. But there was no doubt; he'd felt the unmistakable echo of his own energy as their angel selves had fought. Plus she looked almost exactly like Miranda, the young music student he'd once enjoyed – though nothing like him, thankfully. Raziel groaned aloud, seeing the assassin again. Next time he would move faster. Next time he would tear the energy forces from them both and watch them crumple into lifeless heaps on the ground...

"Hush, hush," whispered a voice. A young human woman was there. She stroked his arm, and even in his current state, Raziel found this irritating and wished she would stop. More voices:

"Is he coming out of it yet?"

"No, I don't think so. I don't know what to do for him; they're so different from us..."

The assassin's finger, pulling the trigger. The searing wrench as the bullet hit his halo. His wings going into flapping, helpless spasm; his body shuddering, closing down in protest – and the *anger* that had seethed through him as he collapsed to the floor and the world turned black. The Second Wave was arriving, and instead of being there to greet them and show off his status in this world, he'd been brought down by the very assassin whose life he'd so stupidly spared for his own purposes. He'd thought he'd been so clever, using Kylar to kill the angelic traitors, letting him think he was following standard orders from the CIA. Who'd have guessed that the young assassin would have such a mind of his own?

It was a mistake Raziel would soon rectify. Oh, yes; he'd relish every second of it. But it was the girl who incensed him the most – the girl who caused his fists to clench beneath the covers. He'd been told she was dead, and instead she'd had the gall to actually try and stop the Second Wave from arriving.

"Shh," soothed the woman's voice. A cool, damp cloth brushed across his forehead. If the girl had succeeded it would have meant death for them all: Paschar's vision fulfilled. And even though she'd failed, Raziel still burned with humiliation – the entire angel community knew that Willow Fields was the half-angel he'd been trying to find for weeks. They'd know exactly what she'd been trying to do in the cathedral; would know he'd been deceived and nearly bested. It was this that made him long to kill his daughter slowly, listening to her screams. And she felt so *close* now – so infuriatingly close. Raziel's head turned restlessly on the pillow. He could sense her energy, even though she was hundreds of miles away, in a sleeping bag with the assassin. The knowledge felt fuzzy; he wasn't sure how he knew it. Why, *why*, hadn't he managed to kill them both when he had the chance?

"Can't we at least make him more comfortable?" pleaded the woman. "He seems so distressed."

"Let's try this – it's very mild, but it might help."

A pinprick of pain in his arm. It did nothing, of course; angels were unaffected by either stimulants or relaxants. Raziel found himself drifting deeper anyway, exhausted by his own thoughts. As he did, other knowledge came to him...the most unwelcome knowledge he could have imagined.

Though individuals, angels were also all linked as if by an invisible web; when one died, they each felt it. Now, with the arrival of the Second Wave, the angelic energy in this world had more than doubled, humming with new life. And at its heart there pulsed a purposeful presence that Raziel recognized all too well.

In his long life he'd only rarely felt fear, but he felt something akin to it now – a jolt of shock and wariness so great that for a moment he almost surfaced back into full consciousness. No one had told him this. It was inconceivable that none of the other angels in this world had known, but the information had not been shared with him. The fact held ominous implications. He hadn't expected this to happen for several more years at least; he'd thought the Council would wait until the last Wave to make their move, holding reign in the angels' old world for as long as possible.

But no, they were here – and it could not bode well for him.

The Twelve had arrived.

*   *   *

Manhunt for Terrorist Suspects Continues, read the headline.

They'd stopped at a small 24-hour service station near the Mexican border; dawn was still an hour away. As he glanced over the story, Alex was relieved by its lack of details – not to mention the photo of Willow with her long blonde hair spilling past her shoulders, reassuring him again just how different she looked now. The picture of Raziel was an old one, he noticed. He felt a grim satisfaction, knowing the angel was probably still incapacitated from the bullet that had nicked his halo. Alex would have far preferred to have killed Raziel, but knocking him out for as long as possible would do for second best.

"Pump three," he told the guy behind the counter. He put down two styrofoam cups of coffee, too.

Willow was waiting beside the motorcycle as he went back outside, her short red-gold hair spiking in the breeze. She had on faded second-hand jeans that she'd bought the day before, and a tight, pale blue shirt with long sleeves that looked great on her. Behind her, the night sky was starting to lighten, the stars fading to the east. Alex smiled, his blood warming as he remembered the silky feel of her in his arms the night before. It had taken a serious effort to get going that morning; all he'd wanted to do was stay in the tent with Willow for a while – like, the rest of his life.

She stood looking off into the distance as he walked up, frowning as if she were thinking about something. She seemed to shake it away when she saw him. "Thanks," she said, taking one of the coffees. "And here, you take this. I hate even holding it." With a quick glance at the empty service-station forecourt, she covertly handed him the pistol.

Alex never felt good about giving Willow the gun. Handing a loaded weapon to someone who'd never shot one before, and was nervous of them anyway, wasn't really the best plan in the world. But it was a million times better than her *not* having a weapon if any trouble happened. He tucked the gun away in his holster, keeping his back to the camera that he knew would be perched on the roof of the service station.

"I need to teach you how to use this," he said, thinking aloud.

He saw her start to protest. Then she looked away and took a sip of coffee, her green eyes troubled. "Yeah, okay," she said finally.

Alex's eyebrows flew up. "Really? I thought you'd hate the idea."

"I do," said Willow. "But I can't not do something just because I don't like it. I don't have that – luxury, any more." She shrugged. "I mean, all I have to do is look in the mirror to see how much things have changed. And I can't depend on you to protect me all the time."

"You protect me too," Alex pointed out. The memory of Willow's angel flying above him, shielding him while putting herself in mortal danger, flashed into his mind. It had been the moment he'd first realized he was in love with her, though he'd been too much of an idiot to admit it to himself. He gulped down his coffee and tossed the empty cup into a trash can.

"Okay," he said. "You ready to become an illegal alien?"

Willow shook her head with a smile and threw away her own empty cup. "This is the ultimate bad-boy date, isn't it? Breaking into a different country."

"Hey, it makes a change from hot-wiring cars together."

"Been there, done that… Alex, seriously, are you sure no one's going to shoot us?"

"Don't worry – if anyone's around, we won't cross," he said. Border guards weren't exactly his number one concern just then, but he still had no intention of taking any risks.

They sped down the highway again; the southern New Mexico desert stretched out around them, silvery in the pre-dawn. A ghostly-looking coyote loped alongside the motorcycle for a few seconds, as if they were running a race, and then veered off on errands of its own. To Alex's relief, he found the dirt road easily, leading off from the highway a few miles further on. He took it, leaning into the turn and feeling Willow's hands tighten on his waist as she shifted her weight behind him.

The border wall came into view. In some places this was a concrete barricade with razor coils glinting at its top; here it was just a tired-looking barbed-wire fence separating the two countries, as if they were neighbouring ranches. The fence cut across a dried-out riverbed; where it came up one of the banks it gave up for a few feet, collapsing onto the ground with its posts sagging.

There was no one around; it was still almost dark. Alex trundled the bike to a stop, and Willow helped him manoeuvre it over the slant in the riverbed, into Mexico. "I thought the wall would be more…wall-like," she said.

"It is, in some places," said Alex. "But in others, it's just like this. And look." He nodded at a rusty metal sign. It said, *You must enter the US by a designated entry point. This is not a designated entry point. If you enter by this route, you are committing a felony.*

Willow stared. "But – it probably cost more to make the sign than it would have to repair the fence. It's almost like they *want* people to sneak in."

"They do," said Alex. Pebbles skittered down as they

got the bike up over the edge of the bank. "Or at least the angels who live around here do. Illegal immigrants mean fresh energy supplies, without them having to go looking." He remembered when Juan, one of the other AKs, had first showed them this route – and how he and his big brother Jake had encountered a border guard here once, smiling with angel burn and talking about how important it was to do the angels' work.

Kara had been with them that time, too – an exotically beautiful AK with nerves of steel; both he and Jake had had crushes on her back then. "Idiot," she'd said as they'd driven away, shifting gears with a tight, angry motion. Sitting in the back of the jeep, Alex had taken in her profile. And despite the easy banter the AKs usually shared, in that instant he could think of nothing at all to say to Kara – but had instinctively understood the mix of fury and sorrow that made her mad at the guard, as if getting angel burn were his own fault.

Now Willow looked slightly queasy at the thought of the predatory border angels. "Oh," she said. He saw her throat move. "That's – that's really…"

"I know," said Alex, understanding exactly how she felt. Unfortunately, there were plenty of angels in Mexico too, and had been even before the Invasion. There was hardly anyplace on earth now that he thought he could take Willow where she'd be really safe.

But he'd do his best – or die trying.

Nearby, he could just see the rough dirt track he remembered, heading off to the east. "Okay, that connects up with the highway eventually," he said, climbing back onto the bike. "Or at least, it used to." He hoped it hadn't been washed out; struggling the Shadow over miles of no road at all seriously wouldn't be his idea of fun.

Willow started to put on her helmet, but hesitated, playing with its straps. "Alex, are there any really big cities in Mexico? I mean – *really* big."

He looked at her in surprise, taking in the worried lines that had appeared on her forehead. "Yeah, Mexico City. It's one of the largest cities in the world. Why?"

She didn't reply immediately. "I'll tell you later," she said at last. "But maybe we could find a place to stop soon, where we can talk."

Apprehension tickled his spine. Whatever this was about, he didn't much like the sound of it already – but hanging around a few feet from the border wasn't the place for a long discussion. "Yeah, okay," he said reluctantly, and pulled on his own helmet.

The dirt road seemed to last for ever, but as the sun came up they finally turned south onto Highway 45. This part of Mexico looked almost identical to the New Mexico landscape they'd just left behind: hard, dry ground scattered with juniper bushes and cactuses, with rugged-looking mountains rising in the distance. Alex grimaced as they passed a billboard: the familiar image of an angel with wings and arms outspread. *La Iglesia de los Ángeles,* it read.

Dusty pickup trucks passed by, driven by men with dark hair and white straw cowboy hats. Though no one gave Willow a second glance in her helmet, Alex knew he wouldn't be able to relax until they were holed up in the Sierra Madre, as far away from the Church of Angels as possible. It was a lot more remote up there, in what they called *el monte*: the wild.

And then he could start trying to recruit people, and train them.

The dread Willow had sensed the night before touched him again with its clammy fingers. *Get a grip,* he thought, irritated with himself. *You have to do it; you're the only one left.* If he didn't get some other AKs trained – didn't somehow get a camp set up and then hopefully other camps too, until they had a network of them up and down the continent – then humanity could just kiss itself goodbye in a few years.

Even so, Alex's hands tightened on the Shadow's handlebars as the wind rushed past. It wasn't that he didn't want to fight the angels – god, apart from being with Willow, it was the only thing he *did* want. He'd willingly give his life; he'd do it a dozen times over, if it meant defeating the angels in this world. He just didn't want to be responsible for the lives of a whole team too. His brother's death shuddered through his mind. Yeah, he'd already shown how great he was at covering someone's back, hadn't he? And if one of his decisions killed someone—

Alex pushed the thought away, hoping that Willow wasn't picking up on any of this crap. There wasn't anyone else who could be in charge, so he'd deal with it. End of story.

The sun beat down on them as it rose higher, chasing the clouds away until the sky was an almost painful blue. He drove until about ten o'clock that morning, wanting to get a few hours between them and the border before stopping. Finally, near the outskirts of Chihuahua, he saw a roadside taco stand and pulled over. He killed the engine and did a quick scan. Good – no angels nearby, at least.

"What do you think, is it all right to stop here?" he said to Willow as they got off the bike.

Her short hair was ruffled as she took off her helmet; she smoothed it absently, gazing around her. "I think so," she said. "There's *something* here, but…" She trailed off with a frown.

Alex kept quiet, letting her concentrate. While she did, he leaned against the bike, smiling slightly as he took in her slim figure, her face with its delicately pointed chin and wide eyes. God, she was so beautiful. He still wasn't sure how he'd managed to get lucky enough to have Willow, but was thankful for it every day of his life. The two years he'd spent alone before he met her seemed like a black-and-white film to him now, a time devoid of colour.

"I think we're okay," said Willow finally, sounding more certain. The day had grown warmer, and she pulled off her blue long-sleeved shirt; under it she wore a green camisole top. She put the shirt away in the Shadow's storage compartment. "Anyway, *Señor*, we're supposed to be saving money on food, remember? What are we doing at a taco stand?"

"It's okay; these places are really cheap," he said as they started towards the stand. Back when he'd had even less money than he did now – it had never occurred to Alex's father that perhaps his sons should receive a salary like the other AKs – he and Jake had used to live off these roadside stands every time they came here.

Tacos, quesadillas, mulitas, tortas, said the weathered sign. Willow gave it a quizzical glance. "Hmm, Toto, I don't think we're in Kansas any more. You choose for me, okay?"

Alex got them each a Coke and a few tacos with *carnitas*: chopped roast pork. "And don't worry, I told her you want extra chillies on yours," he said to Willow, keeping a straight face. They were actually for him – he loved spicy food.

She gave him a look. "Dude, if there are *any* chillies on mine, you're going to be wearing them."

Alex paid with dollars – most places down here accepted US bills, though he knew he'd need to change their dwindling funds into pesos at some point. A worn picnic table stood to one side; they carried their food over. For a few minutes they ate the Mexican tacos with their soft cornmeal wraps, in companionable silence, a light breeze stirring the dusty ground.

Finally Willow sighed and put her last taco down. "So I guess we need to talk."

The remains of their food went uneaten as she related her dream. Alex listened intently, his skin prickling as she described the twelve bright angels, and the sound that was like a million of the creatures screaming.

"It was all so vivid – and there was such an incredible sense of urgency," Willow finished. Her face was tight with worry. "Only I don't even know where this place is, for sure."

"Mexico City," he said absently, still thinking of the images from her dream. He'd been there twice, on hunting trips with Juan and a few of the others.

"Definitely? You're positive?"

Alex shrugged. "No other place is that big. Plus that

square you described has got to be the Zócalo – it's one of the largest squares in the world." He rubbed his forehead, where a dull ache was beginning to pound.

Willow started to say something and stopped, touching his arm. "Are you okay? You look really pale."

"Yeah, I'm fine." He dropped his hand. "Listen, if what you're leading up to is that you think we need to go there—"

"We *do* need to go there," she broke in anxiously. "The Sierra Madre isn't where we're supposed to be; Mexico City is – I'm sure of it. Only, I don't know what's going to happen once we're there. The dream didn't feel very... cheerful, exactly."

Great. He let out a breath. "Willow..."

"Alex, listen to me. It wasn't just a dream; it was a premonition. We have to go."

His voice hardened. "You do know that Mexico City is literally about the last place on the planet I'd ever want to take you, right? The Church of Angels is huge there – and the city was full of angels even *before* the Invasion. Any angel that saw your aura would know exactly who you are. We're in enough danger just sitting here, but at least we can do a scan first. In a city that size? No way."

"I know." Willow was still touching his arm; her fingers felt warm against his skin. "But how often do angels scan auras when they're in their human bodies? Don't they usually wait until they're in their angel form, about to feed?"

"The ones I've tracked usually do," he admitted.

"And you've tracked hundreds," she pointed out. "So it must be pretty typical. If an angel saw my aura when it was about to feed on someone, then we'd probably see it, too. We'd have a good chance of getting it."

When it came to Willow's safety, *probably* and *good chance* were not his favourite words. Looking down, Alex took her hand, playing with her fingers. "How strongly do you feel we need to go there?" he asked at last.

"Really strongly," she said without hesitating. "The sound of all those angels screaming..." She trailed off. Slowly, she said, "Alex, it feels like something's going to happen in Mexico City that could cause the angels serious harm. Only we have to be there for it to take place. We *have* to be."

Alex fell silent. Willow's premonitions had never steered them wrong so far, and if what she'd dreamed was even partly accurate, then she was right, no question – they had to go. And even apart from her dream, he knew it would be a lot easier to recruit people in a city, rather than up in *el monte*. If he were on his own, then Mexico City would be exactly the place he'd head for. Plus there were the rogues: angels who believed their kind didn't have the right to destroy humanity – Nate had told them about how they did something called "marshalling", where they implanted a tiny bit of resistance in a human's aura to make it unpalatable to angels. There were bound to be some rogues in Mexico City; if he could somehow hook up with them, it might be just what was needed to swing the balance in an almost-hopeless fight.

Alex massaged his forehead as the headache jabbed again. Yeah, going to Mexico City was all really logical... except he'd already nearly lost her once.

Willow took in the movement of his fingers on his brow. She didn't comment this time, though he saw the concern in her eyes. "Alex, we have to go," she said instead. "We really do."

"All right," he said finally. He managed a smile. "I mean, if you've got a psychic girlfriend, then I guess you'd better listen to her, right?"

She reached across and gripped his hand; he knew she was only all too aware of how much he dreaded anything happening to her. "Okay," she said softly. She started to pick up her taco again and then stopped, narrowing her gaze. "Wait a minute. So, does that mean you wouldn't listen to me if I *wasn't* psychic?"

She looked so cute that he almost grinned despite his apprehension. He raised an eyebrow at her. "Is that a trick question? Of course I wouldn't – you're a girl."

Willow's mouth pursed as her green eyes flashed with

sudden humour. She started laughing. "Oh, you are in so much trouble for that."

"I am?"

"Definitely." She propped herself up on her elbows and kissed him, stretching across the picnic table. Alex curled his fingers around the smooth skin at the back of her neck, holding her in place for a moment and savouring the feel of her lips on his.

"Is that really your idea of being in trouble?" he said when they drew apart. "Because I don't think you've grasped the whole punishment/deterrent thing. See, you're supposed to make me *not* want to do it again."

Willow was laughing, wiping her mouth with the back of her hand. "I'm the one who doesn't want to do it again. Your *lips* are all spicy from those chillies—" Suddenly her face slackened in alarm. "Alex, the bike!" she cried.

He leaped up from the bench without asking for details. A pickup truck had pulled in front of the taco stand while they'd been talking, blocking the motorcycle from view. As Alex hurtled around the side of it he saw a stocky guy with black hair crouched beside the Shadow, untying the tent. On the ground beside him sat a bulging knapsack, and both sleeping bags.

"What the hell are you doing?" shouted Alex in Spanish. "Get away from my bike!"

Leaving the camping stuff, the guy grabbed the

knapsack and ran, his heels kicking up dust. The jimmied-open storage compartment gaped emptily. Alex swore and took off after him, pounding across the dry soil. The guy was as fast as he was, though, weaving around dumpsters and abandoned cars like a rabbit and finally veering off to the right, scrambling over a high concrete wall. Alex started to follow but stopped, acutely aware that he'd left Willow by herself, when anyone from the Church might stop by the stand and see her. Still cursing the thief, he turned and jogged back to the bike. Jesus, how was that for luck? They'd lost their stuff twice in one week now.

Willow was waiting beside the Shadow looking anxious; the taco stand woman stood beside her, chattering in worried Spanish that Alex knew Willow didn't understand. "He stole your things!" the woman cried as Alex approached. "I'm so sorry – I didn't see him until you shouted. Is there anything I can do?"

"No, but thank you, *Señora*," replied Alex. If they'd been in America, he knew she'd have probably already called the police. Thankfully, running to law enforcement didn't usually occur to people here – which was good, since the Mexican police were just as much in the angels' pockets as back home.

Willow's face was tight with distress as the woman returned to her stand. "God, I'm sorry – I *knew* there was something! I was focusing so strongly on the Church of

Angels, but I could tell it wasn't that, and I guess I sort of disregarded it—"

"Hey, come on, it's not *your* fault," he said, squeezing her shoulder. He squatted beside the bike, shaking his head as he examined the forced-open lock. The thief must have worked fast; he obviously knew what he was doing.

"Well, at least he didn't get much," he said as he stood up. "And I've still got my wallet. We can always buy more clothes; the marketplaces in Mexico City are really cheap."

Willow nodded as she hugged her elbows. "Yeah," she said finally. And then it hit him. Her photo. The one of her as a child, standing beneath a willow tree and tipping up her head in delight at its trailing leaves. It had been taken by her mother – was the only thing Willow had of hers. And it had been in the storage compartment, in the pocket of her other pair of jeans.

He swore, his fists tightening as he glanced back towards the wall the guy had disappeared over. The thought of the slimy creep stealing Willow's photo – tearing it apart to see if there was money in the frame, then throwing it away in the garbage somewhere...

"Alex, it's okay," said Willow, touching his arm. "It's... it's only a photo. You couldn't catch him now, anyway. And besides, we shouldn't draw attention to ourselves – just let it go."

He let out a breath, hating himself. "I almost *had* him..."

"It's okay," Willow repeated. "It really is." Stepping forward, she hugged his waist. As he held her close, Alex knew he was seriously never going to forgive himself for this, even if Willow already had.

"I love you, you know that?" she said.

He managed a rueful smile. "Why, because I let that jerk steal your photo?"

Willow looked up; her eyes were like a forest washed with rain. He could see the happiness in them as she regarded him. "No, actually it's because you're everything I ever wanted."

"I love you too," he said softly, kissing her. Then he sighed. "Anyway, you're right – I won't catch him now. We'd better get going."

He reattached the camping gear. Just as they started to climb back onto the bike, the woman hurried out from behind her stand again with a paper-wrapped package. The rich aroma of roast pork rose up from it.

"Please, take these for later," she said in Spanish. "It's the least I can do."

"*Gracias, Señora.*" Alex put the food in the damaged storage compartment, grateful to have it. They could save some money on dinner now.

"*Gracias,*" echoed Willow fervently. "*Muchas, muchas gracias.*"

A few minutes later they were speeding down the highway once more, leaving Chihuahua in a haze of heat behind them. The houses they passed were small, dusty, in various shades of pastel with black water tanks perched on top of each one. Alex gazed beyond the homes to the rugged shape of the Sierra Madre, looming off to the southwest. And with all his heart, he wished that Willow had never had her dream. He'd have had a decent shot at keeping her safe, up there in that wilderness. Mexico City was going to be anybody's guess.

But they'd made their choice now. As they roared down the desert highway, he reached for Willow's hand at his waist and twined his fingers through hers.

CHAPTER *Four*

"WILL I FIND TRUE LOVE?" asked the woman. She was in her mid-twenties, pretty, with a serious, earnest face.

They were sitting in a corner of the Chihuahua marketplace. Seb considered how to answer as he pretended to inspect her palm – though the information he was getting had nothing to do with the woman's lifeline, and everything to do with her aura; the feel of her energy; sudden flashes of knowledge.

"There's a man in your life – his name's Carlos," he said. He wasn't usually good on names, but he was sure this one was right; he was sensing it so strongly. "You've been hoping he'll propose to you. *Señorita*, I don't see this happening."

Her expression fell. "But…he told me just last night to give him a little more time."

Seb was getting it clearly now. Not only did Carlos have two other girlfriends on the go, he was married already. The woman had no idea; she'd believed everything the *cabrón* had told her. It was hardly uncommon – a lot of men didn't seem to know the meaning of the word "faithful", unless they were talking about what their wives and girlfriends had better be to them – but Seb had given too many readings over the years to stomach this attitude. He knew only too well by now what it did to women; how it made them feel.

"Carlos's life is complicated," he said, managing to hide his irritation at the man. "I'm sorry, *Señorita*, but he isn't in a position to propose to you. I'm afraid he never will be."

He wasn't usually this blunt, but he could tell that on some level the woman already knew it was hopeless; it was why she'd stopped to get a reading from him. Now she winced, and ducked her head down. "I've been praying so hard to the angels that things will work out," she said in a whisper. "I thought – I thought so many more of them arriving might be a sign they'd heard me."

"The angels are very kind," said Seb diplomatically. He

could see that the woman's energy field was undamaged; she was just one of the ones who loved the angels anyway. There were plenty of them, and now that the angels' numbers had increased by so many, he supposed there'd soon be plenty more. "But I can hear them now," he went on, "and they're saying to me that you shouldn't wait for Carlos."

The woman's eyes widened. Okay, he was making this part up – but he had to give her *something*, or else she wouldn't make the break. "They want you to get on with your life," he said firmly. "To be happy. You haven't been happy in a long time, *Señorita*."

By the time the woman left, her expression was thoughtful; Seb could sense the hope that had taken root in her. He leaned back against a palm tree, savouring the mental silence. A few hours of readings had left him as drained as an empty bottle. He wasn't really sure why he put so much into them, for only a hundred pesos. When he'd made the decision to quit thieving, readings had just been a way to keep from starving – and back then, he hadn't bothered to make much effort; he'd cobbled together quick fortunes from whatever he saw. Somehow, as the years had passed, he'd started caring a lot more.

Thinking of the angels' arrival, Seb sighed. When he'd glimpsed some of the TV footage in a cafe two days before, he'd wondered for a heart-pounding moment if the presence of so many more angels might somehow lead him to his half-angel girl after all. But he couldn't see how it might – and so for him, the world hadn't changed, despite how much happiness the angels' arrival might have brought everyone else. The realization had depressed him; he'd avoided looking at the footage after that.

Seb scraped a hand roughly across his stubble – enough of this. As he got to his feet, a female voice called his name. Turning, he saw two girls a year or two older than he was heading towards him – both with bright American smiles and bouncing ponytails. "Hey, remember us?" said the redhead in English as they reached him.

"How could I forget?" Seb swung his knapsack over his shoulder. Lucy and someone else. Amanda, that was it. They were part of a group of American students staying at the same hostel that he was; Seb had sat up with a few of them the night before, drinking and talking. The girls' Spanish wasn't nearly as fluent as they thought, so that he'd found it easier to speak to them in English, which he'd picked up from giving readings to American tourists over the years. He spoke a little French too – was good at languages almost without trying. He knew being psychic helped.

"So, are you finished with 'work'?" asked Lucy the redhead, giving him a flirtatious smile as she made quote marks in the air. They'd thought it was hilarious that he gave psychic readings. He wouldn't have bothered telling them, except that one of their group had seen him here in the marketplace the day before. "Because if you are," she went on, "maybe you could show us the sights."

He hesitated. Both girls were pretty and fun to be with, but all he really felt like doing was going back to the hostel and reading his book – maybe sitting outside with a cigarette. But Lucy was already laughing, pulling at his arm. "We're not taking no for an answer. Besides, you promised last night."

"I don't remember this," he said, smiling despite himself.

"Well, you *practically* did. Come on, give us the grand tour of *el mercado* – we want to see a typical Mexican marketplace."

He gave in. Why not? It wasn't as if he had anything else to do with his time, now that he was no longer searching. The thought brought a wince of pain; he pushed it away.

"All right," he said. He raked his hair back; he could feel the curls hanging over his forehead, annoying him. "The first thing, I think, is that we go and find something to eat."

"Ooh, good idea," said Amanda. She had dark hair and eyebrows that were too perfect to be natural. "Lead the way."

The bright chaos of the marketplace enveloped them:

vendors shouting their bargains; the smell of spicy food cooking; crowds of shoppers. Seb had been in Chihuahua for almost two weeks now. After his decision at the orphanage, he'd hitched a ride with the first truck he'd seen to wherever it was going, but had somehow felt compelled to get off here – so strongly that he'd almost shouted at the truck driver to stop. It didn't make much sense to him now; the town was as dusty and run-down as he remembered. Still, he supposed it was as good a place as any to figure out what to do with the rest of his life.

The problem was, he had no idea – all he knew was that ever since he'd arrived in Chihuahua, he'd had a feeling there was something he was supposed to be doing. It was a constant irritation, like a bee buzzing at his head.

They got tacos and wandered around the stalls. Lucy kept close to him as they walked, frequently touching his arm as she and Amanda chattered about the Copper Canyon train trip their group was taking the next morning, to see the plunging canyons of the Sierra Madre. They were excited about experiencing the "real Mexico", which amused Seb. The Copper Canyon tour – so safe and so geared for American tourists – was not remotely like the real Mexico he knew.

"You'll have a good time," was all he said. "Make sure you don't fall out the window – it's a long way down."

"Hey, maybe you could come with us!" Lucy gave a

little skip to get ahead of him, walking backwards. She was wearing tight jeans, and a halter top that showed off her creamy skin. "Why don't you? I'm sure we can get you a ticket. We'd have a great time!"

Amanda rolled her eyes. "Um, hello – we had to book those tickets months ago, remember? There's no way we can get him one."

"It's okay, I've seen it," said Seb. He crumpled up the wax paper that his taco had come in, pitching it into a garbage can. He was dryly aware that even as he was talking to the girls, part of him was scanning every aura he passed. Yes, he'd certainly given up searching – didn't even think about it any more.

Lucy gave a little pout. "Oh. Well, will you still be here in a few days? Doing your *psychic readings?*" She bantered the words, making it clear that she didn't believe in that stuff for a second.

"Maybe – I haven't decided yet." Or decided what to do with the gaping years ahead of him, either. Not wanting to think about it, he said, "Who knows, maybe I'll give it all up and become a violinist."

"A violinist?" Amanda nudged him. "No way, you look like you're strictly an electric-guitar man. I keep expecting you to whip out your axe and start doing 'Stairway to Heaven'."

Seb held back a smile. He could never resist an opening

like this. "No, my father's a classical violinist," he said seriously. "I guess it's just in the blood, you know?"

She blinked. "Really?"

"Yes, I was raised on that stuff. My mother's an opera singer. She plays too, though. Piano. She says it helps her relax, so she likes to take it on tour with her – it's so difficult getting it on flights. Because it always has to be *her* piano; no other one will do."

Amanda's brown eyes had gone wide. "Wow – are you serious?"

"*No*, he's not serious," laughed Lucy. "Get your brain in gear, Amanda."

The dark-haired girl made a rueful face. "Okay, you got me, Seb. So what do your parents really do?"

"Really? They run a circus training school."

Lucy snickered. "You're not going to get anything out of him. Don't you remember from last night? Seb's the original man of mystery." She squeezed his arm, giving him an arch smile. "I bet your parents are really Mr. and Mrs. Ordinary of Boring, Mexico."

He laughed out loud at that – if only she knew. "Yes, I think maybe you're right," he said.

Leaning close, Lucy traced the thin scar on his forearm, from a knife fight when he was younger. He caught a whiff of her shampoo; it smelled like oranges. "Let me guess – a swordfight with pirates, right?"

"Just a cat scratch. It was a big cat, though." Even without the sultry pink lights shifting through her aura, Seb was very aware that Lucy was coming on to him a little. As she touched his arm, he knew without trying that she was wondering what it would be like to kiss him; planning how she could get him on his own at the hostel later.

From long habit he started to pull gently away – and then stopped. For the last year or so, the sense of his half-angel girl had grown so strong that Seb had stopped having even flings with human girls; it had felt like he was betraying her. But she wasn't real, she never had been – he had to get that through his head. Since giving up his search he'd been even lonelier than usual; achingly aware that he was the only one of his kind. This girl didn't want a *relationship* with him, so why not? She obviously liked him – and it had been so, so long.

As if in response, he caught the sense of his half-angel girl again, like a whiff of perfume floating past. Seb's jaw tightened. Why couldn't she just leave him in peace, instead of taunting him with what he could never have?

He didn't pull away. After a moment he felt Lucy's hand slide down his arm and find his. "Maybe you can give me a psychic reading later," she said softly, under cover of the sound of a *mariachi* band that had just started up.

Seb took in the clear invitation in her eyes. No human

girl could ever give him the true companionship he craved; he knew that. This, right here, was the most he could ever have – and he'd take it, because he wasn't saint enough to spend the rest of his life alone, never even feeling the warmth of someone's touch.

Fighting the wistfulness he felt, he pushed the beautiful phantom out of his mind and let his fingers close around Lucy's. "Are you sure?" he said. "I'll find out all your secrets."

"Promise?" She smiled, and flipped her ponytail back. She said something else, but he didn't hear what it was; in a sudden flash, a blinding white figure had come into view overhead. There was an angel cruising over the crowded stalls. Its wings burned in the late afternoon sunlight as it glided, gazing down at the shoppers.

Reflexively, Seb shifted his aura to the dullest colours he could think of, making it look stunted, unappetizing. He'd fought an angel only once before; he had no desire to ever do it again. "Come on, let's go this way," he said, pulling at Lucy's hand. Amanda was lagging behind looking at jewellery; he took her arm too. "Come, there's a stall over here I want to show you."

"Hey!" protested Amanda as he dragged her off. "I was going to buy that."

"No, don't bother," he said. "This stand's better, I promise."

Glancing over his shoulder, he saw the angel select its victim and land, so dazzling with radiance that the marketplace seemed to fade away. The man stared at the being in wonder as it reached towards him. Smiling gently, it rested its gleaming hands in his aura and began to feed.

Seb led the girls to another jewellery stand. While they stood laughing, trying on rings, he found his gaze drawn back to the angel as it finally flew away in a shudder of light. Though he no longer wanted to be pure angel himself, he couldn't completely hold back his old longing for their strength and power, which had seemed so desperately appealing to him at thirteen. When it came to the creatures' feeding, he had never quite decided what he felt about it. The angels hurt people and he wished they didn't – but they also made them genuinely happy. From the readings he'd given to people with angel burn, he knew this happiness was real, even if their health was damaged. When humans hurt other humans, there was no happiness at all – just pain and misery. At least the angels gave something back. Then Seb sighed as he wondered how the man was damaged now. The issue wasn't an easy one; he'd never resolved it in his mind.

The girls were trying on necklaces now, admiring themselves in a small mirror.

"I like the turquoise one," said Amanda, her dark hair beside Lucy's red.

"Really?" Lucy cocked her head to one side as she inspected herself. "I can't decide; I like the shell one, too. Wait, are there matching earrings?"

Seb drifted to the next stall. It sold a mishmash of things: clothes, old paperbacks, CDs. He took his cigarettes from his knapsack and lit one as he started looking over the books, arranged spine-up in long, battered rows. He'd first started reading for pleasure in the measly library of the orphanage, while checking every book they had to try and find out about others like him. There'd been nothing, of course, but he'd stumbled across a story about a boy and a horse, and been hooked ever since.

Now he found a popular science title that he hadn't read, and propped an elbow on a shelf to his side as he flipped to its opening page. Soon he was immersed.

"I've got some stuff to sell," said a voice. "You buy clothes and things, right?"

Seb didn't look up, distantly aware that the stall owner was going through a pile of goods with someone, the two of them haggling over prices. "Man, you've got to be kidding – this shirt alone is worth fifty pesos—"

Deciding that he'd get the book, Seb took a final puff of his cigarette and ground it out. As he glanced over, he saw the speaker was a stocky guy a few years older than himself, holding up a girl's light blue long-sleeved shirt. Seb frowned. The sense that he was meant to be doing something tickled over him again, more strongly than ever. A price was finally agreed; the stall owner put the shirt to one side.

For some reason, Seb couldn't stop himself – he reached for the shirt. As his fingers touched the thin cloth, he gasped a quick, stunned breath.

Familiar. How could it feel so familiar?

Lucy came dancing up, her eyes alight. "Look, aren't I pretty?" Squeezing his arm, she shook her head at him, showing off her new earrings. Then she glanced down at the shirt and her eyebrows rose knowingly. "Ooh, what's that? Are you buying me a present?"

"I – uh, no," Seb said faintly, hardly noticing she was there. He was still gripping the shirt; he wasn't sure he'd ever be able to let go of it. He watched as the stall owner examined a pair of girl's jeans; the man pulled a small, framed photo out of the pocket and squinted at it.

"Pretty girl. I can sell the frame; the photo's no good to me. Do you want it back?"

The stocky guy glanced at it. "Nah. How much for the frame?"

Seb's throat went dry. Without taking his left hand off the shirt, he said, "Wait – can I see that?" and plucked the framed photo from the stall owner's hand.

The picture was of a little girl with long blonde hair, peering up through the trailing fronds of a willow tree.

For a moment, Seb almost couldn't breathe as he looked at her smiling face; it felt like he'd been punched in the stomach.

Lucy stood staring at him; at the other end of the stall, Amanda had appeared, flipping through the CDs. "Hey, what's wrong?" said Lucy. "I didn't catch all of that."

"I'll take this," Seb managed to get out to the stall owner. "And the shirt – how much do you want for them?"

The man gave a bemused shrug. "A hundred pesos for both? It's a nice little frame."

Seb dug the money out of his pocket, shoved it at him. He put the shirt and photo into his bag, zipping it tightly as if to protect them. "Where'd you get these?" he asked the stocky guy. His voice was shaking. "Who's the girl, do you know?"

The man looked shifty suddenly. "No one in particular. Why are you so interested?"

"Because I *need to find the girl*," gritted out Seb, each word low and distinct. "Did you steal this stuff? Where from – just tell me!"

"Hey, I'm no thief! No, it was just on the side of the road. Like someone had lost it all."

He was lying – his aura had turned a devious mustard yellow. Seb's muscles were trembling; he knew he was close to lunging at the guy and attacking him. He stepped closer. "Don't lie to me, man. I'm asking you one more time – where'd you get it?"

"Seb!" cried Lucy, tugging at his arm. "God, cool it – what's going on?" He shook her off, not taking his eyes from the thief. The man swallowed, a nervous expression on his face now.

"Look, I don't want any trouble," put in the stall owner. "You boys got a problem, take it somewhere else."

"Tell me," said Seb in a low voice, ignoring him. And he knew that his tone was the same as from the dark time when he was thirteen. He'd enjoyed fighting then; he didn't now, but he'd have no hesitation about doing it.

He could sense the guy realizing this, coming to a decision. "You won't find them," he said finally. "It was hours ago – they're gone now, okay? They were *gringos*, they'd only stopped to get some food. And that's all I'm telling you."

It was the truth. Seb let out a breath. Amanda was standing beside Lucy now, both of them gaping at him as if he'd gone insane. Maybe he had. "Sorry," he muttered to Lucy, taking a step backwards. His pulse was throbbing in his ears. "I've got to go."

"Go? You mean back to the hostel?"

"No – no, I've got to go." And before she could answer he turned and took off at a run through the marketplace, leaving her startled face behind him in a blur. He had to get someplace private; had to look at this stuff again. He must be going crazy – this couldn't possibly be true—

The hostel would be full of people. Veering east, he pounded down the streets and into the Plaza de Armas, with its small, pattering fountain, its mix of palm trees and spruce, and the white stone cathedral that looked almost pink in the sunset. There was a bandstand across from the cathedral – an elegant wrought-iron structure from a different age. Seb saw that it was empty and took its four steps at a single leap. Breathing hard, he pulled the photo from his knapsack and then hesitated, clutching it tightly, the image hidden as the small frame dug into his palm. It couldn't be true. He had just wished for it so often that he'd finally gone insane. He was going to open his hand and it would just be a human girl, that was all – just a human girl.

Swallowing, Seb finally dared to unclench his hand and look down. He stared. Without realizing it, he sank to the worn wooden floor, still holding the photo.

From the time of his earliest memories, he'd been able to see auras – the angry, crackling red of his mother's boyfriend's energy as he beat Seb; the soggy blue of his mother's as she'd put him in the orphanage, crying that it was Seb's fault for not getting along with the man. His own aura, whenever he'd brought it into view, was the only one he'd ever encountered that was mostly silver, with forest-green lights shifting through it. The difference had bothered Seb deeply – he'd been convinced that his aura's strangeness had been the reason for the beatings. That had been the start of his lifelong habit of shifting his aura's colours, of learning how to blend in. He hadn't known then that it was pointless around humans – that nobody except him could see the bright shapes of energy anyway.

But he didn't just see auras when he met people face-to-face; he could see them in photos, too. And now…Seb gazed down at the framed photo in his hand, and it was as if the whole world had stopped breathing. It was true. He hadn't been mistaken. The little girl peering up through the willow branches had an aura like his own: silver, with lavender lights.

Another half-angel.

It was her.

Seb's heart thundered in his chest. Jesus god, he had to find her. Where was she, though? *Who* was she? "Them", the guy had said, so she was travelling with someone. He'd seemed certain that they wouldn't still be in Chihuahua, but—

Seb closed his eyes and sent his other self soaring, even though he usually kept his angel self hidden in cities – the violent encounter with the angel years ago had taught him that. Right now, he didn't care. Lifting up through the bandstand's roof, he stretched his shining wings and glided over the city, scanning its roads, its parks, the highway that stretched through town.

There was nothing, of course. Nothing.

His angel rushed back to him. Seb opened his eyes and stared unseeingly at one of the ornate iron posts. The possibility that he might have finally come so close to finding his half-angel girl, only to have *missed* her somehow, made him sick with dread.

His gaze fell on the knapsack near his feet. Suddenly he remembered the girl's shirt – the feeling of familiarity that had swept over him in the marketplace. He pulled it out; the material felt soft against his fingers. With a steadying breath, Seb closed his eyes again.

It washed over him all at once. The sense of an energy so similar to his own was dizzying, and Seb's hands turned to fists, grasping the thin material like a lifeline. His phantom half-angel girl, who he'd spent so many years of his life trying to find – she was real; she had worn this shirt. He could feel her so strongly, her spirit whispering through the fabric. Everything about her that he'd been in love with for so long – her kindness, her strength, her humour – it was all here, and more. Seb's heart was battering in his chest.

When he could finally focus again, he realized that she was about his own age, and that she'd been worried about a dream. Pictures started appearing in Seb's mind; he frowned in surprise at the familiar streets. *El DF.* She had dreamed of Mexico City, and of angels, and a sense of urgency that pulled at her like the tide. They had to go there, she and her human boyfriend – they had no choice. The details from the dream swirled over him; he could feel the girl's fear, her anxiousness.

The final image jolted him with shock.

A boy in her dream stood watching her in a park; he held out his hand, called her *querida.* Seb could feel how much the girl wanted to go to him; the longing that came over her as their eyes met. And the boy's face was the same one that he saw whenever he looked in a mirror.

The dream faded. Seb lowered the shirt, his mind reeling. She had dreamed of him – she'd longed for him just as he'd always longed for her. For a minute he couldn't help it; still clutching the shirt, he slumped against the side of the bandstand, burying his head in his arms as he struggled against tears. Oh god, it was true – it was really true. She was real; he wasn't alone.

The cathedral bells began to ring through the evening, tolling six o'clock. As the last note died from the air, Seb rose shakily to his feet. If the two of them were following the girl's dream, then they were on their way to Mexico City. It didn't matter how much he hated *el DF*; he had to get down there now, this second, so that he could find this girl – even if he had to search every square inch of the place to do it.

Folding the shirt, Seb tucked it into his bag, his fingers leaving it reluctantly. The photo he studied for a moment, drinking in the girl's delicately pointed features, her smile and green eyes. He shook his head in wonder as he touched the upturned face. So this was what she looked like; he'd yearned to know for most of his life. So beautiful, even as a child. Was she with her human boyfriend for the same reason he'd been tempted by Lucy – just because the loneliness had become too much, and there was no one else? Maybe this girl had always felt alone too, the same way he had.

Seb tucked the photo into the pocket of his jeans, wanting to keep it close. Mexico City held twenty million people, but he'd find her, somehow. They had to meet, had to be together. The certainty of it was like a heartbeat drumming through him. No other option was possible – it was meant to be.

She had dreamed of him.

CHAPTER *Five*

THE FIRST THING I NOTICED about Mexico City was the traffic. It was endless, chaotic: cars, taxis, other motorcycles. Horns blaring; red lights being run; hardly any attention paid to the division lines at all, except to see how blatantly you could ignore them. When it stopped for even a second, shouting sellers appeared in the street, striding past with cigarettes and candy. I kept my hands on Alex's waist as he wove us deftly in and out of it all, swerving and putting on the brakes as people tried to blindside us.

The second thing that hit me was the smell – a dizzying cocktail of exhaust fumes, the spices from sidewalk food vendors, dust from construction projects. And the sound: jackhammers, rock music, brakes squealing in protest. I couldn't stop staring, taking it all in. As Alex and I made our way towards the centre of the city, I saw medieval buildings jostling for space beside modern glass structures and art deco ones from the thirties; others that were abandoned, with graffiti-ridden boards covering the windows. I blinked as I noticed something else – a lot of the buildings seemed slightly skewed, as if you were viewing them after a drunken night out. The whole place looked like the aftermath of a giant party.

And there were the angels, of course.

I spotted the first one soon after we entered the city, gliding serenely over a neighbourhood a few streets away. As we got further in, I kept seeing others here and there, circling and occasionally diving downwards in flashes of light. I even saw one feeding on a dingy sidewalk as we passed by, not ten feet away. My scalp went cold; I couldn't take my eyes off it. The old man being fed from stood smiling dazedly; the angel was brilliant white, almost seven feet high, its wings blinding in the sun. It was surreal, the way people on the sidewalk were just shoving past the man; how none of them could see what was so painfully obvious to me.

The next light turned red and we came to a stop. Alex glanced over his shoulder, pushing his visor up.

"We should start thinking about where we're going. Any ideas?"

I swallowed. Not even Alex could see what I saw – not unless he shifted his consciousness up through his chakra points. Feeling very alone suddenly, I looked away from the feeding angel, thankful that the thing was too distracted to notice me. "No, no ideas," I said.

Then, as the traffic started up again, I thought of something. I raised my voice over the noise. "Wait – can we go to that square, the one I dreamed about?"

"Yeah, I guess," Alex called back after a pause. I knew he was thinking about the hunting angels I'd seen in my dream, and wasn't crazy about the idea – but he didn't argue.

It was nearing sunset, the sky spectacular with the pollution: wild streaks of red and pink that swirled across the grey dusk like oil on water. I'd have known the city was seething with angels even if I couldn't see them – on almost every street corner, silver and blue Church of Angels signs were painted on the sides of buildings like giant billboards. And lots of people were visibly sick. As Alex stopped for another light, I watched a young woman pause on the sidewalk, gripping a street light for support. It could have been a coincidence, of course. She could have just had a dizzy spell or something. But I really doubted it. And if it was this bad here *now*, what was it going to be like in a few more weeks, now that the Second Wave had arrived? I bit my lip, hating the thought of it.

Slowly, a massive stone cathedral loomed into view above the other buildings. It had two ornate bell towers; they stood to either side of a central dome, where a golden angel perched on one foot, lifting a garland towards the sky.

I felt Alex's muscles tense; when we stopped for another light, he whipped towards me again. "I don't *believe* it – that angel's the most famous statue in Mexico City! It's always been on top of a column on the Paseo de la Reforma, and now suddenly it's up there on the Catedral Metropolitana."

"The what?"

"The Metropolitan Cathedral," he said. His jaw was tight. "It's the oldest cathedral in the Americas – it's been here for, like, four hundred years. And I've got a really bad feeling it's a Church of Angels cathedral now. It must have happened just recently."

"Oh," I said weakly. That…didn't seem like a good sign.

"Anyway, it's on the Zócalo – we're almost there. And guess what?" Alex added, nodding at a brightly-coloured poster on a street lamp. "That sign says there's a 'Love the Angels' concert going on in the square tonight."

My eyes met Alex's; I knew we were both remembering

the dancing crowd in my dream. A terrible sense of inevitability came over me – déjà vu times a hundred. Just like when I'd realized that I had to go to the Church of Angels in Schenectady, to try to help Beth. The comparison wasn't comforting, when the entire congregation had tried to kill me and I'd only barely escaped.

"So," said Alex finally. He faced forward again, lifting his voice as the traffic started to move. "I guess we should go check it out." I could tell he was thinking about his gun, and how many cartridges he had left.

I cleared my throat. "Yeah," I called back. "I guess we should."

A convertible filled with people wearing angel wings passed by, honking. We turned onto the same road they did, leading to one of the streets that bordered the Zócalo. I stared as the square came into view, taken aback by how accurate my dream had been. The Zócalo was *huge*, with people streaming by the thousands into its broad expanse.

And just like in my dream, a stage had been set up at the cathedral end of the square, bathed in floodlights. There were food stands, and vendors moving through the crowd selling angel wings, holding them up in feathery white clusters like giant dandelion heads.

It didn't look as if you were supposed to park on the streets surrounding the square, but people were doing it anyway. Alex pulled over too, angling the Shadow alongside a car. We got off the bike. We were in front of the long, official-looking building from my dream, with the cathedral rising up to our right. I stiffened as I took off my helmet – there were three angels gliding over the square.

Alex checked his pistol, concealing it between his body and the parked car. I felt him shifting through his chakra points, so that when he turned around again his gaze found the angels as easily as I had. "Okay," he said, regarding them grimly. "Any idea what we should do next? Was there anything else in your dream?"

The only thing in my dream I hadn't told him about was the strange boy, and my reaction to him – it had just seemed too weird to mention. I shook my head, watching the angels as they hunted. I knew if Alex were here on his own he'd be slipping into the crowd to kill all three if he could, before they started feeding.

"Don't let me hold you back," I said, looking up at him. "I'm serious."

He let out a breath; I could see the conflict in his blue-grey eyes. Still studying the square, he put his arm around me. "No, I'm not going to leave you on your own with angels around."

"Alex, it's okay. I can take care of myself."

"Your angel self can," he agreed. "But until you learn how to shoot, your human self is so vulnerable it gives me nightmares. Willow, all it would take would be two angels ganging up on you, and they'd rip your life force away."

I opened my mouth, then closed it again. Okay, I didn't exactly have an answer for that.

Alex squeezed my hand, then glanced at the roof of the parked car behind us. "Come on. Let's sit up here where we can keep an eye on things; see why your psychic powers brought us here."

He vaulted nimbly onto the car's hood and then the roof, leaning over to help me up. Plenty of people around us were doing the same, though presumably in their case the cars in question were their own. Some had even brought coolers full of beer and food, as if the concert were a giant Fourth of July picnic. The night was mild – apparently the weather here was like a perpetual springtime.

Trying to ignore the angels, I stared out at the square, with its buildings that looked so completely unlike anything in the United States. Especially the cathedral. It was actually *two* cathedrals: the massive main one with its tiered bell towers and angel-topped dome, and then another, smaller, one just beside it, with ornate stonework framing a broad wooden door.

"The tabernacle," said Alex, following my gaze. "I think it was built at a later date – I'm not sure why."

I nodded slowly, taking it all in: the ancient-looking stone, the cars, the vibrant crowd. There was a real buzz in the air – and not only here; I'd been noticing it ever since we got into the city. It tickled at my senses like something tangible.

"Mexico City is just amazing," I said, sitting cross-legged on the metal roof. We hadn't had a chance to buy other clothes yet; I was wearing Alex's red plaid shirt over my camisole. "I've never seen anything like it."

Alex shrugged; I knew he wasn't much of a city person at heart. "Yeah, it's like New York on a caffeine jag. Jake loved it when we were here on hunts – he used to drag me clubbing every night we could sneak out."

The momentary sadness crossed his face that always came whenever he mentioned his brother. I pressed against him, slipping my arm around his waist, and he managed a smile. "Anyway, the angels love it here, too – something about the energy really draws them." His eyes went to the cathedral again and he shook his head. "They must have a complete stranglehold here now – and the Second Wave angels probably haven't even arrived yet."

By the time a band called *Los Ángeles Amigos* came on – four guys wearing angel wings and a girl singer with a slightly crooked halo – the square was packed with people and there were over two dozen real angels gliding around overhead. It was ironic, I guess: as rock music celebrating the angels beat through the night, the angels themselves dipped and turned, taking their time as they chose which human to feed from. Occasionally one dove, disappearing into the dancing crowd. On the next car, the people on the roof had their arms around each other, singing along with the music. Alex and I watched in silence, holding hands.

Finally the band stopped; a woman in a short red dress stepped onstage and grabbed the mic. She shouted something about "*los ángeles*" – "the angels" – her voice booming out through the speakers.

"*Sí!*" roared the crowd.

"Let me guess," I said to Alex, leaning close so he'd hear. "*Do you love the angels?*"

He smiled wryly. "Got it in one."

The woman called out something else. "*Are you happy they're with us?*" Alex translated, his lips a warm tickle against my ear as the crowd screamed, "*SÍ! SÍ!*"

The woman crouched down on her high heels, flinging one arm up as she shouted a third time. Noise thundered through the night; the crowd went berserk, screaming and jumping up and down.

Alex started to speak, then broke off, straightening abruptly. I caught my breath as I saw it too. One of the angels had just dodged to the left, its great wings slicing through the air. The angel paused, hovering, as it seemed to look around it. With a sudden flurry it darted aside again.

And then, on the far side of the square, another angel

vanished in a petal-pattern of radiance, like a firework going off over the crowd. Pieces of light drifted to the ground.

I stared dumbly as they twinkled in the floodlights. I could hardly get the words out. "Is – is there anything else that can cause that?"

When Alex spoke, his voice sounded rough. "No," he said. "No, there isn't. Somebody just shot an angel."

We glanced at each other. I felt the tense excitement pulsing through him; it matched my own. There was another AK out there in the crowd – someone else who knew how to fight the angels. More than one in fact, because back towards the stage, two angels were flying towards the one who had first dodged – and suddenly one of *them* lunged to the side too, as if avoiding a bullet. At the same moment, the first angel jerked away again with a bright shimmer.

"At least three gunmen," murmured Alex. The muscles in his forearms looked taut. "Christ, there's a whole team of AKs out there."

"*Can* there be?" I said in a daze. "I thought you were the only one!"

"I don't know – maybe the CIA set up another group down here without telling us, or maybe someone else figured out how to fight them—" Alex broke off, tapping the car roof as he watched the scene. "Jesus, why are you letting them go on the offensive?" he muttered to the unseen AKs. "They know you're there, just *shoot* them already!"

As he spoke, one of the three angels twisted nimbly to the side, wings glinting. I went cold as it hit me: the AKs *were* shooting at the angels; they were shooting at them almost non-stop.

But they were missing.

I knew from Alex that everyone missed sometimes; an angel's halo wasn't an easy target, especially when they were in motion. You had to be accurate a lot more often than you weren't, though. If you missed too many times, then what was going on right now happened: the angels realized you were there, and moved in for the kill.

Distantly, I saw another angel burst into nothingness at the opposite end of the square, but couldn't take my eyes off the disaster that was unfolding here, near the stage. The three angels glided in a hunting pack, and now I could tell they'd spotted the gunmen below: there was a sudden decisiveness to their moves, a deadly certainty in the way they banked as one and started plunging downwards.

The AKs obviously saw it too. There was a flurry of motion in the crowd; a small group of people shoving their way through the throng, panic giving them strength. "Get away, *hurry*," I whispered. My hands were clenched. The gunmen burst out of the other side of the square, and then went racing away down a busy road. They turned into what looked like an alleyway; the three angels headed after them, gliding with an ominous lack of haste.

Alex swore as he jumped off the car. "The *idiots* – why are they going for an enclosed space, where they can get backed against a wall? They're all about to be killed." He yanked on his helmet.

I'd already slid off the car behind him and was grabbing for my own helmet. "Can we get through the crowd?" I asked, raising my voice over the sound of the next band that had just come on. The street was full of hundreds of pedestrians milling around, dancing to the music. Lots of them wore angel wings, feathery and surreal in the half-light.

"We've got to," said Alex shortly. We straddled the bike and he revved it; at the sound of the engine, the people nearby gave way. He nudged the Shadow through as fast as he could, honking the horn. Finally we reached the main road and he opened up the accelerator with a roar. As we sped south, I could just see the flock of three, heading away over the buildings. Alex did too; he took off after them, weaving in and out of traffic. They vanished from view and he took an abrupt turn, and then another, sending us hurtling around corners.

The angels were nowhere in sight.

Suddenly I could *feel* which way we should go,

throbbing through me with absolute conviction. "That way!" I shouted in Alex's ear, pointing to a street off to the right. He took it, and soon we were barrelling down a long road that was mostly businesses, run-down and seedy. Behind a faded pink stucco house, the tips of the angels' wings flashed in and out of view.

Alex screeched to a halt. In the sudden silence we could hear shouts. Bars covered the windows; a wrought-iron gate stood open, showing the drive. No lights – the place almost seemed abandoned, except for a white van. I felt Alex's energy lift again, scanning quickly.

"All three of them are back there," he muttered, flinging his helmet off.

I looked at the house…and the moment froze. My scalp prickled as the darkness of the barred windows reeled me in like a black hole. Something was going to happen here – something that would make both of us so unhappy.

I shook the idea away; it had to just be nerves or something. But the coldness remained, and as the frightened shouts rang through the night, they almost seemed to be coming from inside my own head, dreading whatever was to come.

Willow stood motionless, staring up at the house with wide eyes. "Come on!" said Alex. He grabbed her hand,

and she seemed to return to herself with a start. They raced down the driveway as the shouts grew louder.

"Get away from me!" yelled someone. The words were in English; the voice sounded American. The faint thud of silenced gunfire came from nearby.

The drive ended. Alex pressed against the side of the house, deftly screwing on his own pistol's silencer before peering around the back.

A chaos of scrambling bodies; three angels swooping about like giant moths to a flame. There were five AKs – two girls and three guys – and they were shouting, waving their guns around. The angels were toying with them, Alex saw grimly – laughing as they darted towards their opponents and then away again, biding their time before they ripped their life forces away.

They were in a concrete courtyard; there was a back door with a light over it, casting a circle of luminance like a bizarre stage set. A muscular blond guy stood in the spotlight's centre, grasping a gun with both hands and swinging it wildly.

"Come on, *cabrona*!" he screamed at a female angel. "Come and get me!" His accent was pure Texan.

Alex saw the angel decide it had had enough of playing; it went high and then dove at the guy, screeching. Alex tracked the creature as it moved, aiming for the pure, bright blue at the centre of its halo. Even through his concentration, he was shaking his head. Tex was flailing about so frantically he'd be lucky not to blow one of his friends away.

"Oh god, one's about to get that girl," burst out Willow. With a smooth shiver her angel form appeared; her human body was still crouched at his side, eyes closed now as she concentrated.

"Willow, no," he started. "Seriously, stay back—"

Her angel had already sped away, heading towards the cement wall that bordered the courtyard. Wings outspread, she swooped over a dark-haired girl with a sharp face, protecting her. The attacking angel drew back with a surprised hiss; the girl flinched and gaped upwards.

"I can't just let it kill her!" said the human Willow at his side. "I'll be okay." Alex gritted his teeth and tried not to worry. Willow's life force was in her human body, not her angel one – but neither of them knew what might happen if her angel self got injured somehow.

The diving angel was still corkscrewing down, wings flashing. Aiming again, Alex shot; the creature seemed to sense him, dodging aside at the last moment. He shot again, anticipating the move this time, and the angel erupted into a million pieces of light. Tex gave a yelp as the shockwave blew him backwards, off his feet.

One down, two to go. Alex glanced again at the girl cowering by the wall. Above, Willow's angel darted about like a shining bird as she held off the attacking female. The angel was beating its wings fiercely as it tried to get past her. Willow's angel was smaller than average – only barely larger than her human form – but incredibly nimble in the air, like a kestrel.

"You!" Alex heard the female angel hiss. "Half-human *thing*—"

The remaining angel had been about to dive; overhearing, it twisted in the air, looking for Willow's human form. Alex lifted his gun as it spotted her in the drive. It came at them in a rush of light; Alex shot and the creature veered away sharply…and then it soared off and disappeared over the back wall.

Remembering the dozens of angels in the square, Alex's pulse quickened in alarm. Oh, Christ, the thing had gone to get them – in minutes they'd have an angel army coming down on their heads, all of them intent on killing Willow.

He broke from the shadows, pounding across the courtyard where Willow's angel still feinted with the female. No one seemed to have realized he was there; he saw a rush of startled faces as he lunged at the wall; scaled it quickly and dropped to the ground. He ran down an alleyway, bursting out onto another street. The angel was flying fast, heading away from him.

"Hey!" shouted Alex, his feet pummelling the pavement as he ran. "*Hey!*"

The creature whirled in surprise as Alex shot. Rage creased its glorious face and it came at him, swooping down like a giant bird of prey. It was faster than he'd expected. Alex dove to the ground as the angel screeched overhead, its fingers grasping towards his life force. He rolled and was up on one knee in seconds, wishing for his rifle; it handled ten times better in situations like this. The thought flashed past. He took aim as the angel roared towards him again in a fury of light and beauty, taking care not to look into its eyes, to keep his gaze only on the halo—

He shot.

Leaving the remnants of the angel floating gently behind him, Alex tore back up the alleyway. The whole episode had only taken a minute or two; as he dropped back into the courtyard, he saw Willow's angel still holding off the larger female. Their wings blurred as they fenced and parried, and he could tell that it was Willow's vulnerable human form the angel was now trying to reach. A couple of people stood watching with open mouths; the others dashed back and forth, trying to take aim at the angel. Tex was just struggling dazedly to his feet.

Alex tracked the angel, getting her halo in his sights. "I'm on it!" he shouted to Willow. Immediately, her angel twisted away, plunging back towards her human form. The creature started to follow and then wavered, turning towards Alex as it sensed a trap.

It was all the time he needed. The muffled sound of his silenced bullet thudded around them and the last angel vanished into a fountain of light.

Alex let out a breath as he put his pistol away. He looked towards the drive, and saw Willow rising to her feet in the shadows. Their eyes met. She seemed shaken, but gave him a small smile. She was okay; it was over with. Alex felt himself relax a notch as he smiled back, and for a second there was only the two of them. At a slight movement to his left he glanced over, his gaze leaving Willow reluctantly – and his blood froze.

Tex was aiming his gun right at her.

"*No!*" Alex hurtled forward, tackling him just as the pistol went off. They crashed to the ground together, the gun skittering across the pavement.

"*What the hell are you doing?*" he shouted. "She's on our side!"

The guy writhed under him like a fish out of water, struggling to get free. "Let me up!" he yelled. "She's not human – her aura is angelic—"

"She's on our side!" shouted Alex again. Tex's fists were flailing; Alex held him down, ducking to avoid being hit. "Jesus, will you *listen* to me—"

Tex bucked upwards, half getting away as he scrambled on all fours for his gun. Alex threw himself after him, grabbing him around the waist. The guy twisted and swung, his fist connecting hard with Alex's cheekbone. The world went red; Alex slammed him back to the ground. Drawing his pistol, he shoved it in the guy's face. The struggling stopped as Tex stared at it.

"Do. Not. Move," Alex gritted out.

Slowly, he rose to his feet, still aiming his pistol at Tex. His cheek was throbbing; he hardly noticed. The others stood nearby, staring, not moving a muscle. "All of you – guns on the ground," he ordered without looking at them. Silence. "*Now*," he barked.

They must have heard something in his tone that convinced them. There was a brief hesitation, then the clatter of weapons being dropped on concrete.

"Willow, are you okay?" called Alex, not taking his eyes off the muscular blond guy. He held an arm out in her direction, and felt infinite relief as she appeared at his side, slipping under his arm.

"I'm fine," she whispered. "Alex, I'm fine; he didn't hit me."

Thank god. "Get behind me," he muttered, squeezing her shoulders briefly. Tex's gun was just beside his foot; as Willow moved behind him, Alex kicked it away, sending it spinning into the shadows.

"She's not human!" insisted Tex from the ground, his drawling voice fierce. "She's one of them – you must be on their side, too—"

"Yeah, that's why I just shot three angels, and why she was holding one off until I could get to it," snapped Alex. He glanced at the others. Four of them, all looking shaken. "What do *you* think?" he demanded of the girl with the sharp face. "You're the one whose life she just saved. Do you want to take a shot at her, too?"

There was a slight shuffling as they all looked at each other. "Her aura...and there was the angel, with her face..." stammered the girl.

"That's so great that you know how to see angels," said Alex coldly. "You might want to work on your interpretations a little. Her angel didn't have a halo, or didn't you notice?" With his pistol, he motioned for Tex to get up, sending him to stand with the others. "Now, listen to me: *she's on our side*. Anyone who doesn't believe me, you'd better go for your gun and shoot me now – because I'll kill the next person who tries to hurt her."

His words hung in the air. Nobody moved. In the sudden silence, the drone of traffic could be heard, along with the fluttering of moths as they battered against the naked light bulb over the doorway.

"Good, I'm glad that's settled," said Alex finally.

He took in the tense group, wondering who they were – all the voices he'd heard so far were American. They stared back at him. Apart from Tex and the sharp-faced girl, there was a short guy with wiry rust-coloured hair who looked frozen in place; a curvy brown-haired girl, features tight with worry; a black guy who met his gaze sullenly, arms folded across his chest.

"So who are you all, anyway?" asked Alex. "You're sure as hell not Angel Killers."

Tex bristled. "We sure as hell *are*."

"Yeah? So that's why you managed to kill, like, none of them, right?"

Tex's muscles swelled as he glared at Alex, like a quarterback in a barroom brawl. Before the Texan could respond, the brown-haired girl cleared her throat. "We… we were angel spotters," she offered. "Back in the US."

Alex's forehead creased. "What, you mean for Project Angel?"

She nodded. She had an earnest face and blue eyes, her hair drawn back in a ponytail. "Until just a few months ago. And then—" The girl Willow had saved nudged her, giving her a piercing look; she flushed and fell silent.

Angel spotters. Alex nodded slowly. Yeah, that made sense. The angel spotters had worked for the CIA too, the same as he had – their role had been to locate angels and send texts to the AKs with their locations. They were trained to see angels, but wouldn't have much of a clue about the rest of it.

He scanned the group again. "So what happened – how did you find each other? I thought you guys had to work in isolation too, just like—" He broke off as he felt Willow stiffen behind him. At the same moment, a low female voice came from the drive:

"You want to explain why you're holding a gun on my group, hotshot? And it'd better be good, or I'll blow your freaking head off."

Alex whirled in place, ready to shoot. Instead he just stared.

The dark-skinned girl who stood holding a gun on him was beautiful, and almost as tall as he was, with high, chiselled cheekbones and close-cropped black hair. Her brown eyes widened abruptly as they regarded each other. She wore tan jeans and a sleeveless T-shirt; he could see the slim, hard muscles of her arms, as if she spent half an hour every day doing chin-ups.

On her left bicep was a black *AK* tattoo in gothic lettering.

Time had come to a stop. "Kara," whispered Alex.

The girl opened her mouth; closed it again. "Jake?" she got out. Her voice sounded ragged.

"No," he said. "No, I'm—"

"Alex," she finished for him. "Oh my god, Alex!" The next thing he knew, she had catapulted herself into his arms and they were hugging tightly. "I don't believe it!" Kara gasped, sounding close to tears. "It's really you – you're alive, you're okay…"

"I thought you were dead," he said against her neck. *Kara*. His throat felt too small for speech. "I thought everyone was dead, except for me."

She pulled back and touched his face; her slender hand felt firm and strong. "*Look* at you," she breathed, her eyes shining. "You look so much like Jake! You're all grown up—"

Suddenly they were both laughing. "Yeah, all grown up, just like you," he teased, putting away his gun. Kara was only four years older than him, but when he'd been a love-struck fourteen-year-old, it had seemed more like four decades.

The tension in the courtyard had faded; the AKs stood watching in bemusement. Willow stepped forward. He could see her joy for him that one of his old friends had made it – though the slight tension around her mouth reminded him of when she'd met Cully, back in New Mexico. She'd been worried then that all the AKs would hate her because of what she was.

"Willow, this is Kara Mendez," he told her. "We were at the camp together."

"Hi," said Willow, offering her hand to Kara. She looked almost waiflike in the plaid shirt, her green eyes dominating her face. "I'm Willow Fields."

Kara's eyebrows flew up; she gave Willow a cautious handshake. "Willow Fields – as in, the terrorist who's all over the news?"

Willow shrugged, and tried to smile. "Yeah, something like that. I was trying to stop the Second Wave from coming."

"And she ain't human," put in Tex sullenly. "Check out her aura, Kara; it's *weird*. Plus there was this angel with her face, and—"

"Shut up, Sam." From the way Kara said it, it was a phrase that got used often. But her expression turned wary as she glanced at Alex. "You want to explain what he's talking about?"

Alex started to answer; Willow put her hand on his arm, stopping him. Lifting her chin slightly, she said in a steady voice, "He's talking about the fact that I'm half-angel."

Kara took a sharp breath between her teeth; the others recoiled in shock, staring at Willow. "Whoa," murmured the wiry-haired guy, taking a step backwards. Tex – Sam, apparently – had a mix of validation and stunned horror on his broad face.

"*Half-angel?*" sputtered Kara at last. "That's supposed to be impossible!"

"I know," said Willow evenly. "But it's true. My father—" She stopped, a tautness crossing her features. "My father was an angel," she finished. "I never knew him, though. I never knew anything about any of this until just recently."

Alex knew that Kara's reaction was probably milder than his own had been when he'd first found out about Willow's parentage, but he still hated it. She was staring at Willow as if she were some kind of unthinkable lab experiment.

"Willow and I are together." He put his arm around Willow's shoulders and drew her against his side. "She almost died in Denver, trying to stop the Second Wave."

Kara didn't move, but he had the impression she'd just been rocked to the core; that she was even more shocked at this than at the revelation of what Willow was. "Together," she repeated in a monotone, her chocolate-brown eyes narrowing. "Let me get this straight: you're telling me that you've got a half-angel girlfriend."

"Yeah," said Alex. "That's right." Their gazes collided; he saw the thrust of Kara's chin and suddenly remembered how stubborn she could be. She and Cully had once had a stand-off for hours over a game of poker – the two of them bickering until late into the night, with Kara demanding that Cully take it outside with her. It had been funny at the time; he and Jake had taken bets on who would cave first.

It hadn't been Kara.

Willow cleared her throat. "Look, I don't want to cause any trouble or anything."

"You're not," said Alex, not taking his eyes off Kara. "Is she, Kara?"

Kara didn't answer at first; Alex couldn't tell what she was thinking. With deliberate movements, she put her gun away, tucking it into the holster under her jeans waistband.

"So," she said coolly. "I guess we should go inside, huh? Seems like we've all got a lot to talk about."

It took Alex a second to get what she meant. He glanced up at the dark house beside them. "Inside – what, *here*? This is your base?" He turned and stared at the other AKs in disbelief. "You mean, you actually led them back *here*. To your base."

Kara looked sharply at Sam. "Led who back? Was there trouble?"

Alex couldn't help it; he laughed out loud. "Yeah, let's go inside," he said. "You're right, there's a lot to talk about."

CHAPTER *Six*

KARA TOOK THEM THROUGH the back door and switched on the light. Alex could see cardboard boxes stacked against the wall, and scuffed floor tiles with a blue and white floral pattern. A decorative niche that looked as if it should have a vase in it instead held a flashlight and someone's change.

"What is this place?" he asked. He was carrying their camping stuff and helmets from the bike; they didn't have much else.

"Welcome to AK Central," said Kara. She led the way into a small kitchen. The other AKs hung back in the hallway, watching Willow with distrustful expressions. Sam especially was keeping an eye on her every move, as if she were about to sprout a halo and swoop at him, screeching, to feed. Alex dropped their stuff in a corner and put his hand on Willow's back as she stood against the counter, stroking lightly between her shoulder blades. The small smile she gave him didn't touch her eyes.

Kara introduced them all. Sam, Alex already knew better than he wanted to. The sharp-featured girl was Liz, who had long black hair and a pale, goth look. She kept casting appalled sidelong glances at Willow – apparently saving her life wasn't enough to earn her trust. Trish, the freckled brown-haired girl, didn't seem any less appalled; she also appeared anxious at the tension, gazing worriedly at the others.

"Hi," they each muttered. After a beat, Brendan, the short one with wiry hair, stepped forward to awkwardly shake Alex's hand. With an apprehensive glance at Willow, he stepped hastily back again.

The black guy was Wesley, whose arched eyebrows and wry mouth made him look like he should have a great sense of humour – except that he also looked like he'd never smiled in his life. He shifted his feet, glowering. "Are you going to need us for this, Kara?" he muttered.

"No, I don't think so," said Kara. "Why don't you guys

go into the TV room, or the range or something, so the three of us can talk?"

"You sure?" drawled Sam. He narrowed his blue eyes at Willow in a calculating way. "You might need some backup."

Alex snorted. With an effort, he refrained from pointing out that backup worked a lot better when the person backing you up actually knew how to shoot a gun.

"Yes, Sam, I am sure. Go on, now. I'll tell you guys whatever you need to know later."

After the AKs had drifted away, Kara put some water on to boil. She started getting mugs out of a cabinet, then hesitated as she looked at Willow. "Do you…do you eat and drink like we do, or—"

A cold anger tightened Alex's muscles. "Kara, for Chrissake—"

"Well, *I* don't know!" she snapped back. "How am I supposed to know what a half-angel does or doesn't do?"

"Come on! Do you think I'd even be *with* her if she was like them?"

Kara started to say something else and stopped; a flush tinged her cheeks. Not answering, she banged the cupboard door shut and opened another one, taking out a jar of instant coffee. She thumped it onto the counter.

Willow looked away, hugging herself; the plaid shirt billowed loosely about her thighs. "Yes, I eat and drink like you do," she said in a soft voice. "But I don't want anything."

Wishing he could pull her close against his chest, Alex put his arm around her instead; he could feel the tautness of her shoulders. Kara poured boiling water into the mugs, and added splashes of milk. "Two sugars, right?" she said without looking at him.

He glanced up in surprise as his throat tightened. It was how Jake had taken his coffee. "No, uh – just milk."

He saw Kara realize her mistake; a pained wince crossed her face. There must have been a hundred times on hunts when they'd stopped at a 7-Eleven and Kara had walked back out to the jeep balancing coffees for everyone – teasing Jake about the sugar and saying he couldn't take his java like a man. Now Alex knew she was seeing the same thing he was: his brother's grin as he said, *What you're really saying is I'm sweet enough already, right?* The flirting between Jake and Kara had never come to anything, though if Alex knew his brother, it hadn't been for lack of trying.

Kara handed him a mug without speaking; they sat down at a battered wooden table that dominated half the room. "You sure you don't want anything?" she said to Willow, her voice stiff.

"Maybe some water," said Willow. "I can get it," she added as Kara started to stand up.

Alex and Kara sat in silence as Willow found glasses in

a cupboard and filled one from the bottled water that sat on the counter. Kara was very pointedly not looking at Willow; she sat drinking her coffee, drumming her fingers on the worn wooden table. Her nails were short but shapely, painted bright pink. Memory stirred in Alex as he noticed. Those incongruous feminine touches of Kara's had given him some sleepless nights when he was fourteen or fifteen; he'd speculated endlessly on whether she might wear lacy lingerie too. Kara probably would have decked him if she'd known. No, not "probably".

Willow sat down, slipping into the chair next to him and avoiding his eyes. Under the table, Alex rubbed her thigh reassuringly, wishing they were alone; he hated how tense she seemed. She let out a breath, and darted a grateful glance at him.

"So what is this place?" he asked Kara again. "How did you hook up with the angel spotters, anyway? And how did you manage not to get killed? Cully said—"

Kara's brown eyes turned large. "You've seen Cully?"

"Yeah, just over a month ago." Alex glanced down, playing with the handle of his coffee mug. "He's got angel burn, Kara." Even now, he hated thinking about it. Once Alex's father, Martin, had started losing grip with reality, Cully had taken over as lead of the AK training camp: the place in the remote New Mexico desert where both Alex and Jake had been raised. And he'd done it so tactfully and unobtrusively that Alex's dad hadn't even noticed to take offence. The man had been a father to him in everything but name.

He described the encounter to Kara – how Cully was staying alone at the old camp now; how he'd tried to kill Willow because the angels had told him to.

The news brought a hard line to Kara's mouth, but then her manner turned thoughtful as she took in the pink scar on Willow's arm, where Cully's bullet had struck her.

"So the angels want you dead, huh?" she said.

Willow grimaced slightly. "Yeah, you could say that."

"It's what the terrorist manhunt is about," said Alex. He drained the rest of his coffee in a quick gulp. "They think she has the power to destroy them."

Kara sat watching Willow; even relaxed, Alex could see the muscles in her slender arms. "And? Do you?"

"No one's told me how yet, if I do," said Willow. Her spiky red-gold hair cut across her cheek as she looked down, tapping at her water glass. "Unfortunately, being a half-angel doesn't come with an instruction manual."

"No, I guess not," said Kara. "But my guys saw *something* about you that freaked them out."

"My angel self," said Willow. "I have a – dual nature, I guess you'd call it. My angel form can appear at the same time as my human one. They're both me, though. My angel self doesn't have a halo. It doesn't…feed, or anything."

Alex could tell how bizarre Kara was finding this. "Ohh-kay," she said. "So, you want to show me?"

Willow gave her a level look. "No, not really."

Kara's gaze narrowed for a second, then she shrugged. "Fair enough. But how is it that…I mean, I thought angels couldn't breed."

"I don't know," said Willow. "I'm the only one; it's a mystery to them, too." She managed a tight smile. "I'm just a fluke, I guess."

Briefly, Alex explained how he and Willow had first met; how Willow had almost died trying to stop the Second Wave from arriving. He didn't tell the final part of the story – how he'd held Willow's lifeless body in his arms and somehow willed her back into life. It still made his stomach clench to think how close he'd come to losing her.

When he'd finished, Kara tipped her chair back as she studied Willow carefully, her dark eyebrows drawn together. "So you really are on our side, then," she said.

Willow shrugged. "I don't think my AK boyfriend would want to have much to do with me if I wasn't, do you?" Kara didn't answer. Willow went on, her voice quiet but deliberate, enunciating each word clearly: "My father destroyed my mother's mind. She would have been normal if it wasn't for him; instead she barely knows who I am. Of course I'm on your side – I *hate* what the angels are doing here."

Her hand was clenched on the table; Alex covered it with his own.

"Okay. Got it," said Kara after a pause. Then she frowned, and her chair legs slowly came down to touch the floor. "Wait a minute – what are you two doing down here, anyway? How did you find us?"

"Willow had a dream that we should come here," said Alex. "She's psychic; she knew something was going to happen in the Zócalo."

Kara didn't move. "Psychic," she said finally, and Alex knew exactly what she was thinking: psychic skills were an angelic trait.

"Yes, I've always been psychic," said Willow. "Even before I knew…" She shrugged her slender shoulders, looking tired suddenly. "Even before I knew," she finished.

Alex circled her palm with his thumb. "Are you going to answer some of our questions now?" he said to Kara. "If the interrogation's over with, that is."

Kara rolled her eyes at the word "interrogation". She pushed her chair back and got up. "All right, let's just get settled first. You guys hungry? Liz likes to cook; we've got some leftover spaghetti I could heat up."

"Yeah, starving," said Alex. He let go of Willow's hand and scraped his palm across his face; his cheek gave a throb where Sam had punched him. It felt as if he'd been awake for days.

"Liz?" asked Willow.

"The one with dark hair," Kara reminded her, opening the fridge and taking out a covered casserole dish.

"Oh yeah, her. The one whose life Willow saved," said Alex pointedly, and took a dark enjoyment in the startled look on Kara's face. "Man, Kara, that group of yours needs some serious training," he went on. "What did you even have them out on a hunt for? Are you trying to get rid of them or something?"

Kara rested her hands on the counter; closing her eyes, she hung her head for a second, shaking it. "Okay. I've got to hear all about this, and I don't like the sound of it one little bit…but let me answer your questions first, and then we'll get to it."

She slid the casserole dish into a microwave and punched a few buttons; a low humming noise started. "So, the first thing you should know is – this place isn't mine, it was Juan's originally. He bought it for us to use."

"*Juan?* Is he alive too?" Alex sat up straight, heart thumping. Juan Escobido had been one of the best AKs at the camp – he'd often been the team lead on hunts, especially after the accident that had cost Cully his leg. If he was still alive, it was some of the best news Alex had heard in months.

"No," said Kara heavily, leaning against the counter. The fluorescent light cast the exotic lines of her face into sharp relief. "He was the one who brought us all down here; that white van in the drive is his. But he was killed the day after we finished fixing this place up. He didn't even have a chance to start training the team."

Alex went still. He could feel Willow's eyes on him, gentle with sympathy.

Kara's voice turned rough. "And the way it happened was just – stupid. The two of us had gone out to get some supplies, and we forgot to scan. An angel linked minds with Juan to feed, and he managed to break away enough to try and shoot it…but then it tore his life force away."

Alex didn't speak. "I called an ambulance, but I already knew he was gone," Kara went on. "And you know the worst part? I had to pretend I didn't even know him, that he was just some man I'd found collapsed on the sidewalk. Thankfully, I managed to get his gun, and he never carried ID…" She trailed off. "I got the angel," she added after a moment. "But it was sort of too late by then."

Unfortunately, Alex could picture it all too well; Jake's death had happened because he himself had forgotten to scan. God, it was so easy to do sometimes – so stupidly, criminally easy. Willow touched his arm, and he knew she was aware of what he was thinking.

"So how did he get you all down here?" he asked finally.

The microwave went off; Kara took the spaghetti out

and started piling portions onto plates. "Well, when Project Angel first got taken over, the angels started getting rid of all the AKs and angel spotters – you probably already know that. They sent one of their lackeys out after us; I guess none of them wanted to get near us themselves. And when it came to Juan's turn – well, let's just say that now there's one less lackey in the world."

"Good," said Alex shortly. Willow sat without speaking, listening intently.

Kara handed them both a plate; opened a drawer and fished out forks and spoons. Putting them on the table with a soft clatter, she sat down again. "Afterwards, Juan searched the guy's car and found his phone – and there was a document on it that had the names and contact numbers of everyone who hadn't been killed yet. Me and those five in there." She nodded towards the rest of the house. "We were all next on the list. Juan managed to get to us first, and brought us all down here."

"Why Mexico City?" asked Alex. He wasn't that hungry any more, but knew he should eat; he took a bite of spaghetti. "Juan wasn't from here, was he? I thought he was from Durango."

Kara nodded, tapping the table. "He was – we're here because of an email that Juan found on the phone. Alex, something big is going to be happening here soon. And we have to be here for it – we have to be ready."

Willow shot Alex a quick look. "What's happening?" she asked Kara. Her tone was full of dread; he knew she was thinking of her dream.

"I'd better start from the beginning," said Kara. "Juan didn't keep the phone after he got the information from it, but he wrote the email down – wait, I'll show you." She got up and left the room, her tall, slim form moving almost silently.

As Willow turned to him, her face creased with concern. "Your poor cheek," she murmured, stroking it gently. "Does it really hurt?"

"It's okay," said Alex, his mind half on what Kara had been saying. "I just wish I'd punched him back when I had the chance." Then he glanced at Willow, taking in her face. "Are *you* all right, though? Being here?"

He wouldn't really call the slight curving of her lips a smile. "I'm fine," she said.

Alex fell silent, not knowing what to say. He knew how hard this must be for her – coming into a strange situation where all anyone saw was her half-angel self, and no one trusted her as far as they could throw her. When she was probably the most trustworthy person on the planet. "Listen, they'll get used to you, if we stay," he said. "Kara's a really good person; she just—"

"I know," she broke in. "Alex, it's all right. I can't expect them to just…take it in their stride, I guess."

She was so beautiful, sitting there in his faded plaid shirt. He slid his hand around the back of her neck and leaned forward, kissing her. Her lips were warm and soft; he felt her tension melt as she responded.

They both sensed rather than heard Kara standing there. Alex drew back, not taking his eyes from Willow's. He smiled at her again; her own smile looked a little more relaxed this time.

"So, here it is," said Kara shortly. Her expression was tight as she sat down; Alex didn't know if it was the document in her hand, or what she'd just walked in on. Both, probably.

She pushed a sheet of paper across the table. "The Church of Angels email address this was sent to belongs to the preacher at the Metropolitan Cathedral here," she said. "You might have seen that it's a Church of Angels cathedral now. And you know the tabernacle, right beside it? It's been redone into the office space for the Church. The preacher is the head honcho there – and believe me, he's as devout as they come."

Alex angled the page towards him, sharing it with Willow; a pang hit him at the sight of Juan's familiar looping handwriting. He started to read:

Yes, I can verify that arrangements are underway for the Seraphic Council's planned visit to Mexico City. They have several vital orders of business there; one is to select an angelic head for the Church in Mexico. As we discussed, the utmost security during their stay is vital – the general populace is not to know of their presence. However, rest assured that Church officials will of course be allowed to pay homage to them, as will a few selected members of the public. We shall discuss this when next we speak. Meanwhile, please send a precis of all security arrangements. Remember, their safety is vital for all angelkind.

"Seraphic Council?" said Willow. Her hair tickled his cheek as she bent close to read. "Didn't Nate mention that to us?"

"Yeah, but I'd never heard of it before." Alex frowned down at the page. "We knew all about their habits at the camp – nothing about their politics." It was interesting news that this Council, whoever they were, planned to appoint an angelic Church head for Mexico – Alex had always had the impression that Raziel, who was head of the Church in the US, had simply grabbed all the power for himself. So did that mean this Seraphic Council were above Willow's father, in the angelic scheme of things?

But more than that, Alex found himself staring at the phrase *their safety is vital for all angelkind*. Kara reached across and tapped the words. "That's the reason we came here," she said. "It sounded like if we did away with this Council, then maybe it would be a real strike against the angels – only we didn't know that for sure, or when they were arriving, or even where, exactly."

"Past tense," noticed Alex, straightening up to look at her. "You do now?"

"Some of it," said Kara. "When we first got here, the cathedral had just reopened and I went there a lot, pretending to be a devotee. I, ah…well, I've managed to get kind of friendly with the preacher's main assistant, a guy named Luis."

Alex smiled wryly; he had no trouble reading between the lines. Obviously, Luis was not supposed to be talking to random devotees about this stuff – and just as obviously, Kara had the poor guy so enamoured he couldn't help himself.

She crossed her forearms on the table. "First of all – this thing is huge. Much bigger than we'd even hoped." She took a breath. "The reason the high-ups at the Church are so concerned about the security risk is because the Seraphic Council is like the angels' heartbeat. They're called the Twelve, and their energy is the original angel energy – apparently it's to do with them being the 'first formed'. And the angels can't live without them. *Literally* can't live without them. If the Council of Twelve dies—"

"They all die," finished Willow faintly. She looked at Alex; the blood had drained from her face. "My dream – the twelve angels vanishing, the sound of millions of them screaming…it all fits."

"Jesus," murmured Alex, sinking back against his chair.

His heart started pounding as his eyes locked on Willow's. They had a second chance to destroy them. They actually had a second chance. If they managed to get rid of the Council, then eventually humanity would start to recover; the world would be safe. His family flashed through his head. Willow's mother. They *had* to succeed this time, so that what had happened to the people they loved would never occur again, not to anyone else.

"Do you have any other details?" he asked Kara finally.

"According to Luis, they're going to be coming in early January and then staying for three weeks at the Nikko Hotel," said Kara. "It's one of the most exclusive hotels in the city – the whole top floor is reserved for them. Security's going to be tight, but there's a reception planned for the last day they're here – and apparently the Council are going to be holding private audiences then, so that selected people can worship them in their angel forms. I'm trying to convince Luis that me and some of my friends should be on that list." She gave a hard smile. "Because I'm so *devout*, don'cha know?"

Alex nodded. It definitely sounded like the best time to do it, if the Council were going to be in their angel forms with their vulnerable halos on display.

"And hopefully we can pull it off with as little damage to us as possible – I really don't want this to be a suicide mission." Kara rested her chin on her palm, her face tight with worry. "But everything depends on the team being able to take out the Council – because this is probably the only chance we'll ever get at them. If we fail..." She shrugged. "Well, I doubt they'll let us get away to try again later."

"I think you're right – this is our only chance," said Willow in a steady voice. She told Kara about her dream; Alex watched Kara go still.

"So it's sort of...fated for you two to be here," she said.

"Looks that way," said Alex, playing with his fork. His mind was ticking over everything Kara had said. Depending on Luis the assistant to get the team into the reception sounded a little too flimsy for comfort to him. But even if everything went to plan, the hardest part was going to be escaping after the Council was killed, once people figured out what they'd done. There were almost certainly going to be casualties.

He rapped the fork against the table, and left aside the logistic difficulties for the moment. "Okay, so this reception is around eleven weeks away. If you need your team trained for then, what are you doing sending them out on hunts *now*, before they're ready? Are you trying to get them killed, or what?" He explained what had happened at the Zócalo; as he'd already surmised, Kara had been the lone gunman who'd actually been hitting the angels, at the other end of the square.

"Sounds like the others all stayed together," said Kara morosely. "Damn it – I *told* them to fan out."

"You shouldn't have sent them out there in the first place! God, you should have seen them out back just now, when those three angels were attacking – it was complete chaos. What did you think you were doing?"

Her dark eyes flashed. "What I've been *doing* is being in charge the best way I know how ever since Juan died, okay? And they seemed like they could handle it! They'd all been hitting the bullseye over ninety per cent; they're already experts at scanning; they—"

Alex let out a disbelieving laugh. "Come *on*, Kara, you know how different it is shooting angels for real, instead of just hitting targets! I remember Dad telling you that often enough, anyway."

"Yeah, well, I'm not your dad! And it wasn't exactly my *plan* to have Juan die before we even got started, so that I had to be in charge of training this bunch—" Kara broke off. Exhaling, she ran a hand across her face; there was silence. "Oh, hell, I messed up, okay?" she said finally, her voice weary. "They'd been doing target practice for what seemed like for ever, and I'd just found out about the Council, and this being our only chance – and I guess I sort of freaked. I thought it might be good practice for them, or something – like we couldn't just *sit* here with all this going on; we had to get out and do something."

Alex sighed – he could understand this kind of frustration all too well. "Yeah, I know. Don't beat yourself up over it." He looked down at his plate again; took a disinterested bite. "No one could be like Juan, anyway. He was one of the best leads I ever worked under."

Kara leaned back, crossing her ankle over her knee. She gave him a long, appraising look. "I bet *you* could be like Juan," she said at last. "Maybe even better."

Alex's muscles stiffened; he could see Willow watching him, and knew she was thinking the same thing as Kara. His voice came out sharper than intended. "No way. You're in charge, Kara. I'll help however I can, but I'm not going to come in here and take over your team."

She rolled her eyes. "What about if I begged and pleaded?" she said. "Alex, seriously; I'm barely holding it together here. Give me an angel to shoot and I'm fine – but this?" She shook her head. "Even when you were a kid you were a great AK. I bet you'd be fantastic at all the strategy stuff, and the training – it's just in your blood; you've been around it your whole life. God, I remember you taught *me* the best way to go for a halo, and you were only around fourteen!"

Willow touched his hand; her voice was steady. "You'd be great. I know it isn't really something you want, but you'd be so, so good at it."

"You've got to do it," said Kara. "You have *got* to.

Or else we don't even stand a chance against the Council."

So here it was, the thing he'd dreaded so much – as inevitable as the coldness of ice. Alex's bruised cheek gave a throb. Somehow he'd known this would happen, from the moment he first saw Sam flailing around with the gun, screaming at the angel to come and get him. There was no getting away from it. He couldn't say no, even though he wanted to refuse this more than anything he'd ever faced – because it wasn't just a team's safety he'd be responsible for now; it was all of humanity's.

"If I'm lead, then the first priority is to get floor plans for the hotel," he said finally. "I also need more specific security information. A *lot* more specific; every detail you can find out – how many guards, exactly what's happening at this reception, everything. And as soon as the team is ready, we'll have to start taking them out on safe hunts – the safest we can manage, so they can get some real-life practice. I don't want any of them dying if I can help it." His mouth twisted. "Not even that jerk-off Texan."

"You got it, chief," said Kara softly.

Chief. Alex resisted pulling a face. "Are you okay with this?" he said to Willow.

She nodded. She looked resigned, as if she too found this inevitable. At the same time, apprehension flickered deep within her green eyes, and he knew how worried she was. "Of course," she said. "This is what we have to be doing."

"So, I guess I'll tell the team tonight," said Kara.

Alex started to eat again; the food had lost all its flavour. "Tomorrow," he said. "Let me get some sleep first, okay?"

Kara nodded. And though he was exhausted, Alex didn't know whether that was the real reason he wanted to put the announcement off, or whether he just wanted a few more hours' reprieve before he had to take this on. He glanced at Willow, wishing again that they were alone. He wanted to find out how she really felt about staying here, given the reception she'd received.

Willow seemed to guess what was on his mind; her fingers rested fleetingly on his arm, telling him it was okay. She pushed her chair back. "Is there a restroom I could use?" she asked Kara.

Kara turned, pointing with a slender brown arm. "Yeah – just go through that door and it's upstairs, second door on the left."

After Willow had disappeared, Kara said, "So. She does that too."

Alex didn't look up from his meal. "Yeah, gosh, just like a real human being. Do you think you could stop being such an idiot about this? As a special favour to me?" He shovelled another bite of spaghetti into his mouth.

"She's very pretty," said Kara after a pause.

"I know."

"So…can I ask you a personal question?"

He looked up sharply; her beautiful face was bland. "Yeah, you can ask," he said. "I might not answer, if it's none of your business."

She tapped her pink nails on the table. "Well, I'm guessing you two are – intimate, am I right?"

Alex held back a snorting laugh and took another bite of spaghetti. If Kara thought he was going to discuss his sex life with her, she was insane.

"Okay, fine, don't tell me," she said. "But what I'm getting at is, aren't you worried about angel burn?"

He let out a groan and dropped his fork. Kara went on before he could say anything. "I mean, all right, she's not on the side of the angels; I get that. But that doesn't mean being close to her won't physically hurt you somehow. I'm not saying she'd do it on purpose, but—"

Alex gritted the words out. "Listen carefully and I'll say it again – she is not like them. She doesn't feed. How could she give me angel burn?"

Kara shrugged, her expression arch. "I don't know. Who the hell knows anything about a half-angel? *She* doesn't even know, so how can you?"

"Yeah, well, thanks for your concern," he said, picking up his fork again. "I feel fine."

"Good," she said. "Glad to hear it." She picked up the

sheet of paper with Juan's writing on it, turning it over thoughtfully. "Course, you don't always *know* these things, do you? Some of those cancers, for instance, can take a real long time to start showing themselves—"

He glared at her; he would have happily smashed the plate of spaghetti in her face. "Kara, I'm serious – *shut the hell up.*"

A strained silence fell. "Hey," she said eventually, touching his shoulder. "Don't be mad at me, Al. I mean, just put yourself in my shoes – I really hope that if I came strutting in here with some half-angel boyfriend, you'd start asking a few questions."

He managed a smile at her old nickname for him, and knew she was right. If he had been in her place, he'd have been saying the exact same things. He shook his head. "Kara, Willow is…she's the kindest, most unselfish person I've ever known. She'd die before she hurt me, or anyone else."

Kara lifted a hand. "Okay," she said, and he knew she was holding back from repeating what she'd said before – that it might not be something Willow was doing on purpose. "Just keep it in mind, all right? That's all I'm asking." She changed the subject adroitly. "You know, I really cannot get over how much you look like Jake now – you've actually grown into those shoulders of yours. What a difference a couple of years makes, huh?"

He was glad to feel the tension between them ease. "Yeah, but you still look just the same," he said, scanning her face. Kara was half black and half Mexican; the mix had resulted in stark, dramatic features and a graceful neck. Extremely short hair looked amazing on her; it always had.

She smiled, and pretended to preen. "Thanks – when you get to my age, you kind of like hearing that." Her face grew more serious again. She examined her nails; he saw the same expression in her eyes as when she'd made the mistake over the coffee. "So…do you still think about him as much as I do?"

Alex looked down at his plate; the words wouldn't come. He felt Kara reach across and squeeze his wrist. "Sorry," she said. "Stupid question."

"Every day," he said finally. "I miss him every day."

They both straightened as Willow came back into the kitchen; he could tell that she'd picked up on the mood. She stood with her arms crossed over her chest, and attempted a smile. "Hey, I'm sorry to be boring, but I'm getting pretty tired," she said. "I might just go on to bed."

"Me too," said Alex, stretching. Then he remembered. "Kara, can we borrow some clothes from you guys? Some thieving jerk stole all our stuff, up in Chihuahua."

"Yeah, we can fix you up, no problem," said Kara. She

started clearing the plates away; Willow moved to help. "So, Willow, we've got an extra bed in the girls' dorm that you're welcome to. And Alex, you can take Juan's old room if you want; it's right by the guys' dorm – it's pretty small; it's got a single bed in it—" She stopped, looking flustered as she glanced from Alex to Willow. "Oh, wait. I guess maybe you…"

"We'll both take Juan's old room," said Alex. He saw Kara start to say something and then stop, her lips tightening. "What?" he said sharply. "Everyone knows that Willow and I are together; I'm not going to start hiding it."

"No, it's not that," said Kara. She scraped the remains of the spaghetti into the trash. "It's just…well, Juan thought it was better if people didn't couple up too obviously. For the team, I mean. He sort of laid down some ground rules when we first got here, and that was one of them. But look, you're in charge now; you do what you want."

He started to say *Good, I will*, and then hesitated as he remembered – his father had had that rule, too. It wasn't that Martin had cared who was seeing who – illicit meetings in the broom closet had been fine as far as he was concerned – but he'd said it made the team feel like more of a unit if it was always team first, couples second. And when you were in a combat situation, that could be vital.

"Alex, it's fine – I'll go into the dorm," said Willow, rinsing their forks and knives off without looking at him.

He could just imagine what it would be like for her in there, with the other girls hating her. Then he noticed the tension in her movements, and that she still wasn't meeting his gaze. His eyebrows lowered in concern as a suspicion came to him. "Could you leave us alone for a second?" he asked Kara.

She put the rinsed-off dishes onto a drying rack. "Sure, I'll just go and find some clothes for you both. Back in ten."

Alex leaned against the counter by the sink and gently pulled Willow to him, looping his arms around her waist. "You heard what Kara was saying before, didn't you?"

She gave a reluctant nod. "Just the last part of it, as I was coming down the stairs, but…yeah, enough to get the idea," she admitted.

"Okay, so you know it's a complete fantasy, right? You do *not* cause angel burn. Not to me, or anybody else."

Glancing down, Willow fingered the crystal pendant he'd given her; it gleamed in the light. "Kara's right, though, you don't know that for sure." Her voice was unsteady. "How can you? No one really knows anything about half-angels. I mean, I don't *think* I've ever hurt anyone, but you and I are so close, and maybe— "

"*Wil*-low. Come on. Babe, please, listen to me—" He

lifted her chin with his hand; her eyes were bright with tears. "Of course you're not hurting me," he said. "Do I look unhealthy to you? I'm fine."

"But just because someone looks healthy doesn't always mean they are. And what about that headache you got in Chihuahua? The night before, we almost—" She stopped, flushing slightly. "I mean…we came so close, remember?"

With a sudden grin, he said, "Oh, hey, yeah. Now that you mention it, I do seem to recall that." He bent his head down and kissed her; felt her start to respond and then pull away.

"Alex, I'm serious! What if that had something to do with—"

"Shh," he murmured, kissing her again. His hands were on her hips; gliding them upwards, he could feel the slim cello-dip of her waist. "Listen to me. You don't have a halo. You don't feed. The only way you could hurt me would be to stop touching me. That would hurt. A lot. This feels… really good, actually." The kiss deepened, their mouths moving together. He felt her give in to it, pressing close against him and twining her arms around his neck. He stroked his hands up her spine, relishing her warmth. The thought of sleeping separately from her was agonizing.

When they drew apart, Willow rested her head against his chest; he dropped his cheek onto her hair, caressing her back through the softness of the plaid shirt. "Promise me you'll tell me if you ever even suspect I'm hurting you," she said after a pause. "I mean, if you even have a *cough* that you don't think you should have, you've got to tell me, all right?"

He started to make a joke and then Willow looked up; her expression was gravely serious. "I promise," he said, touching her face. God, he could kill Kara for putting this idea in her head. "But, Willow, it's not going to happen. You're not hurting me. It was just a headache – everyone on the planet gets them sometimes."

She hesitated, her eyes searching his. "I really hope you're right."

"I am," he said. He stroked her cheek with his thumb. "I promise you. I'm completely fine."

Willow let out a breath. "Okay," she said at last, nodding. "Maybe I overreacted a little." She reached up and covered his hand with hers. "I'll believe you until I have a reason not to, how's that?"

"Much better," he said. He drew her back to him again. Lowering his head, he whispered in her hair, "So now that we've got that settled…maybe we should think about finishing what we started the other night."

She glanced quickly at him; her cheeks reddened a little, but she was smiling. "Oh, I'm definitely thinking about it – believe me." She traced a finger over his chest. "But next time, someone needs to be a little more prepared."

Alex nuzzled at her neck. "I bought some on the drive down today," he murmured against her smooth skin.

"You did?"

"Mm-hmm." He nibbled at her ear; felt her shiver.

"Oh," she said faintly. "That makes it…really, really suck that I'm going to sleep in the girls' dorm while we're here."

He pulled away. "You are?"

Willow sighed. "I think I'd better. Don't you, honestly? I mean, I don't want to cause any problems, and it sounds like it's sort of the established thing."

He grimaced. "It doesn't *have* to be. I mean, I'm the lead now…I could always just order you to sleep in the same bed as me."

"Oh, that's romantic."

Alex half laughed, half groaned, dropping his head down onto her shoulder. He felt her stroke his hair. "Yeah, you're right," he said finally. "Dad had the same rule. He didn't care what people did, but…" He raised his head and smiled ruefully. "Maybe we could find a broom closet somewhere."

"It's amazing; this conversation just keeps on getting more and more romantic."

"So…that's a no to the broom closet, then."

"It is a definite, emphatic no to the broom closet."

Alex smiled. "You know I'm only kidding, don't you?"

He found her hand; linked his fingers tightly through hers. "Willow, when it happens, I want it to be just…incredible for you. For both of us. Totally perfect."

"I know," she said, her eyes soft. "We'll find a way soon. Let's get used to being here first, okay? Then we can start sneaking around and checking out broom closets." She sighed. "I'm really going to miss sleeping with you, though," she said, running her hand up his arm. "I mean, just – talking to you. Being held by you."

Alex could hear Kara returning with their clothes. "Yeah, I know," he said, giving her another quick kiss. "Me, too."

And he thought wryly that was probably one of the biggest understatements of his life.

CHAPTER *Seven*

"RAZIEL!" THE FEMALE VOICE WAS low, urgent. A hand lightly slapped his cheek, and then the other one. "You *must* wake up. Hurry, we haven't much time!"

The touch was angelic; the voice wasn't any that he'd been hearing since lying here in bed – and how long had that been? A day? A week? With terrible, sudden clarity, what he'd sensed while unconscious came roaring back, and Raziel's eyes flew open. When he saw who was at his bedside, he struggled upright, his head still swimming.

"Charmeine," he said.

She was sitting on the side of his bed, wearing grey

trousers and a black angora sweater that bared one shoulder, her long white-blonde hair falling in a shining stream. Raziel regarded her, pleasure mixing with sharp suspicion. He and Charmeine had had a thing once and were now friends of a sort, though Charmeine was too much like him for comfort sometimes. They'd kept in touch sporadically these last two years, but he hadn't known that she'd planned to come across with the Second Wave. Given the Council's sudden appearance as well, it wasn't particularly reassuring to find her here now, perched on his bed.

"I know what you're thinking, but you're wrong – I promise you can trust me." Charmeine took his hand and he felt her opening herself to him, showing her sincerity. Which was nice, but meant little. It was standard procedure to let someone in and show them exactly what you wanted them to see.

"The Twelve are here, Raziel. And—"

"I know," he broke in bitterly, pulling his hand away. He still felt dizzy. "And only three or four years ahead of schedule, fancy that. Why? Did someone tip them off?" Like many angels, Raziel had unconsciously taken on characteristics from some of his human energy donors; the English accent had been with him for years.

"No, I mean they're *here*," said Charmeine levelly. "Downstairs. In the cathedral. They sent me to summon you."

Raziel was unable to hide his shock; he felt it leap within him like a flame. "They're *summoning me* – in my own cathedral?" he said finally.

"Yes," said Charmeine. "And yes, they're here in the first place because they were tipped off. I don't know who by, but they know everything you've been up to – they have for months. They've been making plans."

Apprehension tightened his muscles. "What plans?"

She shook her head. "You'll find out soon enough, I'm afraid."

Typical Charmeine: to dangle information, and then not supply it. Raziel frowned, but didn't bother to go searching. Angels had had thousands of years to perfect the art of psychic manoeuvring – Charmeine's defences were as skilled as his own. "And what do *you* have to do with all of this?" he demanded instead. "What do you mean, they sent you?"

"I was, shall we say, strongly encouraged to come across with the Second Wave and serve them," said Charmeine. "They've decided that only family can be trusted. Even a black sheep like me."

Charmeine was one of the "first family" – an angel who had been formed soon after the Twelve. She wasn't as close to them in lineage as some – more of a distant cousin than anything else. But her basic ethereal make-up was still more similar to the Twelve's than other angels', which in theory meant they'd find it easier to have psychic control over her. Hence their sudden yearning to have their "family" around them, no doubt.

"So they've bound you," summed up Raziel. "You're one of their psychic lackeys now, and they know everything you do."

Charmeine shrugged; her exposed shoulder was slim and pale. "They think so. I think they'd be surprised how strong my defences are. The familial energy works both ways, you know – I have layers they haven't even discovered yet."

Raziel regarded her; if true, it was interesting news. "And how long do you think you can keep *that* up?"

"Long enough, hopefully."

Her tone was lightly casual, but he knew Charmeine had never said anything truly casual in her life – like most angels, she thrived on innuendo and subtext. Raziel shoved back the covers and got out of bed. He was wearing a silken pair of pyjamas that he rarely bothered with; obviously one of his human attendants had put them on him.

"Delightfully mysterious as always, I see," he said. "Fine. I've got to take a shower and change."

"Don't be too long," cautioned Charmeine, glancing at the door. "They expect you down there shortly."

"I'll be as long as I like," he snapped. "This is *my*

cathedral – they don't give the orders around here."

Despite his bravado, he still found himself hurrying as he bathed, which enraged him. Lurking below the anger was that same almost-fear he'd felt while unconscious. He hadn't expected the Council to find out the true extent of his power in this world yet. Ever since the First Wave, their knowledge of what was happening here had been somewhat sketchy; only a few First Wavers had the ability to communicate with them across the dimensions. And as time had passed, loyalties had shifted. It hadn't taken long for the angels living here to feel more in tune with Raziel and others who were connoisseurs of this world than with the old guard back home – or to see the enticing possibilities for the power they could all share here.

Because what no one could have foreseen was the Church of Angels: the fastest-growing religion in history. Though founded by humans, the angels had been quick to take advantage of the Church – particularly Raziel, who'd always chafed at the Twelve's automatic reign thanks to their status as the First Formed. You could either spend eternity jockeying for position as one of their lackeys, or try to carve out a niche for yourself elsewhere. The angels' mass presence in this new world had given Raziel the opportunity he'd been craving for millennia; it hadn't taken him long to wrest control of the Church and rise to its head.

With him at its helm, the Church of Angels had soon become the most influential church in the world. Angels were now so firmly fixed in society's consciousness that people who'd never even encountered one were embracing their predators wholeheartedly. In Mexico City, the historic Catedral Metropolitana had recently been converted to become a Church of Angels cathedral – an astounding coup, made all the more so by the relative lack of press attention; it was just seen as a natural course of events. Raziel planned to take over the running of this new cathedral himself in due course, dividing his time between the United States and Mexico. In London, there was talk of St Paul's being similarly converted; in Paris, Notre Dame.

So far, talk was all it was – the angelic presence wasn't as great in Europe yet – but Raziel had had little doubt that in the wake of the Second Wave, these plans would go ahead. By then, he'd expected to be in charge of most of the Americas and imagined setting himself up akin to the Pope, with ruling angels under him. Once the Council had finally settled in this world and seen what was going on, it would have meant all-out war for them to try to wrest control back from him – and by then he'd have had more than enough allies to take them on.

At the moment, the Church stood on the brink: it was poised to take over the world, and those angels who were on Raziel's side could help him do it. And so any reports back to the Council had always carefully downplayed the importance of the Church of Angels, and Raziel's growing power base.

Or at least, that's what he had thought.

As he turned off the shower, it hit him suddenly: Mexico City. The half-angel was there – and she too was aware of the Council. The knowledge was as fleeting as a soap bubble, gone as quickly as it had arrived. Raziel was left frowning, water dripping in his eyes as he wondered whether he was going insane. *Forget the half-angel,* he thought. He could still hardly bear to use the word *daughter.* He had more important things to think about right now.

When he emerged again, Charmeine had moved to the sitting room. After putting on a pair of casually expensive grey trousers, Raziel went in and found her curled up, catlike, in his favourite armchair. He knew they'd made a striking pair, once – her with her delicate moonlight beauty, and him with his crisp black hair and poet's features. If he was the sentimental type, this might have caused him to view her with less suspicion. Fortunately, he wasn't.

"So what are you up to?" he demanded, buttoning a midnight-blue shirt. "Why are you tipping me off that there's trouble?"

Charmeine looked amused. "Old time's sake?" she suggested.

"How wonderfully altruistic of you," replied Raziel, tucking his shirt in. "Please remember this is me you're talking to, and how very, very well I know you. What's your game?"

"No game," said Charmeine. Her beautiful gamine face was impossible to read. She rose and came over to him, lazily circling one of his shirt buttons with a fingernail. "I just have a feeling you're going to need a friend in this world soon, that's all. And I think our mutual needs could work together very well."

Raziel's expression didn't change as he looked down at her. "Does the Council know about you and me?" he asked sharply.

Her hand wandered up to the nape of his neck, playing with his hair. "Of course; they delved my mind and found everything I wanted them to see," she said. "And so they know I hate you very, very much, and would do anything to get back at you."

Raziel started to say something else, then stopped as they both felt it – a harsh tugging at their minds, as if they were a pair of fishes being reeled in by invisible fishermen. "Showtime," murmured Charmeine, dropping her hand. "By the way, your cathedral is about to be used for something pretty disagreeable. Necessary, I suppose, but…disagreeable."

The riddles were doubly annoying when the place under discussion was his own territory. Without answering, Raziel shifted into his angel form and flew from the room, gliding silently through the walls. Charmeine followed with a bright flash of wings. As they soared out into the main space of the cathedral, with its high, arching dome, Raziel saw the Twelve gathered in their human forms below, near the white-winged pulpit. And what fun; they'd brought an audience with them – there were around fifty angels seated in the pews nearby.

Raziel's ethereal eyes narrowed as he saw the results of the half-angel's attempt to destroy the gate: the buckled floorboards; the missing ceiling panels; the metal scaffolding that stood in place. Fury seared through him again that she'd even attempted such a thing – and that the damaged fruits of her work were now on gruesome display for the Council and their sycophants to view. *Mexico City. She's there*, he thought again. And though he shoved the knowledge away for now, he dearly hoped it was true. Knowing the creature's whereabouts would mean he was only a few steps away from having her and her assassin boyfriend destroyed.

He touched down in front of the Council and changed back to his human form; Charmeine followed suit. The Twelve looked nothing alike, yet there was a commonality between them, all the same – a similar bland expression, perhaps, or a certain way they all held themselves. Six males and six females who'd been leading the angels' affairs for millennia, since long before anyone could remember. From what Raziel had heard, most of them loathed each other heartily, though they were far too entwined, both psychically and politically, to ever separate now.

"Welcome to my cathedral," said Raziel, inclining his dark head.

He managed to keep the irony from his voice, but knew they'd pick up on it psychically; he wasn't especially bothering to hide it. "Thank you," said Isda, who was often the spokeswoman for the Twelve. "It's a pleasure to be here." She was tall and statuesque, with sculpted features; her grey eyes rested on Raziel with no visible emotion. "Shall we get the unpleasantness out of the way first?"

"By all means," said Raziel smoothly, trying to bury his faint throb of alarm – what unpleasantness were they talking about, precisely? And now he saw that in addition to the expected hangers-on in the audience, all the First Wavers who'd been in psychic contact with the Council were here too. He could sense their deep tremor of worry; the expectation had been that Raziel would be firmly ensconced in power by the time their betrayal was found out.

"Good. You and Charmeine may take a seat," said Isda, nodding at a nearby pew.

Being given permission to sit in his own cathedral grated; Raziel did so in moody silence. Charmeine perched beside him, looking straight ahead.

Isda and the rest of the Twelve stood in a row, their backs to the pews. The tall stained-glass windows in front of them glimmered in the sun; it was here, exactly, that the Second Wave had arrived, mere days ago. "Now, please," called Isda in her low voice.

The stadium doors to the side opened and a long line of almost a hundred angels were led in – all in their human forms, with their hands cuffed behind them. Raziel sat up straight, his pulse quickening in surprise as he recognized the remainder of the traitors: the angels that he'd been using Kylar, the assassin, to do away with. Though a diverse group, the traitors all believed that angels didn't have the right to use humans for their own purposes, and were committed to helping humanity, even if it meant the extinction of their own kind. Raziel had gotten their names by chance over a year ago, from a rogue who'd been captured and had then turned in the others to save himself. Raziel had had him killed anyway, of course, but it had been a very useful meeting all the same.

The nature of the "unpleasantness" was now only too clear. The Council had been aware of the rogues' identities from the start; it had seemed politic to pass the information across. And they'd know that only a rogue – in this case,

Nate – could have helped the half-angel with her near-disastrous attack on the gate. As a result, the traitors had escalated themselves out of being a matter that could be taken care of quietly, and into one that merited a public statement. The Council would have drawn the rogues to them easily enough; one of the most annoying things about the Twelve was how their psychic call tugged on you, like it or not.

Gazing at the traitors, Raziel wondered why they stayed imprisoned in their chained human forms – and then realized uneasily that the Council had something to do with that too. In a subtle undercurrent that he'd missed before, he could feel them working together to exert some kind of mental hold on the captured angels, preventing them from shifting.

The traitors stood motionless before the Council, awaiting their fate. The cathedral had fallen utterly silent; beside him, Charmeine sat unmoving. The Twelve didn't speak, but a heavy energy was gathering, crackling with power. Gradually, Raziel sensed their mental hold on the prisoners reverse itself, so that now it forced them into their more vulnerable divine forms. Knowing what it meant, they were resisting with everything they had – faces grimacing, muscles straining. Raziel squirmed slightly. He didn't mind watching the traitors' deaths, but the Council's display of power was…unsettling.

A dark-haired angel named Elijah was the first to succumb. His angel form appeared in a rush, its winged figure darting upwards as he tried to escape through the ceiling. A quick mental feint from the Council and Elijah shuddered to a halt mid-air, wings flapping feebly like an insect pinned to a card. His halo began glowing, brighter and brighter – too bright, it was throbbing, trembling under the pressure – and then it exploded into silent fragments. Elijah's scream echoed through the cavernous building as he was torn to pieces…and then there was silence again as the remnants of his ethereal self drifted towards the ground.

Raziel winced – as Elijah died, it felt as if a small piece of himself had been torn away. The Twelve's energy was even stronger now, pulsing through the cathedral like a heartbeat. With an anguished cry, several others lost the battle and erupted into their divine forms. The Council showed no strain in dealing with all of them at once. As their halo-hearts burst one after the other, the remainder of the prisoners followed in a helpless torrent, taking to the air amidst the shining shards that were now falling like snow. Screams echoed; angelic bodies writhed. Raziel gritted his teeth as the pain of death after death clawed at him. Beside him, Charmeine's face was emotionless but pale.

When the last executed angel had faded from view, the

Council shifted and lifted upwards. Their wings moved slowly as they hovered, turning to face their audience. Raziel just managed not to shield his eyes. The divine bodies of the First Formed were painfully bright, their features impossible to make out as they burned blue-white before their audience. A thought came like psychic thunder, twelve voices speaking at once: *This is how we deal with traitors. We are sure you all understand.*

Raziel swallowed, his throat suddenly dry. It was typical of the Council: using a necessary execution such as this one as a helpful little aide-memoire as well. He didn't have to look behind him to know how sick the expressions were of the First Wavers who had been on his side.

The Council stayed aloft for almost a minute, silently making their point. Finally they touched down again and rippled back to their human forms. Though they didn't look at Raziel, he abruptly felt singled out, as pinned to his seat as the rogue angels had been in the air. Still speaking psychically, the many-toned voice that was both one and twelve rumbled through him:

Raziel, may we see you alone, please?

The meeting was short and to the point.

Half an hour later, Raziel sat alone in one of the cathedral's downstairs conference rooms, staring at the gleaming wooden table; the tasteful decorations; the silver water pitcher that had an arched, graceful angel as the handle. He had done all of this; he had made it all happen – and apparently, if he was very, very good and did exactly as he was told, he might be allowed to keep it for a little while.

Or not.

Impotent anger clenched his fists. No. They weren't going to get away with this – not after all his hard work; not after all he'd done in this world and still planned to do. He wouldn't allow it. He *would not*.

"Raziel?" Charmeine had appeared; she stood in the doorway.

"Shouldn't you be off doing lackey work?" he said bitingly. He shoved his chair back and rose, striding for the door.

She shut it with a soft click and leaned against it. "If anyone goes checking psychically, that's exactly what they'll see," she said. "For your information, I'm currently going through your email account upstairs, while the Twelve talk to some of your First Wave chums."

He snorted. "Aren't you noble? As if that's not exactly what you *were* just doing."

Charmeine gave a mild shrug. "It helps to have visual details in mind when you're creating psychic decoys. And let me guess," she went on. "They've told you about their plan to only recognize those angels in power who they've appointed themselves."

"Good guess," snapped Raziel. "And those they *don't* recognize will be dealt with as traitors." He swore and raked a hand through his hair. "Why couldn't this have happened a few years from now? I'd have had enough of a power base by then to take them on, to constrain them in some way—" He stopped, aware that he was saying far too much.

He could feel Charmeine's sincerity again; her anger at the Council. "I really am on your side, Raz," she said softly. "You can trust me."

He slumped against the table, tapping his thigh as he tried to think. Just as Charmeine had said, the Council had apparently known about his schemes for months. They'd informed him that plans were already in place for them to make a state visit to Mexico City soon, where they'd appoint an angel of their choosing to be head of the new cathedral there. Then, once they returned, they'd decide his fate. The implication was clear: he should spend the time in the interim mulling over his wrongs and deciding whether or not he wanted to be their poodle for the rest of eternity.

He glanced at Charmeine, wondering if it was she who'd betrayed him. She'd known enough about his plans here, and could have guessed the details he hadn't told her.

But it could also have been almost any of the First Wavers – several had become increasingly greedy in their demands of late. He supposed he should have dealt with them more diplomatically, played them along until he could get rid of them. But who would have thought they'd go crying to the Council?

"So what now?" asked Charmeine. "Are you going to toe the line?"

Enough of these games. Raziel rose in a quick motion; he gripped her head in his hands and kissed her harshly, shoving her up against the wall. *Open to me,* he thought. Her arms twined around his neck as she responded. Using the connection their past history gave them, he delved deep, deeper into her mind, probing her roughly. He could feel her slight tremor as she allowed him in, opening up layer after layer to him, until there were no more to be explored.

Finally Raziel raised his head, frowning down at her. Her black sweater was askew on her bare shoulder; her white-blonde hair still lay sleek and perfect. He'd seen only that in return for her help, she wanted to share power with him in this new world. He'd have expected nothing else.

"Well?" Charmeine was a touch paler than usual, but her voice was steady.

"All right," he said, letting go of her. "Maybe it wasn't you – and maybe you're actually sincere, for a change."

"Of course I am," she said intensely. "I hate them as much as you do; I always have. So will you answer my question now?" She rested against the wall without adjusting her sweater; he could see the firm upper swell of one breast.

Raziel's lip curled. "No, I'm not going to toe the line," he replied. He sat on the table again and shoved at the water pitcher, sending it sliding across the dark, shining wood. "I'll play their game for now – but that's all."

"That's what I thought," said Charmeine with quiet satisfaction. She traced her finger along the door jamb, watching its movement musingly. "They're overconfident, you know. *You* really did delve me completely, but they only think they have. It hasn't even crossed their mind that the oh-so-sacred family energy might not be enough of a connection for them to get everything. And meanwhile, I've picked up a few things myself."

Raziel studied her. "Such as?"

"Such as, I don't think it's ever seriously occurred to them that someone might want to take them out." Her eyes met his; she smiled. "They're a little concerned about the security risk here from non-devout humans, that's all – at home, we've been hearing stories about Angel Killers, and now there's been that episode with the half-angel and the gate. But other *angels* wanting to destroy them, given the possible consequences to us all? No, never. They'd never even suspect it." She shrugged. "Still, the way I see it, this is a fresh new world, and we need a fresh new start. And we can never have that as long as the Council is around."

Raziel had been thinking the same thing. To hear it put into words, and to feel the passion behind them psychically, gave him a stirring of dark excitement that was like a rich red wine.

If the First Formed died, all angels would die: it had been drummed into them since the beginning of time. And much as Raziel hated to concede it, in their home world this was almost certainly true. But things were different here – the ether in this world was thinner; it was why angels had to feed from humans instead of the ether itself. The truth was that no one really knew what would happen if the Twelve were killed here, rather than at home.

The dominant view was that the exact same result would occur: without the First-Formed's energy, all angels would die. Yet there were other possibilities too. The most enticing of them was that if the Council were killed here, then only the Council would die. Hardly anyone believed this – seeing the Council as indispensable to their existence was second nature to most angels – but Raziel had by now spent so much time in this world that it seemed a real possibility to him. Angels were still linked here, but not as strongly as back home; the thin ether made their bond weaker too. If the assassination of the rogues had happened in their own world, he knew he'd still be reeling from the pain of it; not here. As far as he could tell, the Council's deaths shouldn't necessarily mean the deaths of them all.

As other likely outcomes flickered past, Raziel shrugged mentally. None of them concerned him very much. Even the potential risk to the human world seemed a chance worth taking, when the single constant in every scenario was the death of the Council. And he himself would most likely be executed soon enough anyway, for he had no intention of succumbing to their rule. So if the risk paid off, it would pay off big – and if it didn't, he wouldn't be around to catch the blame.

"You do know what you're saying, I suppose," he said finally, regarding Charmeine as she stood against the door.

"Yes, I know." Charmeine's eyes were alive with challenge. "Are you a gambling man, Raz?"

The question was how.

Late that night, Raziel sat at his desk in a black silk dressing gown, catching up on his emails while he considered the problem. Several messages included links to news stories; he'd learned almost the moment he'd switched on his computer that the half-angel's mother and aunt had been killed in an arson attack. Good – it saved him the trouble of doing away with his damaged ex-lover himself. For of course Miranda couldn't have been allowed to stay alive, now that he knew her identity and that he was the thing's father. The possibility that his secret might get out was sickening.

Around him, the wooden-panelled room was sedately opulent – a plush grey carpet, antique books and furniture, and, in the daytime, a soaring view of the Rocky Mountains. In his bedroom nearby slept Jenny, the devout who'd sat by his bedside while he was unconscious. Raziel had been gratified to discover just how attractive she was when she'd returned with the other ejected humans after the Council's departure earlier – crying and throwing herself worriedly into his arms – and how delectable her energy tasted, after days of not being able to feed at all. Once alone with her, he'd plunged his hands deeply into the turquoise lights of her aura and drunk and drunk, leaving her swaying on her feet but wide-eyed with wonder. Her body was no less delectable, as it turned out – made even more so by the fact that the Council had made its disapproval about this sort of thing clear in their meeting. Raziel felt much more himself again now; more able to deal with the problem at hand.

Unfortunately, there was no easy solution. Though the

Twelve could be killed like any other angels, their powers of psychic control over their brethren were far stronger than he'd suspected – as the mass execution today had illustrated so well. An angelic army, even assuming he could raise one, would fare no better than the traitors. No, what was needed were more…conventional means.

Mexico City.

Remembering the strange glimmer of knowledge that had come as he showered earlier, Raziel frowned. And now he recalled that the moment in the shower hadn't been the first time. He'd had a sense of the girl while he was lying unconscious too – had known then that she and Kylar were in a tent together, near the Mexican border. What was going on?

Clicking a few buttons, he brought up the Church of Angels website. It still showed the girl's image on its home page: blonde and smiling, her green eyes sparkling with suppressed laughter. His daughter. Picturing Jenny lying asleep in his bed, Raziel's mouth twisted wryly. If he thought for a second that such a perverse fluke as Willow Fields could ever be repeated, he'd volunteer himself for death-by-Council immediately. No, the anomaly had clearly been something to do with Miranda, rather than himself, though finding out exactly what it had been was impossible now.

What he *could* find out, though, was how he knew

where the girl was. He relaxed back against his leather chair, then closed his eyes and went searching, allowing any knowledge to come as it would. Images of the moments in the cathedral before the Second Wave had arrived began drifting past. The long line of acolytes from all around the country, kneeling in homage before the gate. A girl's screams. Willow's startled face when she realized her disguise had been seen through; her mad dash to the gate, with her angel self flying overhead. Himself, blocking her angel from its task and feeling the disconcertingly familiar energy as their wings and auras had touched.

In fact…he could still sense her energy inside of him, even now. It was as if Willow had left a small part of herself behind, like pollen brushed from a flower.

Raziel went very still as he considered what this might mean. Then he took a breath and journeyed more deeply within. The room, the chair, the hum of the computer all faded to nothing. Soon he found the spark of his daughter's energy: a silver and lavender glow. Grimacing at the unnatural half-angel feel, Raziel prodded it carefully, touching it with his thoughts. It responded and grew, lengthening into a rich, pulsing stream of information that led to a similar spark of his own energy, now residing inside Willow.

She was lying in a bed in Mexico City – she and Kylar had found other Angel Killers. The thought that had come to Raziel in the shower was correct: she knew about the Council. She and the others thought that to kill the Twelve would kill all angels, but didn't seem aware of the other possibilities – had no clue that it could backfire horribly, as far as they were concerned.

Unconsciously, Raziel swivelled his chair from side to side as he took everything in: how Juan had stumbled on the information; the help of Luis; all of their plans and schemes. A slow smile grew across his face. He'd never have believed it, but he actually had reason to be *thankful* that he'd spawned an offspring, like some animal of the lower orders – because the family tie between them had now resulted in a psychic link, set in motion by their inadvertent exchange of energies in the cathedral. And Willow was completely unaware of it.

Though he had everything he needed for now, Raziel somehow found himself lingering. Willow's energy was unmistakably half-him; he'd have known she was his daughter even if she looked nothing like Miranda. *Strange,* he thought with a frown, letting the feel of it wash over him. It wasn't quite as unpleasant as he'd initially thought.

Willow's angel was stirring – the girl had sensed the rushing energy between them, though she had no idea what it was. Quickly but thoroughly, Raziel hid the spark of his energy that dwelled within Willow, disguising it so that it was as similar to her own essence as possible.

As Raziel opened his eyes again, he was sure the girl would never suspect their psychic connection; he could carry out any further explorations with no danger. Willow's own spark within himself didn't worry him, either – if she hadn't gotten anything from him yet, she was unlikely to. Raziel sensed strongly that his greater psychic experience gave him the advantage here. His daughter's skills were impressive, but sadly for her, they were hardly on a par with someone who'd been refining them for millennia.

Seeing that his computer had switched to the Church of Angels screen saver, he tapped his mouse and brought back Willow's photo.

Maybe Paschar was right after all, he mused, steepling his fingers. Paschar, an angel who'd been killed by Kylar almost two months ago, had had a vision that Willow could destroy all angelkind. A half-angel who might have the ability to annihilate them all: Raziel couldn't hold back a grin. Yes, that sounded like a fair contender for someone to take out the Council.

The first thing, of course, was to tone down the manhunt against Willow and Kylar. Ironically, keeping Willow safe needed to be his top priority now. He'd make a few phone calls tomorrow – get the media to gradually back off. After a few weeks of not being bombarded with her image, the general public would forget; they had the attention span of a squirrel. The other angels wouldn't be nearly so easy to divert, but at least with the human portion of the Church pacified, Willow stood a chance of not being killed by a lynch mob.

The Angel Killers' plot was unlikely to succeed without some help, though. Fortunately, he'd be happy to provide a bit of fatherly assistance from behind the scenes. Soon Charmeine would be travelling down to Mexico City for a brief preliminary trip with some of the other Council lackeys. It would be child's play for her to meet this Luis person and give things an angelic helping hand. And in due course, once Willow and her boyfriend and their little team of assassins had fulfilled their purpose and done away with the Council for him, he'd have them all put to a slow, lingering death.

Assuming anyone was still alive at that point, of course.

CHAPTER *Eight*

THE GIRLS' DORM WAS A large room on the second floor with terracotta tiles underfoot, an arched window and four single beds. Though I was so tired it felt as if I'd been wrung out like a dishrag, I lay awake that first night in my borrowed pyjamas for hours. Curled tight on my side, I tried to tell myself that somehow we were actually going to defeat the Council, and everything would be okay – that the premonition of sorrow that had hit me in front of the house hadn't meant anything at all.

Or the feeling of dread in my dream, come to that.

It wasn't easy to convince myself though, when the

hunting pack over the Zócalo had been exactly like what I'd seen. Recalling the rest of my dream – the strange boy in the park – I frowned into the darkness, a flutter of worry passing through me. If the events in the Zócalo had come true… I shook my head, irritated at myself. There was just no way. The idea that I could ever care for another boy the way I did for Alex was insane.

Forget the dream, I decided. Not all of it was accurate; that was completely obvious – and reality was more than enough for the time being anyway, with Kara and the others all half-afraid of me, watching my every move. *They'll get over it once they figure out I'm basically as human as they are,* I thought. I stared at the window; a street light shone through the thin curtains. *It'll just take time.*

Remembering the atmosphere in the dorm when Kara had brought me in, I sighed. Okay, maybe a whole lot of time. Liz and Trish looked nothing alike, but could have been twins, the way they'd stood watching me side by side with their arms folded protectively over themselves. Liz's expression had been cold, her black hair half hanging over her face. Trish had looked scared and anxious, biting her lip – somehow the look didn't really go with her freckles and cheerful snub nose.

"So she's staying?" said Liz.

"Seems that way," replied Kara shortly. She was putting fresh sheets on the one empty bed; it was in the corner, slightly away from the others. I don't think anyone was too upset about that, including me.

I moved to help her. "Yeah, we're staying," I said over my shoulder to Liz, and caught her whispering something to Trish – who looked almost ready to cry when she saw me watching; she waved her hand at Liz in a frantic shushing motion.

I straightened up from the bed. "Look, I know this must be really weird, but—" I stopped. They'd both frozen, as if a chair had suddenly started speaking. Great. Instead of alarming them further, I turned away and picked up the pyjamas of Trish's that Kara had given me: blue with white polka dots.

"Is there a shower I could use?" I asked Kara. There hadn't been one in the bathroom she'd directed me to earlier, and I was dying to get rid of the grime from travelling all day on the Shadow.

"Yeah, but only one, unfortunately," said Kara, finishing with the bed. I was trying not to stare at her the way Liz and Trish were staring at me – the sculpted lines of her face were so exotically gorgeous. "The boys usually get it at night; we take ours in the morning," she went on without looking at me. "But if you wanted to go ahead, since it's your first night…"

"No, that's all right, I'll wait," I said with an inner sigh. I started towards the bathroom to get changed – the last thing I felt like doing was getting undressed with Liz and Trish scrutinizing my every move – but then I stopped. If I did that, they'd be imagining god knew what about me; that I had angel wings sprouting out of my shoulder blades or something. So I set my jaw and got changed right there, keeping my back to them and feeling their eyes burning holes in my skin.

"I, um…don't need those back, or anything," Trish blurted as I pulled the spaghetti-strapped pyjama top over my head.

"Thanks," I said, as if I didn't know exactly why she didn't want them any more. And as everyone else started to get ready for bed too, the silence in the dorm had felt like a blanket smothering the air out.

Lying awake now, I was starting to seriously regret insisting that Alex and I didn't sleep in the same bed here. I could be with him this very moment, curled up in his arms and talking through the day's events. And then later…my cheeks tinged as I stared at the high, old-fashioned ceiling; I counted its cracks in the glow of the street light to take my mind off the fact that my heart was suddenly beating faster. Yes, good call on not sharing Alex's bed, Willow. Thumbs up.

Then I stiffened.

I could hardly even describe what I'd just felt – it was like a sort of *rushing past*, as if I were standing beside a river and could sense the intensity of its current, ready to knock me off my feet. But it wasn't beside me, it was inside of me, so powerful that it felt like I'd get swept away if I even dipped a toe in.

The feeling lasted only seconds; then it faded. Frowning, I closed my eyes and went deep within, searching. Nothing. I looked again to be sure, carefully exploring every corner of my mind. The weird energy was gone, if it had really been there in the first place – there was no sign of it. I shook my head at myself. Okay, psychic glitch time.

Then I became uneasily aware of my angel. Usually she waited inside me to be sought out, but now, all at once, she was just *there* in my mind, watching me, with her wings opening and closing.

I stared back at her, wondering what was going on. Ever since we'd bonded, her presence had always brought such a sense of love, of comfort. Now it seemed different. Edgy. My angel's shining face was my own, but my scalp chilled as I realized: there were different thoughts than mine behind her eyes. Thoughts I couldn't read.

That sense of rushing power, like something had been awakened.

Shaken, I withdrew and lay huddled under the covers, listening to the sounds of the others sleeping; the faint noise of traffic. I'd never been conscious of my angel having her own thoughts before – or even having thoughts at all, really; she'd always simply been me. What had just happened? And what would have occurred if I'd shifted my consciousness to hers – this radiant twin who suddenly felt like a stranger?

The idea brought a shiver of apprehension, and I hated it. I'd only barely gotten used to having this other part of me, and now suddenly it seemed so…alien. I let out a breath. Had I really just been thinking about how human I was? The irony wasn't funny, somehow.

It took me a long time to finally fall asleep. And even when I did, I could still sense my angel, restless inside of me.

"Okay, today I just want to see what each of you can do," said Alex.

We were standing in the range: a long room on the ground floor that looked as if several walls had been knocked down to form it. There were arched windows down here, too – and though I hadn't noticed when we'd arrived, they'd been boarded up from the inside. Kara had told me that morning that Juan had bought the place outright, plus all of their equipment. Apparently being an AK paid a lot, which wasn't really news, given Alex's Porsche when I'd first met him. And like Alex, Juan had squirrelled away part of his money in cash, though apparently on a far greater scale.

"So we've got enough to keep us going for a while," Kara had said as she got dressed that morning, while I tried not to gape at her perfect body. She was so sleek and toned; she actually had a tiny six-pack. And an *AK* tattoo on her left bicep, just like Alex's. A strange feeling stirred through me at the sight of its gothic letters; I'd always associated that tattoo only with Alex.

She caught me studying her and stiffened, snapping a T-shirt over her head. "What?"

"Nothing," I said. "Sorry. You just…look like you're in really good shape, that's all. I guess I'm not, that much." It was true. I'd always been thin without trying, but I used to get Cs and Ds in PE, because my best friend Nina and I would just sit and talk half the time. Thinking of Nina, I felt a pang, wondering what she thought of me now.

"Huh," said Kara, brown eyes narrowed as if she didn't quite believe I hadn't been up to something. "Well. We'll get you into shape," she'd said grudgingly.

"So what's *she* going to be doing?" asked Sam now as we all stood in the firing range.

"Excuse me?" said Alex coldly. He was wearing faded jeans and a black T-shirt he'd borrowed from someone. I'd never seen him wearing black before; it made his dark hair look a shade lighter, his eyes almost bright blue.

"Her. Your half-angel girlfriend," repeated Sam in his Texan drawl, folding his arms over his muscular chest. His short blond hair was spiky with gel. "I'm assuming she's going to be part of the team, right?"

The news that Alex was taking over as lead had been met with a mix of wariness and something like relief. Everyone seemed to respect Kara, to admire her for stepping in after Juan died – but no one argued that she should stay in charge now that Alex was here. Remembering the apprehension I'd picked up from him that night in the tent, I watched him closely now, trying to send him good vibes. He didn't seem to need them. No matter what he might have been feeling inside, there was no hint he was even nervous as he stood facing the group.

"Okay, I want to get a few things straight with all of you," he said, and though his voice was calm I could tell how irritated he was. "*She* has a name. It's Willow. And yes, she is going to be part of the team. This is her fight too. She cares as much about defeating the angels as any of you."

I tried to smile as everyone glanced sideways at me. I could feel the suspicion in the room, as if a snake had just slithered through it.

"If you're accepting me as lead, then you're also accepting Willow," Alex went on. "Because I'd trust her with my life. So I do not, repeat, *do not* want to hear any crap from anyone about her. Yes, she's half-angel; no, she is not going to harm you in any way. And that is seriously the last time I ever want to have this conversation. Is that understood?"

Mumbled yeses. Sam looked like he was about to say something else, then thought better of it. My cheeks were in flames. I understood why Alex had had to do this, but part of me wanted the floor to splinter open and drop me into the core of the earth.

"Good," said Alex finally. "Let's get started. Kara, can you get everyone going with some target practice? Willow doesn't know how to shoot yet; I need to give her some basic training."

Oh. I'd forgotten that I'd promised to learn how to shoot. But even with my lifelong dislike of guns, it was still ten times better than just standing there while everyone in the room avoided looking at me. Alex took me to the back of the range where there was a table, to show me how to load a magazine.

"You're doing great," I whispered to him. "Seriously."

He made a face as he looked down at the pistol he was holding. "Yeah…I guess we'll see how it goes." He pulled the magazine out with a *click* and discharged the cartridges, then started pressing them back in again in a smooth, rapid motion. "Okay, look, this is really easy – just watch how I'm doing it."

I hesitated, wondering what was bothering him. I knew he must be even more worried about the situation with the

Council than I was, when he was the one responsible for training everyone. But this felt like something else.

He glanced at me; a slight smile appeared. "You know, you sort of have to pay attention if you're going to learn this. Here, I'll do it again."

This time I took in the steady rhythm of his thumb as he pressed the cartridges in. "Like a Pez dispenser," I said. All around us were the faint thuds of silenced bullets. They weren't loud, but they were *intense*, somehow; you could feel the whole room vibrating with them.

"Yeah, exactly." Alex took the cartridges out again and handed me the empty magazine. "And listen, I'm sorry about just now, with the group," he added in an undertone. "Hope I didn't embarrass you."

"It's okay," I said, thinking how strange it was for us to be standing this far apart. I'd gotten so used to touching Alex whenever I wanted – it seemed as natural to me as breathing. I knew he felt the same. Earlier that morning, he'd pulled me into one of the storerooms as I'd come out of the shower room wearing a borrowed bathrobe – stroking my damp hair back with both hands, kissing me deeply, the two of us pressed up against the wall in the shadows.

"I missed you last night," he'd whispered between kisses.

"Me too…me too," I'd murmured. His arms had felt so

safe around me, as if the weird sensations of the night before would never have happened if I hadn't been sleeping away from him. As if they weren't important at all any more.

I swallowed as I looked down at the magazine, struggling to push a cartridge in. I'd been trying not to focus on it, but that sense of my angel being restless was still there. I was so conscious of her as a separate presence that she almost felt loose inside of me; I was reminded of Peter Pan trying to sew his shadow back on. God, I hated this – not knowing what was going on with my own body.

"Hey. What's up?" asked Alex.

I shoved my worries down as far as they'd go and slammed a door on them. There was no way I was telling Alex this; it was too not-human for me to even want to think about it. "Nothing. I'm fine."

He propped a hip against the table, watching me carefully. "Those girls haven't been giving you a hard time, have they?"

"No. Well, a little. Nothing major." I manoeuvred another cartridge into the magazine. It wasn't nearly as easy as it looked. "How did you *do* this so fast, anyway?"

He glanced down at my hands. "Practice. What do you mean, nothing major?"

I shook my head – Liz and Trish staring at me while I put on my jim-jams was really the least of my worries just then. "Seriously, Alex, it's okay. I've got to make my own way with them, you know? It's no good if my boyfriend the lead AK gets all involved every time someone looks at me funny."

I could tell he understood, even if he didn't like it much. "Yeah, all right," he said finally. "But listen, I have to make sure that everything's running smoothly with the team. So if it gets to the point where it might affect that, then I need to know, okay?"

"Deal," I said in a soft voice. His eyes were so warm, so concerned. The rhythm of the cartridges slowed as I took in the familiar strong lines of his face, and the raw-looking bruise on his cheek where Sam had hit him. My gaze lingered on the bruise. I wanted to stroke it better, feather light kisses all over it. In fact, I just wanted to kiss him, period, so much that it hurt.

He grinned suddenly, and my heart turned over. "Oh man, don't look at me like that, or we're going to cause a scandal in the AK house."

And for a minute I felt better, just standing near him and seeing his smile. "Look at you like what?" I said innocently, as I finished loading the magazine and put it down on the table.

"Yeah, you know *exactly* like what. Like you're thinking about the broom closet, that's what." Unobtrusively, he put his hand over mine on the table, stroking my index finger lightly. We smiled at each other; then he glanced over his shoulder and the smile faded. His expression turned serious, intent. "I'd better get over there, see how they're doing. Do you want to practise this for a while? I'll be back soon to start teaching you how to shoot."

He showed me how to empty the magazine, and then went over to the others. My gaze followed him without me meaning it to, drinking in the firm set of his shoulders under the T-shirt; his rumpled dark hair; the sense of confidence that shone through without him even being aware of it, just in the way he walked – so easy and relaxed.

And then I saw something that I really didn't know what to think about.

Kara was looking at him in the same way.

As the days passed, things settled into a routine.

I learned how to shoot. Started target practice with the others. Watched the news a lot, like everyone else, to see what was going on in the world now. And we all tried to avoid bumping into each other like peas in a can. There weren't *that* many of us in the house, but it always felt crowded somehow – apart from the dorms, there was only the range, the kitchen, the TV room and a couple of storage rooms, which were so full of boxes you could hardly get into them anyway. There was also a tiny gym in the basement, with a few exercise machines and free weights. Everyone worked out. I did too, since I was going stir crazy – Alex didn't want me outside on my own until he was satisfied I could defend myself. He wasn't just being protective of his girlfriend; the same thing was true for the other AKs, apart from Kara.

Other AKs. It was strange to realize that's what I was now.

Alex hadn't been satisfied at all with the way the first target practice went. Afterwards he'd told the group they were way too static – great at shooting if nothing was moving, but unfortunately angels had this funny habit of not just standing there motionless when bullets were coming at them. He rigged up targets that swung wildly from the ceiling, and made them start practising with those instead. In no time, the wall behind the targets was peppered with bullet holes, as if the room had been through a war.

"Man, this sucks," complained Sam a few days later, red-faced with frustration as he missed again. The target swung about on its chain: a manic, mocking pendulum. "It's all we've been doing for days! When are we gonna get out there and hunt some angels for real, so we can get ready for the Council?"

"When you're over ninety per cent on the moving

targets," said Alex shortly. He took Sam's pistol from him and aimed at the still-bouncing target; he shot once, twice, a third time. Bullseye each time. Silence fell from the group as they watched.

"That's what I want," said Alex. He handed Sam's gun back. "Until you can do that, you're not getting anywhere near an angel again – period. You're no good to me unless you can actually hit them."

No one said anything as he put them back to work, but it was like a ripple of determination had passed through the group; like they all suddenly got it. He kept everyone practising for hours each day, and when they weren't doing that, he made sure they were working out, keeping in shape. He discussed strategy with the team too, drilling it into them – like, what to do when you're under direct attack, so you don't lead the angels straight back to your doorstep.

He was an excellent teacher – patient and good at explaining things – but I could tell he never forgot that in just over ten weeks, he had to have everyone trained for what might be humanity's only real chance against the angels. Though he never even hinted to the others that he had reservations about being in charge, I knew how heavily the responsibility weighed on him. It showed in his face, his eyes, making him look so much older than eighteen that it wrung my heart. And while I'd never met his father, as I watched Alex explaining diagrams at the kitchen table with everyone crowded around him, I somehow knew he was his dad all over again.

The TV showed that the world had changed already. Before, it was possible to go a day or two without hearing a reference to the angels. Not any more. Almost every time you changed the channel, you got a talk show where *los ángeles* were being discussed, or a documentary about true-life angelic stories, or a music video with everyone bopping around in angel wings. We got CNN and a few other American channels on cable, and it was exactly the same in the US. There were new TV shows galore: *Who's The Angel?*, *Angelic Paths*, *Angels 1-2-3*. They all looked sort of cheesy and rapidly thrown together, but were obviously meeting a huge demand; everyone wanted to drown themselves in images of their predators. On the news, random street shots always showed people wearing angel wings: a new fad meaning you'd seen an angel. The camera often caught someone gazing dreamily into the distance too, basking in the glow of a beautiful creature only they could see.

With all that, it wasn't surprising the problem of overcrowded hospitals was getting worse. I remembered the documentary I'd seen back in Tennessee: the beds lining the hospital corridors; the teenage girl with exhausted, angel-burned eyes. That was only a couple of months ago, and now those images seemed practically upbeat. In both the US and Mexico, people were literally dying on hospital floors. You sometimes couldn't even get an ambulance now, or find a hospital that could take you in. Protests were springing up all over, with people demanding that the government do something. Here in Mexico City, things were even worse, because renovating the cathedral to become part of the Church of Angels had been paid for with taxpayers' money. Most people were all for it, but a group calling themselves the Crusaders for People's Rights were furious that the funds hadn't been used for medical care. Protests here were turning into sizzling confrontations, with the "Crusaders" and the "Faithful" screaming at each other on a regular basis.

We saw Raziel once on TV too.

He was in his human form, walking through the Denver cathedral – apparently pointing out the damage, though the commentary was in Spanish. I sat stiffly on the battered sofa, unable to take my eyes away – and was so, so glad that nobody except Alex knew this was my father.

"*That* jerk," muttered Kara. Often she was out with Luis in the evenings, trying to get information, but she was home for a change – perched cross-legged in the armchair, painting her toenails. "You know, I hate all the angels, but that one is really something else. I want to throw stuff at the screen whenever I see him."

"Yeah, you're not the only one," said Alex, beside me on the sofa. He took my hand, squeezing it as the camera panned around the cathedral. There was scaffolding up, and dozens of workers busy repairing the buckled floor and collapsed section of ceiling. I stared at the spot where I'd crouched less than two weeks before, my muscles clenching as I remembered what it had felt like to die.

Raziel appeared again. Jet-black hair; a refined, sensitive face. And long, slender hands that had buried themselves deep in my mother's energy field when she was only a twenty-year-old music student at NYU. As he spoke, Spanish subtitles scrolled across the bottom of the screen. "Yes, repairs are almost finished now," he said. "We're looking forward to getting back to business as usual, and putting all of this behind us."

"And you, sir, you claim you're an angel yourself?"

Raziel gave a small, wise smile directly to the camera. An almost-dimple appeared in one cheek; his eyebrows arched good-humouredly. "It's not a claim, it's the simple truth. My kind are now living amongst you, to bring hope in these troubled times."

Hatred twisted in my stomach. He sure hadn't brought hope to my mother.

"Will the world see any changes now that more angels have arrived?" asked the reporter. "For instance, will the Church of Angels remain the same?"

Raziel's benign expression vanished as his brown eyes narrowed – and all at once I was looking at the same deadly angel Alex and I had confronted in the cathedral. "No," he said. "There will be no changes to the Church." His smile returned, almost as pleasant as before, though this time I could see the calculation under it. "No changes at all," he repeated deliberately. "That is my promise."

I held back a shudder. For a weird second, it had felt as if he was looking right at *me*, as if he could actually see me through the screen somehow. As usual now, that slight sense of my angel shifting within me was there, and I tried to push it away, suddenly sickly aware of how *not* human I was – with this thing inside me and Raziel for a dad. I'd thought all of this was something I'd gotten used to. It so wasn't.

At least the manhunt for us seemed to have calmed down, though our pictures still flashed on the screen occasionally. I stared at my photo whenever it appeared, wondering who that blonde girl with the bright smile was. Kara always teased Alex about the terrible drawing that made him look like an aging football player – and whenever he managed to unwind a little he teased her too, with stories from their life back at the old camp. I could see the real affection between them, but it seemed so totally brother/sister on both sides that I thought I must have been insane to have imagined how soft and shining Kara's eyes had become as she watched him that day.

Except I didn't really believe I was.

After what Alex had told them, none of the AKs gave me a hard time – but none of them spoke to me much either. And this was not exactly a quiet group. They were always talking, arguing, bantering. Brendan was from Portland and like a terrier, all wiry hair and hyper energy. The only thing he and Sam agreed on was the need to rid the world of angels; they'd bicker about politics for hours, with Brendan clawing at his head and practically shrieking with frustration – "Man, how can you *think* that? Are you even listening to how ignorant you sound?"

Eventually Trish would step in and try to defuse things in her gentle way. Everyone liked her so much that Brendan might subside for a while, grumbling, and then Sam would make another drawling comment and they'd be off again. Liz was just as bad, dropping biting little remarks into the conversation and goading things along.

She was also the self-designated cook, which was something I loved to do too – but when I'd suggested that maybe we could take turns, she'd stiffened as if I planned to sprinkle poison in the food. So I dropped it. It wasn't worth it. Even with the others, "prickly" seemed to be Liz's default setting, though she and Trish got along really well. Once I walked into the girls' dorm to find them talking earnestly together. "I don't think you should blame yourself," Trish was saying. "Everyone's family has issues."

Then they saw me and clammed up. Liz scowled, lifting her chin; as always, Trish looked alarmed and slightly tense to have me around. "Sorry to interrupt," I said. Neither answered, and I held back a sigh as I got my shampoo and towel and left the dorm again. The ironic thing is I think Trish and I could have been friends – she was so *nice*; there was no other word for her. But it was obvious how wary she was of me, and how much she hated the strain I'd brought to the group.

Wesley was the only quiet one; always hunched over his laptop, more given to sullen grunts than talking. At first I thought he hated everyone, then I realized he was just excruciatingly shy. Though there was something else there too – once, I got a sense of sorrow from him so strong I almost said something. The *keep away* expression on his face told me to forget it. Mostly he avoided me, the same as everyone else, while I tried to ignore the fact I was being avoided. As if there wasn't this huge unspoken *thing* about me that made everyone stiffen if I accidentally stood too close.

I mentally gave myself a shake whenever I caught myself thinking like that. I hated feeling this way; it was totally unlike me to be self-pitying. But I was just…really lonely.

I missed Alex, even though we were in the same house together. There wasn't anyplace we could truly be alone here. The dorms and the kitchen always had people going in and out; the range and the exercise room were pretty unideal. The TV room always had someone in it – such as Brendan, who had insomnia and was usually surfing the net on his laptop at three in the morning.

Though Alex's tiny bedroom should have been a haven, it wasn't much of one, because it was right off the boys' dorm. As in, you had to pass directly through the dorm to get to it. When any of the guys were out there we could hear their murmurs of conversation – so obviously we could be heard as well. And somehow Alex being the lead meant we couldn't just tell them to get out; it would have felt like he was getting special privileges or something.

So we could kiss, we could touch…but we couldn't let ourselves get too carried away. I was so aware of the box Alex had bought on our way down to Mexico City, still sitting in his bag unopened. He was too – understatement – but neither of us mentioned it. Like me, I knew how much Alex wanted it to be perfect for us when it happened – not feeling self-conscious because someone might hear, or sneaking down to the sweaty-smelling exercise room.

Anyway, that was bad enough, but not being able to talk the way we used to was even worse. Alex had noticed how things were for me, though. "I'm sorry," he said in a low voice when we'd been there for over a week. "I know you're not very happy here."

We were closeted away in his bedroom for a few minutes before dinner; distantly, I could hear the TV playing. "I'm fine," I whispered back. "Don't worry about me; this is what we have to be doing. And besides…you don't exactly seem happy either." I traced the dark curve of his eyebrow. Obviously *being happy* wasn't the point, not when what we were doing was so crucial to the world. Neither of us would have chosen to be anywhere else, even if we could. But still, it made me sad when I realized that whole days had gone past since the last time I'd seen Alex really smile – that gorgeous, easy grin that melted my heart.

"I do worry about you," he said, ignoring what I'd said about his own happiness. "Willow, listen, if we actually manage to do this – if we defeat them, somehow – it'll be so different for you and me then, I promise…"

He broke off as we heard someone enter the dorm next door, moving around and getting changed. After that we fell silent, just letting the feel of our lips together do the talking for us.

Most of our conversations were like that now – snatched sentences; a quick touching of base with no time for details. I missed sleeping in the same bed as Alex. I missed it so acutely that I just lay awake aching for him sometimes, longing to slip through the dark house and go to him. I hadn't really known before just how much we *talked* as we lay in bed together, or how precious those soft conversations in the dark were to me.

And I thought if I could only lie curled up in his arms again, and know that we were alone – really alone, the way we used to be – then maybe I'd be able to tell him how scared I was.

I hadn't contacted my angel since that first night, but I could *feel* her there, all the time. As the days had passed, her restless shifting had intensified into what seemed like a longing to break free. I became so self-conscious, trying to get through my days without letting on this was happening; without really letting on to myself, even. But it felt like everyone knew anyway – because sometimes the nape of my neck would start prickling, as if they were all staring. Occasionally someone would be there when I checked; more often I'd find myself looking at an empty space. And meanwhile I could sense my angel, straining against me. What frightened me most was that it was starting to take an effort to hold her back, like struggling to hang on to a tugging kite.

My old life in Pawntucket was like something that had happened on another planet: Willow Fields, who, okay, was maybe sort of strange because of fixing cars and being psychic, but who had a pretty boring, ordinary life, actually. And who definitely didn't feel like a stranger inside her own body. I could hardly believe now that such a time had really existed, when I'd just felt…normal.

Human.

Chapter *Nine*

The PARADE TOOK SEB by surprise.

It had been just over two weeks now since he'd hitch-hiked down to *el DF*, and he'd spent every moment of daylight looking for the girl in the photo; he only vaguely knew what day of the week it was any more. But now, as he walked back to his hostel near the *centro*, he saw that it must be Revolution Day. A *mariachi* band was playing, with its warbling singers and the jaunty sound of guitars and horns, and there was a parade passing by, full of schoolchildren dressed as soldiers: the boys in sombreros and bullet belts, sporting eyebrow-pencil moustaches; the girls in long, bright skirts and snowy-white blouses, their hair in braids. Behind them came a group of older girls in green T-shirts, dancing and waving Mexican flags.

With his knapsack over his shoulder – there was no way he'd leave it in the hostel during the day – Seb edged through the crowd lining the sidewalk. A few angel wings brushed him as he passed. Everywhere he went now, there were people wearing them. The mood of the crowd was exuberant, their auras practically bouncing against him; even those that were stunted with angel damage shimmered with excitement.

It was the same city he'd always known, and yet completely different. The angels were everywhere – he'd noticed it even though he was spending most of his time wandering around Bosque de Chapultepec, searching for the same configuration of trees that he'd seen in the girl's dream. It was turning out to be a heartbreaking task; Chapultepec was one of the largest city parks in the world. And in the meantime, hardly an hour went by when Seb didn't see a few angels cruising overhead, like white eagles on the hunt. Each time he passed the Zócalo there were several swooping over it as well; others fed right on the sidewalk. Curiosity had taken him briefly inside the converted cathedral – he couldn't believe what had happened to the place – and there, too, the angels had been hunting. He was so used to keeping his aura dim and unappealing now that he did it almost without thinking.

"Hospitals for all!" shouted a voice. "We need more beds, more doctors!" Glancing over his shoulder as he crossed the street – darting between the girl dancers and a donkey pulling a flower-laden cart – Seb saw a large group approaching, carrying signs: El DF *is Dying for More Doctors*, and *Angels Don't Need Money – The Sick Do!*

Immediately, the mood of the crowd changed, the auras around him almost crackling with emotion. A woman sitting in a wheelchair yelled, "The angels would help you if you had faith!" Her cheeks looked sunken, her eyes fervent. Several voices called out in agreement, booing the group marching past.

Seb was glad to leave it all behind and reach the street that his hostel was on. Though even here, it looked like they were getting ready for some kind of dance later; there was a stage being set up, and green, white and red bunting hanging from the wrought-iron balconies above. The hostel's outer walls were once tan, now smudged grey with pollution. Seb knew he'd been lucky to get a bed. Like every other hostel in the city, the place was packed with Church of Angels followers from around the world, here to see the newly converted cathedral. He passed a few of them now on the way to his dorm – a trio of pretty French girls in angel wings, who he'd encountered a few times in the lounge in the evenings.

"*Bonsoir*, Seb," said one of them, Céline, with a flirtatious smile as they passed. "*Ça va toi?*" He summoned up a smile as he returned the greeting, trying not to notice how sick her aura looked. Being around people who'd been hurt by the angels depressed him; he preferred to avoid it.

Thankfully, his dorm was empty. Seb stretched out on his bed, and lay staring upwards. His birthday had been the week before, making him eighteen now; he hadn't even realized it until the next day. All he could think of was the half-angel girl – she was so close now he could almost feel her, yet in a way she seemed further away than ever. To know that she was probably right here, in this very city – only a few miles away from him at most – but to have no idea *where* exactly, was agony.

The framed photo was a small, solid rectangle in his jeans pocket. He didn't need to take it out to bring back the girl's image; he knew it by heart now. Her spirit was with him already, just as it had been for so many years – and since touching her shirt with its whispers of her energy, this sense felt even stronger: a line drawing brought richly to life with colour. Seb shoved his hair back as he regarded the dingy plaster ceiling. God, he was in love with a girl he'd never even spoken to. But he *knew* her, inside and out.

Could she sense him as strongly? Had she always been in love with a shadow too?

Outside, music had started up. With a restless sigh, Seb swung his feet off the bed and went to the ancient French windows; he swung them open with a creak and stepped out onto the small wrought-iron balcony. On the street below, couples were beginning to dance; paper lanterns cast a festive light. Seb stood against the railing, looking down.

During the day he was single-minded. Mostly he searched Bosque de Chapultepec, but he went to other parks too – always scanning non-stop, not letting himself believe for a second that he wouldn't find her. It was these other, quieter times when doubt swamped him, leaving him cold. What if he'd gotten the girl's dream wrong? What if the park they'd seemed to be in wasn't in *el DF* at all, but somewhere else? She was American; it could be someplace in her own country – which spread across thousands of miles, and contained probably millions of parks. He'd most likely never find her at all, if that was the case. And to know that she really existed, that she wasn't a dream, but to never be able to locate her… Seb swallowed. No. He wouldn't believe that. He couldn't.

The door opened behind him. "Oh, hey Seb," said a voice.

Mike, one of the Americans staying in the dorm – and one of the few people at the hostel undamaged by the angels. "Hi," said Seb from the balcony. Mike joined him;

he was nineteen, with floppy brown hair and a friendly smile.

"So what's this all about, anyway?" he asked, resting his forearms on the railing as he took in the dancing. "Is it like the Fourth of July back home?"

Shoving his thoughts away with an effort, Seb tried to remember what he'd heard about the American holiday. "What's the Fourth of July? You have fireworks then, yes?"

In that way Americans sometimes had, Mike looked surprised that Seb didn't know – even though *he* had no idea what Revolution Day was. "It's when we got our independence from Britain," he explained. "You know – the Boston Tea Party, Paul Revere. And yeah, lots of fireworks."

Seb nodded, remembering now. "It's sort of like that," he said. "It celebrates the day we started fighting to get rid of the *dictador* Porfirio Díaz."

"You got rid of a dictator? Cool," said Mike cheerfully. "And anyway, any excuse for a party, right?"

This made Seb laugh in spite of himself. "Yes, if you're Mexican. We like parties."

"Man, you're not the only ones. You should come to America sometime. Folks *love* to party there."

Seb knew he might have to someday, if his search in *el DF* proved fruitless. Except how could he ever leave, when the rest of the girl's dream had so obviously taken place here? Her light-blue shirt was still folded neatly in his knapsack, but he resisted the urge to bring it out again; its images were becoming fainter each time he touched the soft fabric, diluting the girl's energy with his own.

The evening softened into darkness, the lanterns glowing brightly as the jubilant sound of guitars and trumpets soared around them. Mike had brought some cold beers into the room; he offered one to Seb and they stood drinking them, gazing down at the swirling dancers.

"So I'm planning on going to Tepito tomorrow," said Mike, leaning against the wall and stretching his legs out. "Can't find anything about it in the guidebook, but it's north of here, isn't it?"

Seb was smoking a cigarette as he thought about the park again – wondering if he should focus more on its woodsy third section, instead of the more popular first and second ones. At Mike's words, he blew out a quick breath of smoke and glanced at him, startled. "What? Why?"

"To *see* it, man. I want to see all of this place."

"No," said Seb flatly. "Don't go there."

Mike blinked. "Why not? It's just a market, right?"

"It's the worst *barrio* in the city," said Seb. "A *gringo* with a camera and cellphone, who barely speaks Spanish? They'd think Christmas had come early this year. You'd be robbed in minutes, or worse." It was where he was from. The dark streets of Tepito, with the rustling, plastic roofs of vendors' stalls, were as familiar to him as the various scars on his body – and living there had been just as enjoyable as getting them.

The American looked sceptical. "It can't really be *that* bad, can it?"

"Yes," said Seb. "Trust me – stay away. Go do all the tourist things in your guidebook. They don't put Tepito in there for a reason." He smiled, took another puff of his cigarette. "The paddle boats in Chapultepec Park are very nice."

Mike pulled a face; he opened his mouth to say something else and then glanced at the scene below. "Hey, look at that," he laughed, propping his forearms on the railing again as he looked down. "The little scamp."

Crushing out his cigarette, Seb followed his gaze and saw a street child slipping through the crowd that stood watching the dancers – a girl of seven or so, with tousled dark hair. Seen from above, her hand motion was clear as she dipped it into a man's jacket pocket and then out again, quickly tucking whatever she'd found under her shirt. Seb smiled slightly, remembering all too well the feel of it – the quick flex of the fingers, the grasp and pull, all the while making sure that you didn't touch the sides of the pocket.

Mike went back to talking about Tepito; Seb's eyes stayed on the girl, watching as she manoeuvred through the crowd. Thin, and so young, with big brown eyes and a dirty face. He knew she probably lived in one of the abandoned buildings not far from the *centro*, or maybe down in the sewers. It was a tough life – god, such a tough life, with so many dangers in it. Even now, years later, he was amazed sometimes that he'd made it out alive.

It had still been better than that place they'd put him in.

"Well, what about the Lagunilla market?" Mike was saying. "Is that one all right to go to?"

"Yes, it's not too bad," said Seb distantly. "Just stay in the streets near Francisco Bocanegra and Comonfort; it's safer at that end."

"Okay, thanks." Mike smiled. "Hey, maybe I'll ask those three French girls to come with me, if I can drag them away from the cathedral. You want to come too? I think that one, Céline, has a thing for you."

Seb started to answer, but broke off as he caught sight of an angel gliding overhead. He shifted his aura to dull greys; brought it as close to his body as he could so that it appeared shrunken. On the balcony beside him, Mike's aura looked far too healthy. He found himself edging closer, attempting to hide it a little. The angel cruised silently past, almost on a level with them. Seb tried to look as if he couldn't see it, but its radiance burned itself into his skull anyway – the proud, fierce face; the powerful wings that seemed to glow blue-white, every feather outlined.

"'Cause I heard her talking with her friends yesterday," went on Mike, "and if my high school French wasn't failing me, she was saying that she thinks you're really hot. Wondering if you're a devout or not." He grinned. "My advice? Just pretend that you are, man. Tell her how much you *lo-ove* the angels."

Seb was barely listening to him. Below, the angel had chosen its victim; landed in a flurry of wings on the festive street.

It was the street girl.

Seb went very still, staring. He had never seen an angel choose a child to feed from before. The girl was gazing up at the angel with a look of awestruck joy on her face; her energy was pale blue. It wavered like a soap bubble, looking young and vulnerable.

"Seb?" He felt Mike shove his arm with a laugh. "You awake over there? God, I wish *I* had so many gorgeous girls drooling over me that I could take it in my stride." He stroked his jaw with a musing expression. "Maybe it's the stubble. I could always stop shaving…"

"Thanks, but I can't – I've got some things to do tomorrow." Seb heard his voice say the words. Somehow it sounded normal. Below, the angel was advancing on the girl, smiling, stretching out its shining hands towards her. With no conscious thought, Seb switched his awareness to his angel self and flew out in a rush, swooping down so quickly that the lanterns and the dancers were a blur.

He hovered in front of the girl, spreading his wings wide. The angel drew back with a flapping hiss. It was a male, and its gaze widened abruptly when it saw that Seb had no halo. "You – how—"

"Not this one," said Seb. He had never spoken in his angel form before, but his voice came out with no hesitation, low and hard. Inside, he was screaming at himself. *What are you doing? For the first time in your life, you're so close to finding her – and you're risking it for this?*

"Another one!" snarled the angel. "Half-human *mutant* – you shouldn't even exist!" It came at him in a fury of brightness; Seb fought it back, beating at it with his wings. He sensed that it was scanning in great sweeps of thought, searching for the feel of his energy to find his human form. He could disguise his aura's look, but not its feel; it would be on him in seconds.

A brief, frenzied attack, and then Seb darted away and whirled to face the girl. Her eyes were huge, full of wonder. They stared right through him. His spirits sank; he had meant to tell her to run, but she couldn't see or hear him – only her predator, whose mind was linked with hers. Behind him, he heard the angel cry out in triumph. It had found his human form. Unless he somehow managed to destroy it, it would kill him and feed off the girl anyway.

No, he thought, staring at her small, grimy face. Many things had happened in his life that he couldn't stop – but he would stop this.

On the balcony above, Mike had lifted an eyebrow. "Really? What are you doing that's better than hanging out with three French girls who think you're hot? 'Cause this I have *got* to hear."

Without answering, Seb straightened quickly in his human form, shoving his beer at Mike; he took off at a run just as he saw the angel come swarming up towards him. He flung himself out of the dorm and barrelled down the hallway; raced down the stairs. As he burst out of the front door, he knew that barely seconds had passed. The angel was now nowhere in sight as it searched for him, gliding through the upper floor of the hostel.

And in doing so, it had, for the moment at least, broken its connection with the girl.

Seb came to a skidding halt in front of her; crouched down so he could look her in the eyes. She still seemed dazed – there was a happy smile playing at her lips as she stared after the angel. He gripped her thin shoulders; shook them fiercely. "Run, *niña!* Don't ask questions – just go – go!"

He gave her a shove; the girl gasped and seemed to

come back to herself. With a frightened, startled look, she took off at a run, vanishing into the crowd.

Seb's own angel was hovering overhead, looking out for when the creature reappeared. His human self rose slowly as he stared at the hostel. It was too late for him to try to get away; it knew he was here and would stop at nothing to find him now – and besides, his knapsack was still upstairs, with the girl's shirt inside. He couldn't leave it. Distantly, he was aware of Mike up on the balcony, gaping down at him; the rollicking music; the dancers still swirling past.

The angel came soaring out of the building. It saw him standing on the street below almost immediately, its beautiful face contorting in fury. Seb's angel form darted in front of it and the creature roared and charged at him in the air, burning with light.

The two battled fiercely in the street over the dance, flapping and struggling at each other; Seb felt the sizzle of the angel's energy where their wings touched. The halo. He had to get to it; it was the way he'd defeated the only other angel he'd ever fought. But the creature's great wings kept him at bay as they twisted together in the air – the angel trying to get to Seb's human form with its vulnerable life force; Seb straining to reach that gleaming, pulsing circle.

"Hey, what's going on – are you okay?" Mike had come out and was on the street beside him now, holding both bottles of beer. "Dude, you look like you're seeing ghosts, or something."

Seb shook his head, unable to take his eyes off the invisible battle above. His angel self was fast and strong, but he could feel that he was tiring. The angel snarled at him as they collided again, shoving at him with its wings.

"I'm fine," he managed with an effort. "Mike, go inside. Don't stay out here."

Mike laughed uncertainly. "What – is this another dangerous place like Tepito? Yeah, we've got all these scary grannies and grandads dancing past – don't know what they might do."

Seb started to speak, but knew with a chill that it was too late – the angel had seen Mike standing with him. He saw its eyes narrow; it plunged at the angel Seb with an even greater ferocity, fighting to get past. *No!* Seb's angel held it off somehow, his wings flashing in the light of the lanterns. The angel darted; Seb lunged but it wrenched away, soaring straight at Mike – not bonding with him, just attacking for all it was worth.

Seb grasped the thing's plan instantly; knew it was a trap – but he couldn't let Mike be hurt when he'd only been trying to see if Seb was okay. His angel self put on a burst of speed, whipping in front of Mike to protect him, just as he'd protected the girl. He stretched his wings out, holding the angel off as it feinted at him in a frenzy of radiance. Mike kept talking, oblivious to the drama being played out only feet away.

In his human form, Seb's heart was thumping. He put his hand in the back pocket of his jeans and his fingers closed around his switchblade.

As he'd known it would, the angel went for him while his angel self was still shielding Mike. Seb didn't let himself think. Dodging sideways to avoid its outstretched hands, he flicked out the blade of his knife and went for the halo before the angel could strike him with its wing. The blade glowed white as it sliced through; for an agonized second, his arm felt like it was on fire. An explosion of light that knocked him off his feet – the sound of the angel's screams.

It was gone.

Seb lay where he was on the sidewalk, breathing hard as the remnants of the creature glittered gently over the dance. He brought his angel back to himself, relishing the feel of it safe inside of him. He had done it. Somehow he had done it. The half-angel girl flashed in his mind, and the realization that he was still alive and still had a chance to find her was like diving into a clear mountain pool.

"Uh…Seb?" Mike was squatting beside him. "Tell me that was some kind of Mexican folk dance, right? And that you didn't *really* just start leaping around with a switchblade for no reason at all."

Seb smiled. With an effort, he sat up. He was still holding the switchblade; he flicked the knife away and stuck it back in his pocket. Then he took his beer from Mike, pulling at it in a long sip. "Folk dance," he said as the singers warbled into the night around them, guitars strumming. "It was definitely a folk dance."

Mike shook his head. Settling cross-legged next to Seb on the sidewalk, he said, "You Mexicans are weird."

"But you like us."

"Yeah. Guess I'm weird, too."

Seb gazed at the dancers, watching the bobbing colours of their auras as they spun past – and knew that sometime soon, he was going to have to think about what he'd just done.

He'd always told himself that at least the angels gave something back to humans with their touch – but if he really believed this made a difference, then why did he try to protect every human he ever met from them? Why had he just risked his life for the *niñita*, when for the first time in eighteen years, he might be close to finding the only thing he'd ever wanted? If he'd let the thing feed from her, then the street girl would have been happy for ever, no matter how she might have been damaged. Yet at least she had a choice now. Perhaps she could pull herself out of the streets, and be safe and well – find a happiness that was grittier, more real than anything the angels' touch could give her. Seb shook his head in amazement as he realized: he'd do the same thing again, if he had to do it over.

"Nice night," said Mike, tapping his hand on his thigh in time to the music. "The street dancing, and the lanterns. Nice."

"Yes, it is," agreed Seb. He didn't really understand himself, but he supposed it didn't matter. He reached into his pocket and touched the brass frame of the photo, stroking his finger across its smoothness. And he knew that his half-angel girl *would* understand this, probably a lot better than he did. He could feel her compassion for what had just happened, for both the street girl and himself; see the warmth in her green eyes. He let out a breath, drinking in the sense of her that felt so close now. He needed her; he always had. Somehow he knew that she needed him too.

I will find you, he thought. It was a promise to them both.

But for now, it was enough to just be watching the dancers, basking in their happiness.

Chapter *Ten*

"OKAY, THE RECEPTION'S GOING to be in here," said Kara, pointing. We were sitting around the kitchen table with mugs of coffee, looking at Brendan's laptop – he'd found floor plans for the hotel on the internet. "There's a private reception with just the Church of Angels officials first, then we lowly peons will be allowed in."

Alex and I had been there for just over two weeks, and it was starting to feel like a plan was coming together. Luis, after being hesitant to tell Kara too much, had now become a lot more forthcoming. Not only did he start opening up about security details, but he'd given Kara invitations that would get her and her "friends" into the reception for a private audience. It was a huge relief – if the word *relief* can be applied to something that fills you with utter dread.

"So we'll be entering by the hotel front door at three o'clock," said Alex, lightly touching the screen. "We'll go in with the other guests…then up the elevator to the main function room." His finger trailed along the map, then he glanced down at the printed schedule Kara had gotten from Luis. "Do we know where the private audiences are being held yet?"

Kara shook her close-cropped head. "But it's got to be one of the rooms on the same floor, right? Maybe that one?" She pointed to a meeting room down the hallway.

As they kept talking, my eyebrows drew together… because I wasn't picking up anything at all from the floor plans. I don't always from images, but given the circumstances I would have expected *something* – some glimmer of emotion. But it was like the plans were just empty pixels on a screen, instead of a map showing the location of the most vital operation in the world.

"The reception's not black tie, is it?" asked Liz, chewing her fingernail. Most of her nails were bitten to the quick. "'Cause we can't exactly hide guns under evening gowns."

"Oh god, I hadn't even thought of that," murmured Trish, her freckled face worried.

"Thankfully, no," said Kara. "Luis said the people

representing Mexico City – that includes us – can just wear their normal outfits. Maybe something a little dressier, like you'd go to church in."

I kept looking at the floor plans, trying to feel something – anything – about them. Finally I shrugged it away. Maybe I was just nervous.

"Do you think the angels there will be scanning people's auras?" I asked Alex.

"Some are bound to be, because they'll be feeding." He glanced at me, and I could see the thought in his eyes – that the angels might recognize my aura before the team was ready to make a move. He wasn't really sorry about it. I knew he'd give anything if I wasn't involved in this; if I stayed away someplace where I could be safe.

"Don't even say it," I said quickly. "I'm going." The thought of waiting here at the house while they all left – of not knowing what was happening, if they were going to live or die – no, there was just no way. "Alex, I *have* to," I said before he could answer. "What about Paschar's vision, that I'm the one who can destroy them?" I sensed a wave of doubt from the others, and knew no one took that very seriously – since I so clearly *hadn't* been the one to destroy them last time I'd tried.

Alex sighed and pushed his hair back. I could see how tired he was – how heavily all this was weighing on him. "Maybe," he said. His blue-grey eyes caught mine, asking me to wait until we were alone to discuss it. Reluctantly, I nodded.

Across from me, Wesley sat examining the map in his usual dour silence. With Sam sprawled beside him, they were like an illustrated example of "closed book/open book". "Okay," drawled Sam, squinting at the screen. "Are the Council like ordinary angels when it comes to killing them? Or are they different, or what?"

Kara shook her head. "I don't know, but they must be *able* to be killed, or their safety wouldn't be such an issue. Apparently they do feed, so I'm guessing it's their halo that's vulnerable, like other angels. Who knows if there's anything extra we have to worry about though." She rolled her eyes. "I'm glad Luis is finally opening up," she added dryly. "There's really a limit to how many security questions I can slip in between *Oh, you're so wonderful* and *Ooh, do that again.*"

My cheeks warmed. Kara was so matter-of-fact about her relationship with Luis. Well, not a *relationship*, I guess, though he clearly thought it was. I studied her covertly, wondering again if I'd only imagined the way I'd seen her gazing at Alex that day. I couldn't get that soft-eyed look of hers out of my mind; I just had a feeling about it. Not that I was worried, exactly – every time Alex touched me I could sense how deeply in love with me he was – but it didn't make me feel all that great, either. Kara was so utterly, gorgeously human.

Brendan beat a light tattoo on the table; even when he was sitting quietly, he wasn't quiet. "Hey, wait – couldn't Willow help?" he said suddenly.

I glanced at him in surprise. "I – sorry, help with what? I was off in my own world, I guess."

Thinking freaky half-angel thoughts, said the faces of almost everyone around me.

Brendan seemed alarmed to be talking to me directly – the most we'd ever said was a mumbled hi when we'd almost walked into each other in the hallway once. He cleared his throat, fidgeting with his teaspoon. "Um – help find out if there's anything we need to know about killing the Council," he said. "You're supposed to be psychic, right? So maybe you could get a vision about them or something."

The room went quiet. "Could she do that?" said Kara to Alex.

"You'd better ask Willow," he said tersely, still studying the printed schedule. He got very short with anyone who ignored me.

"It doesn't really work that way," I said before Kara had to say anything. "I mean, yeah, sometimes I get flashes of things, but mostly for me to get anything specific I need to be touching someone. Like, holding their hand." No one said anything. Feeling awkward, I traced the design on my coffee mug. "I, um…used to do psychic readings a lot, back home. People at my high school would come to me and ask for them."

"You went to high school?" blurted Liz. Her pale cheeks reddened when I looked at her. "I mean – that sounds so normal."

Normal. I tried not to think about the fact that, even as I spoke, I was mentally aware of my angel shifting around inside of me. "Sure, I went to school," I said. "I didn't know anything about any of this until a couple of months ago – as far as I knew, I was just like you."

"Whoa," murmured Sam, staring at me. "Half-angels going to high school, and we don't even *know* about it? That's…freaky."

I saw Alex give him a considering look, and decide not to say anything. I shrugged. "I think it's half-angel, singular, actually – as far as anyone knows, I'm the only one."

For the first time, the thought gave me a very strange feeling. It hadn't really struck me before how inherently lonely this was – being the only one of my kind in the entire world. I went on quickly, before I could think too deeply about it. "Anyway, I didn't go as often as I should have – my friend Nina and I used to skip a lot, and just go clothes shopping. I'm into vintage stuff, so there's this store in Schenectady we'd go to…" I trailed off, wondering why I was telling them this.

Open mouths around the table now. I could almost hear the same thought from everyone: *You had a friend?* Followed hard on its heels by the girls with, *Wait – you're into clothes shopping?*

From the look on Sam's face, half-angels going shopping was seriously his idea of conversational hell. "Yeah," he said. "So anyway, can we get back to this psychic thing? Couldn't she – *Willow* – go into the cathedral and start holding people's hands? Like, some of the officials there, or something?"

"It might look pretty suspicious," I said wryly. "I usually have to focus for a few minutes; it's not like a lightning flash the second I touch someone."

"But you said you get feelings sometimes," pointed out Kara, studying me carefully. "So if you did go into the cathedral, you might pick up something useful."

Alex sat reading the sheet with his head propped on his hand, caressing his forehead. "I'm not sending Willow in there; her aura's too distinctive. Any angel that saw it would know exactly who she is – all they'd have to do is sound the alarm, and there'd be a riot. Every Church member in the world wants her dead."

"Yeah, but we could *scan* first, right?" Brendan's voice quickened with excitement, just like when he was arguing politics with Sam. "Make sure there aren't any angels around."

Kara nodded. "Sure, and then you and me could go in with her, Alex, and make sure she's covered."

I was about to say it sounded good to me – and it really did; I'd been painfully aware that so far I was probably the least-contributing member of the team – but Alex glanced up and spoke first, his voice impatient. "You said angels cruise in and out of that place all the time, Kara. What good would scanning do?"

I hesitated. "But Alex, if I did get something, we'd know a lot better how to plan this thing. I wouldn't be in there *that* long; I'd probably know in five minutes if I could get something."

He gave me a look. "It's not just the angels. Your picture's been on every Church of Angels website in the world, remember? Someone could recognize you."

"Not with my hair like this." I touched its short red-gold strands.

He snorted. "Oh, yeah, like that's a master disguise no one could see through."

"But if you and Kara were covering me, then—"

"Do you even know what 'covering' someone means?" Alex asked coldly. "This isn't a movie. Do you really want us to have to start shooting at a screaming mob to get you out of there if something goes wrong?"

Where had this argument come from? "No, of course I don't *want* that," I said. Everyone had gone quiet, watching us. Trish's eyes were wide; her coffee mug paused in mid-air. "But Alex, you know I can usually sense if a place is going to be a danger to me. I mean, okay, it's not foolproof, but—"

"*Willow.*" He lashed my name at me like a whip. "I said *no*, all right? Drop it."

It felt like he had slapped me. In the sudden roaring silence, Alex tossed the sheet down and shoved his chair back. He left the room without a word.

My cheeks were on fire; at first I was too shocked to move. There was a long pause. Finally, Kara lifted a perfectly-shaped eyebrow. "Well. I see that his temper hasn't improved any. I'll go and talk to him." She started to get up.

"No," I burst out. "No – I'll do it."

She regarded me, her expression almost amused. "You sure? I've got a lot of experience dealing with Kylar boys when they get like this. It's kind of an acquired skill."

I hadn't really been certain what I thought of Kara up until then, even with the look I'd seen her give Alex – but now it was becoming clearer to me. I didn't like her very much. "I've acquired it, thanks," I said, getting up from my chair. "I'll go."

I heard the silence in the kitchen erupt into words as I went down the hallway. I let the buzz fade away behind me, not trying to decipher what was being said. I could guess easily enough.

I knew Alex had to be in his bedroom. But when I got there, his door was shut, and I paused as I stood in the faintly sweaty-smelling mess of the boys' dorm. His door was never shut, unless he was asleep or I was in there with him. Despite what I'd said to Kara, this was all new territory to me; Alex and I hardly ever argued. Then I remembered the way he'd snapped at me, and grimaced. We had to have this out.

I knocked. "Can I come in? We need to talk."

There was a pause. "Yeah," he said.

I opened the door, gathering my thoughts for what I wanted to say. It all left me the second I saw him. Alex was sitting on the side of his bed with his shoulders slumped, elbows on his thighs as he massaged his temples with both thumbs. His eyes were closed.

Hurriedly, I shut the door and sat next to him. "Are you okay?"

"Yeah." His voice was distant; his fingers on his forehead white with tension.

I touched his arm and pain jolted through me, so sharp and furious it made me gasp. "Oh god, you're not! Your head—"

"It's just a headache. I'm fine."

It didn't seem *fine* at all. I stood up, my words rushing

together: "I'll go get you some Advil – there's some in the girls' dorm—"

Without looking up, Alex reached for one of my hands; squeezed it hard. "No. Just…stay with me. Please."

I bit my lip, not knowing what to do. I sank back down beside him and we sat in silence, Alex still rubbing his temples. Finally, he let out a breath and dropped his hands. He was pale, with tiny beads of sweat on his forehead. He gave me a rueful look. "Hey, you."

"Hey," I echoed. I could feel how tense he was; the pain that was still thudding through him.

He put his arm around me. "Sorry," he said against my hair. "I was a jerk. I shouldn't have—" He broke off with a wince, gripping his forehead again.

"Alex, I'm going for the Advil now—"

His arm tightened, holding me in place. "It's okay. It wouldn't help." After a pause, he sighed and dropped his hand from his head; shifting position on the bed, he lay back against his pillows, looking drained. "Shit. I thought I was over these."

"Over what?" I propped myself up next to him, gently stroking his forehead.

"That feels really nice," he murmured, closing his eyes again. I moved further up the bed; leaning against the wall, I rested his head on my lap and kept stroking it, soothing the pain away. His breathing slowed, grew more relaxed.

"Over what?" I repeated softly.

"Migraines," he said. "I got them after my dad died, and after Jake died. They went away after a while; I haven't had one in over a year. This one just blindsided me out of nowhere."

"You never told me," I said.

"No. It seemed pretty pathetic."

My heart twisted. I didn't think I'd even be able to keep my sanity if I'd been through everything Alex had – almost everyone he loved in the world dying. Migraines just seemed *normal*, not pathetic.

Then my mouth went dry. My hand stopped on his forehead. "Alex, you don't think—"

"What?" he said, opening his eyes. Seeing the look on my face, understanding came over his features. "Willow, no – don't even think it. It's got nothing to do with you; I started getting them years ago."

I swallowed. Just that morning, Alex and I had managed half an hour alone here in his room together; we'd almost been able to forget anyone else was around. "But to get one *now*, when you haven't had one for over a year…"

"Yeah, that might have a little more to do with being responsible for this mission, and everyone's lives. Not making out with my girlfriend." He reached for my hand. "Willow, you're not hurting me. I promise. It's just this stupid thing that happens sometimes—" He cringed again and went silent. His slight stubble looked inky black against the sudden pallor of his face.

"It's not gone yet?" Fear was curling through me.

"No, it won't be gone for hours." He gave my hand a slight tug, tried to smile. "Hey. That was nice, what you were doing before."

I started stroking his head again, trying hard to believe that this really was just a coincidence. After a few minutes, Alex turned his head on my lap and kissed my wrist. "I'm sorry I spoke to you that way before," he murmured. "Really. I was way out of line."

His eyes were so beautiful; stormy skies reflected in a blue sea. My fears started to fade, looking into them. *You're panicking*, I told myself. *He's gotten migraines in the past, and he's stressed out of his mind right now. He's right. It's got nothing to do with you.*

I ran my fingers through his dark hair. "I wasn't trying to argue with you in front of everyone," I said softly. "It's just that we've always decided things together."

"I know," he said. "We still do – I need you, Willow. But this time it's different. I don't want you going anywhere near the cathedral unless we don't have a choice; it's too dangerous."

I hated pressing the point when he was in so much pain, but I had to say it: "Even if we could find out more information about the Council? So that we know for sure what to expect?"

"How likely is that, though? I've never known you to get anything specific just from being inside a place. The most I've ever seen you get is feelings."

"I know, but there could still be a chance, even if it's a tiny one. Alex, if it wasn't me – if it was someone else on the team who was half-angel—"

"I'd be saying the same thing," he broke in. "Seriously, this isn't about me being in love with you. It's just too risky, for not enough return. That place is full of angels – if they saw that you were here in the city, it could jeopardize everything."

I sighed – when he put it like that, I could see his point. After a pause, I bent over and kissed his mouth upside down; he tilted his chin up to make it linger. Our lips left each other slowly. "Okay," I said. "You're the boss."

"Yeah, I must have been really bad in a past life or something." He smiled, his eyes still in pain. Reaching up, he touched a strand of my hair. "Don't leave, okay?"

"Shh. I'm not going anywhere." I kept stroking his forehead, trailing my fingers across it. His muscular shoulders gradually relaxed, his eyes closing again. His breathing slowed, became more regular.

I could hear the TV on in the other room, the sound of voices. None of it mattered to me. I stayed there until long after Alex had fallen asleep – gently caressing the brow of the boy I loved, trying to keep his pain at bay.

The other AKs kept improving with their moving targets, until Alex started doing combat variations with them – making them run across the room, drop into a roll and then shoot, that kind of thing. Their averages plummeted again, but I saw that this time it didn't take long for their scores to start climbing back up. They were getting there. Sam was the best shot by far; he'd obviously taken Alex's demonstration with his pistol that day as a personal challenge. At first, Wesley had been as awkward with guns as he was around people, but now he wasn't far behind Sam, and Trish was pretty much on a level with him – she seemed to aim and shoot in a single motion, hardly even thinking. I don't know why that surprised me, except Trish was so nice that you didn't tend to think of her and guns in the same sentence. Brendan and Liz weren't doing badly, either – they were both consistent enough to be dependable, at least.

Unlike me. Though I'd gotten pretty good at shooting a stationary target, I still hadn't reached a ninety per cent success rate; I couldn't get over the habit of flinching each time I pulled the trigger. I really didn't think I was ever going to get used to this – the cold weight of the weapon, the acrid smell of gunpowder.

Standing in the target range with the muted thumps of gunfire around me, I braced myself for the kick of the pistol as I aimed – and then that strange prickling feeling nagged at the nape of my neck again. I *knew* no one would be there, but I still had to glance and check. Only the wall of the range looked back. I let out a breath, wishing I could get over feeling so self-conscious in this place.

As target practice continued, part of me wondered why I was even bothering to learn how to shoot now, apart from my personal safety. When Alex and I had talked some more about the Council attack, he'd convinced me that it wasn't a good idea for me to go – that the threat of my aura attracting attention and putting the team in even greater danger in that situation was too great. I hated it, *hated* it. This was my fight too. I couldn't bear the thought of staying behind while Alex and the others risked their lives; of not being there to do whatever I could to help them. But I knew he was right. No one had any idea what Paschar's vision meant, including me…and meanwhile, my aura was like a big neon arrow pointing right at me. This was the only chance we were going to get. My personal feelings about not being included didn't even come into it.

I sighed and squeezed the trigger, felt the report jump through me. A hole appeared just at the edge of the bullseye. "Hey, that's a lot better," said Alex, pausing to watch. He glanced at me; his mouth creased in sympathetic amusement. "You still totally hate this, don't you?"

"Me? No, I was born to be a gun moll." I set my jaw as I started to aim again.

He reached over and corrected my hold on the gun slightly, his fingers warm on mine. For a second he was almost his old self again. "You make a really cute one, you know that?" he said in an undertone. "All you need is one of those thirties gangster suits."

"Ho, ho."

I saw the kiss he wanted to give me in his eyes. Then he was gone again, heading towards Brendan. I held back a smile as I looked after him, wishing as usual we'd had longer to talk. Returning to my target, I squared my shoulders – and somewhere inside of me, my angel gave a flutter, darkly restless. In an awful way I'd gotten used to this by now; only half thinking about it, I pushed her aside in my mind.

Only this time it didn't work.

My angel broke free with a shining rush, soaring out of me. With a startled gasp, I stood gaping up at her as she hovered. *I couldn't feel what she was feeling any more.* Oh my god, what was happening; who *was* this creature with my face? Belatedly, I tore my gaze away, my heart thudding. I couldn't let anyone see me staring upwards – couldn't let anyone figure out what was going on.

Before my angel could do anything, I quickly switched my consciousness to hers. All at once, I was the one hovering overhead, looking down at the foreshortened Willow below, still aiming the gun as if nothing was happening. My angel knew what I was about to do; there was a sudden mental frenzy as she fought against me. Gritting my teeth, I ignored her and swooped back into my human body. A flapping struggle; almost a scream of frustration as my angel tried to wrest free – but for now at least I was stronger, and I shoved her away inside of me.

The whole thing had taken only seconds. I took a few breaths, making sure I really had control. I could sense her frustration now, and that weird looseness again…but my angel had gone silent. Shakily, I flicked the safety on the gun and rested it on the floor. Alex glanced over, and I tried to smile.

"Bathroom," I mouthed, and he nodded.

Upstairs, I splashed water on my face. My eyes in the mirror looked large and frightened; my face pale. Okay. This was not good. This was really, really not good. I had to tell Alex, only what could he do? He wouldn't know what was going on any more than I did. But I couldn't keep this from him any longer, no matter how much I didn't want to face it myself; it had gotten way too serious. The possibility that I really *could* be responsible for his migraine – and that it might be a symptom of something far worse – came to me again, chilling my blood. Suddenly it seemed only too likely. I wanted so much to believe it wasn't true; that my touch wasn't hurting him – but how could I *know*, when I had this thing inside me that I didn't even understand any more?

I caught sight of my crystal pendant in the mirror, and went very still. I heard Alex's voice saying, *Your angel is you; she's a part of you. And that means she's...everything I love.*"

Alex had always believed – always – that my angel wasn't something separate from me; that she was just another aspect of myself. What was he going to think when he found out that wasn't true? That she had separate thoughts from mine; that I couldn't even *control* her any more?

My hands were ice. I slumped weakly against the sink, imagining the look that would be on his face when he found out. Oh god, he'd defended me to the whole team, telling them that they could trust me, and now – I swallowed. The thought that his beautiful eyes might look at me with dread, or suspicion, made me feel sick. I knew how much he loved me, but the angels had killed his whole family. He'd devoted his entire life to fighting them. Could he really still feel the same about me, when he found out my angel self had a mind of its own? I had to tell him; I knew I didn't have a choice.

But how?

CHAPTER *Eleven*

JENNY SAT CROSS-LEGGED ON THE other side of the desk, looking radiant with happiness – if a bit tired and drained. "Would you like to arrange a meeting with him, sir?" she asked.

Tapping a pen, Raziel glanced over the email printout in question. The town of Silver Trail was a few dozen miles up in the Rockies; the weather might be foul this time of year. Still, the proposed idea was intriguing.

"What do *you* think?" he asked, smiling at Jenny. Her almost-demure business suit hugged her figure. He couldn't imagine now why he'd wasted so much time with a male assistant whose energy he didn't even find appealing; he must have been insane.

She flushed, eyes shining. "I think it's a wonderful idea – really wonderful. It could make such a difference to so many people's lives."

Indeed it could; Raziel already had thoughts about how he could put his own spin on the scheme. "I think you're right," he said, handing the email back to her. "Go ahead and arrange the meeting."

Once Jenny had departed, Raziel's momentary good mood faded. Scheduling meetings as if nothing had happened was all very well, but meanwhile he was going mad with nerves.

There will be no changes in how things are run. That is my promise.

Raziel's face darkened as he recalled the TV interview. It had been big news for a few days, with his own image smiling out at him from all the major papers. Not very clever, he supposed. But when the question had been asked, he'd been standing in the same place in the cathedral where the Council had demanded to see him in private, as if he were a naughty schoolboy about to be told off. Anger had bristled through him, remembering, and with the reporter's microphone thrust in his face, the words had come of their own accord. Saying them had given him deep satisfaction at the time, but now he wished he'd been more circumspect. Though the Council probably hadn't had much doubt that he had no intention of toeing the line, they'd have none at all after this.

The Twelve had shown no reaction to his statement. Yet.

The knowledge that they were deliberately keeping quiet to let him do exactly what he was now doing – writhe uncomfortably, wondering how they'd respond – made Raziel's teeth clench. The time for their demise couldn't come quickly enough for him now, in more ways than one. But if his own death was caused by the Council perishing, at least he'd have the pleasure of knowing he'd taken them out with him.

The plan was now securely in place – though Charmeine had found something out that made its probable outcome less uncertain than before, and not in an especially reassuring way.

After her brief trip to Mexico City, Charmeine had managed a day away from the Twelve and spent it here at the cathedral with him, in his private quarters. He'd given orders to Jenny that he wasn't to be disturbed – he'd had a feeling things would resume between him and Charmeine, and had been correct, as it turned out. Enjoyable, but utterly calculated on both their parts; it had cemented their alliance even further, making it easier to read each other's thoughts.

"So I found Luis without any trouble," she'd said later on. Raziel had already gleaned some of this from her mind – flashes of an earnest-looking young man with brown eyes and thick black hair – but still listened with interest as she described the encounter. "He's pretty smitten with this Kara person. It didn't take much to get him to trust her."

"You fed from him," summed up Raziel. They were on the luxurious leather sofa; Charmeine had her long legs draped over his lap.

"Well, obviously. Several times, just to make sure he got the message." She stifled a yawn. She had on Raziel's black silk dressing gown; her pale hair spilled down it in stark contrast. "Sorry. I have to keep myself shielded all the time around the Twelve, without them realizing – it's pretty tiring."

"You're holding out against them though." Raziel's voice had sharpened.

"*Yes*, don't worry. I'm fine, it's all right." Charmeine rolled her eyes, nudging his thigh with a slender foot. "As if I thought for a second that my welfare is what's concerning you."

He hadn't bothered to deny it; she'd have felt the same. Just because he could, he slid his hand up her leg and let his thoughts go wandering through hers, relishing the sense of all doors opening to him – it had a thrill of its own. Naturally, his own mental doors weren't all open to her, though she'd think they were. He'd constructed an elaborate false memory detailing how he'd anonymously gotten into contact with the Angel Killers and gained their trust – the last thing he wanted was for anyone, including Charmeine, to realize he had a link with the half-angel. A good false memory had the same vivid sensory details as the real thing; Raziel was quite proud of the level of attention he'd put into this one. Charmeine could have done something similar, of course, but he didn't think she had. He could sense her loathing of the Council seeping through her almost every thought; there was no way she could fake that. *Hiding* it was just about possible, though not easy. It wasn't surprising she was tired.

For a moment Raziel thought he felt a flutter of resistance. He gave Charmeine a keen look. She lay against the sofa cushions with her eyes closed as he explored, her face untroubled. The faint feeling was gone just as quickly. Probing further, Raziel decided it hadn't been hiding anything in particular.

Then his hand froze on her leg as he came across something. *What?* He checked again; he hadn't been mistaken. He stared at Charmeine wordlessly.

"I was wondering when you'd find that," she said without opening her eyes. "They told us a few days ago; it's why we're spending three weeks in Mexico City. I always thought it was sort of a long time just to appoint a church head."

Raziel shook his head, still half-lost in the images he was getting. "*What* do they think they'll accomplish by such a thing? They must be insane!"

Charmeine sat up as she glanced at him, her expression ironic. "Let's just say they're very eager for angels to remain angels. They think being in this world is turning us all into base gluttons, who indulge ourselves for pleasure instead of necessity. They don't want us mixing with humans too much, except when we absolutely have to."

It was hardly news. Raziel thought of the Twelve's meeting with him in the conference room below, and snorted. Drumming the sofa, he considered the implications of what he'd just seen. Though the two dimensions had split off from each other eons ago, the human and angel worlds had once been one and the same – and this meant the Twelve, as First Formed, had links to this world's energy. On its own, the fact didn't worry him overmuch. The possible cost to the human world after the Council's deaths had always seemed a low risk to him – it was the angels' link to each other that was the main issue.

But now there was this mad plan of theirs: to use their connection with the Earth's energy to bond with it and calm down places that felt "buzzy" to angels, so that angels around the world would be more inclined to resist their baser urges. How noble of them. And how…interesting, in terms of what consequences their deaths might now bring.

With a silken rustle, Charmeine swung her feet off his lap and sat close beside him. "You haven't changed your mind, have you? Because I certainly haven't, even if it does make things more of a gamble."

Raziel had given her a withering look. "Are they going to back off and recognize my leadership here? What's that – the answer's no? Then no, I haven't changed my mind either."

Now, alone in his office, Raziel knew he'd increased their gamble even further by his impetuous statement to the press. Just to reassure himself that all was still well, he reached for the connection to Willow. He checked it often to keep abreast of the AKs' progress, though had to admit that he also found the girl oddly intriguing in a way. Not to mention how surprised he'd been by her angel's anxiety ever since he'd first entered her mind. On some deep level, Willow was obviously aware there was something amiss. While his daughter's distress didn't concern Raziel enough to try to soothe things for her, he did find it interesting. Her psychic skills were stronger than he'd thought.

His cellphone rang before he could get very far, jolting him back to his office. With a glance at the screen, he saw Charmeine's name. She didn't often get a chance to ring with updates; he snapped the phone open. "Yes? What is it?"

"Something's up," she said tightly.

Raziel cringed; he'd been waiting for this. "Let me guess – they saw my TV interview."

She gave a snort. "Raz, the *whole world* saw your interview. Yes, of course they did, and they're more annoyed than you can imagine. But no, that's not what I meant. Something else has happened—" Charmeine broke off; he could feel her tension as she listened to something. "I have to go," she said abruptly. "I'll call you back when I can."

"Wait! What's going on? What—"

She was gone. Raziel swore, knowing he'd get nothing from her psychically now, other than whatever front she was putting on for the Twelve. He shoved his chair away and stood up, propping his hands on the window sill as he glared out at the mountains. In the distance, a heavy rain was falling, obscuring the peaks in dense cloud and heading his way.

"I'm going to take the team on a practice hunt tomorrow," said Alex.

Kara was sprawled sideways on the battered armchair. She turned her head to look at him. "Are they ready?"

The two of them were in the TV room; the others were scattered around the house somewhere. Willow was helping Liz in the kitchen – Liz had thawed towards her enough to let her chop lettuce for a salad, or something. Alex didn't hear them talking much, but supposed it was a start.

He shrugged. "As ready as they can be for now, without angel holographs to help train them. They've got to get some real-life experience." He felt his lips move into a small, wintry smile. "Can you imagine what my dad would say? Taking a team on a hunt before they've had at least a year of training?"

Kara had on sweatpants and a tight, cropped T-shirt, showing the sleek muscles of her arms and stomach. She smiled too. "Vividly. It's different times though, Al. I'm sure this is the right thing."

He made a face, hoping she was right. His mind was already ticking over the details of the hunt; how best to manage it. Bosque de Chapultepec, the large, leafy city park off the Paseo de la Reforma, seemed the best bet to him – parts of it were kind of remote, and quiet during the week. If the team came across any feeding angels, they'd have space to manoeuvre and little chance of being seen. The important thing was keeping them all as safe as possible.

A news story had come on: another confrontation between the Crusaders and the Faithful. Alex gazed at the screen, only distantly taking in the shouting, angry faces. He'd known being in charge of a team would take over his life; what he hadn't anticipated was how much he'd care about all of them – even the ones he didn't particularly like.

It didn't matter. Training them, being responsible for their lives – it just got under your skin; you got to know them in a way that transcended personal feeling. Sam, who Alex could cheerfully clout a dozen times a day, had still impressed him by buckling down these last few weeks and turning into a damn good shot. Liz was really okay, despite being so prickly sometimes – he'd seen how hard she'd worked to gain her shooting skills; how harsh she was on herself when she didn't get it right. Brendan's incessant talking grated, but Alex knew he'd miss him if he were gone. And Trish, with her freckled face and blue eyes, was almost like the glue that held them all together: smoothing quarrels, making sure everyone was getting along, so that the others gravitated towards her like a den mother.

Not to mention Wesley. Alex had sort of discounted him at first, not having time to delve into whatever the guy's sullen deal was, as long as his training was coming along all right. Then one night he'd heard a noise in the range and gone to check – and there had been Wesley, at two o'clock in the morning, shooting targets on his own.

"Hey, aren't I working you hard enough?" Alex had joked.

A flush had stained Wesley's dark cheeks. He'd hastily put the gun back in the weapons cabinet, while behind him the target still bounced on its chain. "Couldn't sleep," he muttered.

Suddenly the truth had hit Alex. "Wait a minute – you do this a lot, don't you? That's why your score's been improving so much lately."

Willow had told him Wesley was shy; Alex hadn't really believed it until now – a scowl was coming over his face, but underneath it he just looked mortified. "Look, I've got to get it right, okay? I'm not keeping anyone awake or anything."

"I didn't say you were." Alex leaned his shoulder against the wall. "But staying up all night won't help; you need to get a good night's sleep."

Christ, he sounded like his dad. Mentally rolling his eyes at himself, Alex had started to say something else – and stopped as Wesley burst out, "You don't understand! I've *got* to get it. It's my only chance to get back at the angels, I can't—" He broke off. The flush crept down to his neck; he crossed his arms over his chest and looked away.

Alex had slowly come away from the wall. "Angel burn?" he guessed.

Wesley swallowed. "My, um…my whole family. My mom was…was CIA; that's how I…" He trailed off.

Painful understanding had stirred through Alex, as he realized how much they had in common. "I never knew that," he said at last.

Wesley was already looking sorry that he'd mentioned it. "Yeah, well, don't tell anyone, okay? I don't want to *talk* about it, I just want to *get* it."

"You are getting it," Alex had said quietly. "You're doing really well. Look, no more practising this time of night, all right? Take an extra hour first thing in the morning if you want; no one will ask you any questions. But I need you in top form – and that includes getting enough sleep."

The target slowly swung to a complete stop; around them the house felt heavy with silence. Finally Wesley had nodded. "Yeah, okay."

There hadn't been any big, dramatic change in Wesley after that; he was still closed-off and didn't talk much. But as Alex stared at the TV, he realized that he felt like he knew the guy now. He knew all of them, just from watching them grow, change, get better – and he'd make sure they stayed safe through this, no matter what it took.

"Is Willow going on the hunt?" asked Kara.

Alex glanced at her; she sat curled up in the armchair with her forearm draped across its back. "I don't know," he admitted.

Though Willow didn't think so, she was doing great for someone who'd never touched a gun before – but she wasn't up to fighting angels yet. Leaving aside his fears for her safety, Alex knew that her angel self was incredibly useful in combat. Yet if an angel saw what she was and got away… He winced, seeing again the battle in the courtyard and the angel speeding off down the street.

"I don't know," he repeated, massaging his temples idly. Not a migraine this time, just a headache that had been grumbling at him for hours.

Kara glanced down at her bright red fingernails, turning them this way and that. "Can I ask you something?"

He gave her a wary look, holding back a dry smile. "If this is about my sex life again…"

"No, not that. It's just – well, I've been wondering why you haven't used her angel to help train them."

Alex shrugged. "It doesn't have a halo. And I don't know what would happen if someone got excited and shot at it – whether that would hurt Willow or not."

"But that could happen on a hunt, too," Kara pointed out.

"Yeah, it could," he agreed. It was another reason why he wasn't convinced about taking Willow: the possibility of Sam or someone getting all adrenalin-rushed and trigger-happy with her angel in flight.

"If you want my advice, I don't think she should go," said Kara after a pause. "I mean, I know you've made it clear to everyone that she's part of the team, but…"

"But she's not, really," finished Alex sharply.

"I'm not saying it's her fault," said Kara. "It's just that the others still don't really trust her."

Alex felt a ripple of annoyance. "Well, then it's about time they got over it. Besides, they trust her a lot more than they did."

Kara sounded like she was choosing her words carefully. "They've gotten sort of used to having her in the house; it's not quite the same thing. Look, I just don't think taking her along on the first hunt would be great for morale when everyone's going to be nervous enough as it is. And she's not that competent with a gun yet anyway – there's more minuses than pluses, that's all."

Her tone was so reasonable that it made Alex's teeth grit together. "Okay, I think you've convinced me," he said finally.

"You're not going to take her?"

"No, I am," said Alex. "Because she *is* part of the team, and you and the others need to start seeing her that way. She already can't take part in the Council attack, or go into the cathedral. But there's not too much danger on a hunt like this, where we're all out in the open and can manoeuvre. There's no way I'm going to tell her she can't come."

Kara nodded, obviously unconvinced. "Okay. Your call." She fell silent, gazing at the TV as a commercial came on. When the news started again, she said, "You really love her, don't you?"

He glanced over, taken aback by the wistful note in her voice. "Yeah, I do," he said. "More than anything."

Kara's mouth twisted; she looked down at her nails again. "I can tell. It's nice, you know? Once I thought that maybe me and Jake…" She trailed off.

Alex sat up a little, staring at her – and then realized he wasn't that surprised. She and Jake had always been close, though he knew his brother had given up hoping anything would ever happen; Jake had told him once how he'd made a play for Kara and been completely shot down. Suddenly Alex felt as wistful as Kara had just sounded. God, Jake had been crazy about Kara, way beyond Alex's own adolescent crush on her. Getting together with her would have made him so incredibly happy.

"So…why didn't you?" he asked.

Kara sighed, propping her chin on her hand. "Oh, I don't know. He still had some growing up to do. Mostly, I think I just didn't want to mess up our friendship. But life's too short; you've got to go for it – what happened to Jake taught me that." She fell silent as she ran a finger along the arm of the chair. Then she said in a low voice, "Speaking of going for it…you're a lot like him, you know. I mean, a lot like how I hoped he'd turn out to be."

Alex's gaze flew to hers. Her brown eyes were serious, unwavering. Christ, this couldn't actually be what it sounded like, could it? He cleared his throat, half sure she was going to burst out laughing. "Look, um…Kara—"

Her hand went up, stopping him. "It's okay. I know

you're in love with Willow. I'm just sayin', that's all." She unfolded herself from the chair and came over to him; kissed his forehead with lips that were warm and gentle. "Don't worry, I won't say it again. I don't want to complicate things for you. You're a good guy, Al. The best. And if things are ever different..." She shrugged, gave a small smile. "Well, who knows?"

As she left the room, Alex stared after her, swamped by confusion. *Kara?* If this had happened a few years ago – no, a few *months* ago – he wouldn't have been able to say "yes" fast enough. Now it meant nothing to him, other than to somehow make him feel guilty even though all he'd done was sit there. Thinking of his crush-ridden younger self, Alex had a wry moment of wishing he could have had this conversation with Kara back then; imagining what that would have been like.

Okay, now he really *did* feel guilty. Mentally cursing Kara, he went and found Willow in the kitchen. She was squeezing a lemon into a bowl; Liz was doing something with a tray of chicken breasts. He stood against the doorway, watching unseen for a moment – taking in Willow's slim curves in her jeans and tight T-shirt; the short, red-gold hair that showed the graceful lines of her neck.

"You should try it some night," she was saying. "The tarragon adds a really nice flavour."

"Yeah, maybe—" Liz broke off as she noticed Alex standing there; Willow looked up too.

"Hi," she said softly.

"Hi," he said, smiling at her. She had a tiny smudge of flour on her nose. "Can I talk to you for a second?"

She hesitated, then nodded. "Sure." She wiped her hands on a paper towel. "Back in a minute," she said to Liz.

He led her into one of the storage rooms and shut the door; the room was shadowy, crammed with boxes. "You might be longer than a minute," he murmured, lowering his head to hers. He felt her tense, and drew back in surprise. "What's wrong?"

She started to say something, and stopped. "Nothing. I just – think I'm getting a cold. I've been feeling sort of strange ever since target practice. You probably don't want to get too close."

Her voice sounded strained. He tipped her chin up with his hand. "Hey. You're not still worried about my migraine, are you? That was days ago."

Willow flinched. "Maybe a little." She took a breath, hugging herself. "Alex, I sort of...I mean, there's something..."

"What?" For an awful moment he thought she was going to say that she'd overheard Kara. Then he saw the expression in her eyes, and fear clutched him. "Willow, what's wrong? What is it?"

A burst of voices from the hallway: Sam and Brendan, arguing about some computer game. Willow bit her lip and glanced towards the door. Finally she shook her head. "It's nothing," she repeated. "Sorry. I – I guess I'm still just getting used to being here."

Unconvinced, Alex took her hands in his, studying her face. "But I thought it was getting better for you. I mean, you and Liz were just in there sharing cooking tips. I'm expecting you to teach Sam how to fix engines next."

Willow gave a short laugh. "Yes, dream on. It's not *that* much better, really – I think Liz has finally decided that I'm not going to use the pepper mill to grind glass into everyone's food at least. I don't know. Ignore me. I'm just feeling kind of weird today."

He didn't understand what was going on; all he knew was that he hated seeing her so upset. He put his arms around her; she buried her face hard against his neck. "I love you," she said in a muffled voice. "I mean – I really love you. You know that, don't you?"

Fear was now laced with complete bewilderment; this was so unlike her. Gently, he took her by the upper arms and forced her to look at him. "Babe, you're scaring me. If there's something going on, you've got to tell me what it is."

"I know," she said in a small voice. Again, she started to say something and then stopped, her eyes anxiously searching his own, her elfin face so lovely that it nearly broke his heart. The moment spun out around them; then Willow sighed and looked down, playing with the edge of his T-shirt.

"I'm just feeling worried about how everything is going, that's all," she said dully. "I mean, what's going to happen – if we'll manage to defeat the Council or not."

Alex watched her. "You're sure that's all it is?"

She let out a shaky breath. "Isn't that enough?"

He snorted. "Yeah," he said. "Yeah, that's enough." He sighed and leaned against a stack of boxes. "Listen, I'll be telling everyone later tonight…but we're going on our first hunt tomorrow."

Willow went motionless. "We are? You mean, me too?"

"Yeah, all of us," he said. "It's time; I've got to get them some real-life practice, or they won't stand a chance when the time comes." Then he saw the worried tightness of her features. "Hey, you're okay with this, right? I mean, I'd sort of rather that you stayed here, actually, but I thought…"

"I'm fine with it," she said after a pause. "Well, nervous. But fine."

"Don't worry, I won't let anything happen to anyone," said Alex. God, he hoped that was true. He pushed it away; the hunt was the last thing he wanted to think about when he actually had a few minutes alone with Willow for a change.

He bent his head to hers again. He felt her hesitate, start to draw away – and then give in to the kiss in a rush. Alex's pulse leaped as she pressed against him. Gently slipping his hand under her shirt, he caressed the silky smoothness of her skin, the soft warmth of her. For a few endless minutes there were only the two of them in the entire world.

Willow pulled away with an abruptness that startled him. "I – sorry, I'm still getting this cold, remember?"

"I don't care," he murmured as he reached for her again. "Germs are good."

"No, really. I don't want you to catch it." She stepped away, her cheeks flushed as she adjusted her shirt, not meeting his gaze. Alex's eyebrows drew together. He was just about to ask if something was wrong again when she gave him a quick, apologetic smile. "I'll see you at dinner, okay? Love you."

Before he could respond she'd kissed him on the cheek and slipped out of the door, shutting it softly behind her.

CHAPTER *Twelve*

THEY TOOK THE METRO TO Chapultepec. In years past, Alex knew they might have been the only foreigners on the train; now, with the city so full of tourists to see the newly converted cathedral, their group hardly even merited a second glance.

Only Trish and Liz got seats on the crowded car. Alex stood with the others, holding onto a looped strap that hung from the ceiling. Willow was next to him; as the train lurched she stumbled slightly and he put his arm around her, steadying her. He could feel her tension. They were all tense. Hanging onto the next strap, Sam stood tapping his thigh with his free hand; nearby, Wesley looked more sullen and closed-off than ever. Brendan was chattering away about not much at all, his voice high and nervous. Alex started to tell him to cool it, then Kara gave Brendan a look that did the job for him. She'd kept her word since their conversation the day before, to Alex's relief – in fact, was acting so completely sister-like now that he almost wondered if he'd imagined it.

They got off at Constituyentes; the entrance to the park stood nearby. Chapultepec was essentially a giant forest, and held everything you could think of – even a historic castle and an amusement park – but right here it was quiet. Alex could see paths, trees, smooth manicured grass. As they crossed the road and entered its grounds, a hush seemed to fall, leaving the noise of the city behind them.

From Willow's silence, Alex knew there weren't any angels in sight yet. Just as he'd counted on, there weren't many people here either on a weekday afternoon – though hopefully enough to attract some angels. The irony of *hoping* for an attack brought a dry smile. Closing his eyes, he lifted his consciousness through his chakra points; felt the others doing the same.

"Okay, we're going to split into two teams," he said. "Kara, you lead Wesley, Liz and Brendan; I'll take Sam, Trish and Willow. Keep out of sight if you can, but keep an eye on the main paths; that's where the action will probably be."

Kara nodded. "How long?" she asked, glancing at her cellphone. Alex had one too; he'd bought it at one of the outdoor markets that morning. He'd also grabbed some more clothes for himself and Willow while he was at it; he knew how sick she was of wearing borrowed stuff.

"An hour, then we meet back here," he said, checking the time. He returned the phone to the pocket of his blue hooded sweatshirt. "Call me if there's any trouble. And happy hunting, guys – keep safe." He spoke the familiar words without thinking – it was what Cully had often said to them before a hunt, and then later on, Juan.

And now him.

From the look in Kara's eyes, he knew she was thinking the same thing. "Will do," she said, and led her team off through the trees.

"Come on, we'll go this way," said Alex to his own group. He took them down another path. "Start scanning, everyone. Tell me what you can sense." He'd already found angel energy about a quarter of a mile away – wanted to see how long it took the others. Angel spotters were supposed to be good, but he didn't know what their training had been like; the CIA had recruited them all.

A moment of concentration. "That way," said Sam and Trish almost in unison, motioning down the path. "Not too far," added Trish with an earnest glance at him. "And more than one, I think."

"Yeah, I got that, too," said Alex. "Okay, let's start cutting through the trees." He looked at Willow as they made their way up a slight rise, wondering if she was all right. She was walking silently, staring down at her purple sneakers. She'd been quiet all day.

As if feeling his gaze, Willow looked up as the other two pulled ahead. To his alarm, he saw that her eyes were miserable, almost frightened. "Alex, listen, I – I can't take part in the hunt," she blurted out. "I know this is really bad timing, and I'm so, so sorry – I should have told you this yesterday – but—"

"There!" called Sam from ahead. "Oh hell, it's a whole goddamn *feeding party!*"

Alex's head jerked up. Whatever Willow had been about to say was forgotten as he saw Sam sprinting off, with Trish following after, both pulling out their guns as they ran. Oh *Christ*, didn't they know any better, after all the hours he'd spent drilling strategy into them?

"Sam!" he called as loudly as he dared. "Trish, wait!" Trish stopped in her tracks, looking sheepishly back over her shoulder; Sam went on, barrelling through the trees like a guerrilla warrior.

Alex pounded after him; caught up with him and grabbed his arm, yanking him to a halt. "*Stop*," he hissed.

"Are you completely insane? You don't just go racing in, you have to scope things out!"

He could see the angels for himself now, a hundred yards away down a small hill where the path curved past. Sam was right, it was a feeding party: four angels clustered around four people. Their touching wings made a shining flower shape, their halos bright and pulsing as they fed.

"We have to hurry!" Sam cried, jerking away from him. "Those people are being hurt, right this second—"

"Get down," said Alex, not taking his eyes off the angels. Sam didn't move. "Get *down*," he repeated in a snarl, shoving hard on the Texan's broad shoulder. Sullenly, Sam lay on the ground beside him, both of them flat on their stomachs. Trish joined them and did likewise, her usually neat ponytail rumpled. Her face paled as she regarded the scene.

"Okay, look," said Alex. "I know it's not easy to watch this, but they're already feeding – we can't save these people. The best we can do is wait for a clear shot."

"But we gotta shoot *now*!" Sam's voice rose. Trish glanced at him worriedly. "We can't just let them—"

"Lower your voice," said Alex, his own voice a knife that cut Sam's protestations short. "Look at how they're standing; their halos are too close to those people's heads. We could blow someone's brains out."

"Yeah, well maybe that's not such a bad thing! They've got angel burn now; what good is—"

Alex swore as one of the angels looked up. For a brief, burning second its eyes met his – and he knew that it knew. He tore his gaze away and reached for his gun. "Well, you've got your wish now; they've seen us. Nice going, hotshot. Stay in position, both of you – shoot when you can, and *don't* look into their eyes—"

There was no time for further instructions; the angels were jetting towards them in a frenzy of light. One banked and soared high, ready to dive; Alex ignored it for now and went for the angel in front. The sun dazzled off its halo, momentarily blinding him, then it flashed back into view and he fired. As the creature exploded into fragments, he felt the familiar rush of energy from angel fallout howl past.

Panicked shooting was going on beside him; a hasty scrambling in the grass. "Whoa!" shouted Sam, flipping onto his side as one of the creatures dove – its female face fierce and beautiful, long fingers straining towards Sam's life force. Alex rolled onto his back and sat up in a single motion, tracking the angel as it wheeled on one wing, ready to return.

Beside him he heard Trish's gun go off, saw a bright explosion out of the corner of his eye. *Yes! Good one!* he thought as he fired. The female angel darted sideways, its wings cutting against the sky. Alex fired once more and got it this time – and as he twisted to track the fourth and last angel, Sam's gun went off again.

Silence. Light, falling towards the ground.

"We…we did it," said Trish, sounding stunned. "We really did it!"

Alex turned to Sam, giving him a long, level look. The Texan's gaze faltered; his face turned red as he put his gun away. "Don't you *ever* do that again," said Alex in a low voice. "If any of us had died, it would have been because you'd drawn their attention to us."

Sam swallowed. "Yeah, but—"

"*Shut it.* I don't want any excuses from you. You do *not* go running off before you know what you're getting into, and you do *not* keep talking loudly when I've told you to keep quiet. Do you understand me?"

"I'm sorry," said Trish in a tiny voice. "I went running off too."

"You were okay," said Alex, still watching Sam. "At least you stopped when I told you to."

"I – I guess I acted pretty stupid," said Sam finally, looking sick. "I got excited – I wasn't thinking." His eyes rose to Alex's. "I'm sorry. It won't happen again."

"No, it won't," said Alex. "Because if it does, you're off this team for good."

Sam nodded, his lips white. "I understand."

"Okay then," said Alex as they got up. "Aside from that...you can both be pretty proud of yourselves." He gave Trish a quick one-armed hug; clapped Sam on the shoulder. "Listen, that was seriously *not* shabby – it's hard when they've seen you. Good work; I mean it."

Trish looked like the adrenalin was still pulsing through her; she managed a shaky smile. Sam winced and ran a hand over his short blond hair. "Yeah, but I – I completely choked at first – goddamn, I could hardly even shoot straight—"

A long-ago day in an Albuquerque park came back to Alex, and his throat tightened as he remembered Cully: *Weren't you listening to me? It's tough when they see you. You did good. You did good.*

"You did good," said Alex quietly. And he meant it. Though their first kills hadn't exactly gone smoothly, he was acutely aware they could have gone a hell of a lot worse. And he still had over seven weeks left to train them. With luck, it should just about be enough time.

Below, the victims seemed to have come back to themselves and were walking away down the path, talking in low, ecstatic voices about *los ángeles*. One girl looked barely sixteen, with long black hair that gleamed in the sunshine. As the group rounded the bend she staggered, and took the arm of the woman next to her.

Trish sighed. "So I guess this is the hard part, isn't it?

When you don't get to them in time."

"Yeah," said Alex. He put his gun away. "But when you do manage to save them — it makes everything worth it, believe me. And now that those four are dead, they can't hurt anyone else, at least."

"Hey, where's Willow?" said Sam suddenly.

Alex went cold as her frightened, unhappy face came back in a rush. What had she been about to tell him? Had something happened? He took off up the hill at a run; burst onto its leafy crest with Sam and Trish close behind. Dread thudded through his veins; he couldn't see her anywhere.

"Willow!" he called, cupping his hands around his mouth. "Willow, where are you?"

"Wait — is that her?" Trish gasped.

"Oh *shit*," said Sam at the same moment. He stood gaping upwards.

Alex spun towards where Trish was pointing. And stared. A girl who looked like Willow was far away down the path, running towards the eastern gate of the park. She was holding hands with a guy who had curly-looking brown hair.

Dimly, he became aware that Sam was tugging at his arm. "Alex! Look *up*."

Somehow Alex tore his gaze from Willow and the strange boy…and saw that high above them both flew a long, shining stream of angels, a hundred strong, searing through the sky.

As Alex ran off after the others, I started to follow him, fumbling for my gun. The movement felt so unnatural, as if I'd somehow morphed into a heroine in a cheesy action flick. Then a thought came, like a drench of Arctic water. I stopped short as Alex's blue sweatshirt and dark hair disappeared through the trees.

What was I even thinking? I couldn't get anywhere near the angels. Before I'd bonded with my angel, she'd emerged without fail whenever others attacked, shielding me with her gleaming wings. What if she came out again now, and I couldn't control her? What if she did something that ended up with someone getting hurt?

As if in response, my angel gave a vicious twist inside me, struggling to break free. *No!* I fought her with everything I had; somehow shoved her back with a mental wrench. I stood shaking, clutching my head and breathing hard. Oh god, was this what the rest of my life was going to be like? I'd go insane. What *was* this – why was it happening to me?

I sank to the ground, pressing against a tree and burying my head in my arms. I could sense rather than hear the sound of gunfire not far away. I'd never felt so helpless in my life. I reached out with my thoughts, searching for Alex – needing to feel him. His energy was there, strong and comforting, and I latched onto it, holding him tight even if he didn't know I was doing it. *Be safe, please be safe. And please don't hate me when I tell you that my angel is a stranger to me after all...that she's not part of the girl you're in love with like we both thought she was...*

Slow, hesitant footsteps were approaching. My head jerked up.

A few feet away stood a boy in faded jeans and a long-sleeved grey T-shirt, staring at me. He was about Alex's height and build, with soft-looking brown hair that had a curl to it – but there was nothing remotely feminine about him. Solid shoulders; a firm jaw with a light coat of stubble; high cheekbones. The boy's eyes were wide, and fixed on mine. As I realized who it was, my thoughts stuttered to a halt.

The boy from my dream.

He closed the distance between us and dropped to his knees in front of me, letting the battered knapsack he'd been carrying fall to the ground. His throat moved as he swallowed. He looked down at my arms; reached out and touched them – I could feel him trembling. He stroked his way down their length, as if to reassure himself I was real. When his hands came to mine he gripped them tightly; his were rough and warm. He said something in Spanish.

"I—" Why wasn't I pulling away? But it was like he'd cast a spell over me. "I don't speak Spanish," I got out. "*No hablo español.*" Then I did start to pull away – but suddenly the energy from him swept over me in a wave and I caught my breath in shock, unable to move. It felt so familiar, right down to my very core, like nothing I'd ever known before.

The boy looked up. His eyes were hazel – warm brown, with green radiating out from his pupils. "Yes, I'm sorry – I knew that, I forgot." His voice was distant, as if he wasn't thinking about what he was saying. He shook his head, staring at me as a wondering smile grew across his face.

"It's really you," he whispered. "I can't believe I found you." Letting go of one of my hands, he touched my cheek. The sun hit his face, turning the stubble on his jaw golden.

I jerked away from him, my heart beating hard. "Who *are* you?"

He started to respond, but then broke off as we both saw it: a flock of at least a hundred angels flying east across the park, in a long, shifting stream that glinted in the light. At their very centre was a small group that shone more fervently than the others – angels so bright I could barely look at them.

As I realized why that seemed so familiar, my pulse skipped. All the elements of my dream were suddenly crashing together at once, so that I hardly knew what was real and what wasn't. First the boy, and now the twelve angels – I could count them, twisting and shining against the sky. My mind felt like it had stalled, trying to take everything in. What were they doing here *now*? They weren't due in Mexico City for five more weeks.

I stood up, gaping; the boy had risen to his feet too. "The Council," I whispered. "Oh my god, it's the Council from my dream. We have to follow them; we have to see where they go – Alex!" I shouted over my shoulder. "Alex, hurry! The Council's arriving!"

At the mention of my dream, the boy gave me a quick glance. He grabbed his bag up from the ground. "Come on – we have to be fast," he said.

"Alex!" I shouted again, but knew he hadn't heard. A small part of my mind was still with him, and I could feel that he was okay; that he was pleased. They'd won against the angels then – and hadn't seen this larger group yet, with the Council gleaming at its centre.

"Come!" urged the boy, grasping my hand and peering upwards.

"Wait – let *go* of me! I have to tell my—"

"There isn't time!" The boy started to run, pulling me along with him; I gave up and started running too. He was right, there wasn't time. And more than that…more than that, I somehow just couldn't say no to him.

We pounded through the trees and onto the footpath – the boy's hand gripping mine, long legs pumping rhythmically. The angels flitted in and out of view; he steered us sharply down one path, then another. We raced past sidewalk vendors, plunged down some steps and skirted a pond. Ducks took off with a startled flapping.

I wanted to tell him to slow down; instead I gritted my teeth and went faster. The boy half turned and put his arm around me, helping me along for a few paces.

"Hurry, *querida*!"

The endearment from my dream stunned me, even as we ran – and suddenly I realized that he'd seen the angels as easily as I had, without lifting his consciousness through his chakra points. Who *was* this boy?

The angels were further ahead now, but still in sight, rippling in the sky. The boy jogged to a stop at a bridge flanked by a pair of black lions on pedestals; he was barely even breathing hard. Ahead, I could see a set of park gates.

We stood side by side, staring. Beyond the park, a solitary tower was in clear view, soaring high over the trees – a half-cylinder of green glass that angled off at the top, reflecting a half-moon shape at the clouds. The angels veered up to this slanted peak, darting about it like moths around a flame, spiralling so brightly that the tower looked on fire.

Dimly, I was aware that the boy had put his arm around

me again, drawing me close against him. It didn't seem strange for some reason. "What's happening?" I gasped. "Is that the Nikko Hotel?"

He shook his head, as unable to tear his gaze away as I was. "No – it's La Torre Mayor; the big tower. It's for business." A woman pushing a stroller strode past, oblivious. Overhead, the angels had started disappearing into the building. The twelve brightest ones were the first to vanish, gliding into the glass half-moon. The others followed gradually, until finally the last angel winked from view with a glimmer of wings.

"I've never seen anything like this before," murmured the boy, his hand gently rubbing my arm. "There were so many of them – and those twelve in the middle were so bright…"

"It's the angels' Council," I said, still staring upwards. "I saw them—"

"Council?" The boy looked down at me with a frown. "You mean their government?"

I nodded. "I had a dream about them. Twelve angels, and…" I trailed off. The boy had gone very still at the mention of my dream, his gaze locked on mine, and I knew he wasn't thinking about the Council any more. Suddenly I noticed that I was standing pressed against him, with my head almost on his chest. God, what was I *doing*?

I jerked away, flustered. "Look, who *are* you, anyway? Because this is just – extremely weird."

Without taking his eyes from me, the boy propped himself against the base of one of the statues. There was a look of lean strength to him, with shoulders as firm as Alex's under his long-sleeved T-shirt.

"My name is Seb."

"Seb?"

"Sebastián," he amended. His eyes held such incredulous happiness, drinking me in as if he'd never be able to look away. "Sebastián Carrera. And you?"

For some reason it hadn't occurred to me that he wouldn't know my name already; he seemed so familiar with me. "Willow Fields," I said.

"Willow," he echoed. In his accent, the word was a soft sigh: *wee-low.* He smiled, seeming almost shy suddenly. "That's a tree, isn't it?"

The expression on Seb's face was the same one from my dream, and looking at him now I saw how accurate my dream-image had been: the loosely curling brown hair, the high cheekbones and perfect mouth. The stubble that defined his jaw, making him even more attractive than he already was. God, what did it *mean*, that he was actually real? And that he was here?

I crossed my arms over my chest, feeling uncomfortable for more reasons than I could define. "Yeah. It's a tree."

"It's a pretty name." Seb's glance lingered on my hair. "It's changed," he said after a pause. "You were blonde before."

"How did you…" I trailed off, swallowed. "I dyed it."

He grinned suddenly, shaking his head. "I can't believe this; I can't believe I'm really standing here talking to you. Willow – you are so, so beautiful." As if he couldn't help himself, he reached for my face again, tracing a soft line down my cheek with the back of his finger.

I yanked away, hating the way my pulse had fluttered at his touch. "Stop *doing* that. Look, what's going on? You said that you found me – what did you mean? Why were you looking for me?"

His hazel eyes widened; I could see that I'd stunned him somehow. "You don't know," he said, almost to himself. "But how can you not know? You've got to see—" He stopped, his gaze scanning over me. "Wait – why aren't you changing?"

"Change? Into what?" I took a cautious step backwards, wondering why I was still standing here talking to this guy. And Alex. What in the world was Alex going to think? As far as he knew, I'd disappeared without a word. I had to get back; he wouldn't even know how to find me.

"Your—" Seb gestured impatiently at himself, sketching a quick circle around his body. "I don't know the word in English. Your energy. Your *self*."

"Aura," I realized.

"Yes, aura. You shouldn't show your true aura out in the open this way – the angels might see you."

Time slowed as I remembered how he'd seen the angels too. The truth hit me like a blow, so that all that existed was the two of us, standing on the bridge. Focusing on Seb, I brought his aura into view. It was pale green with darker green lights.

"Show me," I whispered.

He understood what I meant without me having to explain. A smooth rippling – and his aura changed. Silver, with forest-green lights gleaming through it. In a dream, I put my hand out, running it through the gently-shifting colours as if I could catch them; watching as they played on my fingers. Seb stood very still. I felt him shiver and realized he could feel this, just as if I was stroking his skin.

I lowered my hand, but couldn't stop staring at the beautiful, silvery lights. My eyes were full of tears – the words almost wouldn't come.

"You're half-angel," I said. "I thought – I thought I was the only one in the world."

Seb let out a breath that was almost a sob. "*Yes*. Yes, me too…me too." He tried to say something else; couldn't seem to get out the words. He reached for my hand, squeezing it hard.

I stood with his fingers gripping mine as we stared at

each other. *I should pull away,* I thought...but instead I was holding onto him tightly too. I could sense his energy again, and now it all made sense. It felt so warm and familiar, because, for the first time ever, I was touching one of my own kind. The sensation of like touching like was indescribable, something I knew now that every human being on the planet took for granted. But to have never experienced this at all, and then to suddenly *find* it, after seventeen years...oh god, it was like sinking into a warm bath and not knowing where my skin ended and the water began.

Seb's eyes were so full of wonder that he looked almost frightened, and I knew he was feeling exactly the same thing. Other knowledge came too: snapshots from his life, swirling through my head. The orphanage he'd been abandoned in, life on the streets, a young offenders' place that was so horrific I found myself wincing in pity. More than that, I got a sense of *him.* His inner strength. The teasing sense of humour he'd somehow hung onto, the charm that hid the utter loneliness he felt sometimes. He'd known he was half-angel since he was a small child – had felt alone for most of his life. He'd searched for so many years. So many.

And underneath everything, steady as a heartbeat, was an emotion so intense it took my breath away.

No, I have to be wrong about that, I thought in confusion.

He couldn't feel that way about me – it didn't make any sense. We'd only just met each other.

"How did you find me?" I asked finally.

Seb looked down at our hands together; his fingers tightened. "You dreamed about me," he said huskily. I stiffened. Oh my god, how did he know that? "You dreamed we were in a park in *el DF*, so I came here," he went on. "I've been coming to Chapultepec for weeks, trying to find you."

"But—"

"I've got your shirt, your picture. I saw it was you, and I—" His hazel eyes rose again, and my chest clenched at the expression in them, so that other questions suddenly seemed meaningless. He swallowed; in slow motion, he reached out and touched my hair, as if it were something fragile and precious. "Willow, I've been looking for you for so long. I can't tell you how I felt when I saw your picture for the first time – what it meant to me. I—"

The sound of running footsteps came from the path behind us. "Willow!" called Alex's voice, and suddenly I was hotly aware that I was standing there holding a stranger's hand, staring into his eyes. I pulled away from Seb as Alex came jogging up, but I knew that he'd seen.

Alex stopped in front of us, dark hair ruffled from the run as he looked at me in bewilderment. His glance at Seb was tinged with suspicion. "Willow, what's going on?

Who *is* this guy? I saw you running off with him, and I thought…are you okay?"

"I'm fine," I said, touching his arm. The pure human energy rushed through me; it took me a second to adjust, and then it was only Alex again, warm and familiar. "I'm fine," I repeated. I started to try and explain, then remembered in a rush. "Alex, the Council's arrived! They were part of that flock that was just overhead!"

His jaw dropped. "The *Council*? Are you sure? They're not supposed to be here for another five weeks!"

"Yeah, it was definitely them – twelve shining angels, just like in my dream. They flew into the top of that tower." I pointed, shading my eyes from the sun.

"The Torre Mayor," muttered Alex, staring upwards. "What the hell are they doing *there*, instead of the Nikko?"

"The plans have changed, I guess." Feeble, useless words. "Or maybe they're going to the hotel later?"

Alex let out a strained breath, still gazing up at the gleaming pinnacle. "God, let's hope so. We don't know *anything* about that place – no floor plans, nothing. My team's not even fully trained yet." He shoved his hands through his hair; I could feel how shaken he was.

There was a pause, and then he looked down at me, and back at Seb again. Confusion crossed his features. Slowly, he said, "Okay, so…who is this guy, anyway? Why were you—" He stopped.

Holding hands with him. My cheeks flushed. Seb stood leaning against the statue's base, listening. I could sense how disappointed he was that we'd been interrupted, and in a daze, it hit me just how easily I could read him already. I'd never felt such a strong instant connection to anyone in my life before.

"Alex, this is Seb. He—" I broke off. "Seb, is it okay if I tell him?"

"Tell me what?" Alex's dark eyebrows had drawn together. "Willow, what's going on?"

I glanced at Seb; he gave a resigned shrug. "He's half-angel," I said.

Alex couldn't have seemed more stunned if I'd smashed him over the head with a mallet. "He's *what*?" He looked sharply back at Seb; there was a rapid shift as his consciousness rose through his chakra points. "His aura's green, not silver. But his energy feels…" His eyes widened. "Christ, you really are one. What's the deal with your aura?"

As clearly as if I was thinking it myself, I knew how much Seb disliked Alex knowing this; the fact that he could change his aura was something he'd always kept secret. You wouldn't have guessed it from his body language, though. He looked like the definition of "casual" as he stood there against the statue.

"You can see auras," he said. "Most humans can't."

Most humans. The words gave me a start – Seb didn't see

himself as human. And I still did, somehow, even though I so clearly wasn't.

"I've been trained," said Alex shortly. "Answer the question."

Seb flicked a glance over him; you didn't have to be psychic to see that he didn't like being ordered around. "It isn't smart, with angels around," he said at last. "So I changed it."

"Wait – you can change your aura?" repeated Alex, his eyes narrowing. "Like, at will?"

Seb's forehead creased; Alex said something in rapid Spanish, and he nodded. "Yes, at will." A wry smile. "Your Spanish is very good, *amigo*."

Alex gave him a look at the word *amigo*, and I knew he was still thinking of Seb holding my hand. "Yeah, thanks," he said. "So are there lots of half-angels, or—"

"No," said Seb and I together. "No," I went on, clearing my throat. "Seb – he's never seen another one. He's spent most of his life looking."

I could see Seb realizing the depth of what I'd gotten from his hand. *Did he get anything from mine?* I wondered suddenly. Did Seb know me just as well as I knew him now? At the feel of his steady gaze on me, my face warmed; I couldn't meet his eyes. God, what was wrong with me? Why was I getting all flustered just because some half-angel boy held my hand?

Alex had fallen silent. I could almost see him turning all this over in his head. "Another half-angel," he murmured. "Jesus." Watching Seb carefully, he rested against the railing of the bridge with his arms folded over his chest. The sleeves of his blue sweatshirt were pushed up, showing his toned forearms.

"How did you find her?" he asked finally.

"Someone stole your things in Chihuahua," said Seb, speaking to me rather than Alex. "Some clothes, and a picture. I bought them at the marketplace, and when I touched them I could see…everything."

I have your shirt, your picture. It all became clear. Seb had seen my dream from my shirt – I'd been worrying about what it might mean for hours the last time I'd worn it.

"And after that?" asked Alex after a pause. "How did you know where we'd gone?"

Seb glanced at me. My heart sank as I remembered: I hadn't told Alex about the strange boy in my dream; it had just seemed too surreal. But even though how I'd felt in the dream had been ridiculous, what would Alex think when he heard about it now – when the strange boy had been holding my hand, touching my hair?

To my relief, all Seb said was, "She was thinking that you needed to come to *el DF* – I touched her shirt, and I felt it. So I came too."

"*El DF* is a big place," pointed out Alex dryly.

"Yes, I get feelings sometimes. I got a feeling today that I should come to Chapultepec." Seb smiled; there wasn't much humour in it. "Any more questions?"

Still leaning against the railing, Alex gave a soft snort. "Oh, sorry, am I being too nosy?" The traffic droned past below as he crossed his ankles, keeping his gaze on Seb. "I get like that when I find some guy hanging onto my girlfriend. Weird, huh?"

Seb arched an eyebrow.

"Alex, it wasn't like that, honestly!" I burst out. From somewhere outside of myself, I was shaking my head in amazement that these two gorgeous boys seemed to be having some kind of stand-off over me. From *inside* of myself, it felt awful. "It was just…this moment of realizing that we're both half-angels, that's all."

Still watching Seb, Alex started to say something else, then stopped. He blew out a breath and shook his head. Glancing at me, he held an arm out; we hugged tightly. I could sense Seb's dismay as he watched, and I actually felt *guilty* for a second. It was insane: I'd only known him for about half an hour. Angrily, I tried to shove this weird hyper-awareness of Seb's feelings out of my mind.

Alex's arms were warm around me. "I'm sorry," I said against his neck. "I know it must have looked—"

He kissed me, halting my words. "Hey, come on; you know I trust you," he whispered.

I had a feeling he wasn't including Seb in that sentiment. Not that I could really blame him. Then I thought of something; I peered around us. "Wait, where are Sam and Trish?"

"They're going to meet us back home with Kara and her group," said Alex. "Sam really wanted to come with me, though – he thought I might be beating up whoever this guy was." From his expression as he glanced back at Seb, he didn't think it was the worst idea he'd ever heard. There was more, though; I could tell he was turning something over in his mind.

"So," he said finally, keeping his arm around my shoulders. "What now?"

Seb looked a question at him.

"See, I've got this really bad feeling that we're not going to get rid of you," said Alex. "Call me crazy, but I don't think you're planning on heading back up to Chihuahua now that you've met another half-angel."

Seb's gaze went to me…and all at once I knew that no power on earth would make him leave. Now that he'd finally found me, he'd die before he ever let himself be separated from me again. And to my alarm, what I felt wasn't far off from that. It made me shaky to admit it, but it was true – something primal that I couldn't even control.

Seb might be the only other half-angel I'd ever encounter. There was no way I wanted him to go back to Chihuahua.

"No, I'm not going anywhere," said Seb. "Not unless you want me to," he added to me.

I was so conscious of Alex standing beside me, of what he might be feeling about all this. "No, I don't want you to go," I admitted softly.

Alex glanced down at me in surprise. I tried to tell him with my eyes that this had nothing to do with him and me, and everything to do with needing to know another of my kind. To my relief, I saw understanding cross his face. He didn't look happy, exactly, but I could see that he got it.

"You were holding his hand," he said after a pause. "What did you get? Can he be trusted?"

Remembering what I'd seen, the question almost made me laugh. Seb had been a thief for years; he'd picked more pockets and stolen more cameras and purses than he could count. But I *did* trust him, I realized. I'd trust him with… anything.

"Yeah, he can be trusted," I said.

Alex seemed to make up his mind. "Okay, look," he said to Seb. "If you came back with us, could you teach Willow how to do that aura thing?"

Seb's eyebrows shot up. "You don't know how?" he said to me.

I shook my head, shocked that Alex was even suggesting this – though on second thought, it made perfect sense. My half-angel aura put me in danger every time I went outside; I knew how much he worried about it. "I'm not usually that aware of auras," I told Seb. "I mean, I can see other people's if I try, but I've never seen my own unless I was in my angel form. Trying to change it never occurred to me – I wouldn't even know where to start."

Seb's hazel eyes were concerned. "Yes, I'll teach you. It's much safer."

I nodded, my emotions so mixed I could hardly make sense of them. Part of me was still stunned that Seb was even *real*, much less that he was coming back to the house with us.

There was no sign now of Alex's own mixed emotions about Seb, though I knew he must still have them. "Good," he said, sounding like he was talking to any member of the team. "And you know what we do, right?"

Seb bent down to pick up his bag. "No. What do you do?"

"We're Angel Killers," said Alex. "AKs. Those angels you saw" – he nodded at the Torre Mayor – "if we can get rid of them, we can destroy all the angels in the world. That's our goal."

It was as if he'd knocked the breath out of Seb. He straightened up slowly, staring. "You...this is a joke," he said. "You're going to kill all the angels? Really?"

"No joke," said Alex. "There's a group of us; that's what we're trying to do. If you come back with us, then you help us fight them; that's the deal. All right?"

Seb stood gazing up at the tower. From nowhere, I got an image of a young girl with big eyes and a grimy face. Seb would have come with us no matter what it was we did, I knew that – but something about this young girl in his thoughts made his shoulders straighten a little.

"Yes, all right," he said. "I'll help you fight."

We started heading back through the park, Seb walking on the other side of me from Alex. I could tell how much he still wanted to be talking to me, but he stayed quiet, his steps long and loping. Alex took my hand, weaving his fingers through mine and letting Seb go a few paces ahead of us.

"So what happened?" he asked in an undertone.

I explained as best I could, from Seb first finding me to Alex finding us together. Uncomfortably, I was aware of how much I was having to leave out – such as Seb putting his arm around me and me not even minding at first, because it had felt so natural.

"But Alex, are you really sure you're okay with this?" I finished. "I mean – Seb doesn't have to come back to the house with us." Though I knew if he didn't, I'd be counting the seconds until I saw him again. There was so much I was aching to ask him; so much I needed to find out.

Alex glanced at Seb. I caught a hint of resigned dislike; then it faded as he seemed to push his own feelings aside. "Yeah, I'm sure," he said quietly. "If he can teach you how to change your aura, so you can be safe…that's all that matters, Willow."

I hesitated, not totally convinced – but before I could say anything else, Alex looked down at me again. "Hey – what were you going to tell me before Sam and Trish ran off? You seemed so worried: I almost had a heart attack when we got back and you weren't there."

My angel. I swallowed hard. Ahead of us, Seb was standing against a tree, waiting for us to catch up. *Seb, please, please have some answers for me*, I thought. *I really need you to.*

"Nothing," I said to Alex. "Sorry, I was just having a freak-out moment about the hunt. I mean, thinking about actually having to shoot something." I forced a smile. "I wasn't born to be a gun moll after all, I guess."

He searched my eyes; I felt both guilt and relief when he believed me. "Yeah, I know how much you hate the thought of it," he said, squeezing my hand. "Just promise me you'll try to shoot if an angel's ever actually coming at you, all right?"

"Promise," I said. More than that, I was promising

myself that if Seb *didn't* have answers for me, I'd tell Alex about all of this immediately.

We caught up with Seb; he peeled himself off the tree and joined us again. When we reached the Metro station, I glanced at him as we headed down the concrete stairs. He was jogging slightly, with his curly head down, knapsack bouncing on one shoulder. He looked so normal – so totally human. I could see why the team still felt wary of me; to look at Seb, there was no hint he wasn't completely human. And in his case, even his aura blended in with everyone else's.

His aura. As we jostled our way to the ticket machines, it suddenly struck me exactly what it would mean if I could learn to disguise my own. I knew it wasn't what Alex had had in mind when he'd asked Seb to teach me – it hadn't even occurred to him; he just wanted me to be safe. But if I somehow managed to get my angel self under control – and if my aura looked human, so that I blended in with the rest of the AKs... I swallowed hard, feeling almost dizzy.

I could take part in the Council attack.

CHAPTER *Thirteen*

ALEX WASN'T SURE WHICH CAUSED a bigger ruckus back at the AK house – the news that the Council had arrived five weeks early and were at the Torre Mayor, or that there was another half-angel in the world, and hey, here he was in their house with them. He explained everything to the team as best he could; it still felt like he'd set a bomb off. Soon after, Kara cornered him in the kitchen.

"Another half-angel – perfect, that's just what we need right now," she said, her hands on her hips. "Who *is* this guy? Can we even trust him?"

Alex was making himself a mug of instant coffee; he

made another one for her without asking – she was as addicted to caffeine as he was. "I don't think *I* can trust him as far as I can throw him," he said dryly. "The guy's got serious designs on Willow. But I think the team can trust him, yeah. And if he can teach her this aura thing, it'll be worth it."

Kara stood against the counter beside him as she sipped her coffee. She rolled her eyes. "You know, that's so reasonable it makes my head hurt."

Alex touched his forehead, where – speaking of hurting heads – another headache was starting to throb. "Reasonable – right. I'm just trying to talk myself out of taking a swing at the guy next time I see him. If you'd seen the way he was looking at her…" And for that matter, the way Willow had been looking at Seb, with her green eyes so full of wonder. Annoyed with himself, Alex pushed the image away and took a gulp of coffee. "Anyway, even if I threatened the guy at gunpoint, he's not going to just go away – he's spent his entire life looking for another half-angel. So I might as well keep him close, where I can keep an eye on him."

"Keep your friends close, and your enemies closer," Kara murmured. She shook her head, looking deep in thought. "God, this is just unreal. And if there's two of them, then there must be more, don't you think? They can't possibly be the only ones – or can they?"

The thought of Willow and Seb being the only two of

their kind brought a small chill; it sounded like Noah's ark and creatures going two by two. "No way, there have to be more," said Alex. "It must be pretty rare, though, when the angels themselves think Willow is the only one."

"And somehow the two of them found each other," mused Kara. Alex gave her a dirty look, and she shrugged. "Sorry. But it is sort of…poetic."

"Yeah, how'd you guess? I feel so much like writing a sonnet right now."

"Okay, okay. I *said* sorry." Kara sighed, and ran a hand over her close-cropped hair. "Anyway, I'd better go and meet Luis – see if I can find out what's going on with the Council."

Alex nodded. "Be careful."

"Always am." She went to the kitchen table where her leather bag lay and pulled out her gun, briefly checking its cartridges before tucking the weapon back into hiding. "All right, see you later," she said, hooking the bag over her shoulder. "I'll text you in a while to check in."

Once Kara was gone Alex stood where he was for a few minutes, worry over the Council throbbing at his skull. He'd thought he had almost two months left to train everyone, but if the Twelve were following their original plan, they'd only be in Mexico City three weeks. *Three weeks.* And he still had a team that who went running off without thinking.

He closed his eyes, squeezing his temples with one hand. *Don't panic,* he told himself. *It's not as long as you thought you had, but you can do it – you can get them ready in time. And maybe Willow got it wrong, and it wasn't even the Council at all.*

That last one seemed like way too much to hope for. Alex let out a breath. Anyway, no point in worrying about this just yet – he'd have to wait and see what Kara came back with.

The only other half-angel in the world.

He frowned as he looked down, swirling the coffee in his mug. It couldn't really be true, could it? And if it was, then Christ – what were the odds of Seb being around Willow's age, and just happening to stumble on her things in a marketplace? Or getting a "feeling" that he should go to Chapultepec, on the only day of Willow's life that she'd ever been there?

Remembering what Kara had said, about the two of them finding each other, a prickle ran up Alex's spine.

He shook his head at himself in irritation; he didn't even believe in fate. Seb was obviously as psychic as Willow was, that was all. And had been determined to find another half-angel. Once he had, learning that she had a boyfriend must have ruined the guy's day – because although Alex was certain that for Willow, the moment when he'd found them staring at each other really *had* just been about meeting another half-angel, he severely doubted the same was true for Seb. No guy looked at a girl the way Seb had been with only species solidarity in mind.

And now he was here in their house...and would be alone with Willow all the time, teaching her how to change her aura.

Alex put down his mug, a little harder than intended, and went to find them. He eventually discovered Willow and Seb up on the second floor, where a small balcony overlooked the concrete courtyard. Seb stood lounging in the doorway with his hands in his jeans pockets; Willow was on the balcony itself, leaning against its metal railing. They'd obviously been deep in conversation, but Willow broke off with a smile when she saw him.

"Hey, you," she said, resting a hand on his chest and craning up on her tiptoes to kiss him. Alex saw how carefully blank Seb's face went, and knew more than ever that he'd been right *Yeah, take that, angel boy*, he thought before he could help it.

Willow sank back to her feet. "I'd better go see if Liz wants help with dinner," she said. "We'll talk later, okay, Seb?"

"Yes, I'd like that," he said softly. He watched her go, his eyes lingering on her petite form.

Alex propped himself against the metal railing where Willow had just stood. "Okay, let's get something straight," he said in Spanish. "If you think I don't know you're after my girlfriend, you're crazy. And if you try to put any sleazy moves on her while you're here, you're going to regret it."

Seb's knapsack was at his feet. He took out a pack of cigarettes; tapped out the last one and lit it. Settling back against the door jamb, he gave Alex a considering, faintly humorous look. "Sleazy moves?" he repeated. "Don't worry, I don't do sleazy moves."

"Let me rephrase," said Alex coldly. "Any moves. Just keep your hands off her."

Seb was silent as he blew a stream of smoke towards the sky. "This isn't really any of your business, you know," he said finally. "Whatever happens between Willow and me is up to her. Not you."

Alex gave a short laugh. "Not my business? Think again – this is my girlfriend we're talking about. And I want to make sure that *you* know it's up to her."

"Well, you can put your mind at ease then." Seb's voice was mild, but with a thread of steel through it. "Because I don't pressure girls, and I don't make moves where they're not wanted. If Willow only wants to be friends, that's all we'll be."

Alex nodded slowly, watching him. "Okay," he said at last. "But if you do *anything* to hurt Willow – if you make her uncomfortable in any way while you're here – I will seriously make you wish you hadn't."

Seb took another another puff of his cigarette. "Be my guest. Look, I really don't want to discuss this with you. But I'd die before I did anything to hurt Willow – or before I let anyone else hurt her, either. End of conversation, okay?"

Watching Seb as he smoked, Alex wondered, despite himself, what it would be like to finally find another of your own kind, after searching for so many years. He knew that if he were Seb, he wouldn't be prepared to just walk away from Willow either. The realization didn't exactly make him warm to the guy.

"No, not quite end of conversation." Alex shifted on the railing, his arms folded over his chest. "How long have you known you're half-angel?"

Seb's eyebrows rose. "Is that any of your business?"

"You're training my girlfriend how to disguise her aura? Yeah, it's my business."

Seb regarded him for a moment. The look on his face wasn't amused, exactly, but it was heading in that direction. "You're big on the girlfriend thing, aren't you?" he observed. "She's not your property, you know."

The comment brought Alex up short; irritatingly, he knew Seb was right, and that Willow would say the same thing if she'd heard him. "No, she's not," he said at last. "But as the leader of this team, I need for you to answer my question."

Seb stretched across to the railing to tap ash off his cigarette. "You know, I'm trying my best to think of the possible relevance here...fine, whatever. I've known I was half-angel since I was five."

"So, that's what – around thirteen years?"

"Yeah, I just turned eighteen."

"Okay. You've known for thirteen years. Willow has known for about three months. When she first found out—" He broke off, remembering Willow's despair, her struggle to deal with all of this. "It was really hard for her," he finished. "So what I'm getting at is – I think she probably needs you, okay? She needs someone who can help her with this."

Seb went silent, his hazel eyes thoughtful as he smoked. "I understand," he said. "I'll do whatever I can."

For some reason, the two-by-two thing flickered into Alex's head again; he shoved it away with a mental grimace. "I'd like you to start training her tomorrow," he said. "The sooner she can learn to hide her aura, the better."

"I agree; it's no good that she doesn't know how." Seb studied him. "Seriously, man, how do you even sleep at night, knowing she's so exposed all the time?"

"She's not *that* exposed – I'd die before I ever let anything hurt her, either," said Alex dryly. "But yeah, it's not easy sometimes."

"I believe you," said Seb. "Because I won't be sleeping

well now myself, until she learns." His cigarette was almost gone by then; he took a final puff, seeming to savour it.

It was childish, but Alex couldn't resist: "Oh, and she hates cigarette smoke, by the way."

The look Seb shot him was now definitely amused. Breathing out a last plume of smoke, he twisted the butt out on the metal railing. "You know what? I had a feeling she did. Good thing I just quit, isn't it?"

Alex could tell he was serious. "So, that would be because you're not after her in the slightest."

Seb shrugged as he propped himself back against the door jamb. "It would be because I've just found the girl I've been looking for my entire life, and she hates cigarette smoke. It's not exactly a complicated decision."

The girl I've been looking for my entire life. Alex resisted the urge to throw Seb off the balcony and see if he could fly. "Here's a tip: you might as well keep smoking. Have four packs a day; knock yourself out. Nothing's going to happen between you and Willow. Or haven't you got that yet?"

Seb stood with his hands in his jeans pockets; a breeze ruffled one of his loose brown curls. He shrugged. "Yeah, that must be the only reason I want to stick around – because I think she's going to fall into my arms tomorrow. You know what, you're right. Now that I've met another half-angel, why don't I just leave? Willow won't care. Neither will I."

Alex had a feeling that Willow *would* care – a lot, actually. God, why had he even suggested letting this guy stay? But he knew why, and it was still the most important thing, bar none.

"Don't go anywhere until you teach her how to change her aura," he said. "After that, I'll help you pack. Anyway, back to business. Have the guys helped you figure out where you're sleeping?"

Seb looked unsurprised at the change of subject. "Yeah, they said they could put a camp bed in the dorm for me. It looks pretty crowded in there already, though. Plus I don't think anyone likes the idea very much, you know?"

Alex didn't like the idea either; Willow was self-conscious enough already about being in his room, without him wanting Seb out there in the dorm too. "You can take one of the storage rooms," he said. "It'll be pretty cramped, but if we pile some boxes up, we could probably just about squeeze a camp bed in."

"Sounds good. I'd like that better, anyway," said Seb. And apparently with that, he considered the conversation closed. He bent to snag his knapsack from the floor; swung it over his shoulder in an easy motion.

Seeing Seb's knapsack reminded Alex of something. "Hey, have you still got Willow's picture?" he asked. "The one of her when she was a little girl? Because I think she'd really like it back, you know. It means a lot to her."

Seb regarded him; suddenly his eyes were almost impish with humour. "Don't worry – I'll keep it safe, and give it back to her soon. But for now—" He shrugged, smiled. "Hey, you've got the girl, I've got the picture. That's fair, right?"

As Seb walked off, Alex was tempted to yank him back by the strap of his battered knapsack and take out Willow's picture himself. Thinking about what he'd told Kara, Alex knew that it was true – he was certain the team could trust Seb; Willow's psychic insights were never wrong about that kind of thing.

Whether he'd ever *like* the guy was a totally different matter.

I helped Liz with dinner that night, though things had gone pretty stiff between us. Not that we'd ever become bosom friends, but we'd at least started talking a tiny bit when we cooked together. Now her mouth was a thin line as she made the salad, and I knew it was because of Seb. When we'd first gotten back to the house, Alex had told everyone what had happened, his tone as matter-of-fact as if this kind of thing occurred every day. Even so, the team had been…surprised to have another half-angel suddenly appear. To put it mildly. That, plus the Council arriving early, had put everyone seriously on edge.

I set the table in silence. My own thoughts were still way too confused to try to alleviate whatever was going on in Liz's head.

We both looked up as the door opened and Kara rushed into the kitchen. "Where's Alex?" she said, yanking off her jacket. Without waiting for an answer, she called out towards the boys' dorm, "Alex! Alex, we've got to talk!"

"What's going on *now*?" asked Liz, wide-eyed.

"Luis is gone," said Kara tightly. She paced the kitchen. "Totally gone; no sign of him. I went to his apartment and it's just abandoned, like—" Alex came in, and she whirled towards him. "Alex! Luis is—"

"I heard," he said tightly.

The others started arriving behind him as Kara explained. "He was visiting his family this weekend, but he was supposed to be home by now; I already had a date with him tonight," she said, her words tumbling over themselves. "But there wasn't any answer, so I let myself in, and…he's just gone. I mean, his bag's there, so he got home all right, but it's still unpacked. There was a half-eaten sandwich on the table, and a cold cup of coffee…" She trailed off.

I bit my lip and glanced at Alex; he was standing behind one of the kitchen chairs, leaning on its back with both arms. "You didn't try to call him, did you?" he asked sharply.

Kara shook her head. "No, and I didn't touch anything

in his apartment either – just got out of there as fast as I could." She took a deep breath. "Plus the Council's not staying at the Nikko Hotel – I headed over there and couldn't feel any sign of them. So then I went to the Torre Mayor, but to get past the lobby you have to have a pass for the card reader. I don't know if the angels are still there or not – they're really high up if they are; I couldn't tell."

There was a long pause as we all took this in. "So. Looks like the Church must have gotten wind of your boyfriend giving out security information," said Alex wryly.

"Less of the boyfriend, please…but yeah." Kara looked more shaken than I'd ever seen her.

"Okay, this is not good, this is officially really, really not good," muttered Brendan, scraping at his rust-coloured hair.

For a change, Sam didn't argue with him. Neither did anyone else. Wesley was glowering even more than usual; Trish and Liz looked as pale and stricken as I felt. At least Kara had never given Luis any information about us – though I felt guilty even thinking that, just then.

"So…I guess the same invitations for the reception won't be any good now," said Trish faintly.

"No way," said Alex. I could hear the strain in his voice, though I doubted anyone else could. "Basically, we don't have a plan any more – we're back to square one."

"Wait – what does *that* mean?" demanded Wesley. He hardly ever spoke with more than a few people around; now his fists were clenched at his sides. "Are you saying the attack can't go ahead? Because there is *no way* that—"

"Of course I'm not saying that," cut in Alex in a low voice. "This is the only chance we're going to have at the Council. We'll find a way to get to them, no matter what."

I swallowed hard, but knew he was right. Everyone glanced at each other. Three weeks – that was all we had now.

"Don't worry, we'll find out what's going on." Kara's voice was matter-of-fact again, back in control. "What do you want me to do? Should I go over to the cathedral tomorrow, see if I can get any information? Any change to the Council's visit was sure to have been organized by someone in the office there – they've been coordinating everything."

Alex nodded, looking deep in thought. "Yeah, good idea – we need anything you can get. Won't they recognize you, though?"

"No, I don't think so. I usually met Luis at his place. He didn't have my cell number or anything." She managed a small smile. "I was a woman of mystery."

I watched Alex's eyes scan over her. "Can you get hold of a wig or something, just in case? If the angels have him, they'll see you in his memories. And you're pretty distinctive."

Another time, I knew Kara would have bantered with Alex over this; now she just nodded. "I'll get one tomorrow. See what I can do with some make-up too."

"Good," said Alex. "And I'll do some checking around myself. Plus keep training these guys – maybe take them on another practice hunt."

Sam was shaking his head. "Yeah, but what about—"

He broke off as Seb came into the kitchen, looking like he'd just taken a shower – his chestnut curls were damp, shoved away from his face as if he'd raked his fingers through them. When I saw him, something in me tightened...because I realized that the whole time we'd been talking, part of me had been thinking about Seb, wondering where he was.

Silence choked the room. Seb obviously noticed, and knew it was because of him. His eyes found mine and he smiled slightly. Despite my discomfort, I gave him a rueful one back; I knew exactly how he must be feeling. The team's stony faces were bringing back some not-so-pleasant sensations of déjà vu. Clearly I *had* made a little progress with them, even if I hadn't been all that aware of it – because now Seb was here, it was obvious that was something else that was back to square one.

Alex sighed. "Hey, Seb," he said, and I wanted to hug

him just for managing to sound normal. "We were talking about something that's come up; I'll fill you in after dinner. You finding everything all right?"

Seb's eyebrows rose at "something that's come up", but he didn't comment. "Yes, fine, thanks."

As we all started sitting down to eat, Seb took the seat next to me – the place where Alex always sat. Obviously he didn't *know* that, but I could see everyone sort of glancing at Alex, to see what he would do. As if there was some sort of competition going on.

My face went hot, and I cleared my throat. "Um, Seb, that's—"

"It's okay," said Alex briefly. He took the seat to my other side, the one where Trish usually went, and Trish squeezed in next to Wesley, where I'd put an extra chair. I saw Seb get what had happened then; he looked like he was holding back a smile despite himself.

Hardly anyone spoke. The clink of knives and forks against plates sounded deafening. My own awkwardness around Seb wasn't helping much either, to be honest...and I was feeling a lot of it.

When Seb and I had been talking on the balcony earlier, there'd been so much to say that we'd just kind of skirted around the edges of it all, with the unspoken understanding that as soon as we could, we'd be sitting down for a long talk. I wanted that desperately. There was so much I needed to know: to ask if what I'd been experiencing with my angel was normal; to find out more about his life; to compare a thousand and one experiences and see if things had been the same for him.

But as we'd been talking, I'd also been scalp-tinglingly *aware* of Seb, even standing several feet away from me. It wasn't because of how attractive he was – and he really was gorgeous; you'd have to be unconscious not to notice – it was just…him. His energy, so like my own. The memory of our hands together; how that had felt. It had been a huge relief when Alex had shown up and I could make my escape.

You don't even know him, I told myself.

Except that wasn't true. I did know Seb. Maybe not all the details of his life yet, but the kind of person he was, yes. And now I could feel him sitting beside me. Not only his physical presence, but his energy. We were close enough that our two auras were touching, and though I never really noticed this with Alex unless I concentrated, with Seb it was like I'd just gained an extra sense – one that tingled through me like electricity. His aura was so alive, so buoyant. I could feel it drifting through my own, just like mine was drifting through his. Intermingling. Exploring.

My cheeks heated. Abruptly, I tried to bring my aura back to myself but we couldn't avoid each other – we were sitting too close. I felt Seb notice; try and fail to pull his own aura completely away. Now there was a sense of gentle, teasing apology where his aura mingled with mine, and I gritted my teeth. Wonderful. I was inadvertently playing aura-footsie with him.

And meanwhile, the silence had not become any less deafening.

"Okay, come on everyone, this is stupid," said Alex finally. "He's a member of the team. We can trust him. Just...act normal, all right? Please, for the love of god, before my brain starts to bleed."

For a moment no one spoke. Finally Kara she said, "So, Willow, maybe you could tell us more about what you saw today, when the Council arrived."

Relieved, I started to answer – but before I could, Sam jumped in. "No, wait," he growled, tossing his fork down with a clatter. "Alex, I want to know how it is you're so sure we can trust this guy. At least with Willow, we all saw her angel defending Liz. Who *is* he, anyway? He's just appeared out of nowhere, and now he's on the team?"

Seb glanced at him. "I'm Sebastián Carrera," he said, cutting a piece of his pork chop. "I'm not from nowhere; I'm from right here, Mexico City. And if I say I'll help you fight, I'll help you fight."

"Willow's read his hand," added Alex as Sam opened his mouth to respond. "We can trust him."

"Got it," said Sam, giving me a look that wasn't

massively friendly. "So I guess that's why she was holding hands with him when they went running off together this afternoon, right? 'Cause she was giving him a reading on the hoof?"

My face went bright red as everyone stared. "Oh, *that* sounds nice and cosy," muttered Liz. Trish gazed down at her plate, obviously hating the tension.

On either side of me, I felt both Alex and Seb bristle. "That was my fault," said Seb in a voice that was calm, but had a challenge under it. "I grabbed her hand to help her run when we saw the angels. We had to go fast, you know?"

Sam snorted. "Yeah, you sure did go fast," he said to me. "You were in an awful hurry to go tearin' off with this guy, weren't you? Guess we must not have heard you when you tried to tell *us* what was going on."

"I *did* try!" I said, stung. "I shouted Alex's name, but—"

"Stop – you don't have to explain anything," broke in Alex, reaching for my hand. He enfolded it in his. "Drop it, Sam. Willow's already told us what happened."

Sam opened his mouth.

"*Drop it,*" repeated Alex.

Silence fell again. I'm not sure whether the quality of it was any better than the last one. More crackling with tension around the edges, maybe.

"Well," said Brendan finally. "Acting normal was fun."

I could still feel Seb's aura mingling with mine; he was concerned for me, wanted to soothe me. On my other side, Alex's hand felt so warm, so safe. I held onto it tightly. I longed to be someplace alone with him – really alone, the way we used to be. Things had been so simple when it was just the two of us, with no one else around. Nothing felt very simple at all any more.

After a pause, Alex squeezed my hand and released it. His voice as he addressed the team was steady. "Look, guys, we're coming up to crunch time on the Council – if they're sticking to the same plan they're only going to be here a few weeks. So we don't have time for this. Seb's here – that's it. Either you trust my judgement on this one, or you don't. You decide."

"We trust you," said Kara quietly. "Don't we, everyone?"

Mumbled yeses, nods. Sam's face was stormy, but he didn't say anything. Trish glanced at him, her gentle eyes anxious.

"Sam?" said Alex, watching him too.

The Texan let out a long breath. "Yeah, okay," he muttered, pushing his blond hair back.

"Good." To my surprise, Alex stretched across me, offering his hand to Seb. "There, they've accepted you. Lucky you."

Seb's smile was wry as he reached across me too. "Yes, I'm very honoured."

And as he shook Alex's hand, I knew two things. One, the team still wasn't happy about this, despite their trust of Alex. And two, somewhere deep down where I didn't want to think about it...was the terrible feeling that being caught between these two boys might be my fate for a long time to come.

CHAPTER *Fourteen*

THE EXERCISE ROOM WAS SMALL — just a corner of the basement really, with a couple of treadmills, a weight machine and some dumb-bells. It smelled of must and sweat. When some of the guys got going on the treadmills — Alex and Sam, especially — the sweat would be literally flying. I saw Seb glance at the floor; it was cement, and not all that clean, I guess. It was also the only place where we could sit. "We could go to my room," he suggested.

Seb's "room" was tiny; it would be both of us on his camp bed. The thought was way too intimate, especially after the aura-mingling of the night before. I felt my cheeks warm.

"No, in here is better," I said. "We've got more space. Wait, though." I ran up the stairs, grabbed the cushions from the sofa in the TV room and carried them back down.

"Here," I said as we spread them out. "This'll be fine."

Above us, I could hear target practice going on with a vengeance. Kara was at the cathedral like she and Alex had discussed, seeing what she could find out. And meanwhile, everyone was comforting themselves by getting as good with their weapons as they possibly could.

The night before, Alex and I had managed to talk on our own a little, while the others were all getting ready for bed or watching TV. As I'd stood against the closed door of the other storeroom, I'd been very aware of how strongly Seb was in my thoughts. Even though I *knew* it was just because he was another half-angel, it still made me feel guilty.

"It's been a weird day, hasn't it?" I'd said, clearing my throat.

"Yeah, understatement," Alex had agreed. I could feel the tension in his muscles, even though we weren't touching. "God – a half-angel and the Council, both in the same afternoon."

I tried to smile. "Hey, have you got something against half-angels?"

I saw him wince as he realized what he'd said; he shook

his head at himself. "Not this one," he said, taking my hand and drawing me to him. "I like this one a lot, actually." He looped his arms around my neck, dropping his head to mine. "Look, I really am glad he's here. I just want you to be safe, Willow."

And all I'd wanted to do was hold him as tightly as I could. I'd hesitated, still worried about angel burn. Sometimes, like when I'd kissed him earlier, I thought I must be going insane to even be thinking about it; other times, the fear was an ocean of ice inside me. Then Alex had pulled me gently to his chest, and I'd given in to it. We'd stood against the wall holding each other for a long time, while the rest of the world faded away. Nothing else seemed to matter, apart from being in Alex's arms.

Now, sitting in the basement exercise room with Seb, I was desperate to get some answers about what had been happening with my angel. Perversely, she seemed to have calmed down a little since I'd met him, but I was still so aware of her, there inside me – so conscious that I didn't know what she might do.

Seb and I settled ourselves on the large, square sofa cushions, sitting a few feet from each other. He was wearing faded jeans again, and a blue T-shirt that had a swirling white logo in Spanish. The words looked slightly crumbled, like they'd ridden through the wash too many times.

"What does your shirt say?" I asked.

He glanced down at himself as if he couldn't remember. "It's for *Cinco de Mayo* – when we threw the French out of Mexico."

"The French were in Mexico?"

"A long time ago." Seb shrugged. "I bought it at a marketplace."

I nodded, realizing how very little I knew about this country. It wasn't exactly something that was covered at school, which was sort of strange when you thought about it – Mexico was so close.

Then, still gazing at Seb, I noticed something that was different. "Hey, you shaved," I said. He looked less like a rock star today; more like an actor playing the sexy new boy at school.

He touched his jaw, looking embarrassed. "Yes – I guess it's been a while."

"I think I liked you better before," I said, studying him, and then wished I had said *anything* except that – I'd just been making conversation, but his hazel eyes looked delighted suddenly. He grinned as my cheeks flushed.

"I'll never shave again," he said.

I grimaced, aware that my face was on fire. "Seb, look – you know Alex and I are together, right? I mean – I like you, but—"

"Yes, I know that," he said quietly. "It's all right." I had the sense of some deeper emotion being buried; then Seb smiled and ran a hand over his jaw again. "But, you know – if you think not shaving would *help*…"

To say I wasn't used to boys making their interest in me so obvious – even in a humorous way – would be the understatement of the century. I wasn't even used to boys *having* any interest in me, much less ones who looked like Seb. Back in Pawntucket, I had always been Queen Weird, the outcast of the school. I opened my mouth and then closed it again, trying to think what to say.

Seb saw my discomfort, and the teasing look in his eyes vanished. "Willow, I'm only joking," he said. "I mean – yes, I *would* like to be more than friends; I'm not joking about that. But I know you're in love with Alex. If friendship is all you want, that's okay. It really is."

I shifted on the cushion. My cheeks were still warm, especially remembering what I thought I'd sensed in him the day before – the depth of his feelings towards me. Thankfully, I couldn't pick up on any sign of that now, though admittedly I didn't go looking very hard. If by some insane chance I'd been right, I seriously didn't want to know.

"Are you sure you're all right with that?" I said finally.

"Yes," said Seb. The corner of his mouth lifted. "My whole life, I've been looking for another half-angel. Believe me, I don't want to leave now, just because you haven't realized yet that you can't resist me."

My eyebrows flew up. "Yet?"

"That was a joke too," he said hastily. "I mean – well, no, I *do* hope you'll realize that someday, but—" Half laughing, he broke off and put his hand over his face, shaking his head. "Ah, *caramba,* I'm not doing very well, am I?"

Somehow I was smiling too. Seb dropped his hand. "Okay, let me start over," he said. "Willow, just to be here with you – to be your friend – that's enough, I promise."

"You're really sure?" I asked, scanning his face. "Even if friends is all we'll ever be?"

Seb's eyes were steady, without even a hint of teasing. "Yes, I'm very sure," he said. "I'll be your brother, how's that?"

He meant it. I let out a breath, relieved that he understood – and even more relieved that he still wanted to stay. "A brother sounds…really, really good, actually."

"You've got one, then," he said. "For life, if you want."

"Thanks," I said softly. And even though we'd only just met, I knew I probably *did* want that – already, I felt such a connection to Seb. Even more, I knew that I needed his help. Feeling shaky, I pushed my hair back; suddenly my words were coming out in a rush. "Seb, I've got so much I want to ask you about. I've been so worried—"

Seb had been sort of half-lying on his pillow; now he sat up, immediately concerned. "Worried?"

"More like terrified," I admitted. "Your angel. Can you feel him inside you? I mean…present, but *separate* from you. Not thinking your thoughts. Like he has a mind of his own."

He frowned, watching me. "Not for a long time," he said. "But when I was younger, I felt that."

I sat on the edge of my sofa cushion. "What happened when you were younger?"

Seb's body language was casual: one wrist on his knee; the other hand resting on the cushion, propping him up. But there was a swirl of emotion from him – and all at once I knew I was the only person in the world who he'd ever tell this to. "Maybe you saw some of this when we touched yesterday," he said. "When I was eleven, I was arrested for stealing."

"Yeah, I did," I admitted. "And that place they put you…" I trailed off.

"Here in Mexico they're called *reformatorios.*" Seb pulled a face. "They used to say to us that we should be thankful to be there – because now we could be improved."

Improved. Remembering what I'd glimpsed of the young offenders' place – running water for only two hours a day; vicious beatings; being strapped to the bed at night – my throat tightened. Irony wasn't the word.

Seb ran a fingernail along a thread in his jeans. "I saw a lot of things happen there," he said finally. "Things much worse than stealing a wallet, I think." He smiled again; there was a hard edge to it this time. "I saw a boy try to escape, and they caught him – they tied him to a tree and left him there for days. No food or water. None of us were allowed to help him."

I picked up a sudden image of this, and desperately wished I hadn't. Oh god, the boy's eyes. His face. I could hardly get the words out. "What…what happened to him?"

Seb gave a small *I don't know* motion with his hand. "After a week, he was gone. We didn't see him any more after that."

"But – is that even *legal*? How can they be allowed to do that? Couldn't you have told the police when you got out?" My voice had gone high-pitched with horror.

Seb's eyebrows shot up in surprise – and with something almost like pity, that I'd think this might be a solution. "No one would care," he said. "We were thieves and runaways – street boys, with no families."

I hugged my knees tightly, feeling shaken. Above us, I could still hear the others practising in the target range. The exercise machines around us looked weirdly ordinary, as if they belonged to a completely different life than the one Seb had been through. I supposed they did.

"How did you get out?" I asked finally.

He shrugged. "There was a loose piece of metal on my bed frame. I got it off, and sharpened it against the wall when no one was watching. It took months, but finally it was sharp enough. I threatened a guard with it, and I got out. Then I ran as fast as I could," he added, his mouth twisting. "I ran so fast I could have been in the Olympics."

I stared at him, amazed that he'd somehow held onto his sanity enough that he could joke about this, even a little bit. *I threatened a guard.* The words didn't surprise me, yet I knew what a fundamentally good person Seb was – a gentle one, even. Thinking about my own life when I was eleven, I mentally shook my head at the contrast. Even with all my problems, I'd had it so, so lucky, and I'd never even known.

"Did you hurt the guard?" I asked.

Seb shook his head. "No, he was a coward. And I think I probably looked very determined. Like I wasn't going to take no for an answer." Faint amusement crossed his face, remembering.

"Would you have hurt him?"

The amusement faded. As his eyes met mine, I knew Seb wasn't going to lie to me – that he never would. "Yes," he said quietly. "I would have done anything to get out of there. And I hated humans, back then. For what they did to each other – for what they had done to me."

My eyes went to a small scar on his arm, just where the sleeve of his T-shirt ended: a deep, dimpled hole, white against his tanned skin. About the size and shape of a cigarette burn. My heart chilled. Oh god, had they done that to him there?

Seb noticed me looking, and glanced down at the scar himself. "No – this was from my mother's boyfriend, when I was small." He shrugged; fingered the scar lightly. "My mother didn't have very good taste in men."

There was no real bitterness to his tone, though I sensed how much he hated the boyfriend. Fleetingly, I wondered about his angel father, but now didn't seem the time to ask. I swallowed. "Seb…" I couldn't finish the sentence; there were no words.

He saw my face and instant regret came over his, that he had upset me. He reached out and put his hand over mine, gripping it gently. "*Querida*, it's all right," he said. "No one has hurt me in years."

I hated it that anyone had ever hurt him at all. I squeezed his hand back and then drew away, wishing my traitor pulse hadn't skipped at his touch. "Hey, you're supposed to be my brother," I said, trying to joke. "Brothers don't hold their sisters' hands or call them *querida*."

Seb smiled, his hazel eyes starting to dance. "Yes, they do," he said. "This happens all the time."

"Well, I guess things are different in Mexico then," I said. "Because in America, no way. And I'm an American."

"But you're in Mexico now," he pointed out.

"Right. And you're saying that here, boys hold hands with their sisters and call them *sweetheart.*"

"Oh, yes. We're very friendly, we Mexicans."

I laughed then; I couldn't help it. Seb grinned. I could sense his pleasure to see me smiling again, and something stirred deep inside me, a feeling I didn't really want to analyze. I just knew I was very glad that Seb was in my life now. Aside from anything else, it felt wonderful to have a friend again – apart from Alex, I'd felt like such an outcast these last few weeks.

"So what about your angel?" I asked.

A few soft-looking brown curls were hanging over Seb's forehead; he shoved them back impatiently. "After I escaped the *reformatorio,* I went back on the streets. And for three or four months…" He shook his head. "I wasn't a person you'd want to know. I hated humans; I wanted to hurt them. All I wanted was to be pure angel, so nothing could hurt me. I got into fights all the time – I almost dared people to look at me wrong, so I could jump them. I smashed windows, I burned cars, I stole…" He fell silent, his eyes troubled. "Not a good time," he finished finally.

And all I could think was…before he went to get

improved at that place, the worst he'd ever done was pick pockets.

"Anyway, my angel didn't like this," said Seb. "Before, I never really felt him inside me. He was always just me. There when I needed him, but me."

"Yes!" I burst out. "Yes – that's exactly what it was like at first."

Seb nodded. "But then my angel saw I was going to die young if I kept on the way I was. So he was always—" He frowned in thought; reached over and pushed lightly at my arm a few times. "Like this, inside of me, day and night."

"Nudging," I said. "*Yes*. Yes, me too!" I was sitting straight up now; it felt like electricity was coursing through the room. "But Seb, what does that *mean*? Does it mean they're separate from us? That they're *not* us?"

He was shaking his head before I'd finished speaking. "No, they're us. Definitely us. I think it's like…sometimes you have two thoughts at the same time, you know? You might be thinking, I should do this thing, and at the same time you're thinking, I'm hungry, or I don't like this person – deep down, but both at the same time, do you see what I mean?"

I understood exactly. "So sometimes our angels have their own thoughts? Or they don't agree with us about something, but they're still just a part of us – like having mixed feelings about something?"

"Yes, I think so," said Seb. "That's how it is for me." He was sitting with one knee up, his arms draped loosely around it.

I told him about my angel breaking free during target practice, and he looked like he was trying not to laugh – though in a friendly way that made my tension ease. "I think your angel must want you to notice her very badly," he said mildly. "What's she nudging you about?"

I tried to think. "I don't know. This started a few weeks ago, when I felt this sort of…rush of energy." I told Seb what had happened – about the river inside me that had trickled to nothing; how I hadn't found anything when I'd gone searching. It was such a relief to finally be talking to someone about all of this that the words tripped over themselves.

Seb listened carefully, his eyebrows drawing together. "I don't know what that was," he said once I'd finished. "I've never felt anything like that before."

"Oh." I looked down at the yellow sofa cushion. The disappointment wasn't easy to bear. I'd been hoping he'd say, *Oh, that. Yes, that happens all the time.*

"But *querida*" – he caught himself with a grin – "Willow, whatever it was, your angel feels different about it than you. You need to listen to her, that's all."

I let out a breath. "She's felt so separate from me lately," I admitted. "Scary. I've thought…I don't know *what* I thought. I guess that whatever it was had…set her off, somehow, so that she can't be trusted now."

I could see that not trusting his angel had never even occurred to Seb. "She's part of you," he said simply. "She'd never do anything to hurt you. She might feel separate and nudge at you sometimes when you don't listen to her – but hurt you? No. Never."

He made it sound like my angel was pure intuition, or a conscience or something – which actually made a lot more sense than whatever ominous ideas I'd been freaking myself out over. The relief was so overwhelming I almost went limp – but I still had no idea what my angel wanted me to listen to her about. With a flash of guilt, I knew that I hadn't given her much of a chance to explain. The second she'd seemed separate from me, I'd just shoved her away and built a wall around her. No wonder she'd felt restless.

"Give me a minute," I said to Seb.

I closed my eyes and went deep within myself, reaching tentatively for my angel. She was there in a burst of light, like sunshine on crystal – my own face gazing back at me, wings glimmering. We gazed at each other. The only movement was the soft shifting of her hair, as if a slight breeze was blowing.

I'm sorry, I thought, mentally stretching my hand out to her. *Can you tell me what's wrong?*

We touched, and my muscles relaxed as the oneness

between us rushed back – our thoughts swirling together, merging again. Forgiveness, understanding. But she'd been so, so frustrated; so desperate to get me to listen to her. The dark power of the energy stream I'd felt had alarmed her greatly. And now she had a feeling something was wrong. She didn't know what; she'd looked, found nothing – but it was a constant worry she couldn't get rid of.

Frowning, I carefully searched my mind again, exploring every corner. There was nothing there that shouldn't be – genuinely, truly, nothing. *I really think it's okay,* I said to her.

She didn't respond; I could feel she wasn't convinced. Leaving her for the moment, I explained to Seb what had happened. "I don't know what to think," I finished. "She seems really positive, but I just can't feel it."

Seb's expression turned thoughtful. "No, I don't know either." Sitting up cross-legged, he held his hands out to me. "Yes? Maybe I can sense something."

I hesitated, looking at his hands.

"I'll be very brotherly," he assured me. His eyes were teasing, but they were also concerned – I knew how much he wanted to help.

"All right," I said finally.

Moving my cushion closer to him, I put my hands in his. Again there was that jolt of energy, of like touching like. His hands were warm and firm, and so reassuring as they held mine, as if just his touch could make things better. I closed my eyes, keenly aware of our two auras mingling again too, and wishing I could shut all this out. Especially the part about how good it felt – how right. I shoved the thought away almost before it formed, hating myself for even having it.

Seb's hands tightened in mine; I could sense his concentration. I tried to just drift, and not think about much at all. I kept getting snippets from him anyway, such as the fact that he'd given up smoking recently – his unconscious desire for a cigarette was coming through loud and clear. Some of what I picked up made me smile, like the stories he made up when anyone asked about his past. I didn't think he'd ever given a straight answer in his life. An opera-singing mother who took her piano with her everywhere?

And yet with me, he'd been so unhesitatingly honest.

Finally Seb let go of me, and I opened my eyes again. We were still sitting close together, our faces only a foot or so apart, and I saw that his eyes had flecks of pure gold in the green. I moved hastily back, scooting my cushion several inches away.

Seb pretended not to have noticed. "I can tell how worried your angel has been," he said, leaning back on one hand. "I didn't feel anything wrong though. Something's been bothering her, yes, but I can't see what."

I could sense my angel's puzzlement as she checked again for herself and found that what Seb had said was true: she couldn't feel what had been bothering her any more either – it was as if it had simply vanished. Or maybe it had never been there in the first place. She hesitated for a long moment within me, her wings gently stirring. I could still feel her confusion, though it was fading now to relief. Maybe she'd been mistaken, she thought at last. Because everything seemed all right now – really all right.

She was nowhere near as relieved as I was. Oh, thank god, things might actually go back to normal for me now – or at least as "normal" as being a half-angel could ever be. "It's okay," I said to Seb. "She thinks maybe it's all right now. Thank you – thank you so, so much."

His eyes were warm. "I didn't do anything. But that's good. If she's happy, there's no problem."

I crossed my legs, pulling them up to my chest. "So I wonder what the energy was that I felt? It was so strong – it just came out of nowhere. It's not something that's ever happened to you?"

"No, never. Maybe it was just – ah, I can't think of the word." Seb tapped his brow and said something in Spanish, looking frustrated.

I smiled slightly, watching him. "Do you want me to go get Alex to translate?"

At the suggestion of bringing my boyfriend down here, Seb gave me a comically incredulous look from under his hand – like, *Are you kidding?* "No, we can't take Alex away when he's teaching the others," he said in a voice so serious that I almost believed him for a second. "It would be very selfish of us. I'd feel so guilty."

"Oh. Well, we wouldn't want that."

"No. The guilt, it would keep me awake at night." Seb straightened up. "The word I'm trying to think of – it's like when something happens only once, then never again. If it happens, you're so surprised. You know? What's the word?"

"A fluke?"

"*Sí!*" His smile was like sunshine bursting through the clouds. "Maybe it was just a fluke. Just a strange thing that happened. Or, I don't know – maybe it was a *girl* half-angel thing."

Somehow "a girl half-angel thing" made me think of Alex's migraines, and the other worry of these last few days. My hands clenched in my lap. I cleared my throat. "Listen, what about…what about hurting other people?" I asked. The words didn't want to come out. "Us, I mean."

Seb's eyebrows came together. "I don't think I understand."

"Do we…" I took a deep breath. "Do we cause angel burn to people when we touch them?"

Surprise spread over his face. "You mean hurt them, like the angels do? No, I don't think so. I've touched a lot of people – holding their hand, giving them readings – and I think I'd have seen."

"I know, I've given a lot of readings too," I said. "But what I've been worried about is whether it might be different for us. The angels only have to touch someone's aura for a few seconds, but maybe with us it's a matter of how close we get to someone physically. I mean...close like when you're in a relationship." My face was a forest fire. I hoped he got what I meant, because I really didn't want to be any more explicit.

"Oh." Seb rubbed the back of his neck. Yes, he'd gotten it. "No, I've never noticed that."

Suddenly I knew he'd had a lot more opportunities to notice it than I had, and I felt my face blaze even hotter. "I'm sorry, I'm not trying to pry—"

He dropped his hand. "You're not prying," he said, though he still looked a little embarrassed. "I'll tell you anything you want to know."

I tried to push my own embarrassment aside and think where to start with all this. Or how to even word it. "Well – did you ever notice any of your girlfriends getting sick? Or damaged, like from the angels?"

"No, never," he said firmly. "I would never have touched any girl in my life if I'd thought I was hurting her."

"And have there…been a lot?"

He grimaced, scraping a hand through his hair. "Not *that* many, but – well, more than I like to tell you," he admitted. I could sense he wished the answer was different. "Not for a long time, though," he added.

"Why not?" The words came out without thinking. Seb was so good-looking – it was hard to imagine he couldn't have any girl he wanted.

He hesitated as he regarded me; again I caught that feeling of something being buried deeply. "I don't know," he said finally. "Always being with the wrong girl…I guess it made me feel lonelier than being by myself, after a while."

A pang went through me. Alex was the only boy I'd ever been involved with, but it still seemed like Seb and I had something in common. I'd been lonely for so much of my life too.

"I get that," I said softly. "I really do."

His smile was rueful. "I wish I'd figured it out sooner," was all he said.

I was aware of what a personal conversation this was, when we'd only met the day before – but it didn't feel that strange somehow. And if Seb had had a lot of experience with girls, and he'd *never* noticed anything like what I was talking about…

Seb was still studying me. "This is about you and Alex, isn't it?" he said. "You're worried about him; I can feel it."

"He got a migraine a week or so ago," I confessed. "And he's been getting headaches a lot. I've been so scared it's because of me; that I've been hurting him just by being with him."

Seb had closed his eyes, shaking his head at himself. He half laughed. "Ah, *caramba*. I gave the wrong answer, didn't I? Can I change it? Yes, we cause terrible harm to humans. You should break up with Alex right now, so that you don't injure him. Do you want me to go upstairs with you, and help you tell him? As your brother, I would be very happy to do this."

"Seb!" I almost laughed, though I still wasn't totally convinced that I didn't have anything to worry about. "So...you're really sure?" I asked. "You never noticed any of your girlfriends getting migraines, or headaches, or anything like that?"

Seb's expression turned gentle. "Yes, I'm sure. Willow, we're half-human – why would our energy hurt them?" He touched my hand again briefly, his fingers comforting on mine. "Please don't worry any more, *querida*. It's all right, I'm certain of it."

Relief. Soaring, total relief. "Oh, thank god," I whispered. "I've been so scared these last few days that I've been hurting him, and hating myself for not saying anything. I've felt like such an awful person—"

"You?" Seb gave a sudden grin. "No, you couldn't be

awful if you tried. You're much too sweet for that."

"*Sweet?*" I made a face, laughing despite myself. "I am not."

"Oh, yes. I've seen this about you from the start. You like to help people; you care about them a great deal. You're very—" Seb stopped, regarding me for a long moment. "Special," he finished finally.

I winced at the look in his eyes. "Seb—"

"I'm saying this only as a brother," he added firmly. "Brothers are allowed to say these things sometimes."

I couldn't help smiling, even though I was shaking my head at him. I wasn't hurting Alex – I really wasn't. It felt like a million sunrises inside me. "So, you didn't finish telling me what happened with your angel," I said after a pause. "Did he keep nudging at you until you listened to him?"

Before Seb could answer, I heard the basement door open. "Hey," called Alex's voice down the stairs. "We're about to go out."

I scrambled up from my cushion and went up the stairs to him. He'd been checking his gun, and was tucking it back into his holster. "Another hunt?" I asked, watching apprehensively.

Alex nodded. He had on his white thermal T-shirt with the red plaid shirt hanging open over it, and just looked so…gorgeous. "Yeah, I thought I'd take them out again –

maybe to a different park this time, so the angels can't start to predict what we're doing."

I rested back against the wall, half conscious of Seb sitting just below. "Be careful," I said in a low voice. "Please."

He smiled and touched my face. "I'll be fine; don't worry. I've been doing this for years. They've just got to get some more practice, that's all." A cloud crossed his features, and I knew he was thinking about the Council; hoping Kara could find out what was happening – otherwise it wouldn't even matter how much practice the AKs got. "Anyway, how's it going?" he asked, nodding down the stairs.

"Really well," I said. "I mean, we haven't started the aura work yet, but…Alex, he's helping me a lot." I stopped, realizing that I couldn't say much without going into a long explanation; I hadn't told Alex about how worried I was in the first place.

"Good," said Alex. "I'm glad." And I knew he really was, though it was clear Seb still wasn't his favourite person. He smiled, and brushed a strand of my hair back. "Got to make sure the guy earns his keep, at least."

Earns his keep. Was I even earning mine? I tried to smile back, but suddenly it wasn't easy.

"What?" said Alex.

"Nothing. It's just…here I am, hanging out in the

house with Seb, while you and the others are going on another hunt, maybe risking your lives—"

"Stop," he said firmly. He reached for my hand; gripped it reassuringly. "What you're doing here is just as important, Willow – I mean it." He hesitated, looking down at our linked fingers. "And…I sort of wanted to talk to you about that. Now that the Council's here in the city, I think maybe it's better if—"

"I know," I broke in. "Don't worry, I'd already decided. I'm not coming on any more hunts until I've learned how to change my aura." Though the thought of sitting at home while the others put themselves in danger grated at me, I couldn't justify the threat that my half-angel energy posed, not when I knew it was possible to change it.

Alex nodded, looking conflicted. I could feel his relief that I wouldn't be going out with them for the time being – but at the same time it bothered him that the team hadn't really accepted me yet, and we both knew this wouldn't help. Just then we heard the sound of the others, congregating in the kitchen.

"Better go," he said. Leaning forward, he kissed me and I linked my arms around his neck, relishing the warmth of his lips on mine. It felt like it had been years, not days, since I'd been able to kiss him without worrying; I had a burst of relieved pleasure that was almost giddy. Now that I knew everything was okay, all I wanted was to be alone with Alex – really alone, for as long as possible.

"See you later," he said when we drew apart. The look in his blue-grey eyes melted me. He kissed my nose. "Love you."

"Love you too." I stood against the wall, watching as he walked back through the firing range and disappeared into the kitchen. The sound of voices, the door opening and closing. My happiness faded and I sighed, hoping they were going to be okay. It felt so strange, Alex going someplace without me – this was almost the only time it had happened since we'd first met.

He'll be fine, I told myself. *If anyone knows what he's doing, it's Alex.*

Behind me, I heard Seb get up and move to the bottom of the stairs. "They've gone out?"

"Yeah, they've gone on a hunt." I jogged down the stairs, brushing past Seb as he stood there, and started gathering up the cushions from the floor. "So I guess we can go upstairs to the TV room, where it's comfier."

Seb took the cushions from me, tucking them easily under his arm. "Yes, that sounds better."

Upstairs, we put the cushions back on the sofa and then went into the kitchen to get some Cokes. There was always plenty of stuff like that in the house – half the supplies in the boxes upstairs were things like canned food and drinks;

the other half was ammo and combat gear. It was like Juan had been preparing for a siege.

I handed Seb a Coke and then kept the fridge door open a second, peering in. "Do you want anything to eat?"

He made a face as he popped the Coke open. "The food here is very…American," he said.

I glanced at him over the fridge door. "What? Like what?"

Seb shrugged. "Cheetos, Doritos, stuff like that," he said, leaning against the counter. I saw the muscles of his chest flex under his T-shirt and looked quickly back into the fridge again. *What is* wrong *with you?* I demanded of myself, irritated. *You're in love with Alex – why are you even noticing Seb?*

"Doritos are sort of like Mexican food though, aren't they?" My voice sounded thankfully normal.

Seb laughed, and picked up a bag from the counter. "Willow – they're *orange*," he said, holding them up. "And the Cheetos are also orange. They're both bright, bright orange." He shuddered. He had a point, actually.

I laughed too, and felt my tension ease. "Okay, I admit the nacho cheese Doritos probably aren't very Mexican," I said, still scanning the fridge. There wasn't much in there – the guys all ate like horses, so that we didn't have leftovers very often. "I meant the plain ones, that you eat with salsa."

"Maybe a little," Seb conceded, tossing the bag back onto the counter.

I closed the fridge door and grabbed a bag of chocolate-chip cookies from the counter behind him. "Here – *everyone* likes chocolate-chip cookies," I said, handing them to him. "Including Mexicans. And there's no orange in them."

He grinned. "You promise?"

"*Sí*, I promise."

In the TV room, I sat on the sofa. Part of me was hoping Seb would take the armchair, but he sat beside me. Not *right* beside me, but I was very conscious of him there, just a few feet away. Trying to ignore it, I kicked off my shoes and settled back in the corner of the sofa.

Seb bent over to take his sneakers off too, and I saw another scar on his forearm: a thin white slash this time, like from a knife blade, stark against his tanned skin. Time seemed to slow as I stared at it, thinking of everything Seb had told me – hating everything he'd been through.

"I wish we'd known each other when we were children," I blurted out. Immediately, I was embarrassed that I'd said it, but it was true. I wanted to go back in time somehow and just…be there for him, so that he knew he wasn't the only one of his kind.

A few loose brown curls fell over Seb's forehead as he looked up at me. He didn't seem surprised, just sort of wistful. "Yes, I wish so too," he said softly. "All my life, I've wished that." He gave a regretful smile. "But I think it would have been better if I had been with you as a boy in your home in the mountains. Not for you to have been where I was."

And for a second, all I wanted to do was hug him. I looked away and crossed my arms over my chest, ignoring the treacherous voice that was whispering *friends can hug*.

"So, you were telling me about what happened with your angel," I said, hoping that Seb wasn't picking up on any of this. God, this must be what it was like for Alex, having a psychic girlfriend.

If Seb sensed my confusion, he didn't let on. "Yes. My angel saved me, I think." He settled himself in the opposite corner of the sofa, stretching his legs out and crossing them at the ankles. The sofa was long enough so that his large boy-feet in their clean white socks weren't touching me.

I sat cross-legged as I faced him. "He saved you?"

Seb nodded. Propping an elbow on the arm of the sofa, he took a gulp of his Coke and then stretched over to put it on the coffee table. "I was in a bad fight, and I think I must have had—" He frowned and touched his head. "Concussio? How do you say it?"

"Concussion?"

"Yes." He shrugged. "I was an idiot; I'd fight with

anyone. And so I fought with someone twice my size, and he got me down and kicked me in the head. Once, twice – I don't know how many times. When I woke up, I was bleeding; I didn't know where I was. I lay there for a long time, and thought I was going to die. I didn't really care, but I was furious that a human had done this to me."

The house felt so still around us. I could see it all clearly – the angry young half-angel who'd been so badly hurt, in every way. Seb's expression was thoughtful; his body relaxed. I could tell that he had understanding for his thirteen-year-old self, but no real connection to him any more.

"Then my angel came to me," he went on. "He wasn't happy, because I'd been acting so stupid that I'd almost gotten killed. He helped me up—"

"Wait – he *helped you up*?" I stared. "Can they do that? Touch you, I mean, so that you feel them?"

"It only happened that one time," said Seb. "I don't know, I think he—" He broke off, frowning, and finally sighed in frustration. "No. I can't say what I mean in English."

"Wait, I think I know," I said slowly, remembering how the angels of the Second Wave had wanted to be seen by the masses when they first arrived, even though angels can't usually be seen except by those they're feeding from. "You mean he…changed his frequency, somehow. Slowed himself down so that he was closer to the human plane, and could touch you."

Seb lightly slapped the sofa arm. "Yes! That's exactly what I was thinking. You read my mind."

"Yeah, I guess we're both sort of good at that," I said, playing with the ring pull of my Coke. As we smiled at each other, warmth curled through me.

"So, my angel helped me up, and..." Seb paused as he remembered. "He showed me what might happen if I didn't change. Like, pictures in my head, you know? He showed me I would die – that someone would knife me in a fight, or maybe shoot me when I stole from them. But what would really kill me would be the anger. It was eating me up inside."

"You mean you saw your own future? I've never been able to do that!"

"No, I can't, either. This was just a warning." Seb fell quiet, his eyes still in that other time. He took another sip of his Coke; put it back on the table. "And so I looked at these pictures of how I might die, and then I knew – the only thing I wanted was to find another of my kind. It's all I've ever wanted, my whole life. When I was a young boy on the streets I was always looking, but after I escaped from the *reformatorio* I hated the world so much that I forgot. So then I thought, to hell with humans; I don't care about them enough even to be angry at them any more –

I'm going to find someone like me, no matter what."

I hugged a faded throw cushion, imagining it all. I knew what came next from what I'd seen in him yesterday – the years of searching, up and down the country. "I'm glad you found me," I said after a pause. "Seb, I really am – I'm so glad. I've been lonely too."

"I know," he said softly, studying my face like he was memorizing every detail. "I feel as if…I've known you for ever. The whole time I was searching, I always knew how much we needed each other."

He was so right that tears came to my eyes. I couldn't help myself this time, and I sat up, clearing my throat. "Seb, can I – I mean, don't take this the wrong way or anything, but—"

Understanding came over his face; he sat up too, swinging his legs forward. "Come," he said in a quiet voice. "A brother can hug his sister, yes?" He held his arm out to me.

I wiped my eyes. "Yeah, he can. And – I'd really like that."

I shifted towards him on the sofa and we hugged tightly for a minute. It felt so good just to hold each other – like something I'd been missing my whole life. Seb's arms around me were strong; he smelled of soap, and a sort of clean woodsy scent. I closed my eyes and pressed against him, feeling his heart beating against mine; the gentle shiver of our auras as they mingled. Seb let out a breath and dropped his head to my shoulder. "Willow…I can't tell you how I feel, to find you after so long," he whispered. "I'd stopped looking. I told myself, *You'll never find this girl; she doesn't exist.*"

I pulled away. "'This girl'? But—"

He hesitated; I noticed again the gold flecks in his hazel eyes. "I always knew it was you I was looking for," he said finally. "I always felt so strongly there was only one other half-angel: a girl my own age. Then I saw your picture, and your dream – and I knew I was right."

My dream. Feeling flustered, I looked down at the sofa, at our legs almost touching each other. I didn't even know how to explain my dream to myself, much less to Seb. Had I been reaching out to him in some way, without realizing I was doing it? I didn't know – the only thing I was sure of was that somehow we were meant to be in each other's lives.

"Why didn't you tell Alex about my dream?" I asked suddenly.

Seb looked surprised at the question. "It felt too private. Like something that's just for us."

Unfortunately, he was right. I let out a shaky breath. If Seb's feeling had been right too, and it really was *me* he'd been looking for all this time…then what did that mean? When I was in love with someone else?

"But there must be other half-angels," I said after a pause. "We can't really be the only two in existence, can we?"

"I've never seen another one," said Seb with a shrug. "Never."

For a fleeting second I wondered if Raziel had ever been to Mexico, but I knew it didn't matter if he had been. Because I was positive that Seb wasn't my half-brother, or even related to me in any way – there was no familial sense to him at all, the way I used to notice with Mom and Aunt Jo. No, Seb and I were just what we seemed – a half-angel boy and girl who had no connection to each other, beyond whatever force had somehow drawn us together.

I could tell Seb knew it too.

Neither of us spoke. I stared at Seb, taking in his high cheekbones; the beautiful shape of his mouth – and I thought, *My god, what if we really are the only two half-angels in the entire world?* My dream flew back to me again – the way he'd held out his hand to me, called me *querida* – and how all I'd wanted was to be with him, how just the thought of being apart from him, ever, had filled me with despair. And Seb *knew* I had dreamed this.

His eyes were very steady on mine. Remembering what I thought I'd sensed from him the day before, my cheeks caught fire. My dream couldn't mean what it seemed; that was all there was to it – so if Seb thought he and I were destined to be soulmates or something, he was wrong. No matter what kind of connection the two of us had, it was still Alex I was in love with – Alex who I wanted to be with for the rest of my life.

I moved away from Seb and snagged the bag of cookies from the table, busying myself with opening it. The plastic made a comforting crackling noise that filled up the silence. "You know, my dream wasn't – I don't think it meant anything," I blurted out. "Or it did, but just that you and I are really close – really good friends. Because that's all it *can* mean."

"Willow, it's okay," said Seb quietly.

Embarrassment wasn't the word; I could hardly even meet his eyes. I cleared my throat. "Listen…maybe we should start doing the aura work. All we've done so far is talk."

Seb got the hint that I really wanted the subject to change – like, yesterday. He nodded. "Yes, you're right," he said. "But first I think I should try one of these – see if there's any orange in it." Stretching across, he reached for the bag and helped himself to a few cookies.

He bit into one. There was a pause.

"Well?" I said finally.

"Maybe it's all right," he said with an uber-casual shrug. "I'll have to try again to make sure." He took another bite, chewing slowly. "Hmm. No, it's hard to tell."

My embarrassment faded a little. "Yeah, you big phoney," I said. "You just won't admit you like them."

He raised an eyebrow at me. "You need to be careful, you know," he said mildly. He gave me a warning glance as he licked a crumb from his finger. "I saw from your hand that you're very ticklish."

"Oh, now *that* is just completely unfair. I didn't get any of your weaknesses."

Seb looked smug. "Maybe you'll find out someday." And as he popped the rest of the cookie into his mouth, my tension melted away at his teasing look. It was what he'd been trying to do, I realized – make me see it was all right; that he wasn't going to pressure me, not ever. No matter what else he might hope for, Seb was my friend. He'd told me that before, and he really meant it.

"Thanks," I said, before I could stop myself.

He didn't ask what for, though I knew he knew – he just *tsk*ed and shook his head. "I don't think you'll thank me when you see what a tough teacher I am."

"Are you?" I said with a smile.

"Oh, yes. Very strict." Seb sat up, brushing his hands off. "Okay – let's get started."

That night I lay in bed in the darkness, listening to the soft sounds of sleep around me. Even with the worry about the Council, I felt happier than I'd been in a long time. I could trust my angel again; it was just me inside of me after all.

And even better, earlier that night Alex and I had slipped away to his room for half an hour and the world had fallen away into nothingness. I let out a shivering breath, hugging myself under the covers, and wished I was with him right now; that I could sleep wrapped up in his arms all night. But meanwhile, just having been close to him for a little while, without the gut-wrenching anxiety that had been chewing me up inside…well, it wasn't enough, but it was still pretty amazing.

Rolling over onto my side, my gaze fell on the small framed photo of myself when I was a little girl, peering up through the feathery leaves of the willow tree. I gently touched its frame. After I'd had a few fruitless hours of working with my aura that afternoon, Seb had finally stood up from the sofa and stretched.

"Come on, you need to take a break," he said.

"Come on where?" I asked, getting to my feet. It was a relief to stop for a little while; I hadn't really expected this to be so hard.

"There's something I need to give you."

I glanced at him in surprise – and then I understood. "Is this what I'm thinking?" I asked as we left the room.

His face was a picture of puzzled innocence. "How could I know what you're thinking? Do you think I'm psychic or something?"

"Yes, very funny."

Seb's storeroom bedroom was filled with boxes; his camp bed literally took up the only empty space, so that when we got there he had to crawl over it to grab his knapsack from where he'd stowed it on the floor. I watched from the doorway, taking in the strong lines of his back and shoulders despite myself.

There was a ragged sound as Seb unzipped the knapsack, and then he stood up and handed me my shirt and photo. His fingers seemed a little reluctant to leave them, but he smiled. "Here, these are yours. And I lied; I could tell what you were thinking," he added. "You were right."

My eyes went straight to the photo of myself and the willow tree. I'd been so sure I'd never see it again. "Thank you," I said softly. Then I gave a small laugh, clutching its frame. "You know, it's so funny – this photo keeps getting stolen and then finding its way back to me somehow."

Seb didn't say anything, but I could feel his emotion – the photo had been how he'd known he wasn't the only one of his kind after all. Looking down at my seven-year-old self, I was so glad that fate, or whatever, had led him to that Chihuahua marketplace that day.

"Thank you," I said again, and tucked it in my jeans pocket. Then I glanced at the shirt in my hand and thought of something. "Wait – you paid for these things, right? So I need to pay you back."

Seb's expression turned gravely serious. "Well, they were very expensive, you know," he said, stroking his chin. "But I'm sure we can work something out. What do you call it – a payment plan? Perhaps if we make an agreement for how much you'll pay me back each month – but no, we need to think about interest, too—"

He broke off with a grin as I started laughing. "Okay, okay," I said. "Why don't I just say, 'thank you very much'?"

"You have said that," he said, his eyes warm. "And you're very welcome."

CHAPTER *Fifteen*

SILVER TRAIL, COLORADO, WAS A small mining town high in the Rockies. The place had had a heyday once, complete with several brothels and saloons – now, its silver depleted, it was home mostly to artists and people who wanted to get away from it all. There were also, Raziel believed, several llama farms, though thankfully he hadn't encountered one. The field he was currently examining appeared to have had cows in it at some point, though. He stepped carefully as they walked, surreptitiously checking the bottoms of his shoes at times.

"See, we could have the school here – and maybe a

library or something nearby," said the man, motioning around him. He was named Fred Fletcher, and his round face was flushed with sincerity.

Raziel had almost cancelled this meeting, but decided it might take his mind off the news about the Council he'd gleaned from Willow's thoughts two days before – with not a single word from Charmeine meanwhile. Not to mention that there was another half-angel in the world; he'd barely even begun to get his head around the implications of *that*. The boy's energy as experienced by Willow hadn't rung any particular bells for him, though he'd dearly love to know who the father was – it could be a useful little piece of blackmail material if he ever found out.

Raziel took out his phone again as Fred continued to talk. Nothing from Charmeine. Obviously this was what she'd tried to tell him – that the Council was in Mexico City weeks ahead of schedule, at a totally different place than planned. He could sense she was still alive, at least, so presumably their alliance hadn't been discovered. But what was going on?

"So that was my idea, Mr. Raziel, sir," Fred summed up finally. "Because you see, as wonderful as it is for people to pledge themselves to the Church and live there, not everyone can do that – lots of us are just as devout, but have families, y'see."

"Yes, naturally," said Raziel absently. He linked his hands behind his back, scanning the frosty fields that sparkled in the late afternoon sunlight, with the Rockies a dusky purple rising up behind them. Forcing himself to focus, he saw that Jenny was right. It wasn't a bad idea at all. Camp Angel: a community where entire families could live in honour of the angels, with schools, a church, a library devoted to angelic works – everything.

"We could have them all across the country," he said, thinking out loud.

Fred's face lit up. "Really? You like my idea that much, sir?"

"It has definite potential," allowed Raziel. Since the dramatic Second Wave TV footage, the demand for all things angel was exploding. A gated community where families could purchase homes and enrol their children in schools devoted to the angels would take off like wildfire.

And as he'd thought before, the idea would allow for another possibility, one he'd been mulling over for some time – something that, if the Council knew about it, he was sure would cement whatever plans they might now have in place for him. It didn't exactly go along with their vision of angels not giving into their baser urges.

"Yes, I'd like to go ahead," he decided. "I'll be in touch soon to discuss the building work." Though everything had now been cast into uncertainty, Raziel still held out hope that soon there wouldn't be a Council to worry about. Meanwhile, in the same spirit of reckless defiance that had caused him to say too much on TV, he refused to put his various schemes on hold.

Fred seemed almost incoherent with gratitude and excitement; he stammered his thanks non-stop as they made their way back across the fields. "Think nothing of it," said Raziel, shaking his hand when they reached his black BMW. "You have the angels' gratitude."

One of the angels' gratitude, anyway. Grimly, Raziel checked his phone again as he got in his car.

For distraction on the drive back to Denver, he found himself exploring the psychic link with Willow once more. When both she and Seb, the half-angel boy, had gone looking for the spark of Raziel's energy – even if they hadn't known that's what they were looking for – he'd cloaked it even further, putting so many shields and disguises in place that even a pure angel would have struggled to find it. Now Willow's angel self seemed puzzled by her former fears, and Raziel was free to wander about the girl's mind without causing even the least misgiving. Willow's own spark of energy within him remained unsuspected by her, which was fortunate: if she ever stumbled on the risks to humanity that destroying the Council now posed, the Angel Killers would never go ahead with the attack.

Willow was currently talking to Seb, trying to learn

how to disguise her aura's colours. It had been news to Raziel that this was even possible. The boy seemed unusually gifted with auras – though who knew what "usual" might be when it came to half-angels.

Steering his way down the mountain roads, a considering almost-smile came over Raziel's face as he listened to Willow's thoughts and feelings. At first he'd told himself he was only delving to find out what was going on with the Angel Killers, but now he had to admit that his daughter's mental processes had become strangely addictive to him – like one of those reality TV shows humans loved so much. He'd never have guessed any progeny of his could be so *nice*. The idea was as alien as having a daughter at all. Raziel had spent days looking for some kind of edge to Willow – the angle from which she operated. There was none, unless it was her love for Kylar, or her desire to help others.

Yet she was no doormat – the girl had a steely strength that Raziel was sure came from him. Miranda had been beautiful, but a limp dishrag of a woman. In short, Willow was a worthy adversary, which irrationally pleased him. If he had to have something as base as a daughter, he at least wanted her to have some wits about her before he put her to death.

Even so, Raziel was deeply thankful no one suspected he was the father. His mind went back to the day he'd first woken up, and his meeting with the Council in the cathedral conference room: their expressionless faces that never seemed to smile or frown. They'd brought up the half-angel, of course – it had been almost the first thing they'd thrown at him.

"We Twelve have tried to find her psychically but can't; her energy is once-removed from ours." Isda's grey eyes had been as impassive as when she'd called for the traitors to be brought out. "How was she able to get into the cathedral and then escape again, Raziel? Exactly what kind of security do you have here?"

Raziel had gritted his teeth, but kept his tone mild as he explained about his traitorous human assistant. He could feel the Twelve's minds craning towards each other; undercurrents of thought that he couldn't catch swirled about the room.

That's not good enough, said someone. The words weren't spoken aloud; the meeting had apparently shifted to the psychic level, which was always a bad sign. If Raziel hadn't already had psychic defences in place, he would have slammed them down at that moment, like a castle portcullis.

The voice became several voices, all communicating with him at once. *This kind of sloppy work isn't acceptable, Raziel. The girl should have been destroyed weeks ago. Who's the father? How was this even able to happen?*

Raziel had managed to keep the surface of his thoughts concerned, wanting to help. Far below, his mind was ticking away. *I have no idea,* he replied. *The girl's existence is obviously a fluke – believe me, I'm as concerned as you are.*

We're relieved to hear you share our concerns, said Isda's voice. Isda herself was leaning silently back in her seat, giving away nothing. Other mental voices chimed in as she continued: *Because, as you know, we have never approved of angel–human relationships. It's unacceptable for angels to demean themselves in this manner.*

Yes, I'm aware you believe that, said Raziel smoothly. *But as newcomers to this world, you have to understand it's quite an ingrained thing by now – traditional, if you like.*

There was a further cooling of the room's atmosphere. *You've spent far too long here, if you think that makes it in any way acceptable,* chided the many voices in his head. *We are angels; we do not cavort with pigs in the dirt.* He could feel a few of them beginning to tendril about, searching for anything interesting, and he put up a few extra defences, retreating deep into the recesses of his mind.

Moderation is the key, Raziel, continued the mental chorus. Every face in the room was stony; he was uneasily reminded of the dozens of angels exploding in mid-air. *You'd better remember that if you want to keep your position here.*

Now anger touched him again as he pulled into the cathedral parking lot; how dare they have sat there and threatened him in his own cathedral? Striding back into his office, Raziel felt a smug satisfaction at the sight of Jenny, remembering that their liaison had begun the same evening the Council had left. After several weeks, she was almost as lovely as ever – though she looked more tired these days, and had developed a nagging cough. Raziel shrugged as he sat down at his desk. Perhaps it might be time for a new assistant soon. If so, there'd be no limit of enthusiastic volunteers.

Still no word from Charmeine. With another restless glance at his phone, Raziel tossed it to one side and brought up his emails.

His forehead furrowed at one of the title lines: *Some Information You Ought to Know.* As he scanned the message, his eyebrows shot up. Now, *this* was interesting: it was from the security guard who'd been stationed at the cathedral's back door when the Second Wave arrived. Raziel regarded the words on the screen thoughtfully.

…The day of the attack, she was one of the ones who brought in Willow Fields. I'm sure it was her this morning, even though her hair was different. She showed me a badge and started questioning me about that terrorist guy who came running in. She sure seemed anxious to find him. She gave me a card and said to get in touch day or night if I thought of where he might have gone. I haven't told the police yet, I just feel better going to an angel with this information…

The phone did a vibrating dance on his desk. Charmeine. Raziel lunged forward, snatching it up. "What's going on?" he demanded.

"I'm fine, thank you for asking," said Charmeine's voice, sounding weary. "I'm in Mexico City. I don't know if you heard about it from your contacts or not, but the Council came here early, with hardly any warning."

Raziel didn't correct her assumption that his communications with the Angel Killers went both ways. "I've known for two days!" he gritted out. "I've been going mad, waiting to hear from you – what happened? Did they find out there was a security leak?"

She sighed. "Yes – our darling little Luis. He let slip to a woman in the office how curious his girlfriend is about the Council, and that he'd promised to get her and some friends in for a private audience."

Raziel groaned aloud; remembering the earnest face he'd seen in Charmeine's thoughts, he could just picture it. The warning not to tell anyone about Kara must have worn off in the time that had passed since Charmeine's encounter with him. Or else the lad had been so dizzy from angel burn he'd forgotten he wasn't supposed to talk.

"Anyway, the woman told the preacher, who went straight to the Council," went on Charmeine. "Apparently there'd always been a contingency plan in place. They switched to it just to be on the safe side."

"The Twelve didn't get hold of Luis, did they?" asked Raziel warily.

"*No*, they didn't. Do you think I'd still be around talking to you if they had? He'd gone to visit his family for the weekend; by the time they figured it out, I'd whisked him away."

Raziel's shoulders slumped with relief. If Luis had been turned over to the Council, they'd have seen what had happened in seconds. "So what did you do with him?"

She snorted. "What do you think? I wasn't going to keep him as a pet."

He nodded to himself; Charmeine might be maddening at times, but she never balked at necessities. Something about her tone worried him, though. "*Are* you all right?" he asked abruptly.

Charmeine sighed. "Yes, I suppose. It's just...this isn't easy, Raz. They delve me almost every day, to make sure I'm still compliant. It's draining, having to keep them psychically at bay and act like nothing's wrong. But I'll keep holding out, don't worry. It's only for a few more weeks."

"Do *I* have a few more weeks?" he asked bluntly. "Or are they going to call me down there and execute me anyway?"

There was a pause. "I don't know," said Charmeine finally. "They're planning some kind of response to your interview soon, but I'm not sure exactly what – they want to make you squirm for a while longer. I do know they'd prefer to take care of you in your own cathedral; they feel it's only fitting. If you lie low, you might be okay for now."

Raziel nodded, grimly hoping she was right. Before the Council had a chance to come for him personally, the tables would have turned.

"Anyway, they're pretty preoccupied with their own plans at the moment," added Charmeine.

Raziel's chair squeaked as he leaned back with a frown, remembering the images he'd seen in her mind. "They're still going ahead with that?"

She gave a short laugh. "Have you been to Mexico City lately? The angels here aren't exactly an advertisement for behaving with decorum. The Twelve are more concerned about our 'baser instincts' than ever. They're going to link with the energy here first, calming it down, then spread out to all the other places in the world where they think things are out of control."

Raziel's gaze narrowed at a painting on the wall. If the Twelve's energies were linked with those of Mexico City, and then the Twelve were destroyed…he gave a mental shrug. All right, so the Mexican capital would definitely take some damage; it could even be levelled. As for the world's other angelic "hot spots", who knew? The kind of long-range energy work the Council was planning wouldn't be instantaneous; maybe it wouldn't have had time to fully take effect. Thankfully, at the rate humans bred, the angels' food supply being curtailed wasn't really an issue either way.

He could almost hear Charmeine coming to the same conclusions; her identical mental shrug. "Anyway, we've got to get the new information to your little band of thugs," she said. "And it can't be someone that close to the Council again; I only barely got to Luis in time. Should I just give it to them myself?"

"They can see auras," pointed out Raziel.

"So? I'll pretend to be a rogue. They were all pally with Nate, right? I'll just put on my sanctimonious, holier-than-thou face."

Raziel clicked a silver pen open and shut as he considered it. Though the entire angel community knew of the rogues' mass execution, the Angel Killers did not – and he knew from Willow's thoughts that Kylar had once had hopes of joining forces with them. But remembering how the young assassin had refused to simply obey orders and kill Willow when he'd been told to, the idea made him uneasy nonetheless.

"No," he decided. "Kylar can get too suspicious – the last thing we need is him poking around in things. We need to find a way to get him the information so he can trust it." Recalling the email he'd been reading, he brought it up on the screen again. A slow smile grew across his face.

"I might have an idea," he said. "Leave it with me."

"Not too long," cautioned Charmeine; he could hear her tension. "It makes me nervous, not even having a plan in place. I'll call you as soon as I can get away again."

After they hung up, Raziel wrote several emails; a few were from anonymous accounts. Finally he hit *Send* on the last one, pleased with himself. A week or two was all it would take, he was sure of it – there was no way she'd be able to resist the lure he'd just cast. Once in Mexico City, she'd be the perfect liaison between themselves and Kylar, even if she thought her role there was completely different. And far less expendable, once she'd served her purpose.

Turning back and forth in his chair, Raziel allowed himself to daydream about what it would be like if his gamble paid off, and the assassination meant only the deaths of the Twelve. On the whole, angels were conservative beings. Once they got over the shock of the Council being gone, he didn't think he'd encounter a serious challenge to his leadership – just lots of angels asking for positions in his new reign. The thought made him smile. He had so many plans for this world.

The newest, Camp Angel, was particularly exciting. Raziel had long wished there was a way angels could savour the energy of all humans, not just the ones who'd reached some semblance of maturity. The energy of childhood was so particularly delicious, though of course it wasn't really the done thing: to feed on too many children would soon spell the angels' own destruction. But with families encased behind gated communities, he could keep track of exactly who was being fed from – and so with careful management, angels would be able to indulge their tastes regardless of their victims' ages.

Like a veal farm, thought Raziel in satisfaction. And remembering the Council's admonition to him about the importance of moderation, he laughed out loud.

CHAPTER *Sixteen*

ALL KARA WAS ABLE TO glean from eavesdropping at the cathedral was that, yes, the Twelve were here for three weeks, but everything about their stay was top-secret; hardly anyone in the Church offices knew more than that. So, after some research on the internet, Alex had made an appointment at an insurance company based on the Torre Mayor's fifty-fourth floor – one floor from its top.

He'd taken the Metro, then walked. The Torre Mayor was the tallest building in Mexico, and looked it, soaring up over its surroundings. Approaching from the Paseo de la Reforma, Alex saw that the half-cylinder of green glass was only the front of the building – its back was a tan, rectangular slab. The entrance – a graceful arch, several storeys high – mirrored the half-moon shape at the building's top; slim grey columns marched across it.

Going in, Alex had found himself in a lobby with a slanting glass ceiling overhead. Like Kara had said, there were scanners in place; employees passing through briefly touched their passes to them. "Richard Singer," said Alex to a receptionist at a glass-topped desk. "I've got an appointment with Prima Life."

No flicker of suspicion; the woman made a phone call to verify, then pushed a clipboard at him to sign in. Alex took the temporary pass she gave him and went through the scanners. As he did, he noted the several cameras that were tucked away in various corners, watching his every move.

Going online, the team had found out quite a few things about the Torre Mayor: apart from being extremely secure, it was the most earthquake-resistant building in the world – it could withstand up to a level *nine* on the Richter scale. There'd been no floor plans to be found though, not anywhere online. But while it wasn't mentioned on the Torre Mayor's website, they'd found a reference on someone's blog that said its top floor – right under that slanted half-moon – had high-security VIP suites and meeting rooms.

In the elevator there'd been another camera, and an

attendant who asked him what floor he wanted. "Fifty-five," said Alex, just to see what would happen.

The man's eyebrows had knitted together as he checked Alex's pass. "Sorry, *Señor* – you need a special card for that."

Alex feigned confusion, taking out the piece of paper from his pocket where he'd scribbled down the details of the meeting. "Sorry, I meant fifty-four," he said, putting it away again. As the elevator hummed upwards, he took in the keyhole beside the button for the highest floor. Okay, so what would happen if the team overpowered the attendant and got the key? But, remembering what they'd found out so far, he knew: computers ran everything here; the security staff would just stop the elevator.

The elevator reached his floor and he got off. To avoid raising suspicions any further, he actually kept the appointment – talking to an agent for half an hour about his insurance needs (he had many, apparently), while mentally scanning the floors above.

Angels, all right – more than he could count. And some of their energy was stronger than anything he'd ever encountered, hitting him like a physical slap.

On his way out, Alex had asked where the restroom was and then went wandering, keeping an innocent, slightly distracted look on his face. In a distant corner he'd found the door for the stairwell and started to push it open. A woman coming out of another office stopped him, flashing an apologetic smile. "No, no, *Señor* – don't go out this way. You can't get back into any of the floors without a code."

Alex had the heavy fire door half-open by then; glancing at the outside of it, he saw it had a digital keypad for a lock. "Sorry, wrong door," he said, smiling like a clueless *gringo* and letting it swing shut again. "Could you tell me where the restroom is, *Señora?*"

Now, standing in the target range with the team clustered around the table, Alex explained what had happened as he spread out the two blueprints he'd managed to get hold of. One showed the Torre Mayor's top floor – which unfortunately was depicted as an almost empty area; the VIP suites and meeting rooms seemed to have been added at a later date.

"The Council's definitely still up there," said Alex, tapping the plans for the top floor.

"I thought so," said Willow softly, her red-gold spikes framing her face as she took in the blueprints. She and Seb stood next to each other. Alex tried to squelch his slight irritation; though Seb had only been here two days, he already stuck to Willow like glue.

The others shifted as Willow spoke, glancing warily at the pair of them. Alex knew that half the team thought the two half-angels must have known each other before, somehow. It bothered him, but he didn't know how to combat it. He couldn't *order* them to trust Willow and Seb.

"That top floor just feels...dangerous," Willow added. She looked up at Seb, who nodded.

"It feels like a place where something will happen," he said in his quiet voice. Frowning slightly, he touched the symbol for the service elevator – then slid his finger across to the same icon on the other blueprint, which detailed the ground floor. "Here too, I think." He circled the service elevator with his fingertip.

Despite his dislike of Seb, Alex was glad to get the confirmation. The building's service elevator was accessed from the loading bays where deliveries were made. He'd already earmarked that route as the team's most likely way in: if there was a weak spot in the building's security, he was pretty sure it would be there.

Liz brushed a strand of dark hair from her pale face. "How'd you get the blueprints, anyway? Aren't they classified now, with the Council staying there?"

Alex was studying the delivery entrance that led to the bays; he felt itchy with impatience to go check it out in person. "Town hall – I told them I was a design student, interested in how the building uses that half-moon shape. And yeah, they're supposed to be, but the clerk thought it must have been a mistake." It had been a stroke of luck, though Alex knew he wouldn't like to be the clerk once the error was found out.

"Well, I found out something today too," said Kara. He glanced up; he could see her excitement. "I followed a couple of the Church secretaries at lunchtime, and got a table next to them at the cafe. The reception's still going ahead on the last afternoon of the Council's stay here, on the nineteenth. They were both hoping they'd get to go."

Alex felt his shoulders slump. Relief – that had been the one piece of information they couldn't do without. "Okay, excellent," he said. "So that's still the best time for us to break in and make our move, since we know they'll be in their angel forms during the private audiences."

"And you definitely don't think we can just get invited to the reception again?" ventured Trish.

Alex had been racking his brains for days trying to think of a way. "I don't see how, without someone on the inside helping us. No one's even supposed to know the Council's here." He massaged his eyes; he'd hardly slept these last couple of nights.

The team fell silent, digesting this. Glancing at Willow, Alex saw the sympathetic support in her gaze; it felt as if she'd reached over and squeezed his hand. She understood, if no one else did, how worried he was about all of this. Fleetingly, he wondered how the hell his father had managed it – being in charge on his own, with no one to confide in.

"So we need all the information we can get our hands on," he summed up. "Whether the same schedule for the reception is still being followed; floor plans for the VIP level; where exactly the private audiences are going to take place; any security details we can find out – anything."

Kara nodded. "The only people who'll know will be the Church officials. The preacher, maybe one or two others."

"Could Willow find out psychically?" suggested Brendan. Alex bit back the automatic *Ask her yourself.* It wasn't needed; Brendan caught himself. "I mean...could you?" he asked Willow awkwardly. "If we found out who had the information, then you'd just have to hold their hand, right?"

Willow's forehead creased. "Maybe, but like I said before, it's not instantaneous. Getting that level of specific detail would take me a while. I mean, a few minutes of really concentrating, at least."

"Yes, for me too." Seb stroked his stubbled jaw. "And even then, you don't always get what you're looking for."

"Don't you?" Willow's voice held mild surprise.

"*I* don't, no," he clarified, glancing down at her. "I get many images, but only what's on their minds. And sometimes not very specific. I hardly ever get names, things like that."

Alex could see how interested both Seb and Willow were by the fact that their psychic skills seemed to vary – if nobody else had been around, he knew they'd have spent the next hour discussing it in great detail.

Meanwhile, Kara had pulled a face at "not very specific". "Alex, what do you think? Is it worth a try?"

He brought his attention back to the plan as he considered. In the wake of the security breach Luis had caused, he'd bet money that only the Church preacher knew all the details they needed – and the man would have been taken into the angels' confidence enough to know that Willow Fields the terrorist was psychic, and worked by holding people's hands. Trying to manoeuvre the guy into a scenario where either Willow or Seb could grasp his hand and concentrate for several minutes was far too likely to raise suspicions; all the Church high-ups would be on red alert now for anything strange.

"No, we can't risk them figuring out what we're up to," he said finally. He glanced at Seb, knowing it was a long shot even as he asked. "Could you sense anything if you went into the cathedral? Willow can't go in there with all the angels around, but you'd be okay if you changed your aura."

Seb's eyebrows shot up. "You mean get security details, just from being there?" He shook his head. "I can try, but I don't think it will work – I think all I'll see is that it's a dangerous place."

That wouldn't be much of a newsflash. Alex sighed. "Okay, so we can't count on that. Kara, how easy will it be to break into the offices?"

"Not easy at all, but it sounds like it's our only hope." Kara's face held a wry expression, as if she wasn't surprised the half-angels weren't turning out to be more useful. She picked up a pencil and started sketching on a spare piece of paper.

"Okay, here's the cathedral, with the tabernacle beside it. The tabernacle still has a small chapel people can use – the new office area is behind that. You reach it from inside the cathedral, from this door." She darkened a line with the pencil. "The information should be on the preacher's computer or in his files. Unfortunately, digital keypads seem to be in vogue – they've added one to the door now. So if we're getting in there, I'll have to find the code for it somehow."

"Maybe a video camera?" suggested Wesley. As everyone turned to look at him, his cheeks darkened; he went on, his voice gruff. "I mean – hundreds of tourists take videos in there every day. So we could use the zoom lens to focus on the door whenever someone's punching in the code."

Alex nodded. "Yeah, good idea. Nice one, Wes." Kara was busy adding more details to the cathedral and office area – hallways, another few exits. He propped his hands on the table as he studied the home-made map. "How accurate is this? Can we get actual floor plans showing the office area, or is that classified too now?"

"Extremely classified, now that the cathedral is Church of Angels central, Mexican style," said Kara gloomily, putting down the pencil. "This isn't too bad, I think. Luis showed me around the office area once."

"No, it's not too bad." Seb stood scanning the map. "You've missed some things though."

Kara gave him a cool look. "Like what?"

He picked up the pencil. "There are doors here, and here." The lines he drew were precise, unhesitating. "This one's very small, easy to miss. And I don't know if it's still there, but in the tabernacle there used to be a fire exit here. You could go out through it, but not in."

Alex had straightened up, watching carefully. "Are you sure? How do you know all this?"

Seb shrugged and tossed the pencil aside. "The *catedral* was a good place to pick pockets. All of us on the street knew every inch of it."

It wasn't a surprise to Alex; Willow had told him a little about Seb's past when he'd asked her. He hadn't mentioned it to the others though. Now Trish and Liz stared at Seb speechlessly; the guys all gave each other *Did you just hear what I heard?* looks.

Kara shot Alex a glance that said she held him personally

responsible for this. "So you're telling us you were a pickpocket," she said.

"Oh, yes," said Seb mildly, pushing back his loose curls. "For many years. When I wasn't breaking into houses."

Alex had a sudden feeling Seb was enjoying this – that the guy was perverse enough to delight in making everyone even more suspicious of him than they already were. From what Willow had said, he hadn't even broken into houses that often; it'd been mostly for a few months when he was thirteen, or something. Naturally, Seb did not volunteer this information.

"A thief," summed up Sam, his broad face creased with disgust. "Now, why doesn't *that* surprise me? Alex, did you know this?"

"Shut up, Sam." Alex leaned against the table, watching Seb. "Do you think you could help us get into the offices?"

Seb gave a one-shouldered shrug. "I don't know. My skills weren't very…" He glanced down at Willow beside him; she seemed to sense the word he wanted.

"Subtle," she volunteered.

"No, not very subtle. Just smash the window, grab some things and go, you know? As much as I could carry." Alex managed not to roll his eyes at Seb's guileless tone. Yes, he was definitely enjoying this. Willow seemed to think so too; her mouth had pursed, as if she was trying not to laugh.

"Well, that's not very helpful here, unfortunately," said Kara stiffly. "Alex, believe me – we're only going to get one chance at that office, and it'd better be a good one."

The larger map of the Torre Mayor was still spread out, sleek and professional next to Kara's hand-drawn lines. Looking at it, Alex thought he'd find some way to get the team in there if it was the last thing he ever did – but without more information, it wouldn't be much better than a suicide mission.

"Okay," he said finally. "I'll keep checking out the Torre Mayor, in between training the team. Kara, I want you to start casing the cathedral. Figure out the routine there, and find a way for us to break into the offices – we'll get you a video camera like Wesley said. But we've got to know what we're going to be walking into."

"Will do," said Kara. Glancing at Seb, she hesitated, her reluctance clear. Like the others, she hadn't warmed to him; Alex doubted that his little revelation just now had helped. "Seb, if you wouldn't mind – would you go over the map with me, see if I've missed anything else?"

From the amused spark in Seb's eyes, he knew exactly how much Kara didn't want to be dealing with him. "Yes, I'd be happy to."

Everyone started dispersing, heading off to the kitchen or the TV room. Alex gave Willow a wry look as they walked across the firing range. "The guy doesn't like making things easy for himself, does he?"

Willow glanced over her shoulder as Seb and Kara bent over the map. "He just…is who he is, I guess."

Alex could hear the unmistakable note of fondness in her voice. Unbidden, a conversation he'd had with Kara that morning came rushing back. She'd been standing at the kitchen counter, long legs crossed at the ankle. Blowing on her coffee, she'd said, "Sooo…how are things going?"

His eyes had narrowed at her arch tone. "What do you mean, 'how are things going?'"

Kara's shrug had been elaborately casual. "Willow and Seb seem awfully close already, don't they? They're always talking whenever I see them."

They were always talking whenever Alex saw them, too. "They're friends, that's all," he'd said shortly as he took a teaspoon out from the drawer.

"You said he wants more though. And, boy, he's really good-looking, isn't he? Those eyes, and that sexy stubble. Willow has to have noticed."

Alex had made a face before he could stop himself. Earlier, he'd seen Willow's cheeks go pink when Seb had come out of the shower room wearing only his jeans, his chest slightly damp. And though her cheeks probably would have gone just as pink if it had been Sam or one of the others, Alex still couldn't help wishing that the only other half-angel in the world had been short, with acne.

"I'm glad you've got the hots for Seb," he'd told Kara coldly, jamming a piece of bread in the toaster. "Do you actually have a point you're trying to make?"

She'd given him a level look. "Just be careful, okay? I don't want to see you get hurt."

The genuine concern in her voice had grated on Alex. It still did; he pushed the memory away. He and Willow had reached the stairwell by then, where it was relatively quiet for now. She reached for his hand. "Alex, look – I know you and Seb haven't really hit it off, but he's a good person, okay? And he's my friend."

"Yeah, but—" Alex broke off; he'd been about to say, *But you know the guy's in love with you, right?* It was completely obvious; Seb couldn't take his eyes off her.

"What?" said Willow.

"Nothing," said Alex finally. He shook his head, irritated with himself. "Sorry, it's just all this Council stuff – I guess it's getting to me. Yeah, I know you're friends. I'm fine with it."

She seemed to smile despite herself. "What – really?"

He smiled too. The love in her eyes was so obvious that he felt like a jerk for caring about Seb at all. "Yeah, really," he said. "I'm glad that you've got another half-angel to talk to. Anyway, how's the aura training going?"

Willow's green eyes sparkled suddenly. She stood on a step so that she was taller than he was, and wrapped her arms around his neck. "I'll tell you if you kiss me."

He grinned in surprise, slipping his hands around her waist. "I don't know, you drive a hard bargain…all right, I give in."

She trailed her fingers over the back of his neck as they kissed; Alex shivered, pulling her closer. "Maybe we could sneak away into your room later," she whispered against his mouth.

"Maybe we could just spend the rest of our lives in there, and never come out again," he murmured back. Nothing sounded better. His lips travelled down to her neck, lingering against her warm skin; he couldn't help smiling. "And don't get me wrong, I definitely like the idea – but you always used to be so worried about us not having enough privacy in there."

"I still am," she said faintly. "But Alex, I just—" She pulled away to look into his eyes; he saw deep happiness in her expression. "I just really want to be close to you. I mean—" She touched his cheek and smiled ruefully. "Well, as close as we can be, with a dorm full of people just outside."

Which unfortunately wasn't as close as either of them wanted – but was a lot better than nothing. "Oh man, it's a date," said Alex, drawing her back against him. Then he stopped as his responsibilities crashed over him like a freight train. They had less than three weeks now. *Three weeks.* He glanced tensely towards the range. "But I should probably head over to the evening service at the cathedral first and check the place out; then look over the blueprints for the Torre Mayor again, see if I've missed anything—"

Willow put a finger over his lips. "It's okay."

He made a face. "No, it really isn't. You deserve—"

"I deserve to be with you, and I am. Always. Alex, it's fine – this is so important, don't you think I realize that?" He could hear her frustration though, and knew how much she hated it that she couldn't go to the angel-filled cathedral with him and try to pick up something psychically. From the moment they'd met, they'd been a team – having to sit at home with her half-angel aura must gnaw at her.

"Of course I know you realize it," he said softly. "God, if anyone in the world understands what's at stake, it's you." He tucked back a short strand of her hair and smiled. "So, have I earned the right yet to know how the aura work is going?"

Willow sighed. "Still not that well, actually," she confessed. "It's a lot harder than I thought."

Discouragement was clear on her face. Alex squeezed her hand, and shook his head in joking disbelief. "After all that? You got – wait a minute" – he counted on his fingers

– "one, two, three, four, *five* kisses out of me? And the aura work isn't even going well?"

She grinned, and pressed close to him again. "So sue me," she murmured against his lips.

My psychic skills had always come so effortlessly that I'd thought disguising my aura would be easy too, once Seb explained it to me. It wasn't – just *seeing* my aura took practice at first. It seemed so unnatural to even notice it, like being awakened by your own snores. After three days, I could finally bring my aura easily into view, but now trying to change it made me feel like I was in the second grade attempting advanced calculus. And for Seb it was all so simple – not to just see his aura, but to then sort of mentally grasp it, changing its colours with his thoughts.

"You have to be friends with it," he said for about the dozenth time. "Be *simpático*."

We were down in the exercise room again, where Seb sat straddling the weight machine. Stubble covered his firm jaw; he'd apparently taken me at my word about the shaving thing. All he needed now was a leather jacket and screaming groupies, though that would be so un-Seb-like as to be completely unreal.

I nodded, determined to get it this time. "All right. Let me try again."

Perched cross-legged on a sofa cushion, I closed my eyes and took a deep breath. My aura swam into my mind's eye. I sat still, noticing the way it radiated out from my body: buoyant when I was happy, drawing in closely if I was upset. It was kind of medium-sized now, with a focused sense that matched my own. I watched its lavender lights drifting through the silver…and then I mentally reached out, frowning as I strove to catch hold of it.

Blue, I told it. *You need to be sky-blue now.*

The aura in my mind's eye stayed calm, intent…and silver. As usual. Opening my eyes, I gazed at it glumly.

There was a creak from the weight machine as Seb got up. "Maybe we should try something different," he said. The sofa cushion dipped as he settled next to me; as always, a pleasurable tingle went through me at the mingling of our auras. "Just feel what I'm doing, yes?"

As we sat there together, I could sense Seb's light concentration, so different from my own grim focus. His state of mind was almost like an afterthought, or daydreaming. Gently, he nudged his aura; I felt it shiver as the colours he was imagining swept through it. Green. Then a dull grey. Green again. Silver.

Neither of us moved as Seb changed his aura over and over. Almost without realizing, I began to echo his sense of relaxed detachment, so that after a while I was practically losing myself in my own aura: whispers of silver and lavender trailing over my skin, gleaming with emotion.

"I think I get it," I said softly. "I've been trying too hard, right?"

Seb nodded, propping himself back on one hand. His hazel eyes were teasing. "Perhaps just a little, *querida*."

"Don't call me *querida*," I said automatically. "Okay, let me see if I can do it now."

Closing my eyes, I merged dreamily back into my aura's glow. *Don't force it*, I cautioned myself. When I felt ready, I mentally stroked its shimmering lights and imagined them turning blue.

I caught my breath as my aura wavered and gave a flicker. Close, but no cigar. My heart started beating more quickly. *No, don't get excited – stay detached*. It was easier said than done, though; when I tried again, my life energy didn't even flutter. Or the next two times I tried. In my mind's eye, I stared at the silvery glow in frustration. Oh god, I *had* to get this. How was I supposed to be there for the Council attack if I didn't?

There was a ripple of emotion from Seb…and when I opened my eyes, he was watching me very steadily, all trace of humour gone. With one of those undercurrents that happened more and more often between us now, I knew he'd heard my thought – and that he hated the idea of me taking part in the attack every bit as much as Alex would.

Just the thought of me being hurt made him turn as fierce as those months when he was thirteen, so that he'd do whatever it took to protect me.

We each knew what the other was thinking. A little shaken by the depth of his feelings, I started to say something, then stopped. There was no point in arguing. I'd learn how to change my aura in time, and I'd be there when the team confronted the Twelve – that was all there was to it.

I could tell Seb had picked up the gist of that, and was letting it go for now – though from the tension around his mouth, he wasn't happy. "Do you want to try again?" he asked finally.

And for then, that was all either of us said about it.

CHAPTER *Seventeen*

HAVING SEB IN THE HOUSE changed everything for me.

Though Alex was, obviously, totally on my side, he was often too busy to really notice everything that went on with me and the others: the minor snubs, the sideways looks. It was all so stupid that I hated the fact it even got to me sometimes, and I didn't blame Alex in the slightest for not always noticing – god, I wouldn't even have *wanted* him to. Because, let's be honest, he had one or two more important things on his mind just then.

But Seb noticed it all. Suddenly there was someone whose gaze I could catch when Trish tensed if I came too close, or Brendan got that deer-in-the-headlights look. Seb's eyes would be smiling as we glanced at each other, the corner of his mouth lifting almost imperceptibly. If we were near enough, I might even catch what he was thinking, which was always something like, *Madre mía – and you look so harmless. Have you got a machete up your sleeve or something?* Once or twice I gave in to the laugh tugging at my lips – which then had the others staring at me in alarm, while Seb just quietly stood there, looking innocent. The difference all that made to my sanity was… well, not small.

Just having Seb to talk to helped. There were so many things about my life that made sense now: strange feelings that had always set me apart, but that I hadn't even known to question until I met him. Like how I've always been sensitive to the moods of places, when other people hardly seem to notice them; or the feeling of duality that I now realized I'd had all my life – the certainty that there was more to me than just the "me" I knew, even if I hadn't been sure before what the rest of it was. These and a hundred other things were just part of being half-angel, it turned out – because Seb had always felt exactly the same way.

"Did you know your father?" I asked.

We were in the TV room, about a week after he'd arrived. The others were out, and as usual when they were on a hunt, frustration nagged at me that I couldn't be there with them. I kept reaching psychically for Alex, needing to know he was safe. We all had cellphones now, but texts weren't the same. Every time I found his energy, the familiar feel of it was like an embrace.

Meanwhile, Seb had finally forced me to take a break from aura training, and he was right – after hours of no luck, my brain felt limp. Being gentle and offhand sounded like it should be the easiest thing in the world, but the problem was that it *mattered* so much. My pulse kept skipping the second my aura started to change, which then sent it snapping right back to silver. Frustrating wasn't the word. How was I supposed to convince myself that I didn't care about this?

At my question, I was aware of Seb's mind opening to mine, without him really thinking consciously about it. He shook his head. "No, I never knew my father. I always knew he was an angel though – I'm not sure how. Maybe my mother told me."

"Did you ever see him in her thoughts, like I saw Raziel in Mom's?" I'd told Seb about Raziel, and the Church of Angels.

"Not really." He pulled a wry face as he sprawled back against the sofa, settling himself on the cushions. "I didn't have much of a...link with my mother, I think is the word."

I got a sense of isolation; a brief image of a woman in

her twenties who looked like him. I wasn't surprised Seb hadn't been close to his mother – in all the pieces of memory I'd seen, she'd either been crying while her boyfriend hit him, or shouting that it was Seb's fault. It was a relief to glance at him now, so healthy and relaxed. I felt my gaze lingering on him, and looked away.

"How badly did your mother have angel burn?" I asked.

Seb propped his wrist under his head as he thought; the firm muscles of his arm flexed slightly. "Very badly," he said. "It was different from your mother though. I think my mother's mind was damaged, but she could still talk, still do things." He knew I'd had to hide my mother's mental illness from everyone when I was younger. Apart from Alex, he was the only person I'd ever shared that with.

"The main thing was that my mother had cancer," he went on. "That's what killed her."

I nodded. He'd told me before that when he was nine and living on the streets, he'd found out his mother was dead. She hadn't visited him even once after leaving him at the orphanage – not in all the years he was there. It made my throat tighten whenever I thought of it.

Seb stretched his white-socked foot so that it nudged at my ankle. "Willow, don't. It's all right."

This happened a lot now, so that our half-psychic, half-spoken conversations would have sounded very weird to anyone else. I shook my head. "It so isn't. I hate that you were in that place."

"The *reformatorio* was much worse," he said with a shrug. "And it was in the orphanage that I found out about my angel. There was a room they locked me in…he first came to me there. So it was worth it."

He wasn't as relaxed as he sounded. I felt his slight tension as he remembered, and got a flicker of fear – a dark, cramped room where he'd been imprisoned for days. Oh, Seb.

"Besides, I would never have started to read books without the orphanage," added Seb. "Never. And I think reading has been to me what fixing cars is to you."

I slowly shook my head. "You're never going to convince me the orphanage was actually a good thing. I've seen it, remember? I know what you went through there."

"Yes, I know you do," he said softly. He gave a small smile. "You're the only person in the world who's ever known me."

Our auras were mingling where his foot rested near me on the sofa; I could hardly feel where mine ended and his began. I smiled too. "Maybe that's because you've never told anyone the truth in your life. A gondolier? Really? *And* you stole his cigarettes."

Seb looked genuinely surprised. "But it's true, what I told him. My people were Italian. There was a gondolier strike in Venice, in eighteen-forty – they came here by the thousands."

My eyes widened. I almost said, *Really? A gondolier strike?* And then felt how teasing his aura had become, and burst out laughing. "Oh, you're good," I said. "Real good."

"So are you," said Seb, his voice casual. "Look at your aura."

Startled, I brought it back into view. Its lavender lights had shifted to forest green, companionably matching Seb's. "Oh!" I gasped, sitting straight up. The second I did, it flicked back to lavender. I stared at Seb. "How long has it been like that?"

"The last few minutes, maybe," he said with a grin. "So you see, you *can* change your aura."

I half laughed, groaning. "When I don't know I'm doing it – great."

But the tiny victory helped, and I started practising with Seb every spare moment I had – even in the evenings sometimes, while Alex and the others went over whatever video footage Kara had managed to take that day, trying to get the door code. I helped with that whenever I could, but I was so aware of time ticking away, and the days passing. I *had* to learn how to do this.

Not that the others seemed broken-hearted that I was doing something else. I kept trying to act normal around everyone, but knew that nothing I ever did would be "normal", as far as they were concerned. With Seb there, I didn't feel nearly as self-conscious about it now, at least. That prickling, too-aware feeling that I often used to get had faded away completely. It was a relief; I'd hated feeling so vulnerable and scrutinized.

Seb never said much when the others were around. If he did, it was always some mild comment that sounded innocent on the surface, but then you could see the person frowning as they thought about it, like, *Wait – what did he mean by that?*

It made me laugh, but it also exasperated me. I knew from his hand that Seb usually got along with people perfectly well; there was just this spark of mischief in him that couldn't resist a situation like this – everyone being so suspicious of him when he hadn't even done anything.

"Playing with their minds doesn't actually help, you know." We were out in the courtyard, where there was a battered picnic table; the Shadow stood parked near the back door. In the evenings, when the rest of the team was home, we usually ended up out here, or up on the balcony.

"I can't help it," said Seb seriously. "I say things without thinking, all the time – the words, they just fly right out of my mouth. It's very unfortunate. I think there must be a medical name for it."

"Really? Maybe we should donate you to science so they can study you."

Seb's mouth twitched. He was sitting up on the tabletop, wearing a cotton long-sleeved shirt with his *Cinco de Mayo* T-shirt over it. "Yes, maybe. But I'm the teacher, so you can't. Come, *querida*, try again."

I nodded, though it was getting pretty hard not to feel discouraged. I could change my aura's colour for a few minutes at a time now, but only if Seb was right there, sort of bolstering it up. Whenever I attempted to shift it on my own, it collapsed right back, no matter how relaxed I thought I was. My dreamy state felt like a self-imposed con now – and it was like my aura knew it. With a mental sigh, I closed my eyes, gearing myself up for another bout.

"No, stop," said Seb suddenly. "You're all—" He laughed as I looked at him. "Like this," he said, hunching his shoulders tensely. "It's a gentle thing, like play. Look, forget about changing your aura tonight. Let's try this."

He jumped down off the table and went over to the back door; leaning inside, he flicked off the light that hung over the doorway. The courtyard plunged into dimness, still lit by the ambient glow of nearby street lights, but much more mysterious now – shadowy.

"All right, are you ready?" said Seb as he returned. His eyes were impish.

I shook my head, smiling now. "Ready for what? Is this some secret half-angel thing?"

"Yes. Well, sort of. Here, stand up." He tugged me to my feet. "Okay, look at my aura."

I brought it into view. He'd shifted to his natural colours – the bright, shining silver and the deep forest green. "Now watch," said Seb. He held up his hand, wrapped in a silvery glow. Then he whipped it through the air. A silver trail followed, so quickly it seemed to glitter. He lashed his hand back again; made gleaming circles and loops.

My mouth had fallen open. "Oh my god, let me try that—" I focused on my own aura, and a few seconds later was doing the same – swirling my hand and making silver trails all around me, as if I were one of those gymnasts with the long, streaming ribbons. I laughed to see Seb writing his name in the air; my own name followed, shimmering and vanishing in a heartbeat. We were like two kids with sparklers. I couldn't stop smiling; I wished I'd known about this when I was a little girl. How cool would that have been, to have had a perpetual sparkler?

"That is so…amazing," I said when we finally sat back on the picnic bench. I stroked my hand through the air, watching it shimmer, aware that this light-hearted feeling was exactly what I'd been struggling to find. "How did you figure that out?"

"Just messing around, when I was boy." Seb sat beside me as I played with the silver glow; he looked delighted at my delight. "We weren't allowed to talk in the orphanage at night – I'd lie in bed doing that instead." He lowered his voice confidingly. "The other boys thought I was very strange."

A flash of my elementary school playground: a group of girls standing in a cluster, whispering and giving me hard looks. I nodded ruefully. "Join the club. I freaked people out a *lot* when I was little. I thought everyone was psychic; I didn't understand why people got upset when I told them things." I glanced at Seb with a smile, wishing more than ever that we'd known each other as children. I wouldn't have cared about the playground at all back then, if I'd had him as a friend. We could have just sat under the jungle gym and been weird together.

Seb's expression had turned warm as he looked at me. He started to say something else, then we both looked up as the back door opened and Alex poked his head out. My heart leaped – I'd hardly seen him all day; he must be finished with the security stuff for the night.

A flicker of resignation showed on Alex's face to find Seb and me out here together; then he smiled. "Hey," he said, walking over to us with his hands in his back pockets.

"How's it going with Kara?" I asked as he sat up on the tabletop beside me. I had a feeling he wanted to put his arm around me but was restraining himself; it would seem too much like *This is my girlfriend, back off*. Meanwhile, I could practically feel Seb closing off, becoming aloof and watchful.

"Not great," admitted Alex, touching his forehead. "She keeps getting video footage that shows a number or two, but not the whole thing. We can't even tell how many digits there are yet; people's hands and fingers are always in the way."

I knew; I'd seen a lot of the footage. "Are you sure I can't help?" I said, touching his leg. "I could try looking through the videos again."

"Maybe," said Alex. He knew as well as I did that I didn't get anything psychically from film – it felt totally cold and flat to me. It was similar for Seb; though he could see auras on film, he didn't get much else. "But I think we're just going to have to keep trying to piece it all together," Alex went on. "Brendan's making a spreadsheet that might help. Oh, and Kara said the church map is a lot more accurate now," he added to Seb. "So thanks for that."

Seb nodded. "Anytime."

A silence fell. I racked my brains for something else to say, but it felt like a lost cause. Conversation did not exactly flow when these two were together. Finally, Seb rose in an easy motion. "Maybe I'll go read for a while," he said. He glanced at me. "Remember what I said. Don't practise any more tonight, okay?"

I made a face; I'd been planning on trying again that night in the dorm, once the others were asleep. "Seb, I feel like maybe I could really do it now—"

"No, just relax," he broke in firmly. "Tomorrow's soon enough."

It was frustrating, but I knew he was probably right – I needed to savour just being friendly with my aura for a change, before plunging back into trying again. "Yes, okay," I said with a sigh.

"See you in the morning," he said, his eyes gentle. I sensed him almost add "*querida*" and stop himself just in time; felt his flash of humour that almost had me smiling too, though it shouldn't have. "Goodnight," he added to Alex.

"Night," said Alex.

Once Seb had gone inside, Alex put his arm around me, kissing my head. "Hey, you," he murmured into my hair. I could feel that he was glad Seb had left. Though I was happy to be alone too, I wanted to say, *You know, you and Seb could get along if you just gave each other a chance.* Except I wasn't really sure it was true. They were both such strong personalities – Seb in his quiet way, and Alex in his direct one – and neither liked being pushed around.

I caught myself; time alone with Alex was too rare to spend it thinking about Seb. I wrapped my arms around him, slipping a hand under his T-shirt and caressing the smoothness of his skin – relishing how my fingers glided over the warmth of him. "Remember the cabin?" I said after a while. "What the sunrise was like there?"

There'd been a few times at our refuge in the mountains when we'd stayed up all night talking, then sat outside with the sleeping bags draped around our shoulders, watching the sun come up – pink and golden fingers that edged up the peaks like fire from within. The memory made me wistful. I'd known then how lucky we were to have that time together, but I'd had no idea how soon it would be before we hardly even got a chance to talk.

"Of course I remember." Alex kissed my neck. "We'll go back someday, Willow. I mean it. If we defeat the Council…"

He stopped. I felt the worry grip him again; the grim tension that was never far away. I hugged him hard, wishing desperately I could say something that would help. We had less than two weeks now – and whether we managed to get further security details or not, we were going to have to enter the Torre Mayor and make some kind of attempt against the Twelve.

We. Because mentally, I was including myself in the attack. I'd learn to change my aura in time if it killed me.

"What are you thinking?" Alex had pulled away slightly, watching me with a considering smile. "You look like you've got a million thoughts whirring around in there." He tapped my brow.

I smiled. "Maybe not quite a million." I wasn't about to tell Alex. He was already worried sick about all this; there was no point adding to it until I knew how to disguise my aura at will. I was just glad he wasn't psychic – he'd have picked up on what I was planning in about two seconds, the same as Seb had. I thought of the steady look that had been in Seb's eyes, that moment in the basement. We hadn't discussed the issue out loud yet – it didn't really feel necessary; we both knew exactly how the other felt.

Without trying, I got a sudden image of him. He was sprawled on his bed reading a book – I could picture him so vividly that I could see the Spanish title on its front cover; the brown hair falling over his forehead in those loose curls that I knew drove him crazy. The image made me smile; he looked so engrossed. I closed it away as quickly as it had come. I don't know when I'd first realized that I could sense Seb's whereabouts when he wasn't around – somehow it just felt natural to know where he was.

Why was I thinking about Seb again? I pushed him away, irritated, and studied Alex's face in the faint glow of the street lights – its strong, beautiful lines. I kissed his nose. "You have a very nice nose, are you aware of this fact?"

He laughed for the first time in days, warming me like a hot drink on a winter's evening. "No, I can't say that I am. I don't think my nose has ever gotten a compliment before."

"Poor nose. It deserves lots of compliments." I kissed it again.

Alex shook his head with a grin. "My nose and I both thank you. Why do I get the feeling you're trying to distract me? You know, I did actually notice that you didn't tell me what you were thinking."

"Maybe that's because I didn't want to. Maybe I'm busy having lots of secret, private thoughts."

"Hmm, very mysterious…" As Alex drew me to him again, a sound came from inside the house, almost like someone shouting.

We glanced at each other, startled, and then it came again and this time there was no doubt. Sam's voice, bellowing: "Guys! You guys, get in here! Everyone, *now!*"

The TV showed a reporter facing the camera, speaking in rapid Spanish. Behind him was a broad conference table with twelve well-dressed people sitting around it, though you couldn't really make out their faces. Sam sat hunched on the sofa, his muscular forearms resting on his thighs. "They're talking about *el Consejo de los Ángeles*," he said tersely. "That's the Council, right?"

"Oh my god," murmured Trish.

No one else said anything. Everyone was there, including Seb, still holding his book: Sam's shouts had brought us all running. I sank down on the arm of the sofa, staring at the TV. Alex stood next to me, frowning; I was glad to feel the warmth of his arm against mine.

From the doorway, Kara began to translate. "...I was brought to this secret location blindfolded, to maintain the security of the group that claims to be the Seraphic Council – the government of those heavenly beings here on earth. I'm talking now to their spokesperson."

A woman with intense grey eyes appeared on the screen. A chill went over me. This was actually one of the Twelve: one of the ones we hoped to kill. Yet somehow the features of her face were oddly difficult to grasp hold of; it was like you kept forgetting them every second you looked. In a daze, it struck me that I didn't know what this angel looked like, even though I was staring right at her.

The angel spoke in apparently flawless Spanish – but her voice had a strange resonance, almost like several people talking at once. My mouth went dry. "We are speaking to the world today because statements have recently been made which are false, and must be corrected,"

Kara translated. "This will be our only public statement."

"Okay, these are some seriously creepy angels," muttered Brendan. The faces of the others said he'd taken the words right out of their mouths. I reached for Alex's hand; felt his fingers squeeze around mine.

"We are the angelic ruling body. We want to let the world know that regardless of what you may have heard, things are indeed going to change. We speak for all angelkind – and we are the only angels with the authority to do so." She paused to let that sink in.

And suddenly I got what this was about. Raziel. He'd appeared on TV and promised nothing would change – as if it were up to him.

The reporter's face was pale. "What changes can we expect?"

The angel gazed directly at the camera for the first time. Her chorus of voices turned lower, more deliberate. "Primarily, there will be imminent changes in how the Church of Angels is run."

"Do you mean—" started the reporter.

She spoke right over him. "We'll keep on with the tradition of an angel heading the Church for the time being – and in fact, will soon appoint an angel to head the Church here in Mexico. However, this angel's name will not be released; from now on, we'll be keeping a much lower profile in your world. Any angel who you know by name will soon be retiring from public view. That is our promise."

The grey eyes burned as the angel echoed Raziel's words. I swallowed. I had no sympathy at all for Raziel, but I was glad I wasn't him, just then. I could imagine his impotent fury so clearly that for a second it was almost like the emotion beat through me.

Beside me, Alex's expression was intent as he took it all in, trying to see if there was anything here that could help us. Seb stood frowning. His feelings about the angels were a lot more complicated than mine – he'd had a love-hate relationship with their fierce, powerful beauty for years – but I knew he was as disconcerted by the Council as I was.

The angel seemed to remember the reporter's presence. She gave something I think was meant to be a smile, though it made him visibly recoil. "This is *your* world – we angels will allow you the running of it. Our administration of the Church is only in response to your unavoidable worship of us – beyond that, we have little interest in associating with you."

Kara stopped translating for a second; she let out a short, disbelieving laugh. "Man, I never thought I'd dislike any angel *more* than Raziel." Then she continued as the reporter stammered, "Is…is that why you're in Mexico City – to appoint a head for the Church here?"

The eyes turned aloof. "Partly," said the angel. "We are currently conducting other business here too – vital business for all angelkind. You humans here in Mexico City, and then also around the world, may notice certain affects. This interview is at an end."

"What does *that* mean?" yelped Brendan.

"I don't know – but they're already *affecting* humanity more than enough," Wesley ground out. He was glaring at the screen, his normally closed-off face alive with anger. Remembering what Alex had told me in confidence, about his entire family having angel burn, I didn't blame him.

"Quiet, you guys," said Alex.

The final image showed the Twelve in their angel forms, their winged figures glowing brightly. "We *chilangos* can be proud that the Seraphic Council chose Mexico City from which to address the world," the reporter said in a voice-over. "But for now…we can only wait, and wonder."

"God, we can't do away with *them* soon enough," Liz burst out as two commentators in a newsroom appeared onscreen, talking excitedly. "Talk about doing the world a favour!"

"At least they don't seem to like that smarmy Raziel very much." Kara still stood in the doorway, her nose wrinkled in distaste. "It sounds like he may not even be holding onto the Church much longer."

"Yeah, but none of this *matters* unless we can actually

get into the Torre Mayor," growled Sam. "Alex, what's up with that? You've got a plan, right?"

I glanced at him, wondering what he'd say. When Alex wasn't taking the team on practice hunts, he'd been hanging out around the rear of the Torre Mayor, watching the service entrance. Though I'd had the sense for days now that a plan was forming in his mind, he didn't seem to want to talk about it yet.

He obviously didn't want to talk about it now, either. "I'm working on something," he said shortly. "Don't worry, we'll get in. But first things first, guys. We've got to get the security info, or we'll be working blind once we *are* in."

Seb spoke, his quiet voice searing through the room. "What I want to know is, what is this 'vital business for all angelkind' that they're up to?"

"No idea," said Alex. "But for now, I'm only concerned about it if it affects the attack." As he kept his gaze on the TV screen, he looked relaxed enough – but taking in the faint lines on his forehead, I knew he wasn't.

"Hopefully it won't," I said.

Alex glanced down at me and I could almost see his tension ease; for a second, we were the only two people in the room. With a small smile, he briefly touched my back, his fingers warm through my shirt. "Yeah, hopefully," he said.

Things became even tenser after that, more determined: the team had actually seen who they were going to be fighting. Alex was still taking them out on daily hunts – which made me curse my inability to disguise my aura more than ever. I hated just staying at home when the danger was increasing with each day that passed – because the angels had to be aware by now that there were AKs in the city. I could never really relax until everyone was back again. Alex was careful to never fall into a predictable routine, though. He always took the team to different places, and at different times; they even went at night sometimes. And the AKs were improving by leaps and bounds. I knew Alex thought that if we could just get the security information, we'd have a real chance against the Council now.

When asked, all he would say was that he had a plan to get us into the Torre Mayor, but he was working out the details.

"*Do* you have a plan?" I whispered one morning when we were alone in his bedroom. I was lying in his arms, savouring the feel of his skin against mine. I'd slipped into his room while the others were having breakfast – I knew Alex would already have had his; he was an early riser. When I timed things right, we could sometimes have almost half an hour alone together. It was incredibly precious to us both – and not just as a time to talk. Now I stroked his bare chest. "Or are you just trying to keep morale up or something?"

Alex sighed. Keeping an arm around my shoulders, he stretched up a hand to bat at the dust motes that were drifting past. "Yes, I've got a plan – but I don't like it very much," he admitted. "I don't want to say anything to the team until after we get the security information. I'm hoping we'll find out something that'll improve on it."

I bit my lip. That bad. I didn't say anything; he clearly didn't want to go into it. After a pause, he rolled towards me, and we lay gazing at each other without speaking. I felt myself falling into his blue-grey eyes, so vivid under their black lashes. As I caught a wave of his emotions, my throat tightened: a deep yearning; a suppressed fear that the two of us wouldn't have the long life together that we both wanted. The thought filled me with dread.

He reached out and touched a strand of my hair, as if he'd never seen it before, and then lowered his lips to mine. I could feel how much he needed to lose himself in me; it was what I needed too, with him. I held him to me tightly as we kissed, and wished there were no time limits and no other people, and that we could just do exactly what we wanted. Because even though I tried not to think about it, in my darkest moments I couldn't help wondering if we'd really survive all this. And I didn't want to die without ever truly giving myself to the boy I loved.

"Alex, maybe…" I whispered now. My heart was thudding; my body felt flushed and prickly.

He rose up on his elbows, scanning my face. Before he could say anything, we heard Sam and Brendan come back into the dorm, arguing about basketball. *Basketball*, when we were a thousand miles away from the NBA. I closed my eyes tightly; I felt like crying. Alex let out a breath, and then kissed me.

"Soon," he said, and I could tell from the determination in his voice that he was going to make it happen, no matter what.

With only one digit left to crack on the six-number security code, it turned out that they changed the code every week, knocking us back to square one. Everyone was stressed – especially Kara, I think, whose task of finding the new code couldn't be hurried, though we all longed for it to be. There was just over a week left now. The rest of the team spent any spare time either grimly working out or watching TV in near silence.

But the success of the plan wasn't my only worry. Once or twice now, I'd gotten glimpses from Seb of the same powerful emotion I thought I'd felt in him the first day we'd met – warm, deep flashes, which told me exactly how much he still hoped that something more than friendship would happen between us.

He usually kept it hidden far below the surface, though. And selfishly, I was glad of it. I didn't want to face his feelings for me. I didn't want anything to change between us, not ever – because Seb and I just clicked, on every level. He really did feel like a brother: a soul-twin who'd somehow found me again, after a lifetime apart.

Blue. I imagined an airy light blue, like the sky on a summer's day. As we sat outside in the courtyard, I focused only on my aura, lightly keeping the sense of oneness, of play. My aura shifted, its silver lights turning obediently to the colour of the sky. Somehow I kept myself detached, ignoring the distant pounding of my heart. For a change, Seb's energy wasn't bolstering me up, though I could feel him sitting nearby, silently willing me on.

Then a car alarm went off and I started; my aura snapped back to silver. When I tried again, I knew I'd totally lost the sense of light-heartedness – I'd have to go into aura-sparkler mode again to get it back. I sighed as I opened my eyes. Now that I'd reached this stage, Seb kept saying I needed to lock away the aura part of my mind and keep it separate, so that nothing could distract me, but I just couldn't seem to get the hang of it.

"You really are doing much better, you know," he

commented. We were at the picnic table again; Seb was sitting backwards on the bench with me up on the tabletop beside him.

"Yes, but—" I broke off, scraping my hands over my face. "Oh, *argh*. Why can't I get this, when you can do it so easily? This is worse than being back in algebra class!"

"I learned when I was a small child – I think this made it much easier," Seb pointed out mildly. He sat back against the table edge, propping his elbows to either side as he gave me a curious look. "You took algebra?"

I shrugged. "Not by choice. It was required." I'd told Seb a lot about high school; like Alex, it was something he'd only seen on TV. I pulled my knees up, sitting cross-legged. "Would you have wanted to go, if you'd had the chance? To high school, I mean."

A ripple of surprise, so that I knew the answer before he said it. "Yes, of course. Even if I'd felt alone there, the way you always did – I'd still like to know more than I do." He pulled a wry face, like he didn't want it to matter too much to him. "I could have learned how not to get caught at stealing, maybe."

Actually, Seb read so much that he knew a lot more than I did about some things. I studied him, trying to picture him in high school. Like Alex, he'd have had every girl in the place after him if he'd gone. Though I had a feeling Alex would have been out on the basketball court, while Seb would have been holed up in the library somewhere.

He pushed lightly at my leg. "Anyway, I know *you* didn't like school very much, but there must have been something about it you enjoyed."

"Enjoyed" was pretty strong. I started to laugh and say *Guess again* – and then I remembered my art class. I'd always loved making things with my hands. When the whole Church of Angels thing happened, I'd been working on a kinetic sculpture that used pieces of old engines. If I'd managed to do it right, the different pieces were actually going to move on their own.

I described my sculpture to Seb; he listened with interest. "Yes, I can imagine you doing that." Then he stroked his stubbled jaw, looking deep in thought. "You know, I think this means I was right," he decided. "There *is* something you enjoyed."

"Yeah, I guess," I admitted. I glanced down at him with a smile, shaking my head. "How did you even *know* that?"

He gave me a smugly arch look. "Ah, you see – I know you better than you know yourself."

And he really did sometimes; that was the funny thing. In some ways, Seb knew me better than anyone in the world, even Alex. I rested my arms on my thighs; in the background was the never-ending drone of traffic. "Can I ask you something?" I said after a moment.

"You know you can."

I cleared my throat. I'd been dying to ask him this ever since we first met, but had felt embarrassed for some reason. "I was just wondering...if I could see your angel."

I felt a leap of emotion from him. "I've been wanting to ask you that too," he admitted. "Very much."

Both of us were shy suddenly. My cheeks heated. I tucked back a short strand of my hair. "Um...so how should we—"

"We'll go at the same time," suggested Seb, straightening up.

I shifted down to the bench, and perched cross-legged, facing him. "Okay, on the count of three."

He nodded. "One...two...three."

I closed my eyes briefly on "three", bringing my angel to me in a bright burst of energy. I merged with her, sent her flying gently from my human body to hover above me.

I opened my eyes. Seb was sitting beside me...and above him was his angel.

I stared with both my angel and human eyes. Seb's angel looked just like him – lean and powerful, with loose curls and a high-cheekboned face – except that he was radiant with light. His wings stretched out over the table, stirring the night air. I could hardly breathe at the wonder of truly seeing another of my own kind for the first time; I thought I could never drink him in enough. From Seb's face, I knew he felt exactly the same. More, even – he'd been longing for this for so many years.

Seb's angel wore jeans and a T-shirt, and suddenly I realized my angel could be clad in anything I wanted. I shifted my angelic robes to a vintage dress from the sixties that I'd always loved; saw Seb's slight smile as he noticed. Hovering in my angel form, I took in Seb's ethereal hands, and how strong and shining they looked. I longed to reach out my own hand – to see what it was like to touch another of my kind in this form too. Something held me back and, with an effort, I kept my arm where it was. It just seemed… too much, for now.

On the bench, Seb's eyes were steady on mine. They caught and held me; I felt almost dazed with wonder that somehow the two of us had found each other – that he had found me. My mouth went dry as I sensed again the true depth of his feelings for me, but I couldn't have looked away from Seb just then to save my life. I was so aware of how much I wanted to send my angel self soaring with his, the two of us flying so far up that we'd find the stars beyond the city lights – but we both knew it wasn't safe here.

Finally, with a last long look at each other, our angels returned to our human bodies in a rush of gleaming wings, so that once more it appeared to be just Seb and me out in the dingy concrete courtyard together. Neither of us moved as we sat there, our gazes still locked. It felt…I can't describe how it felt. We'd seen this innermost part of each other, shared our true selves.

I saw Seb's throat move. His eyes were bright. Without speaking, he reached for my hand; I was reaching for his in the same moment. Our fingers met and twined together, gripping each other hard. It didn't even feel like we had a choice. Seb and I had to touch just then – had to somehow try to express what we'd just experienced. Letting out a ragged breath, I leaned against the firm warmth of his arm, our fingers still tightly linked.

We sat that way for a long time, with the urban night humming gently with life around us.

CHAPTER *Eighteen*

"SO HOW ARE WE GETTING into the Torre Mayor?" demanded Sam for the hundredth time. "'Cause with as long as Kara's taking, I'm starting to think we'd better forget the security stuff. Hell, let's just bust in there, do what we gotta do, and get out again!"

They were returning from another hunt, at Alameda Central this time. The Metro was less crowded than usual, allowing the AKs to sit together in an almost-empty car. Alex groaned and dropped his head back against the window. "Sam, we've had this conversation," he said. "Tell me again, why is it a good idea for us to go storming in there without any idea what we're walking into? Oh yeah, I forgot – we're in a Rambo movie."

"Well, we can't just keep waiting for Kara to get the goddamn code," grumbled Sam. He sat sprawled back in his seat: a large, disgruntled Texan. "The Council'll be gone before she gets it at this rate."

Alex didn't answer, fully aware that if worst came to worst, they'd have to make an attempt on the Council anyway. He sighed, massaging his eyes. The angels in the city were definitely on the alert now. There weren't nearly as many out feeding as there'd been just a couple of weeks ago, and those that were seemed to be feeding somewhat perfunctorily; were less inclined to savour their prey. Even so, the team had managed to bring down four today – and three of them had blasted straight back at him. Distantly, Alex wondered what kind of damage he was taking from all the angel fallout lately. Martin, his father, used to be riddled with it sometimes.

To Alex's side, Liz and Trish were talking in excited, low voices about the hunt; Wesley and Brendan sat across from them, joining in occasionally. Wesley in particular looked psyched, almost smiling for a change – he'd gotten two of the creatures. The team wasn't doing badly; they really weren't. But they had less than a week to go now.

"You still haven't told me what the plan is," observed Sam, tapping his fingers on his leg.

"No kidding," said Alex shortly. He had no intention of telling Sam or anyone else until he had to; morale would plummet. Well, maybe not Sam's morale. But the sane members of the team's, definitely.

He'd spent days scoping out the Torre Mayor's deliveries entrance while pretending to be fiddling with the Shadow's engine in a nearby parking lot – and by now, he thought he had a pretty solid plan for how he could get the team in there and up the service elevator. Juan's white van would be perfect; half the deliveries came in white vans. Though the service elevator would be sure to have that top floor locked off too, they could reach the floor below, then take the stairwell, where he'd shoot out the security cameras immediately. The sudden blank screens in the security office would no doubt bring someone to check the cause within minutes, but they'd be in by then – it would take no time at all to get up the stairs and shoot the door open with a silenced pistol. If they could get to the Council quickly after that, Alex thought their chances of getting in and out alive weren't terrible. It was conceivable that they could get down in the main elevator and be out the front door before anyone even figured out what had happened – especially in the chaos of all the angels suddenly vanishing.

It was that word "quickly" that kept him awake at night and made him keep the plan firmly to himself. Because they just didn't know what was going on now. They couldn't be sure of getting to the Council quickly when they had *no idea* if the schedule was still the right one; *no idea* what the layout was, or what room the Twelve would be in. Alex had nightmare visions of the team wandering around, looking in doors, while security came racing towards them, having tipped off the angels that there were intruders in their midst.

The train came to Zócalo station; Alex stood up abruptly. The others looked at him in surprise – their stop was still several stations away. "Let's get off here," he said, shoving his hands into the front pockets of his sweatshirt. "I want to check something out."

As they came up the stairs from the station, they could hear shouting on the sidewalk – there was a shoving match going on between some of the Crusaders and the Faithful. "My mother is dying!" screamed a man. His face was wild, contorted with fury. "There are no beds for her, no doctors—"

"If she had true faith, the angels would help her!" bellowed someone back. There were signs waving; elbows flying as people scuffled. Alex and the others skirted around them; a man in a business suit lurched backwards and just as quickly flung himself back into the fray. Trish looked worried as they passed, glancing back over her shoulder. Alex could see that she wanted to somehow defuse the tension, just as she always wanted to smooth things over for the group.

"Alex, that looks like it could get serious—" she started.

"I know, but ignore it," he said, not breaking his stride. "We don't want to get involved." The police mostly seemed to ignore the Crusaders, unless things got violent – then, undoubtedly, whoever they arrested got dragged off to the angels.

Trish bit her lip, but nodded. When they were directly across from the slightly tilting mass of the Catedral Metropolitana – no, the Catedral de los Ángeles; he kept forgetting – Alex dug his cellphone out of his jeans pocket. Tapping the buttons with his thumb, he sent Kara a text: *We're at Zocalo. Where r u? Can u check out cathedral with us?*

A few seconds later a reply came: *I'm here 2. Meet u outside cathedral in 5.*

Alex texted a quick *Yes* and tucked his phone away again. Good – he'd thought she'd still be here. Though he'd been to the cathedral several times now to study the layout, he felt twitchy with impatience suddenly – he wanted to see the place again; see if he'd missed anything. "Come on, we're going to check out the cathedral," he said to the others.

"Well hallelujah, we're finally doing something," said Sam with a grin.

Alex gave him a level glance. "Yes, we are. We are going to go in and *look*. Not start shooting. Got it?"

Sam gave a slight grimace, but nodded. "I got it, don't worry."

They headed across the broad stretch of the Zócalo, accompanied by the incessant beat of drums from Aztec dancers. Alex knew that in December the city usually erected a giant ice-skating rink in the square, but this year there was nothing – either *el DF* no longer had funds for it, or they'd decided it would detract from the glory of the converted cathedral. There were hardly any Christmas decorations up around the city, either; he'd heard on the news that a lot of people saw the holiday as lacking in meaning now. Many were planning to start celebrating Arrival Day – October 31st – as their main holiday instead, to honour the angels. *Great*, thought Alex in distaste, picturing it.

They passed through the cathedral's wrought-iron gates; the faded red and black tiles that had once been underfoot were now celestial silver and light blue. Wesley glanced up at the golden angel.

"I still can't believe they did that," he muttered to Alex. "That angel was the most famous monument in Mexico City."

"It still is," pointed out Liz, overhearing. "Even *more* famous now. But that empty column on the Paseo de la

Reforma just looks weird – like it's waiting for something to happen."

Kara was standing beside the cathedral's massive wooden doors. Despite his worry, Alex held back a smile when he saw she had on a pair of pink satin angel wings. "They're really you," he said as they reached her. "Or have you got angel burn, and I should shoot you?"

Kara rolled her eyes; the long, braided wig she was wearing made her look like Cleopatra or something. "It's called camouflage, dear. You should probably all get some too, so our group doesn't attract attention. This *is* Church of Angels central – where the people are whacked-out and the angels are plentiful."

Sam recoiled. "What, *us* wear those things? No way."

"No, it's a good idea." Alex reached for his wallet; taking out a few hundred pesos, he handed the notes to Sam. "Here, go and get us some, okay?" As Sam opened his mouth, he added, "And no complaining, Tex, or I'll make you wear the pink ones." The others snickered; Sam gave him a dark look and headed off to one of the angel-wing vendors wandering around the square.

"Listen, I was just about to text you myself," said Kara in a low voice. "I finally managed to get the security code today – the whole thing, first try. If they only change it once a week, it should be good for another three days."

Alex's heart leaped. "Really? Are you sure?"

"Yeah. And I've got an idea of when the best time might be for us to try to break in too, but…meanwhile, something's come up."

"What?" Alex felt his exhilaration fade. The look on Kara's face did not herald good news.

She fell silent, her beautiful features twisted in thought. "Let's wait till we get inside," she said finally. "You can see what I mean for yourself."

Sam returned with a cluster of angel wings and they put them on, helping each other straighten them. "Perfect – you all look like real devouts now," said Kara. "Just gaze around wonderingly, and you'll fit right in."

The white wings on his back felt ridiculous. But the team looked ready, Alex saw with approval – alert and reasonably relaxed; a big change from only two weeks ago, when they'd had their first hunt.

"Okay, I want all of you scanning and prepared, in case any of us is attacked," he said. "Stick together – don't anyone go wandering off. If we do have to defend ourselves, try to do it without being noticed; I'd sort of like to avoid starting a riot today."

"Riots, bad – got it," muttered Brendan.

A cavernous coolness fell as they entered the cathedral. When Alex had been here years ago, an altar had stood just inside the entrance. Now it was gone, as was the organ behind it, turning the cathedral into a vast airy space.

White pillars marched in a silent line to the single, lavish golden altar far away down the aisle – it stretched from floor to ceiling, ornate with detail, glinting like liquid. A golden angel took pride of place here, holding a trumpet to its lips as smaller angels cavorted around it. From some unseen source, harp music fluttered through the air.

Hundreds of people were inside, though the cathedral was so large it didn't seem crowded. Many sat praying in the long pews; others wandered respectfully about, taking photographs and videos, or lighting candles that stood on small winged stands. Alex spotted one or two being fed from, their faces alight as angels stood beside them – hands buried deep in the humans' life forces as their halos burned brighter and brighter.

Sam had seen too; Alex could practically feel him twitching for his gun. "Steady," he whispered to him.

The AKs moved down the central aisle, their feet echoing on the marble floor. Kara gazed dreamily up at the domed ceiling with its newly-painted pink and white rococo angels that soared between the round windows. Alex knew he couldn't do the blissed-out look as well as she was; he just tried not to look like he completely hated this place.

To either side, the space where chapels to individual saints had once stood was devoted to different aspects of the angels' love. Pretending to be showing them the "love for our planet" chapel, Kara led the AKs to a painting of three angels holding a globe of the world between them.

She pointed upwards, as if indicating a detail of the artwork. "Okay, don't look now, but that door behind me leads to the main administrative offices," she said to the team. Alex had seen it several times before; he took a sideways glance anyway at the dark, arched door in the corner.

"You can see the keypad right beside it," went on Kara. "Like I was just saying to Alex, we've got the code now and it shouldn't be changing again till Thursday – and from what I've seen, there's a few times during the day when we might be able to slip in without being noticed. Evening service is the main one – everyone seems pretty distracted then. There's another issue that's come up though."

Alex had been standing with his back to the stone wall as he listened, pretending to look at the cathedral while he kept an eye out for angels. The two that had been feeding were gone now, at least in their angelic forms. Scanning, he didn't sense any of the creatures in the main space – but a tingle crawled up his spine at the number of them in the unseen office area.

He bent his head towards Kara. "Jesus, how many of them are *back* there?" he muttered.

"That…is the problem," said Kara. Her eyes met his. "It's a new development we have to deal with – 'cause I've got a bad feeling it's here to stay. Come on, let's give the rest of these guys a quick look around at the layout, then maybe we can all go to a cafe or something. I've seriously had enough of this place for one day."

They exited the cathedral about twenty minutes later, climbing up its worn stone steps into the late afternoon. As they crossed the road and started across the square, Alex took out his phone and texted Willow: *Home in a while. We're OK. I love you.* Her response came promptly, making him smile: *Hurry back, I miss you!*

He'd bought cellphones for the rest of the team the day after Seb arrived, not wanting to ever again be in a position where someone was missing and he had no idea what was going on. Now he and Willow often sent a few texts back and forth during the day – tiny notes that made him feel more laid-back about Seb's presence in the house. Not that much more, though, if he was honest.

Alex shook his head at himself in disgust as he walked. He'd never thought he was a jealous person – and he trusted Willow completely. But knowing she and Seb were alone together all day, even though all they were doing was working on her aura, nagged at him like a pebble in his shoe. Not to mention that he'd lost count now of how many times he'd walked in on them having one of their long, intimate conversations. Just a few nights ago, he'd found them up on the balcony; Willow had been wearing

Seb's sweater draped across her shoulders as they talked. Though they'd been sitting at least four feet apart, the sweater had irritated Alex far more than it should have; he'd found it an effort to even be civil to Seb. It wasn't the kind of thing you could mention though, without sounding like a jealous jerk.

But he couldn't have held back what he *had* said to save his life – the words had finally burst out of him, after two weeks of biting them back. "So you know he's in love with you, right?" he'd asked once Seb had gone back inside, leaving his sweater on Willow's shoulders.

Alex had been sitting beside Willow on the cool concrete floor with his arm around her. She'd gone still as she stared up at him. "I know he cares about me a lot," she said finally. "But Alex, we're just friends. I told him that the first day."

"Willow. Come on, seriously – haven't you noticed? The way he looks at you all the time – plus, you must *feel* it, right? With both of you being psychic?"

Her cheeks had tinged with pink. She'd fingered the sweater's sleeve with one hand, apparently unaware she was doing so. With an effort, Alex had managed not to yank the thing off her shoulders.

"No, not really," she said, her voice soft. "I mean, once or twice maybe, I guess I've gotten a flash of something, but—" She stopped; then seemed to notice she was holding the sleeve and dropped it, rubbing her hand on her jeans. "We're friends," she repeated. "He knows that's all it is."

Alex had stared down at her, taking in the short spikes of hair that looked almost cherry-coloured in the half-light. Right then, they'd almost matched her cheeks. And looking down at her face as she gazed out over the courtyard, Alex had longed to be psychic himself – to be able to just reach into her head and find out what she was thinking.

Walking across the Zócalo now with the rest of the team, Alex told himself for the hundredth time that he was being ridiculous – because he *knew* how much Willow loved him. And unlike she and Seb, when they were alone together they didn't sit four feet apart. Just that morning, they'd managed some time in his bedroom: soft words; Willow's body against his; her lips as she kissed his neck, his tattoo, his chest. He went warm, remembering…and tried not to dwell on the fact that if she didn't talk to Seb so much, they could be alone like that more often.

Alex's phone beeped again in his jeans pocket. Pulling it out, he saw another text from Willow: *Did I tell u I love u, by the way? It was a HUGE oversight if I didn't.*

His irritation over Seb faded. Christ, he really was an idiot. *Oversight corrected,* he texted in response. *Did I tell u that I want to kiss u for a very long time later?*

Her reply came in seconds: *That's definitely a plan I can get behind.*

Alex smiled as he put his phone away, but felt slightly wistful too. He wanted it all with Willow, everything – and he'd never realized it more than in these last few weeks, with the fate of humanity hanging in the balance. If they managed to defeat the angels, the only thing he'd ever want would be to live the rest of his life with Willow. Marry her, if that's what she wanted. Just *be* with her, for ever.

But for now the present was all they had, and the only promise he could make was that he loved her. Because the reality was that no plan they put into place would be foolproof: when the AKs made their strike, there was a very real chance that he and the team could die. Alex didn't let his thoughts go down this path very often; the idea of any of his team being hurt was agony. He shoved his hands in his pockets, trying not to think about it now.

Anyway, maybe he didn't know what the attack on the Council would bring – but at least now that the team was trained he could leave them on their own without worrying too much. And so, for just one night, he and Willow were going to have some real privacy, like he'd promised. Alex's blood quickened at the thought. She didn't even know yet; he wanted to surprise her.

No Seb, no other people. Just the two of them in each

other's arms, being truly together in the way they both longed for.

I nudged gently at my pale-blue aura, watching it shimmer and change to a vibrant rose. It wavered before me for a few minutes, the colour of sunrise. Okay, how about green now; green would be nice…and though I'd thought I was totally immersed in my aura, somehow my thoughts drifted then to the Council attack. Alex. How important it was that I got this. And the playful mood was gone, slipped away like mist in the wind.

I opened my eyes and stared at my silver aura. The house was silent around us.

"Willow, stop – you're doing so well," said Seb, responding to the silent berating that was going on in my head.

He had on the same long-sleeved grey T-shirt he'd worn when I first met him, with the sleeves pushed up slightly. The hair on his tanned arms was lighter than on his head; almost golden – from years spent on the road in the sun, maybe. Pushing the thought away, I slumped back against the sofa. "It doesn't feel like it."

Seb shrugged. "You must keep your aura separate from everything now, that's all. Like, you can walk and talk at the same time, yes? You don't think about walking. It's like that."

He was always so patient – he'd told me all this about a hundred times now. But as he stretched across to rustle another cookie out of the bag, I could sense again the conflict that had been with him since almost that first day: he wanted me to be safe around the angels, yet as far from the Torre Mayor as possible when the team attacked.

I sighed. I hadn't really meant to discuss this with him, but I heard the words come out anyway. "Seb, I've got to be there when it happens. For so many reasons. I can't just sit here at home."

His eyes met mine. He didn't ask what I was talking about. "If you learn how to hide your aura in time, then I'll be there too," he said.

I bit my lip. I hated the idea of anything happening to Seb, almost as much as I did anything happening to Alex. "You're part of the team now, though," I said. "Wouldn't you go anyway? Whether I did or not?"

"No." Seb looked down, turned the cookie over in his hands and then rested it on the table uneaten. "When the attack happens, I'll be wherever you are – doing whatever I can to protect you." He gave a small smile. "I wouldn't be anywhere else."

On the one hand, I was touched – enormously. On the other, I felt a little irritated that he seemed so convinced I couldn't take care of myself. "Seb—"

"*Querida*, no, that's not it," said Seb before I could say

131

anything else. "You know I don't think that; you can take care of yourself very well. But if there's an attack and the team fails, the angels will find out everything. I won't leave you on your own in that kind of danger." He shrugged again; his eyes held a gleam of humour suddenly. "You can try to make me if you like. You won't have much luck, I don't think."

My chest tightened – what I felt was far too deep to put into words. Thankfully, with Seb I didn't have to try. I let out a long breath.

"You're still calling me *querida*," I pointed out finally. "Brothers don't do this."

"Sorry. I'm very forgetful sometimes." He picked up the cookie and took a bite; stretching back against the sofa, he rested one long leg out in front of him.

I smiled; if there's an opposite of *sorry*, that's how he looked. "Seb…you know I appreciate everything you've just said. God – so much. But when we attack the Twelve, I have to be there with Alex. I *have* to be. I've got to learn this."

Seb's eyebrows drew together in thought as he finished eating; I could sense him putting aside his own feelings. "You will – I'm just not sure how else I can explain it to you," he said. Brushing his hands off, he sat up and held them out to me. "Here, see again what it's like for me."

I wasn't sure what good it would do – we'd tried this so

many times. I moved beside him on the sofa anyway; putting my hands in his, I closed my eyes. The half-angel energy felt completely familiar now, wrapping around me like a comforting blanket. And the sensation as Seb changed his aura was like second nature to me too by then...but this time, as I drifted into the lights of my own aura, I realized I could feel something different.

In a daze, it came to me: Seb and I had been growing closer every day, so that now I was able to sense what he was doing on every possible level, almost as if I *was* him – and it let me grasp a detail I hadn't managed to catch before. He'd told me this over and over, but for the first time I was experiencing it for myself – the way he kept his aura locked safely away, where it couldn't be disturbed. I could feel how protected that part of his mind was, how cradled away from everything. He'd almost built a sort of barrier around it, though I knew he wasn't even aware of it; he must have done it instinctively as a child.

Mirroring him just as I'd done over two weeks ago, when we'd only barely started, I carefully constructed the same mental shield. Immediately, I felt a calm come over me – as if on a deep level I knew, really *knew*, that whatever I did with my aura now was totally secure.

Blue, I thought, and felt it shift.

I could tell Seb had sensed what had happened, and why. His hands tightened in mine. "Look," he said in a whisper.

I opened my eyes. My aura was a clear sky-blue, with lavender hues. I swallowed, half-expecting it to crash back to silver. Deliberately, I thought of the Council attack; of how much I needed to be there; of every distracting, worrying thought I could throw at myself.

My aura stayed blue.

I reached out in wonder, and watched the blue lights gleaming on my fingers. Exhilaration rushed through me.

"Seb, I've got it! I've really got it!" I lunged forward, hugging him. He returned my hug with a laugh; I could sense his deep relief that I had it now, despite his reservations.

I sank back onto the sofa, staring at my still-blue aura. I experimented with changing it to a dull, stunted grey. The colours dimmed and shrank. It looked like used dishwater clinging to me. I hated it. So would an angel.

I'm not sure how long went by as I sat playing with my aura, shifting its colours with my thoughts. Seb watched in silence. Finally we glanced at each other, and my excitement faded. The closeness between us that had let me finally learn this suddenly seemed like a double-edged sword – because when the team attacked the Council, Seb would be there too now, risking his life. Alex and I didn't have a choice, but Seb did. I wanted him to be safe, just as much as he wanted the same thing for me.

He shook his head, responding to my unspoken

thought. "*Madre mía,* Willow," he said softly. "Do you really think I'd go somewhere and be *safe* while you're taking part in that?"

My chest felt tight. "Seb…you could die. And it would be for a cause that isn't even yours, really."

Almost the moment I said the words, I got a flash of a small girl with big eyes – the same girl I'd seen once before. *Run, niña!* With a frightened gasp, she took to her heels, darting away through a whirling, dancing crowd.

I stared at Seb. "Who is that?"

He shrugged, his eyes distant. "I don't know. A street child." He told me what had happened; how he'd saved her from an angel. I sat without moving as I listened, picturing it all so vividly – and feeling limp with relief that he'd somehow managed to kill the angel with only a knife.

As Seb finished, he pulled a face at himself. "The whole time, I was thinking, *You stupid* cabrón, *what are you doing? You're finally so close to finding her, why are you risking it for this?* But I knew afterwards that I'd do it again. That it was worth it."

"Because she could have been you," I murmured, watching him. He sat with his head down, playing with the cuff of his shirt; the strong features of his face looked almost sculpted. "You helped her when she needed you, the way you always wished someone would help you."

"Yes, I guess that's it." Seb turned his head to look at

me; he seemed to be studying me down to my soul. He smiled slightly. "Even when it happened, I knew you'd understand."

My face heated; we didn't talk much about how it had always been me who he was looking for – as opposed to just any half-angel girl.

He glanced down again, pushed his cuffs up to his elbows. "Willow, I'll be wherever you are when it happens," he said. "Let's not bother arguing, okay?"

"Okay," I got out finally. And in a way it felt inevitable that Seb would be there. But, oh god, I hated it – the two people I cared about most in the world would be risking their lives at the same time.

I'd stopped being aware of my aura as we talked, and now I brought it back into view. It still looked the way I'd last imagined: grey and unappealing. *Purple,* I thought, and watched it turn a rich plum colour. "So I guess I've got the hang of this," I said at last.

Seb was gazing at my aura too. "Yes. Maybe a few more days, to make sure."

I nodded, though I think we both knew I really had it now. But Alex would be sure to insist on the same thing. I sighed, suddenly wanting him here so badly. No, actually, wanting both of us to be somewhere else. Up at the cabin, maybe, going for a walk in the mountains – knowing that we had all the time in the world together.

As if brought on by my thoughts, my cellphone beeped. I pulled it from my jeans pocket and found a text from Alex: *Home in a while. We're OK. I love you.*

I smiled and texted a quick response, then put the phone away. "They'll be here later."

As I glanced back at Seb I saw how he was looking at me – the depth of feeling in his eyes. The wave of emotion from him felt suddenly cut off, as if he'd quickly tried to stifle it, but it still made me catch my breath. I looked away, pretending I hadn't noticed, even though all at once my heart was banging in my chest.

"So, um…we've got time for me to keep practising for a while," I said. My throat felt too small to get words through.

"Yes, all right," said Seb. He sat up, not looking at me as he reached for another cookie. "We'll see how fast you can change it."

I swallowed, taking in the slight flush that had appeared in his cheeks. "Actually…actually, I'll be right back," I said, jumping up. "Do you want a Coke or anything?"

Without waiting for Seb to answer, I went out to the kitchen, where I opened the fridge door and let its chill waft over my face for a few minutes. Finally I took out a pair of Cokes, bumping the fridge door closed with my hip. Then for some reason I found myself putting them on the counter and sending another text to Alex, telling him that I loved him.

When I went back into the TV room, the awkward moment had thankfully passed, and I could tell myself that Seb was just my brother again.

CHAPTER *Nineteen*

"OKAY," SAID KARA ONCE THE AKs were settled in a cafe; the view was of Aztec ruins, with the cathedral rising up behind. She blew on her coffee. "That gang of angels back in the offices appeared a couple of days ago." She glanced apologetically at Alex. "I wanted to get more information before I said anything, with how tense everything's been lately."

He nodded, not really able to fault her for it, though he'd have preferred to know earlier. "And?"

Kara sighed. "From what I've managed to pick up, it's the angel who's been chosen to run the cathedral, along with his groupies. And I don't think they're going anywhere. I don't know if they're discussing details or what, but they mostly seem to be hanging out in the reception area – that means anyone who goes into the main office has to go right past them."

"Are they still there at night?" asked Trish, fiddling worriedly with a packet of sugar.

"I don't know," said Kara. "It doesn't matter; after evening service they kick everyone out and lock up – and their security set-up is a lot better than we're equipped to deal with. Here, look." She showed the team a series of photos taken surreptitiously with her phone – state-of-the-art motion detectors, and steel doors installed above the ancient wooden ones, which looked like they slammed shut automatically if anything went off, trapping you inside the building.

Alex had seen the photos before, but still found himself grimacing as he scrolled through them. Despite his distrust of the CIA, he wished they had some way to get in touch with Sophie – they could seriously use some of the high-tech toys those guys had right about now. He handed the phone to Sam, who'd been craning to see over his arm. "So even with the security code, it's not looking great, is it?" he said grimly. "Not if the offices are chock-full of angels now."

They'd all taken their angel wings off, which were now

lying in a small, satiny pile between their table and the wall. Kara still had on the long wig though; she absently twirled one of the braids around her finger. "They haven't been feeding as much as I'd expect, really, but...yeah, getting past them is definitely going to be high-risk. Between them, I think they've sampled everyone in the offices by now."

Glancing around him, Alex saw that the team looked a little sick. He didn't blame them.

"*But*, I think there could be a way," went on Kara. "Because I don't get much sense of these angels interacting with humans at all, if they're feeding from them – so they can't be that familiar with the workings of the offices. And during evening service, I don't feel any people back there – just these angels. So if someone walked past them into the office then, and looked sort of official – like they had an after-hours job to do – then I don't think they'd challenge them."

"No, just feed off them," said Brendan with a shudder. "This really isn't my all-time favourite plan that I've ever heard so far."

Suddenly Alex knew. He dropped back against his seat. "Seb," he said.

"And/or Willow," agreed Kara. Her voice was businesslike. Whatever she thought about half-angels, she was hiding it for the moment.

Alex shook his head, his mind already ticking, thinking through possibilities. "No, she still hasn't gotten the hang of the aura work. But *Seb*…God, if he'd do it…" The irony of having to ask Seb for assistance wasn't lost on him; he and Seb barely spoke if they didn't have to. Seb had agreed to help them though – and he'd have to see that this was too big for their personal feelings to get in the way of.

Sam's face was screwed up in distaste. He took a slurp of his beer. "Does someone want to explain to me what's going on? Why are we talking about that half-angel guy?"

"Because he can change his aura, idiot, remember?" said Liz, shoving lightly at Sam's solid arm. "That's what he's training Willow to do – remember?"

He glowered at her. "Yeah, but I thought that was just to make it look *normal.*"

"No, he can make it look really unappetizing, too," said Alex. "You know – like the last aura in the world an angel would ever want to feed from. Willow said it's what he does when he sees one on the hunt."

Wesley's habitual frown was back in place, his expression intense. "What about the computers? Won't they have passwords on them?"

Kara sighed. "I think, unfortunately, that's the part we're going to have to play by ear."

Alex blew out a soft breath. He'd known already that breaking into the Church offices wasn't as sure a bet as he'd like when it came to getting the security plans. But it was their only real hope.

"I'll talk to Seb when we get home." He circled his finger through the condensation on his beer glass as he considered how they could best provide Seb with backup. No immediate way sprang to mind – not with that many angels in the office area, and in the narrow hallways that Kara had described. If any trouble broke out, it would be slaughter to have anyone posted back there; Seb was most likely going to have to be on his own.

"Jesus, this is going to be risky as hell," he muttered. He felt a short, fierce relief that Willow hadn't learned to disguise her aura yet.

"Well…there *is* something else we might try, but I don't know how well it would work," said Kara slowly. "The evening service two nights from now is going to be a special one, to celebrate the appointment of the new angel head – and the preacher's going to be giving blessings on behalf of the angels."

Her eyes met Alex's as he took in what this meant.

Liz blinked. "Yes? And?"

"A blessing's seen as a really serious thing to ask for, so probably not that many people will go up," explained Alex. "But for the ones who do, the preacher will hold their hands, maybe for as long as a minute. So Seb could try to get the information psychically first." Even though

Seb had said he didn't always get specific details, it was definitely worth a shot. Not that this option was without risk, either; the angels might decide to make an appearance and sense something amiss. But at least in the main cathedral, the team could provide Seb with cover.

"Will we be able to get in?" he asked Kara. "Every devout in the city's going to want to go to this service."

She nodded. "It's a ticketed event. They're on sale from tomorrow; I'll go down there first thing."

"Listen, are you *sure* we can trust that guy?" put in Sam, leaning on his forearms. "What if he gets in there and starts talking or something?"

"He wouldn't," said Alex. He was sure of that much, at least; Willow would never speak to Seb again if he betrayed them. He drained his beer. "Come on, we'd better get back so I can talk to him."

They left the cafe and started walking towards the Metro station. It was coming up to rush hour, with a steady flow of people all heading in the same direction. Far across the square was a pair of circling angels. Though the AKs couldn't bring them down in daylight with such a crowd around, Alex saw several of the team glance at them speculatively. Good – they were doing scans now without being told.

He hung back a little, walking with Kara. "Can I ask you a favour?" he asked.

She glanced at him in surprise. "Sure."

Alex cleared his throat, wondering how to phrase this. "Well…you know Willow and I don't get much time alone together. So I thought I'd take her out for the night on Friday. Would you be in charge while I'm gone? We'll just be at that hotel on Alfredo Chavero; if anything comes up I could be home in five minutes."

Though he knew Kara still had reservations about him and Willow, she smiled. "No problem – I'll babysit the troops." She gave him a thoughtful look. "Planning a romantic evening, huh?"

Alex's ears reddened; he jammed his hands in his back pockets as they started down the station stairs. "Yeah, sort of." He'd booked one of the hotel's nicest rooms, and arranged for flowers and chocolates to be put in it, plus ordered a special dinner to be delivered by room service. It had pretty much cleaned out his personal funds, but he wanted it all to be so completely perfect.

"Sounds nice," said Kara, her voice neutral. "I hope you have a really good time." As they bought their tickets, Alex was glad she was keeping her thoughts to herself – and even gladder that the issue was settled. Because to be alone with Willow, really alone with her, for an entire night… god, right now there was nothing on the planet that he wanted more.

* * *

When they got home, Willow and Seb were both in the kitchen; Willow was peering into the fridge. "Hi," she said, straightening up as they came in.

Her green eyes lingered on Alex's, smiling. He smiled back. Knowing that just a few nights from now they'd be alone together made it easier to see Seb standing there against the counter. Like always, he'd gone quiet, though Alex had heard him and Willow talking as everyone came in.

Alex had the impression there was something she wanted to tell him; then she glanced at the others and seemed to decide to wait. "I was just thinking about fixing dinner," she went on. "How does chilli sound?"

"Thanks, but I've already got some chicken marinating," said Liz, coming into the kitchen. Her tone was so polite it was practically an insult.

Alex saw Willow give a small sigh as she closed the fridge door. "Well, just let me know if you want any help."

The others passed through without saying much, heading to their dorms or the TV room. As she disappeared, Kara gave Alex a *tell me what he says as soon as you talk to him* look, and he nodded. Meanwhile, Liz had taken Willow's place at the fridge and was pulling out a covered dish. With a flash of irritation at Liz, Alex went to Willow and kissed her, though they didn't usually in front of the others.

He saw her look of pleased surprise as they pulled apart, and resisted the urge to kiss her again. "Hey, can you do something for me?" he said, caressing her arms. "The Shadow's been acting kind of funny – would you take a look?"

Liz glanced up, startled. "What – you fix *motorcycles*?" she blurted out.

"Yes, when I'm not fixing dinner," said Willow mildly. Liz coloured and looked away. Still propped silently against the counter, the corner of Seb's mouth twitched, and Alex knew that none of this had passed him by either.

"'Funny', how?" Willow asked. She was wearing jeans and her green camisole; the pendant he'd given her caught the light with a tiny sparkle.

Alex described how draggy the Shadow had been behaving the last time he'd driven it to the Torre Mayor. He'd forgotten to mention it afterwards, and now he was glad – the look on Liz's face had been pure gold.

"The air cleaner might be blocked," said Willow thoughtfully. "Or it could just be the spark plugs. But I don't have a toolkit, remember?"

"There's one in the hall closet – I saw it the other day." Alex went to the hallway and dug it out. "The Shadow's parked out in the courtyard."

"There's not enough light out there now, though," said Willow. He held back a smile; he could see she was itching to start tinkering. "Could we bring it into the range, maybe?" She smiled. "You can be my able assistant. And there's something I want to tell you – we can talk while I fix it, okay?"

The desire to pull her into his arms was almost overwhelming. Alex managed to restrain himself, and squeezed her hand instead. "Okay, I'll be in with it in a minute." He glanced at Seb. "Can you give me a hand?"

Seb's brown eyebrows rose, but he nodded. "Yes, sure."

Out in the dimly lit courtyard, Alex briefly explained the situation. He spoke in Spanish – Seb's English was good, but he wanted to make sure there were no misunderstandings about this. As the moths battered against the bare light bulb overhead, he could hear the sound of a TV from one of the nearby houses.

"What do you think – will you help us?" he finished finally.

Seb was lounging against the Shadow with his arms crossed over his chest; Alex could see a long, thin scar on his forearm. Seb gave a wry smile. "Yeah, I'll help, but I hope I can get the information psychically – 'cause I really can't say I like your backup plan very much. Search the office with twenty angels hanging around outside? *Amigo,* you have got to be kidding me."

"No, I'm not kidding," said Alex. "But yeah, I'm not crazy about it either. Look, what I need to know most is what time the private audiences are going to be at the celebration and where exactly on the fifty-fifth floor, so that we can head straight for the Council once we're in – if you can get that from the preacher, then forget about breaking into the offices. Do you think you'll have enough time?"

"Yeah, hopefully," said Seb thoughtfully. "I mean, it'll probably be on his mind anyway, so with any luck—" He broke off. A troubled look flickered in his eyes; he went silent, frowning.

"What?" asked Alex sharply.

"Oh, hell." Seb rubbed at his stubbled jaw. "Willow."

"What about her?"

"She's going to want to come, too."

Alex shook his head, picturing the ornate cathedral with its crowds of people; the cruising, feeding angels. "I don't want her anywhere near there. Her aura's way too distinctive with so many angels around."

"Believe me, I don't want her anywhere near there either. She's told me about how those Church of Angels *cabrones* want her dead. But her aura's the whole point. She finally learned how to disguise it today."

Alex went still as he took in what this meant. So this was what Willow had been going to tell him. "She's really mastered it?"

"Once you've got it, I guess you've got it." Seb grimaced

as he kicked at the concrete. "And I know she'll tell you this if I don't," he added gloomily. "She's better than me at getting details from people. If both of us went to the cathedral, you'd have a lot better chance of getting what you need – unfortunately."

Alex saw that in this one thing at least, he and Seb were totally united – neither of them wanted Willow exposed to any danger. He pinched the bridge of his nose, wishing he could just not tell her about the plan. He couldn't even use the possibility of someone recognizing her as a reason to keep her away now; Kara had been disguising herself with wigs and make-up every day to get in there.

Somewhere in the darkness, a cricket was creaking. "Maybe I'm wrong, and she won't want to do it," ventured Seb, not even sounding like he believed it himself.

"Oh, she'll want to do it," said Alex.

Seb exhaled. "Yeah...I know. God, I should just search the office – she couldn't help much with that; she doesn't speak enough Spanish to read the documents."

Now, *that* was appealing. But he couldn't let Seb take that kind of risk unnecessarily – and it was true that if Willow helped, they'd have better luck in getting what they needed. No matter how fervently he might want to, he couldn't put his girlfriend's safety over that of the entire mission; not if there was a reasonable chance she'd be all right.

Reasonable chance. Fear lurched through him; he pushed it away. "We'd better go and talk to Willow," he said finally. "Come on, let's get the bike inside."

Seb detached himself from the Shadow and flipped up the kickstand. "At least this isn't as dangerous for her as the Council attack," he muttered as he wheeled it over to the back door. "When *that* happens…"

Alex had just been moving to the step to help lift the bike through the doorway; now he stopped in his tracks, his spine stiffening. "The Council attack?"

Seb looked at him in surprise, then shook his head with a soft snort. "*Hombre*, how well do you actually know your girlfriend? I know you're not psychic, but come on – you *have* to realize what she's been thinking, don't you?"

Alex hadn't, but suddenly it dropped into place with icy certainty: the Council. With a human-looking aura, Willow could be there when they attacked. He swore as he slumped against the outside wall of the house. "Oh, Christ, I'm an idiot." He scraped a palm across his face. "I can't believe I didn't see this coming…I am such an idiot."

"No argument from me," said Seb. He twisted at the bike's throttle. "Still, you couldn't have *not* wanted her to learn to disguise her aura," he added grudgingly. "Or even put it off, really. She had to know how; it was vital."

"How long has she been planning this?" Alex asked, massaging his temple, where a distant ache had started.

Seb shrugged. "I picked it up from her a couple of days after I arrived. But knowing her, probably from the second she heard about it being possible." His gaze went over Alex, considering him. "She's determined to be there, you know," he said finally. "And not just to help the team – she loves you very much."

Coming from Seb, this should have given him a feeling of satisfaction; instead he was just worried sick. "Yeah, I love her too," said Alex. "So much that I think I'd rather see her get together with *you* than come along on the Council attack."

Seb's mouth quirked into a humourless smile. "That wouldn't get an argument from me either. Just say the word; I'll kidnap her and take us both far away from here."

"Don't tempt me." Alex dropped his hand and let out a breath. "Okay, look – we still have to get the security info if we hope to even have a chance. Let's just focus on that for now."

Seb helped him get the motorcycle into the house, then they wheeled it down the hallway into the range. Willow was crouched on her haunches, inspecting the toolbox. "I'd thought you'd both absconded," she said, glancing up with a smile. Then she took them in more closely. "Hey, is everything all right?"

Alex propped the bike up on its kickstand. "So I hear

you've got something to tell me," he said, stalling for time.

Willow raised an eyebrow at Seb. "You already told him?"

"Yes, I'm sorry," he said. "I should have let you do it." Alex was impressed despite himself by how relaxed Seb seemed – there was no hint anything was wrong.

But Willow's forehead had creased. Slowly, she rose to her feet. "Something's going on, I can feel it," she said to Seb. "You're really worried."

Seb's smile faded. "Willow…"

"Something about me, and the cathedral." She moved closer to him, her eyes searching his. "Seb, what is it?"

Alex watched, his emotions suddenly off-kilter. Why was it Seb's feelings that she was picking up on so strongly, and not his own? Meanwhile, Seb stood almost motionless, looking down at Willow's delicately pointed features…and at the expression on his face, Alex's jaw tightened. Couldn't Willow see that being her *friend* was the last thing on Seb's mind?

Only seconds had passed; Willow was gazing at Seb, frowning intently. Alex almost had the sense they were still communicating. Then she shook her head; fleetingly touched his arm. "You're blocking me out. I can feel it."

Seb sighed. "We'd better tell her," he said to Alex.

Yeah, thanks for the newsflash, Alex thought. Suddenly

his skin felt like it was prickling with heat. What the hell did "You're blocking me out" mean? Was Willow really that used to wandering around in Seb's mind now, sharing everything with him?

Willow's face was tense as she turned to him. She wove her fingers through his, squeezing his hand. "Alex? What's going on?"

Her touch was warm, grounding. With an effort, he shook away his thoughts. *Stop being ridiculous,* he told himself. *Yes, they're close – they're both psychic, for god's sake. It doesn't mean anything, at least not as far as Willow's concerned.*

"Why don't you start fixing the bike, and we can talk about it?" he said. "You stay too," he added tersely to Seb. As much as he wished he could drop-kick the guy into another country, he had a job to do; this concerned both Seb and Willow.

While Willow got to work on the bike, Alex explained, occasionally handing her tools when she asked. Seb sat against the wall, his legs crossed at the ankles. Soon Willow had disconnected a pair of leads and taken off two small, grimy units he presumed were the spark plugs; she inspected them briefly. Even through his distraction, Alex was impressed. He'd never seen her work on an engine before; he himself would have been totally clueless.

"So…that's what's up," he finished.

Willow rested the spark plugs to one side. "Are you asking me to go there with Seb? And see what I can get psychically?"

"Yeah," he said after a pause. "I guess I am."

He could see she knew exactly what this was costing him. "Of course I'll help," she said. "And Alex, it'll be okay."

"I know it will," he said. Picking up a wrench, he rapped it hard against the floor. "Because I'm going to have the whole damn team in there, covering both of you." *Especially you,* he thought, and was grimly grateful she couldn't read his thoughts as easily as she seemed to read Seb's.

Choosing a screwdriver, Willow removed the air cleaner cover, ducking her head down to take a look. "Ah-ha," she muttered as she extracted a plastic bag that had somehow gotten caught in the filter. Then, as if to prove what Alex had just been thinking she looked over at Seb, who hadn't even moved as far as Alex could tell. Her mouth moved in a faint smile. "Hey – I won't be in any more danger than you are, you know."

Seb didn't deny whatever he'd been thinking. With a sigh, he shoved back the brown curls from his brow; Alex saw again the scar on his forearm. "Yes, that's probably true – but you see, I don't care if *I'm* in danger," he said. "When?" he added to Alex.

Sometime next decade, Alex wanted to say. "Day after

tomorrow," he said instead. "That's when the special service is. We couldn't wait any longer anyway, in case we need to use the security code after all. At least it gives you a little more time to practise," he added to Willow.

She nodded. "I will, but I really think I have it now." She darted him an impish look, her green eyes dancing suddenly. "What's your favourite colour?"

He couldn't help smiling. "Blue."

"Okay, check it out."

He concentrated, and Willow's aura came into view – a clear, sky blue, with lavender lights floating through it. Alex stared. He'd been expecting it, but wasn't prepared for his own reaction. Seeing Willow's aura looking so different, as if she was just an ordinary girl, not the girl he loved…it was as if she'd somehow moved far away from him, to someplace where he couldn't get her back. As he took in her life force's gentle blue glow, he felt ridiculously close to tears.

"Alex?" She rested her hand on his thigh, then winced and pulled away, glancing down at her smudged fingers. She wiped her hands off on a rag, giving him an anxious look. "Are you okay?"

"It's great," he got out. He was uncomfortably aware of Seb, who sat watching with an expression that seemed to understand far too much. He cleared his throat. "Seriously… it's great. How about one that the angels wouldn't want to touch?" He'd barely gotten the words out before her aura turned a sickly greyish-brown. It shrank in front of his eyes, hanging listlessly near her body.

Alex blinked. "Wow," he said. "That's – pretty amazing." The realization rushed through him: no matter what else this meant, he'd never have to worry about Willow's aura again. For the rest of her life, she could walk down the street and be safe from the angels.

"Thank you," he said to Seb, and he could hear the relief in his own voice. "That's going to save her life someday."

"You're welcome," said Seb. "I didn't teach her how to do it because of you, though."

"Yeah, I know you didn't," said Alex. There was a beat while they regarded each other – then they both seemed to remember at the same time that Willow was there. Alex saw her watching them with a faintly exasperated look. She shook her head and scrambled to her feet, grabbing up the spark plugs.

"I have to go find a wire brush and clean these off; they're way too dirty," she said. "I'll just be a few minutes."

She left the room, her short cherry-gold hair gleaming in the light. Alex watched her, taking in her narrow shoulders; the green straps resting on her smooth skin. Then, turning, he saw that Seb's eyes were following her too. He'd known they would be, but suddenly it felt like the last straw.

As Willow's footsteps faded away up the stairs, he said in Spanish, "You could give it a rest sometimes. I mean, you don't *have* to watch her every move, do you?"

Seb's voice was mild. "I don't know. Maybe I do." He closed his eyes and leaned back, crossing his arms over his chest.

Alex picked up a screwdriver, tapped it against the floor. "So how's that whole unrequited love thing working out for you, anyway? Hasn't she figured out you two are meant to be yet?"

Seb lifted his head and gave him a long look. "Please tell me that you don't seriously want to have this conversation. Because, personally, I can't think of anything I'd rather do less."

"Yeah, I do want to have it, actually." Alex tossed the screwdriver aside. "Does Willow know you're just biding your time, pretending to be her friend?"

Seb's gaze was cold. "I'm not just biding my time. I *am* her friend."

"Oh, sorry. No, I guess it's never even occurred to you that if you hang around long enough, being the perfect *friend*, she'll come to her senses and fall for you. Right?"

Shaking his head in disgust, Seb closed his eyes again

and settled back against the wall. "You are so far off base, *hombre*."

Remembering his conversation with Willow on the balcony – her pink cheeks as she tried to explain away Seb's feelings for her – Alex had an insane urge to ask Seb if Willow felt the same way about him. Just having the thought made him feel like an idiot. God, he was glad Willow wasn't listening to any of this.

"What's the scar from?" he asked after a pause, nodding at Seb's arm.

"*Dios mío.*" Seb gave a soft, snorting laugh. "Have I told you how much I enjoy these conversations of ours? It's from a sword fight. Or a knife fight, take your pick. The other guy won, if you're interested."

"Not really. Can you shoot a gun?"

Genuine amusement flashed in Seb's hazel eyes as he lifted his head to look at Alex. "Are you challenging me to a duel? Pistols at dawn, best man gets the girl?"

"Dream on," said Alex. "No, I'm thinking about when you and Willow go into the cathedral – if I should give you a gun or not. I'll be right there on the other side of her when you both ask to be blessed, but if anything happens to me, you'll be the best-placed person to defend her. Because she's not bad when it comes to shooting at targets, but if she had to take a shot at another person—"

"She wouldn't," said Seb immediately. "Not unless

someone was threatening you. Or maybe me. But it's so totally against her nature – I can't see her doing it to protect herself; I think she'd hesitate."

It made Alex's jaw tighten to realize how well Seb knew Willow – not to mention that he'd included himself in that list. Though Alex had an uncomfortable feeling he was right. "I know; that's what I'm afraid of," he said. "So – can you?"

"I've shot one a few times," said Seb. "Tin cans in fields, that kind of thing. I couldn't do what you do, but I could probably peg someone who was coming at me. Or Willow," he added.

Alex made a face. Why was he not feeling reassured? "Are you any better with a knife? You've got one, I'm assuming."

"Yes, and yes." Seb pulled a leg up and rested his forearm across his knee; his expression as he regarded Alex wasn't friendly, exactly, but it held understanding. "Look – you really don't have to worry about this," he said. "If Willow's with me, I'll keep her safe. No one will hurt her while I draw breath."

"Yeah, I know that," confessed Alex. And he did – it was one good thing about knowing that Seb loved Willow as much as he himself did. The *only* good thing, in fact.

Willow came back downstairs then. She gave them an arched-eyebrow look, as if she knew they'd been talking about her, but didn't comment. "That should do it; they were completely *black*," she said as she started reconnecting the spark plugs. "Between them and that bag choking the flow to the carburettor, it's no wonder the poor Shadow was acting draggy...it could hardly breathe."

Alex smiled, but was uncomfortably aware of what he and Seb had just been talking about, and what Willow would think if she knew. Meanwhile, smells of dinner were starting to drift out of the kitchen – he could hear Liz moving around in there.

Seb stood up, stretching silently. His T-shirt lifted, and Alex glimpsed another scar on his flat stomach – a raised, ugly one this time, like a twisted worm on his skin.

As Seb dropped his arms again, Willow gave him a teasing look. "Aren't you glad you quit smoking?" she asked, her eyes innocent.

Seb shook his head slightly. "You can always tell," he said.

Willow began putting the air cleaner cover back on, twirling the screwdriver deftly. "Well, it's not difficult. You are practically *oozing* with nicotine cravings, dude." There was a smudge of grime from the spark plugs on her cheek. With her short hair, it gave her an urchin-look that made Alex want to pull her into his arms.

He saw the same warm look in Seb's eyes; then Seb gave a sigh, mock-resigned. "Thank you for the sympathy, it's very comforting. I'm going to go take a shower before dinner. If we're finished?" he added to Alex.

Alex nodded. And as Seb headed off, all he could think was: Willow could sense Seb's nicotine cravings, but not the fact Seb was in love with her? When it was completely evident even to *him*, who wasn't psychic at all? *No way*, he thought, gazing at her. *She just doesn't want to face it for some reason.*

Why not? Was it to protect herself somehow? Maybe if she let herself see the depth of Seb's feelings, she'd have to acknowledge her own. The thought came from nowhere, slithering coldly into his stomach. No way; he *knew* that wasn't true.

But Willow's pink cheeks on the balcony. Her hand on Seb's arm. *You're blocking me out, I can feel it.*

Willow peered up at him from the bike. "So, what were you and Seb talking about just now?"

The words came out with no thought. "Couldn't you sense it from him?"

She briefly closed her eyes, and then gave him a level look. "I didn't try. We don't get *everything* from each other psychically, you know. It's just flashes when we're talking sometimes."

"Okay," he said. It felt like there was something hard and icy lodged inside him. He picked up one of the screws from the floor; rolled it between his fingers. "It sort of seemed like more than a flash, though. The way you were looking into each other's eyes, before."

She touched his hand. "Alex…he's just my friend, that's all. You *know* that."

In what universe does that guy only want friendship from you? Alex didn't say it. "Yeah, I know that," he said. "It's just that it's a pretty intense friendship, isn't it?"

She went still. "Is it?"

He shrugged, putting the screw down. "In each other's heads. Talking together all the time."

"We don't talk *all* the time. But yes, I guess we do talk a lot." Willow drew her hand away from his. "Look, it's just being with another half-angel, and both of us being psychic. I suppose there's a sort of bond between us, without us even thinking about it."

"You really care about him."

Her green eyes were steady. "Of course I do."

"I mean, not just because he's half-angel. Because he's him." Jesus, why was he *doing* this? Why couldn't he just shut the hell up?

"Alex, will you—" Willow broke off, looking frustrated. "Yes. Okay? I care about Seb a lot. I'd care about him a lot even if he wasn't half-angel. The fact that he *is* just makes it an even stronger connection. But I don't—" She worked the screwdriver against the panel again, turning it almost angrily. "I don't want that to make you feel pushed out, or ignored. I love you. My friendship with Seb has nothing to do with our relationship."

"No, except that it feels like there's three of us in it sometimes." He'd been thinking that for weeks; it was a relief to finally say it.

"*Alex.*"

"Well, sorry, but it does. I hardly have *any* time with you now, do you realize that? We hardly had any time together before, and now we have even less. And even when we're alone together—"

Her eyes had gone very large. "Even when we're alone together, what?"

"You're always thinking about him."

"I—" She stopped abruptly, cheeks reddening. Flustered, she glanced down; he saw her swallow.

Alex stared at her. It was something he'd wondered, but hadn't really believed. He'd expected her to tell him he was being ridiculous. "You do, don't you?" he said slowly. "When we're alone together, you're still thinking about *him*. Do you think about him even when we're—"

"No!" she burst out. "God, of course not! How can you even say that?"

"Well, I don't know what to think! Help me out here, okay? How exactly are you thinking about Seb when we're alone together?"

"I don't! It's – there's this sort of link between us, that's all. Like, I can see what he's doing, or where he is in the house…" She trailed off at the look on his face.

"Say that again," he said, the world ringing in his ears. "You have a *link* with him? You can psychically see whatever he's doing?"

"Not *all the time!* Just – I might get a flash, sometimes."

"Like when you're thinking about him," he said acidly, and saw her cheeks turn redder. "So what about him? Does he have this link too? Can he watch everything you do?"

"Alex, you're getting totally the wrong idea about this, I promise you—"

"Answer the question!"

"I don't know!" she burst out. "I haven't asked him."

"So give me your best guess," he gritted out. "Yes or no – can he do this too, with you?"

There was only one screw left on the cover; Willow shoved it on. Her hand on the screwdriver was unsteady, her jaw tense. "I don't want to talk to you about this now. You're too upset."

"Oh, man, you haven't even seen *upset.* This is a 'yes', isn't it? You're telling me that all he has to do is think about you, and he can see you, no matter what you're doing."

She looked close to tears, but also angrier than he'd ever seen her. "It's not like that! You're making it sound really sleazy or something."

"Yeah, sorry – this is just a pure friendship thing, isn't it? So if you thought about Seb right now, in the shower—"

She jammed the tools away in the toolbox and jumped to her feet. "Stop it," she snapped. "You're acting like a lunatic. Which part of *we are just friends* do you not understand?"

He rose too; he could feel the blood beating at his brain. "Oh yeah, because it's really my comprehension skills that are the problem here – I just don't get it, do I? You know what? Maybe I get way more than I want to."

Her face went white. "What's *that* supposed to mean?"

Alex gripped her arms. "It means *he is in love with you*," he hissed into her face. "And now you're telling me you think about him even when you're alone with me, and the two of you share this amazing psychic bond that means he can picture whatever you're doing, whenever he wants – and I'm supposed to be *happy* with that? I'm supposed to go, 'Oh yeah, I guess all that's just *normal* when you've got a half-angel girlfriend'."

Willow was struggling against tears. "Alex—" She took a breath. "Look – please, *please*, can we talk about this later, when we've both calmed down? I promise you, it isn't like what you're thinking."

Alex stared at her for a moment, and then swore and

started out of the range. She caught up with him, grabbed his arm. "Wait – where are you going?"

He pulled away from her. "Where the hell do you think? To throw him out of the house."

"No! Alex, *stop.*"

"What? Are you saying you don't want me to?"

"Of course I don't want you to!"

He could not remember ever having been this angry; it was like a fire raging through him, sizzling his thoughts. The rarely-used front door was nearby, he grabbed her hand and pulled her along to it with him; got it open and them both outside, slamming it shut behind him.

"Let me get this straight," he said in a low voice, with the night air suddenly cool around them. "You don't want Seb to leave. You've just told me that he can *conjure you up in his thoughts* – but that's okay with you, and you want him to stick around."

She had her arms crossed tightly over her chest. Her voice was thin, but steady. "You're making way too much of this," she said. "It's just *flashes* sometimes. And I think our angels would stop it from ever being too…intimate, if neither of us wanted that."

Alex was too angry to even be relieved. "He *does* want that, though. Did you hear me, about him being in love with you?"

Her cheeks went pink. "Yes, I did. Look, I know he

wants to be more than my friend. But he's okay with just friendship – I told him it could never be more than that the very first day."

Alex stared at her. How could she actually believe that? She and Seb were each the only half-angel the other knew – there was no way the guy was going to be happy with just being friends for ever. And the two of them were so close already, after less than three weeks. What would happen when Seb finally made his move? They'd be so entwined in each other's minds and hearts by then – how was she supposed to resist feeling the same?

He stood against the door, rubbing his forehead against a vicious headache that was starting to pound. "I'm not happy with this," he said finally. "I don't care if you have friends who are guys, okay? I really don't. But this, this is something else. You're in each other's heads. You have this intense...*need* for each other, or something."

She seemed to have turned into a statue. "What exactly are you saying?"

He dropped his hand. "I'm saying I want it to stop," he said. "You know how to change your aura now, so you don't need to be alone with him all the time any more. And once this is over with, I want him gone."

Willow started to say something and stopped. She gazed out at the shadowy street, her face tense. "Alex, this isn't fair. He's my friend."

"And I'm your boyfriend. Which is more important to you?"

She gave a short laugh, looking at him in disbelief. "You're not seriously saying *it's him or me*, are you? This is ridiculous!" She took his hand, held it tightly. "Please, please listen to me – I am in love with you. I love you more than anything in the world. I want to grow old with you. Seb is just my *friend*."

Her fingers felt warm in his. For a moment, all Alex wanted to do was hold her; then he pulled away. "Yeah, and you want him around when you're old too."

"Not in the same way!"

"Yes, but you *do*, don't you? You want him around too."

He watched her let out a long breath. "If he wants to be, yes," she said finally. "I don't want him to...to hang around when nothing else is going to happen between us, if that doesn't make him happy. But if he wants to be with me—" She swiped the heel of her hand harshly across her eyes. "Look, you're right; I *do* need him – he's the only other half-angel I've ever met. I need to have someone in my life who understands what this is like. I felt so alone here, before. I—" She stopped, hugging herself.

Alex didn't let himself feel the tenderness that washed over him; the urge to take her in his arms. "Yeah, except it's not even just that he's half-angel, is it?" he demanded. "It's that he's *him*. Look, I'm sorry you've felt alone; I do get that. But I can't handle this. It used to be enough that it was just us, but if that's not good enough for you any more—" He broke off.

"What?" she whispered.

Part of him couldn't believe he was saying the words, but he was helpless to stop them. "Just choose. You can have your wonderful friendship, or you can have me. You can't have both."

She didn't move as she studied his face. "Is this really how much you trust me?" she said, her voice dull.

He felt like punching the door. "Oh, don't even play that card! After everything you've just told me? You can't stop thinking about him! You're attracted to him – do you think I haven't noticed?"

The anger was back in her eyes. "Maybe I am," she said. "In the same way you're attracted to Kara."

"*What?*" He stood staring at her. Where had *that* come from?

She gave him a level look. "Seb's attractive. So's Kara. You'd be blind not to notice Kara, and I'd be blind not to notice Seb. That doesn't mean I don't trust you around Kara – even if she wants more than friendship too. Or did you think *I* hadn't noticed?"

His head felt like it might split in two at any moment. "Jesus, what is this – the best defence is a good offence? I have done nothing wrong here—"

"Neither. Have. I," she gritted out. "I'm sorry you don't trust me. I will do everything possible to make you see that you can trust me. But you are not going to tell me who my friends can be."

"Yeah, and what if you weren't with me, what then?" he said, his voice low and fierce. "Would you still just want to be friends with him?"

She started to answer; stopped abruptly. "That's…not a fair question."

Deep down he knew she was right, and that if the same question were posed to him about Kara, his reaction would have to be the same. It didn't matter. "No, but you just answered it anyway," he ground out. "Like I said: choose. I don't want that guy in my life."

Willow's chin snapped up; he saw again how furious she was. "No, I won't choose – you're being completely unfair. Seb's the only other half-angel I know in the world; I'm not going to cut him out of my life just because you're acting like a jealous jerk." As he stared at her, she let out a breath, pushing her hands through her hair. "God, look, I'm sorry – *please* can we forget all of this, and talk about it tomorrow? We're both upset; we're saying things we don't mean."

There was a pause, with the sounds of the city thrumming around them like a living heartbeat. "No, I'm not," said Alex finally. "I'm saying exactly what I mean."

He opened the door to go back inside and glanced at her as she stood there, with the backdrop of the street behind her. She was so beautiful that it wrung his heart, even now.

"Enjoy your friendship with Seb, Willow," he said quietly.

CHAPTER *Twenty*

I DON'T REALLY KNOW HOW you can come back from an argument like that one.

I didn't eat any dinner that night; there was no way I could have choked food down. Instead I went into the girls' dorm and stayed there, lying on my bed and thinking, *Have Alex and I just broken up?* The words brought back with a chill my premonition from the first time I'd ever seen this house; the unhappiness I knew I'd find here.

God, I hated being psychic sometimes. I lay curled on the faded blue bedspread, listening to the traffic; the distant sound of rock music playing somewhere. And I wished that I'd never even *met* Seb. Then I sighed. No, I didn't. I couldn't wish that; I could never wish that.

Had Alex and I really broken up?

I kept coming back to that, like a scratched record. We couldn't have, could we? Because he still loved me, I knew he did – and I loved him so completely that the thought of not being with him was like not having air to breathe. Surely he'd calm down by tomorrow and see how unfair he was being. Wouldn't he? I'd go downstairs and his eyes would meet mine – I'd see the apology in them, and we'd slip off somewhere alone together and he'd hold me and say, *I'm so sorry, of course I trust you, forget every word I said.*

I stared at the ceiling with its uneven plaster, taking in the shadows cast by every lump and bump. It was a nice fantasy, but I had a feeling that's all it was. I'd never seen Alex so angry. It wasn't like I didn't understand *why*. I knew I wouldn't be thrilled if he'd told me that he and Kara shared a psychic bond. Understatement. The thought would probably gnaw at me day and night, and that's with me being psychic and able to tell whether anything else was going on. Alex couldn't do that – I could hardly blame him for being upset.

No…but I could blame him for not trusting me. For so obviously thinking I had a thing for Seb, and that it was only the fact he and I were together that was keeping me from disappearing off into the sunset with him.

Seb. I swallowed as I lay there. Somewhere in the back of my mind I was aware of how badly I wanted to psychically seek him out. He had to be aware that Alex and I had fought, and I knew how concerned he'd be; he'd want to know I was okay. Almost without realizing it, I started to reach out to him – and then stopped, my cheeks catching fire as I heard Alex say, *So if you thought about Seb right now, in the shower…* Oh, god. There was no way now I could ever feel comfortable again about what had seemed such a natural thing – something that, for all I knew, *was* a natural thing between half-angels; just an extension of our friendship. Feeling completely and miserably alone, I pressed my face against the pillow.

There was a soft knock at the door.

I sat up, my heart pounding. I knew instantly that it was Seb, and I hated the relief that rushed through me; it seemed to validate every accusation Alex had flung at me. But I couldn't help it – I really needed someone right then, and I should have known Seb would sense it, and that he'd be here. That nothing would keep him away.

I'd hardly even known I was crying, but there seemed to be streaks of dampness on my cheeks. I wiped my face and swung my feet off the bed; as I started across the dorm, I scraped my hair back with both hands. It was probably standing up in wild, burning spikes, like a bunch of lit matches.

When I opened the door, Seb stood in the hallway with his hands tight in his jeans pockets, his brown curls tousled. His gaze scanned me worriedly. "Can I come in?"

Oh god, I am so glad to see you. Please, can you just hold me for a while, and let me turn into a blubbering mess on your shoulder? With an effort, I didn't say it. I nodded and opened the door wider. As he stepped inside I hesitated, then closed it behind him. Regardless of what anyone might think, I needed privacy right now; what was going on between me and Alex was nobody else's business.

We sat on my bed; I leaned against the wall. For a few minutes neither of us spoke, and it was such a relief – to be with someone who understood me so totally without words.

"So, this pretty much sucks," I said at last.

Seb grimaced. "It's because of me that you fought, isn't it? You don't have to answer," he added dryly. "Everyone heard. Half of them could hardly wait to tell me about it."

Great. I gripped my arms. "I can't really blame him for being upset," I said. "He's just found out that—" I stopped. I'd never mentioned to Seb that I could sense him even when he wasn't around. Heat swept my skin.

"Oh," said Seb softly, picking up the thought from me. "That – can't be easy for him, I guess." His tone was neutral; I knew he didn't like Alex much more than Alex liked him.

"Is it the same for you?" I asked after a pause. I felt shy suddenly. "With me, I mean?"

Seb nodded slowly. He was sitting on the bed with one foot on the floor, the other leg bent at the knee in front of him. "Even when I'm not thinking about you, you're always in my head somehow." He gave a small shrug. "With anyone else in the world, it would be too much. But with you, it just seems...natural."

It was exactly how I felt. Oh god, I *could* see why Alex was so upset. What if he had this with Kara?

"I don't know if it's because we're both half-angel, or—" Seb shook his head. "Perhaps it's a mix," he said. Though he'd left out a thought, I knew what he meant. Some of this had to be from being half-angel and psychic, but maybe it was enhanced by just – who we were. The closeness we shared.

"How were things left between you and Alex?" asked Seb finally. "What was said at the end?"

I gave a short laugh, swiping at my eyes. They seemed to be leaking again. "A lot of things that hopefully weren't meant." Because Alex couldn't seriously expect me to shun Seb's company, could he? The only other half-angel I knew?

Seb sat silently, studying my face. "Willow...would it be easier for you if I leave?"

I went very still. *No – please, please, no.* "Leave?" I echoed.

"It's me being here in the house that's making things so bad, yes?" He stroked a tear from my cheek with a finger that couldn't have been gentler. "I don't want you to cry any more, *querida*, you see?"

Even through my mental turbulence, I could sense Seb's mixed emotions: how much he hated seeing me unhappy, versus what he hoped could happen between the two of us. Remembering Alex's words, and the look that had been on Seb's face just that afternoon, my chest clenched. Oh god, I didn't want Seb to be in love with me. I didn't want him to be unhappy because of me, ever, not in any way.

"It doesn't matter what's easiest for me," I choked out. "What matters is – I don't want to be unfair to you, Seb. I can't ask you to stay just because I want you here. Not when I don't..." I trailed off. It was the first time I'd told him, however indirectly, that I knew how he felt about me. It was practically the first time I'd really admitted it to myself.

He knew what I meant. He always did. "You're not being unfair," he said, his voice level. "You've been honest with me from the start. I know that you're in love with Alex. And I—" He touched my hair; I saw his throat move. "I love you in all the ways there are to love someone," he said finally. "That includes as a friend and brother. If you want me here, then I'll stay. I just don't want to make things harder for you."

"I love you too," I whispered. "As a friend, I—" My throat closed; I couldn't finish. It all seemed so hopeless – Seb being in love with me when I only loved him as a friend; the argument with Alex that was still pounding at my skull. Oh god, what if we really *had* broken up?

As I started to crumple inside, Seb moved beside me on the bed and put his arm around me. I rested my head on his shoulder gratefully; it felt strong against my cheek. "I shouldn't – I shouldn't let you do this," I got out as I started to cry. "I can't expect you to comfort me when I'm in love with someone else; it's too much—"

"Be quiet and let me hold you," he said firmly.

We sat like that without talking for a long time, Seb's hand stroking my arm as I cried, his cheek against my hair. I concentrated only on externals: the comforting warmth of him as I pressed against him; the slight prickle of his stubble; his clean, woodsy smell. And I tried hard not to think of anything at all.

Finally he smoothed the hair away from my face and said, "The others will be coming upstairs soon...will you be all right?"

I nodded and sat up a little, wiping my eyes. "I'll be fine."

His gaze scanned mine; he knew I wouldn't be. Not really. "I wish I could stay here with you tonight," he said.

"I know. I'll be okay."

Seb's mouth moved in something that tried to be a smile. His arm still around me, he leaned close and kissed my hair, his lips warm as they pressed briefly against my head. I could feel how much he cared – the depth of it embraced me, held me close. Something fluttered inside of me; I pushed it away and closed my eyes, letting Seb's kiss comfort me.

"I'll see you tomorrow," he whispered.

"Okay," I said. "And Seb – thanks."

He rolled his eyes as he stood up. "You would have had to board up the door to keep me out, *querida*."

I hugged my knees to myself, watching as he started across the room – so different from Alex, with his loosely curling brown hair, but his back and shoulders just as firm. As he reached for the door, it swung open.

Kara stood there.

Her eyebrows shot up as she took in Seb, me, the empty room around us. She didn't say anything, and neither did Seb – I saw him start to, and then I think he realized it was pointless; Kara was not going to be too interested in anything he had to say. Instead he glanced back at me. I knew he was saying *I'll see you tomorrow* again with his eyes, and I nodded.

As he left, Kara came in and shut the door. She lounged against it, crossing her ankles. "Well," she said. "That looked interesting."

"Yeah, I'll bet," I said shortly. I unfolded myself from my bed and slid open my dresser drawer, taking out my pyjamas.

"So…are you with Seb now?"

I stiffened, and turned to face her. She met my gaze blandly, her exotic face impossible to read. She had on black jeans; a pink top that showed every line of her sleek body. I could see her *AK* tattoo peeking out from under her shirtsleeve, and suddenly hated it fiercely. It was Alex's – it didn't belong to her.

"No," I said. "Seb is just my friend." *Just* my friend – when, except for Alex, he was the most important person in my life. Language is so stupid sometimes.

"Okay," said Kara, glancing down at her nails. "I was just wondering. 'Cause Alex seems to think so. And, you know…Seb was just up here in the room with you for over an hour, the two of you alone together. Kind of easy to get the wrong impression."

I tried to ignore what she'd said about Alex, even though it made my heart fall off a cliff. "You may find this difficult to believe, but it's actually possible for friends to be in the same room and not do anything," I said.

She gave an elaborate shrug. "Look, *I* don't care what

you do. But I'll tell you one thing – Alex doesn't need this kind of stress right now. So if you wouldn't mind figuring out which one of them you want, that would be a good thing."

"I *have* figured it out," I snapped. Angrily, I yanked off my top, childishly glad that I'd been working out for the last few weeks and was looking more toned myself now. "Look, do you think I don't know you've got a thing for Alex? I noticed it the very first day."

She nodded slowly, watching me. "And do you know he's got a thing for me?"

For a split second, ice froze my veins, and then I caught myself and laughed out loud. "That is a total lie. I'm *psychic*, remember?"

"Okay. So what do your psychic powers tell you about his first crush? Or his first kiss, actually?"

I just stood there in my bra and jeans, staring stupidly at her.

"Alex had a crush on me for years," she said, speaking slowly like I needed it explained in small words. "I used to catch him looking at me sometimes, and he'd blush – it was cute. And now that he's older…well, I think there could definitely be something there." She peeled herself away from the door. Long and lithe, like a jungle cat. "You know, I would never try to make trouble in his relationship if I thought he was happy. But this? Right here, now, with you? Nuh-uh." She shook her close-cropped head. "You are not making him happy, Willow. You're playing mind games with him – you and that other half-angel. God, just flap off out of here together, why don't you, and leave Alex alone? It's not like he hasn't got *enough* on his mind."

My mind was reeling, caught in a storm. "I am not playing mind games," I said in a low voice that somehow didn't shake. "I'm in love with Alex, not Seb. Is that really so hard to understand?"

Kara snorted and turned away. "Yeah, seems to be," she said coldly. "'Cause I don't think *you've* got a handle on it."

Alex was gone when I got up the next morning.

I'd been planning to get him on his own so that we could talk about all this again, calmly this time. But I could tell he wasn't there the second I went downstairs; there was an empty feel to the house, even though it was full of people. I made a mug of foul-tasting instant coffee and drank it slowly in the kitchen, trying to take in the fact that he'd actually gone somewhere without telling me. It seemed even more final than his parting shot the day before – *enjoy your friendship with Seb.*

Trish came in, her hair damp from her morning shower;

she stiffened when she saw me. "Um – where's Alex?" I asked. Heat crept over me, that I even had to ask the question.

"He went to check out the cathedral again." She moved past me to the loaf of bread that sat on the counter. Putting a couple of slices in the toaster, she gave me a tense, sideways look. "So...have you two broken up, or what?"

"No," I said shortly, and walked out of the kitchen.

I wanted to find Seb, but was so aware of what everyone would think now, if they saw us together. Correction: what they'd been thinking all along, from the sound of it. Finally I went into the TV room. Everyone else was there already, apart from Seb. Then, with a sinking heart, I saw that everyone else *wasn't* there – Kara was missing. Of course; she'd gone to the cathedral with Alex. My muscles tightened at the thought of the two of them alone together; what she must be saying to him.

The room had gone silent as I entered. Sam glared; the others didn't look much friendlier. I tried to ignore them all and perched on the footstool, still sipping my coffee. The TV was on. I couldn't tell what was being said, but it was obviously about the Crusaders and the Faithful again. There were crowds of hundreds on the screen; signs bobbing in the air; people shouting in frenzied Spanish.

"Shouldn't you be with *Seb*?" said Liz. I looked up. She was watching me, her sharp-featured face hard. "I thought you were supposed to be practising your aura stuff."

"We're practising outside today," said Seb, appearing in the doorway. He had on faded jeans, and his blue sweater with a white T-shirt peeking out from under the collar. He nodded at me. "Are you ready?"

Relief. We hadn't discussed going outside, but it sounded like heaven; the atmosphere in the house would choke me if I had to stay here all day. I put my coffee down and scrambled to my feet. "Yeah, I'll just get my sweatshirt."

He held it up, and I felt like hugging him. "When's Alex back?" he asked the others as I moved to join him.

For a change, Brendan was sitting almost without moving, staring stonily at the screen. "He said around three."

"Yeah, so that gives you two lots and lots of time to be alone together," drawled Sam. His muscular body was sprawled on the sofa; he flicked a glance over us. "Don't go runnin' off again."

I stiffened; decided not to answer. "I can see all your secrets, you know," Seb said to him mildly as we turned to leave. And nothing was funny just then, absolutely nothing…but even so, the look of guilty alarm on Sam's face was priceless.

Outside it was a gorgeous sunny day, with a cool breeze.

I shifted my aura to dull, lifeless grey and pulled on my hooded sweatshirt. As Seb and I started to walk, I took my phone out and sent Alex a quick text before I could think about it: *I'm sorry we fought. We really need to talk. I love you.*

No reply came.

Seb and I walked for blocks. The shabby businesses around us turned into department stores made of sedate old stone, with bright signs and large windows. The sidewalk grew busier, bustling with people. Satin angel wings, briefcases, morning bags of shopping. I clutched the phone in my hand, glancing down at it every few seconds while my heart slowly died in my chest.

Finally Seb gently pulled the phone away from me and tucked it into his jeans pocket. "I'll tell you if it goes off," he said. "Come on, are you hungry? Let's get some breakfast."

I had never been less hungry in my life. "No, I'm fine," I said distantly.

He ignored me, and steered me towards a sidewalk vendor selling tamales. I could see steam rising from the metal cooking cart. "You didn't eat last night," he said. "And I'm hungry, even if you aren't. So you can keep me company, yes? And then I'm going to show you around *el DF*. You've hardly seen it at all since you've been here."

I managed a faint smile. "You hate Mexico City."

He shrugged as we waited at the tamale stand. "It has some nice places. The only rule is you can't ask if you've gotten a text, all right? I'll tell you, I promise. Just forget about it for now."

Thank god for Seb that day. If it hadn't been for him I would have slowly gone insane while I waited to hear from Alex. Instead, he showed me things he knew would interest me, so that even though the sick worry never went away for a second, it didn't completely drown me. An art museum that was all towering ceilings and baroque gold gilt. A plaza where Aztec ruins sat side by side with a medieval church and a modern office building. Another church; a small stone one that tilted so dramatically I felt dizzy just walking through it. "This is what happens when you build a city on mud," said Seb, smiling at my expression.

We went to a park across the street and sat drinking Cokes on the steps of a monument. Someone was playing guitar, and the smell of cornmeal and spices from the food carts wafted past. The afternoon had grown warmer, so that Seb had pulled off his sweater and tied it around his waist; I'd done the same with my sweatshirt. We hadn't seen many angels feeding, which was a relief. The city seemed to have a calmer feel to it than usual, or something. I wished I could say the same for my thoughts.

"I think you've saved my life today, you know," I said.

"I've saved mine too, then," he said easily. "So I'm being very selfish, really."

He sat leaning back against the white stone steps with his legs stretched out. I saw a girl about our own age eye him appreciatively, and suddenly realized again how attractive he was – his lean, firm body; his high-cheekboned face and curly hair.

If you weren't with me, would you still just want to be his friend?

I flushed and looked away, trailing a finger over a crack in the worn steps. Because just like when Alex had asked me that before, I didn't really know what the answer was. All I knew was that from the moment I'd first touched Seb's hand and sensed him so strongly, I'd felt so incredibly drawn to him – and each day that passed had brought us even closer. He was such a basic part of my life now; I could hardly imagine being without him. I went cold as I thought of my dream, and the flutter that had gone through me the night before.

My god, I wasn't falling in love with Seb, was I?

I shook the idea away in a daze. No. I wasn't. Because I *was* with Alex, and that's all there was to it. I loved Seb as a friend – that was all.

My stomach had gone guiltily tense anyway. "What time is it?" I asked, praying that Seb hadn't been picking up on any of that.

He pulled out my phone again. "A little after two."

Still no text. My gaze met his. Seb's eyes were concerned; beyond that, I couldn't really tell what he was thinking. I was glad, given the direction my own thoughts had been taking.

And I'd see Alex in less than an hour now. Anticipation mixed with dread. The textless screen on my cellphone seemed louder than any shouting from the night before.

Soon after that, Seb and I walked through the park and headed home, taking the Metro. I sat on the hard plastic seat in the crowded subway car, staring at the signs in Spanish. *Home.* It was the only word that fitted for where we were going...yet right then, it didn't feel like a home at all.

"Okay, here's the layout," said Alex.

We were all in the firing range, gathered around Kara's map of the cathedral. Alex had one hand resting on the table, his dark hair hanging over his forehead. He tapped the cathedral's altar on the map. "About halfway through the service, the preacher will ask if anyone wants to be blessed by the angels; probably only about a dozen people will go up. Willow, I don't want you and Seb to be the first ones, or the last either. Let a few other people go up first."

He glanced at me as he spoke; his voice was neutral, professional. Deep down, his blue-grey eyes held a flicker of something else – mostly they just looked as if I was a member of his team and he was giving me instructions. I nodded, trying to focus on what was being said instead of my rigid muscles. Every word, every action of Alex's confirmed it: his cellphone had not been turned off, and my text had not just vanished into the ether somehow.

"I'll be sitting with you and Seb; when you go up, I'll go too," went on Alex. "Willow, I'll be on the other side of you as you're being blessed, ready to cover both of you if you need it. Seb, I'm going to give you a gun, but I want you to spend the rest of today and tomorrow practising with it."

"Yes, all right," said Seb, his voice just as detached. Though we weren't standing right next to each other, the edges of our auras were touching; I could feel his anger at Alex, like a low, simmering fire.

"That doesn't affect you, does it, Willow?" continued Alex. "You can do the aura work on your own now, right?"

The sentence seemed laden with meaning, but again, his tone was bland. I cleared my throat. "Yeah, I think I've got it now. In fact, maybe I should get in some target practice, too." I was heat-pricklingly aware of the rest of the team standing right there watching all of this – and what the topic of the day must have been once Seb and I left that morning. Kara's brown eyes were aloof as they flicked over me, her face giving away nothing.

"Fine, if you think you need it," said Alex. "But don't stop practising the aura work; maybe do half and half." He turned back to the map, pointing. "Sam, I want you and Trish stationed here, about five rows back – in aisle seats, if you can get them. Kara, I want you in the front row like we discussed, or at least as close to it as possible. Wesley, Brendan and Liz—"

I tuned out as I stared down at the map. Alex had already returned by the time Seb and I got back to the house. He'd been in the TV room watching the news with the others – there was a special on about the Crusaders for People's Rights, who were planning a rally the next day, to coincide with the cathedral's special service. No one seemed to have been paying much attention, though. There'd been this awful sense of everyone *waiting* for us…and an even more awful sense of Alex being unsurprised that I'd been out with Seb all day. He'd said hello to me coolly, not moving from the sofa where he sat with Kara and Sam; it had felt impossible to ask for a few minutes alone with everyone staring at us.

Taking in the smooth line of Alex's neck where it disappeared into the collar of his T-shirt, a spike of anger pierced me. Was he really willing to throw away what we had this easily? How could two people who loved each other so much be communicating so badly? When one of them was *psychic*, even?

"Okay, I think that's it for the plans," said Alex, tossing down the pencil he'd been holding. "But there's something else I have to say." He let out a breath, and glanced around the table. "A lot of you overheard Willow and me fighting about Seb last night."

It was the last thing I'd expected. I stiffened, my throat going dry. Around me, the team went utterly still. I could sense Seb's aura stretching out towards mine, wanting to comfort me.

"It was personal; something just between the two of us," went on Alex. "What we fought about has nothing to do with the workings of this team. Willow and Seb are getting the security information for us – that means our lives are in their hands. I wouldn't do that if I didn't trust them completely. So forget whatever you heard; it's irrelevant."

Silence from around the table. Kara had a look on her face that said it was kind of hard to forget it, but she nodded. "We understand." Looking at her starkly beautiful features, for a second all I could think of was Alex's first kiss. It *hadn't* really been her – had it? He'd never even told me that he'd had a crush on her. Meanwhile, I could feel from the slight shifting of mood in the room that Alex had defused the situation a little. But only a little. It was going to be a very long time before anyone actually forgot our argument.

"That's all," said Alex. "Target practice now, if that's what you're doing. Otherwise, just take the rest of the day off and relax. Anyone who wants to go out for a while, go for it – but go in pairs, and watch each other's backs."

As everyone began dispersing, I started around the table to him, but he was already striding away across the range. "Alex!" I called, putting on a burst of speed to catch up with him. "Alex, wait."

He stopped and looked at me. I touched his arm. "Listen, we really need to talk."

"Not now," he said.

"No, we *do* have to talk now. Look, can we go to your room, and have this out? We can't just—"

"*Not. Now,*" he gritted out, kneading his temple with his eyes closed. I stared at him, taken aback by the low vehemence in his voice. He left the range without waiting for a reply. I heard him go upstairs.

No. This wasn't going to happen, not when we hadn't spoken in almost twenty-four hours. He wasn't going brush me off. Seb was standing at the table, loading a magazine; as I glanced at him, I saw that he was looking after Alex with an odd expression on his face. He shook his head slightly, as if to clear it. Our eyes met – and though I knew Seb's mixed feelings must be gouging at him, he motioned almost imperceptibly with his head: *Go after him.*

Upstairs it was quiet, bathed in shadow; everyone was either downstairs or had gone out. As I came up onto the landing I thought at first that Alex must have gone into the storeroom, and I started towards it – but then my neck went cold as I heard him. No, he wasn't in the storeroom; he was in the bathroom.

He was throwing up.

I stood outside the bathroom door, my heart tight with sudden worry. I started to knock and found myself resting my hand on the old wooden door instead, swallowing hard.

"Alex?" I called.

No answer. The noises went on; I had to force myself not to go in. Finally there was silence; the sound of the toilet flushing. Water running in the sink.

The door opened and Alex stood there. His hair looked black against the unnatural pallor of his skin; his face was damp, as if he'd splashed water on it. "What do you want?" he asked, massaging his head.

"You've got another migraine," I said softly. He'd told me how they made him throw up sometimes, the way the pain slammed into him so unexpectedly. I could feel it now, stabbing at his skull like a dagger. "Are you okay?"

He snorted as he dropped his hand. "Yeah, I'm so okay. Willow, seriously, what do you want?"

Did I really have to have a reason to want to talk to him now? I hesitated, taking in his face. "You, um…didn't answer my text."

Around us, the house suddenly felt hollow with silence. "I didn't know what to say," he said finally.

What about that you love me, and you're sorry, too? The words wouldn't come. "Look, can't we just – the girls' dorm is empty; can we go in there and talk?"

A muscle in his cheek moved. "I thought that space was reserved for Seb," he said.

I stiffened; it was as if he had slapped me. I *knew* Kara would tell him about that. "Well, you thought wrong," I said steadily. "He was in there last night because I was upset, okay? You can't actually think anything happened."

"Upset," Alex repeated. "So it's, like, *my* fault he was in there. Got it."

"There was no *fault* – nothing happened!" I stopped and let out a breath. "Alex, please. Don't do this." I couldn't help myself – I slipped my arms around his waist, pressing close against him. "Please. I love you; I know you love me."

I longed for him to lift his arms and wrap them around me. They stayed at his sides as he stood without moving, his heart beating against mine. "Of course I love you," he said. His voice was so emotionless that it sounded like he was saying the opposite. "But I meant what I said last night, Willow. I can't do this. And you've just spent, like, every waking hour alone with Seb since I told you that. So obviously you've decided."

I drew away from him, staring. He was serious. He was actually serious about me never talking to Seb again. I gave a short, disbelieving laugh. "So I was supposed to just do what you told me, even though I think you're completely wrong? Alex, I get how you feel, I really do! But Seb is just—"

"Yeah, just your *friend*, I know," he interrupted. "You keep telling me."

He rubbed his temples again, his eyes closed. I could feel how much physical pain he was in – and despite everything, all I wanted was to cradle his head on my lap and stroke the hurt away. Yearning went through me for that time in his room only a few weeks ago, when I'd done exactly that. It was funny. Things had seemed complicated then – and everything had really been so simple.

"Look, I can't do this now, and neither can you," said Alex at last. "We've got to focus on the job tomorrow. If there's still anything left to say, we'll say it after that."

The lines of his face were so beautiful, so familiar. I remembered being with him in the tent in New Mexico – the things we'd said to each other, the way we'd touched – and something inside of me was dying. But when I spoke, my voice was steady. "There won't be any point. Seb is my friend; he always will be. And with the Council attack coming up…" I stopped, remembering Seb's quiet insistence that he'd be there. "We could all die during it," I said finally. "And I'm not going to live what might be the last few days of my life ignoring someone I care about."

Alex's eyes were cold, stormy seas. "No, just ignoring someone you're supposed to be in love with."

"That's not my choice. It's yours."

He snorted. "Yeah, if you say so." His gaze scanned over me, his jaw tight. Then he shrugged. "I guess that's it, then," he said.

"I guess it is."

And this time, I had no doubt: Alex and I had just broken up.

CHAPTER *Twenty-one*

"SHE'S HERE — WE'VE MADE CONTACT several times now," said Charmeine's voice.

Raziel was in the parking lot behind the cathedral; when Charmeine had called, he'd been about to drive back up to Silver Trail to go over proposed blueprints for the first Camp Angel. "Excellent," he said, resting his forearms on the roof of his black BMW. "So she believes you then."

Charmeine sounded more tired than ever. She managed a low laugh; it tickled at his ear. "Oh, yes. It was a case of 'fish, meet barrel'. I thought you said the woman was a trained CIA agent."

The day was cold, with a gun-metal sky; Raziel climbed into the car for warmth and settled against the comfortable leather seat. "Now, now, give her some credit," he chided. "Hardly anyone knows Nate worked with her. It must have seemed quite the definitive proof that you're a rogue too. So she's got the information now?" From what he'd gleaned from Willow, Kylar actually hadn't been doing badly on his own, though Raziel knew he still needed several crucial pieces of information.

"Yes, everything they'll need," said Charmeine. "Plus one or two little details that'll get your Angel Killers trapped inside the building once they're finished, so that we can take care of them."

"Perfect. But she hasn't actually made contact with Kylar yet, has she?" Raziel was sure she hadn't; Willow's thoughts lately had been preoccupied with the plan to try to get the information from the Church. That and her love life, which was fascinating in a sickly way.

"Not yet," said Charmeine. "I thought it would be best if she could track him down on her own if possible, so that it doesn't seem like I know too much. Fortunately there's a mass demonstration scheduled in the Zócalo around the same time as that special service at the cathedral you said they're going to – she's already decided it's a likely place for him to be, with so many angels liable to be around. So with luck, they'll encounter each other. If not, I'll have to tell her my rogue angel powers have figured out where they live."

Raziel frowned. "Just stay away from the team yourself," he cautioned. "My— The half-angel is extremely psychic."

Charmeine's tired voice snapped with irritation. "Raziel. She's what, seventeen? I know I'm under daily psychic attack here, but come on – you don't think I could outwit a complete novice?"

In the car, Raziel was still shaking his head at himself for his near-slip. "There's no need to take chances, that's all."

"Fine, I wasn't intending to go near them anyway. People who can shoot halos make me nervous. Which reminds me; you really might have told them to ease off a little. There've been over twenty angel deaths in two weeks here – and that's with not as much feeding going on as usual, now that the roots the Twelve have been putting down are starting to take affect."

"Oh?" said Raziel uneasily. "Is anything going to be done about it?"

"No, I don't think so. Angels here are up in arms, but there's not much that *can* be done, the way they're striking – there's never any knowing where, or what time."

Raziel was unsurprised; Kylar was nothing if not a good strategist. "Well, I'll do my best to reign them in," he said. "But they're very keen, you know."

He heard Charmeine snort. "Thanks, that's good of you," she said. "Anyway, in a few more days it might not even matter any more."

"How are you doing?" Her weary tone worried him; she sounded like a woman struggling to hold on.

He could almost see her making a face. "All right, I suppose. But I'm glad the reception's soon. I'm counting the hours until I don't have to keep up a psychic barricade any more."

Anxiety prickled over him. "It's getting harder for you to hold them off, isn't it?"

Her voice turned crisp. "Don't worry – I can hold out till the bitter end, I promise. Meanwhile, I suppose you've heard about Tyrel."

"Yes, I've heard," said Raziel shortly. The news in the angel community was that the Council had recently appointed Tyrel to run the Church of Angels in Mexico – an angel who'd been a hated adversary of Raziel's for eons. Doubtless, this was exactly why the Twelve had appointed him.

"Well, we're going to have the last laugh," said Charmeine. "You'll be travelling down for the fun, won't you?"

Raziel gazed at the mountains, looming sharply against the blue sky. No matter what other consequences the attack might bring, the Council would soon be dead – and if their deaths killed him too, he wanted the last sight he ever saw to be the twinkling shards of their destruction. Thinking of their TV appearance, with their thinly-veiled death sentence to him – *That is our promise* – he gave a hard smile.

"Oh, I'll be there," he said. "I'll book a flight tonight."

"Good. Because you know, I think we actually have a chance. It just feels *different* in this world, doesn't it? We might really survive this."

Once he and Charmeine had hung up, Raziel took his laptop out of his briefcase. With a silent click of a button, he turned it on and opened the files from Project Angel, the covert CIA department which had funded and overseen the Angel Killers. He'd managed to take it over months ago; the special agents now all had angel burn, or had been killed.

Except one.

A few strokes on the mouse pad, and a photo appeared on the screen: a résumé head-and-shoulders shot of an intense-looking young woman with shoulder-length brown hair. Sophie Kinney – a junior agent who'd been quickly elevated by the angelic invasion of her department; she and the traitor Nate had barely made it out in time to save their lives. From his exploration of Willow's thoughts, Raziel knew about Sophie's role the day the Second Wave had arrived. She and Nate had taken Willow to the cathedral by helicopter; Nate had stayed behind to help Willow with the attack on the gate – and been killed, as it turned out; the memory filled Raziel with satisfaction. Meanwhile, Sophie had escaped to a safe location. Smart girl.

But she'd been seen by the security guard at the back door. The same security guard who she'd later tracked down to question in disguise, in an attempt to find out where Kylar had gone – because as far as she knew, he was the only Angel Killer left in the world. Raziel's response to the security guard's worried email had praised him for his devotion to the angels and asked him to keep his encounter with Sophie confidential.

Just send me the contact details that were left with you, and the angels will take care of the matter, he'd finished. And he had done so to perfection. His email to Sophie had, he thought, been something of a masterpiece.

I understand you're looking for Alex Kylar. So am I. I was a friend of your former colleague Nathaniel, and share Nathaniel's goals. There are several of us in Mexico City – where, as you might not be aware, there have been multiple angel killings recently. We believe Alex Kylar is here, and that he's formed a new group of Angel Killers. There are further details that I cannot disclose via email, but as a matter of extreme urgency, we feel that you, our group, and his need to join forces in order to battle the threat that faces this world.

As he'd thought, Sophie had taken some time to

respond – he smiled as he imagined her frantically checking out what details she could on her own, before she'd finally, cautiously written back – but eventually she'd bitten, and he'd deftly reeled her in. And now she was down in Mexico City, in touch with Charmeine the friendly rogue angel – and doubtless very, very excited that she and Kylar were about to rid the world of the angel menace. Bringing back Sophie's image, Raziel smiled. *No need to thank me,* he thought. *Really. I'm only too happy to help you find him.*

Because Kylar knew Sophie. He may not like her, but he knew her. He'd trust information that came from her. And that, thought Raziel as he snapped off his laptop, was the only way to beat Kylar at his own game.

Seb really couldn't believe that Willow's boyfriend was this stupid.

As the team took the Metro to the Zócalo, Seb stood beside Willow in the crowded subway car. Dozens of angel wings surrounded them, looking bent and bedraggled in the throng. The team was scattered throughout; Alex stood with Kara and Wesley, half a car-length away. He and Willow had barely spoken since officially breaking things off the day before – when they'd had to, they'd been cool and professional with each other. Now Willow stood quietly as the train sped them all towards the cathedral, her face expressionless. The crystal pendant she'd always worn was gone from around her neck. Though she'd made it clear that she didn't want to talk about what had happened, Seb could sense her anger; the depth of her hurt.

The train lurched. Willow grabbed his arm briefly to steady herself, then offered him an apologetic smile; conversation wasn't an option with the noise. She was wearing make-up, which she never did. It made her look older, though no more beautiful. As Seb smiled back, he wished that he had the right to put his arm around her for no real reason, just to feel her pressed closely to his side. And he thought he could cheerfully throttle Alex, who *had* had the right, and apparently cared so little about it that he was willing to break up with Willow simply for being friends with him. Seb mentally shook his head in disbelief. God, if Willow was his – if he could be with her the way he longed to be; if he could actually go into a room with her and shut the door and tell her how he felt with words, with his lips; hear her say the same things back while she stroked her fingers through his hair – then he wouldn't care *who* the hell she was friends with. Who in his right mind would? No matter how much Willow cared about him, she would never cheat on Alex, never; did the *cabrón* not *know* that?

By now, Seb had a lot of practice in keeping thoughts like these buried. As he entertained himself with fantasies of dragging Alex to one side and telling him in great detail exactly what an idiot he was – perhaps throwing in a punch now and then to emphasize the point – the uppermost part of his mind was busy concentrating on the car around them; the advertisements; the people. Willow could have sensed what he was feeling if she'd tried, but Seb knew she wouldn't. From the start, it was as if they'd had an agreement: he wouldn't make the fact he was in love with her too obvious, and she'd pretend not to notice it.

As the train rattled its way through the tunnels, Seb supposed he should be glad that Willow and Alex had broken up. But it was obvious how deeply they were still in love with each other. Even across the crowded car, he could sense the emotional ties that bound them; he was sure they'd manage to patch things up soon. Meanwhile, feeling how much pain Willow was in was agony to Seb, so that he found himself in the bizarre position of wanting to pummel Alex until he saw reason and made things up with her. Seb smiled wryly. He wouldn't really have believed it, but he wanted Willow's happiness more than he wanted his own.

He wasn't a saint, though; sometimes it was all he could do not to just pull Willow into his arms and start kissing her. And he prayed with everything he had that she'd get Alex out of her system soon and see what was so blindingly obvious to him. Because thinking of her dream – of the whole sequence of events that had led him to her, spiralling back through his life for years – Seb couldn't believe that fate had brought them together only to be friends. It was clear to him that he and Willow were meant to be, not just because they were both half-angel, but because of who they both were, their personalities. It was as if their souls had been crying out for each other their whole lives.

Seb knew if Willow never felt the same, he'd deal with it somehow – being in her life as a brother was a lot better than not being in her life at all. It was becoming more difficult by the day, though. He'd never have dreamed he could fall *more* in love with his half-angel girl. But actually being with Willow in person, feeling the effortless depth of their connection that was like nothing he'd ever experienced – and knowing that it could still be so much more; a whole world more, if she'd only open her eyes and see it too – Seb let out a breath as the train started to slow. He wasn't sure if it made things better or worse that he thought he'd caught glimpses of attraction from her sometimes; thoughts so fleeting, it was as if she had no control over them. On the whole, he thought it made it worse, given how much she was in love with Alex. And it definitely made it harder for him to be brotherly towards her.

That's exactly what you're going to do though, he told himself. *Until she tells you she wants something different, you are only her brother.* He glanced down at Willow's red-gold hair, her face. She'd see it for herself someday, he thought. She had to.

She just had to.

The train reached Zócalo station; the doors unfolded with a pneumatic hiss. "I guess this is it," murmured Willow, her forehead creased with apprehension.

"This is it," agreed Seb, pushing his thoughts away.

They jostled off the car. Everyone in the world seemed to be going to the Zócalo. Alex and the others had exited further down; the group rejoined each other near the station stairs. As they started up, they could hear a thunder of voices chanting: "El DF *is dying! Funds for doctors, not angels!* El DF *is dying! Funds for doctors, not angels!*"

The Crusaders rally, Seb realized. As they came out onto the Zócalo, they could see it – a solid, fist-waving mass of people gathered near the Palacio. Their auras were blood-red, merging together and throbbing towards the sky as the people chanted, so that the crowd looked like a single, angry creature. Seb stopped in his tracks, neck prickling. He'd seen auras like that before – usually around street gangs before a fight. Never around thousands at once.

Nearby, hundreds of people wearing angel wings had gathered, screaming just as furiously: "*The angels will provide! If you have true faith, the angels will provide!*" Though mostly damaged, their auras were a furious red too, straining towards the Crusaders. Dozens of grim-looking security guards patrolled the edges of the crowd, while overhead several angels cruised, with glinting wings.

Willow glanced at Seb. Her green eyes looked larger than usual, accented with eyeliner. "This really isn't good," she whispered to him, and he knew she meant the seething auras, rather than the angels on the hunt. Like him, she had to be picking up on the vibes of the rally too – the organized fury surging all around them.

"It'll be all right," he muttered back.

"Did we know this was happening?" demanded Sam, frowning at the scene.

Seb rolled his eyes. Sam had been watching it on the news with the others when he and Willow returned to the house the previous day. "Yes, we knew," said Alex briefly, leading the way towards the cathedral. "It doesn't affect us."

Except that it did.

As they neared the Catedral de los Ángeles, they could see slow-moving lines snaking out the entrance; stretching all the way down to the tabernacle. "That doesn't look right – the doors are supposed to be open by now," said Kara. "Alex, I'm just going to go and check." Before he could respond, Kara was running off, her long braided wig bouncing down her back.

Alex glanced towards the cathedral with a frown. "Here,

everyone," he said. He was carrying a large plastic bag; he dipped into it, passing out angel wings. As he handed a pair to Seb, their eyes met – Seb could see Alex's controlled dislike of him. The feeling was mutual.

Alex gave Willow a pair of lavender wings, avoiding her gaze. Willow avoided his too, accepting the wings silently. She had on a short black skirt and top she'd borrowed from Liz, with a jean jacket over it and a pair of unfamiliar heeled sandals that gave her a long-legged look. Seb was in a pair of grey trousers and a crisp white shirt he'd borrowed from Wesley. The others were dressed similarly; Alex had wanted them to blend in with the churchgoing crowd as much as possible. While it grated to take orders from him, Seb had to admit Alex was good at what he did. It was a job he himself would have had no desire to take on.

"Are these straight?" Willow asked him in an undertone. She presented him with her back, where the lavender wings hung askew. Seb straightened them for her, adjusting an elastic strap where it had twisted on her shoulder and trying to ignore how the short skirt showed off her figure. Out of the corner of his vision he saw Alex watching them, and held back a snort. If Alex was jealous, it was his own stupid fault. Willow would never normally have asked for Seb's help instead of Alex's own.

"They're straight now," he told her. *You look beautiful,* he managed not to add.

He'd come so close to saying the words that Willow caught them easily; her cheeks coloured. "Thanks," she said, and he knew it was for the compliment too. "Yours are fine," she added, glancing at his white wings.

Kara came sprinting back. "Alex, it's bad," she panted. "There's been a security alert at the cathedral; they're worried about a terrorist attack with the Crusaders rally going on. They've installed a metal detector."

"*What?*" Alex's head jerked towards the cathedral doors. He swore under his breath.

Seb went still, thinking of the switchblade in his pocket. He was carrying a gun too – the holster felt strange under his waistband – but knew he'd have been likelier to go for his blade in case of trouble.

"So…what does this mean?" asked Liz finally.

"It means we'll take our guns off and go in anyway, right?" offered Brendan.

Alex's frustration was almost palpable. "What good would that do? If there's any trouble, we need to be able to shoot. *Damn* it." He shoved both hands through his hair. "We can't put it off," he muttered to himself, staring at the line of people. "The security code will change tomorrow…"

"We might not need the code," pointed out Willow, her voice cool.

"Yes, but you might," he gritted out. "We can't take the chance; the Council will be gone in just four days." He blew out a breath. "Okay," he said finally. "We're going to have to wait outside the doors for you. Both of you, give Kara your weapons. Willow, hand me your cellphone."

After covertly handing Kara her gun, Willow dug in her jean-jacket pocket for her phone, her mouth tight – Seb knew without trying that she was irritated at having orders snapped at her. Keeping his back to the crowd, he drew out his own gun and switchblade, passing them to Kara. She tucked them away wordlessly in her bag. Her opinion of him was so obvious that Seb couldn't resist smiling and saying, "You won't steal my blade, will you?"

Her brown eyes turned even chillier. "Don't worry. *I'm* not the one who steals things."

Across the square, the sound of chanting was still going strong, pounding through the air. Alex fiddled with Willow's cell, punching buttons on it. As Seb glanced at him, the moment froze.

Though he could see auras without trying, he didn't check out each one he encountered in detail; it would have been information overload. But the day before, as Alex had left the range to go upstairs, Seb had thought he'd seen something strange in his aura's blue and gold hues. He'd dismissed it as a trick of the light – yet now, in the pure, slanting sunlight of late afternoon, he was seeing it again.

Alex's aura was damaged.

CHAPTER *Twenty-two*

SEB STARED AT THE COLOURS of Alex's life force. He'd never seen anything like this before. He'd encountered thousands of auras with angel burn in his life – was all too familiar with the grey, sickly look it caused, with the aura's natural colours trying to regain themselves through the pallor. This was similar, but different: the colours themselves looked faded. The blue – which Seb was sure had been a rich ocean-blue when he'd first met Alex – now looked dull and greyish; the gold almost tarnished, with faint black spots.

The damage looked as if it had been caused by angels… and yet not.

Willow's question barrelled back to him: *Do we cause angel burn to humans?*

It wasn't something Seb had noticed; certainly none of the girls he'd ever been involved with had shown anything like this. But then his chest went cold as it hit him. He'd never been with a girl for any length of time, had he? He'd only had flings; a day or two at most. Willow had been with Alex for months.

Only seconds had passed. Alex handed the phone back to Willow. "Here – I've put my number on speed dial. Keep it in your pocket; we'll be right outside once the service starts. If there's any trouble, just hit the *call* button and we'll get in there somehow."

Seb tore his gaze away, his thoughts spinning as he remembered Alex's migraines, his constant headaches, and thought of the dozens of ominous issues those things could mean. His first and main concern was for Willow. If this was what he thought, it was going to kill her to find out she'd been hurting Alex.

Willow hesitated as she took the phone, scanning Alex's face as if searching for a hint of softness. There was none. She slipped the phone into her jacket pocket, her made-up face abruptly aloof.

"Yes, all right," she said.

She glanced down, buttoning her jacket. And then Seb saw the look she'd been waiting for flicker across Alex's features, turning them young and vulnerable – and he knew Alex was in as much torment as she was, but too stubborn to admit it.

Willow cleared her throat. "So I guess we'd better go get a place in line," she said. The rest of the team was standing a little apart now, talking among themselves; Seb could feel Sam's disappointment in particular that they weren't going in.

Alex's face was expressionless again. "Yeah, all right. We can't wait with you; it would look suspicious if we peeled off before we hit the metal detectors. Be careful, okay? We'll be right outside." Though he sounded sincere, he also sounded like he was talking to any other member of his team, and Seb longed to take a swing at him. *Just apologize, you stupid jerk.*

Except that it was too late for that now, wasn't it? Studying Alex's aura again, Seb could see more clearly than ever that he hadn't been mistaken. His throat felt like sand. How exactly was he supposed to tell Willow this?

She nodded stiffly at Alex's words; he could feel the depth of her hurt that he wasn't backing down even now. "Seb, are you ready?" She turned towards him – and her expression slackened in surprise as she picked up on his anxiety.

"Yes, I'm ready," he said, burying his thoughts as best he could. His gaze met Alex's. A fierce look flashed in the blue-grey eyes, and Seb knew Alex was telling him to take care of Willow, to keep her safe in case some rabid Church member recognized her and raised the alarm. As if he really had to be told that.

"Okay, you've both got your tickets – and you know the code if you need it, right?" said Alex out loud.

Seb nodded; he and Willow had both memorized it. "Don't worry," he replied evenly. And added in his head, *Believe me,* hombre, *I'm not keeping her safe for you – but I'll keep her safe with my life.*

He and Willow started across the uneven expanse of the square; she was taller than usual in her heels as she glanced at him worriedly. "Seb, what's wrong?"

"I'll tell you later," he said.

"But—"

He heard the strain in his own voice. "Please, *querida.* I'll tell you later, I promise."

Willow wavered, searching his face, and finally nodded. "Okay."

The line moved slowly once they joined it, but everyone seemed cheerful, chatting happily about the angels and how exciting it was to be going to such an important service. He and Willow fitted right in with their satiny angel wings. After a while, they could see the stairs that led down to the cathedral entrance, with the rectangular shape of the metal detector set up at the bottom of them.

"I'm relieved to finally be doing something, you know," said Willow in a low voice. Her gaze was fixed on the metal detector and the guards flanking it either side as people shuffled through, showing their tickets. "I've hated, *hated*, having to just sit at home while all this is going on."

Her aura, like his, appeared grey and listless. Seb wasn't surprised that she hadn't noticed Alex's. Her natural psychic focus just wasn't centred on auras; she didn't tend to bring them into view unless she thought there was a reason to. And in Alex's case, why would she? Seb had told her himself that she wasn't causing him any harm.

Seb cleared his throat. "Yes, I know how much you've hated staying at home."

At his non-committal tone, Willow smiled. "Let me guess, you wish I was still there. Honestly, you're as bad as—" Catching herself, she broke off with a sudden wince, her expression pained.

Seb couldn't help himself; he put his arm around her, squeezing her shoulders as he drew her against his side. *It'll be all right, mi amorcito*, he wanted to say. But he didn't really see how it could be, now. Oh god, this was going to destroy her. And what did it do to Seb's own hopes? True, it probably meant Willow would never get back together with Alex, but for it to happen like this – when she was still in love with him; when she knew she'd hurt him with her touch – she'd never get over him then. Never.

Willow was gazing up at him, her expression full of dread. "You're thinking about...whatever it is again," she said softly. She swallowed. "It's something to do with me and Alex, isn't it?"

He was saved from answering. Just as they reached the top of the stairs, there was a squeal and a flurry of angel wings. Three pretty girls raced up to them. "Seb! *Bonsoir!*" exclaimed the one with dark hair. Before Seb quite knew what was happening, she was kissing him on both cheeks; he reciprocated automatically. The other two girls followed suit. Willow blinked, looking taken aback by the social kisses.

"You left the hostel!" laughed the dark-haired girl in French, her tone mock-chiding. Céline, that was her name. "None of us knew where you were; one day you just vanished." Her gaze went to Willow, taking her in curiously.

Seb was acutely conscious that the three girls were devouts, and had almost certainly seen Willow's photo on the news, or the Church of Angels website. "*Oui*, I met my girlfriend," he said, his arm still around Willow's shoulders. "Maria." It was the first name that came to mind. In English, he said, "Maria, this is Céline, and – I'm sorry," he said to the blonde. "Is it Nicole?"

The girl *tsk*ed and shook her sleek head; she looked pale and too thin. "Ah, you see, he forgets all about us once he has you," she teased, glancing at Willow. "Maria, *this* is Nicole" – she indicated the third girl, a tall redhead – "and I am Adèle."

"Hi," said Willow, offering her hand to them.

They started moving down the stairs; to the irritation of the people behind them, the trio showed no signs of leaving. Céline was still gazing at Willow. "You look so familiar," she said suddenly. "Are you an actress?"

Seb's muscles went tight as Willow tried to smile. "No, but everyone says that," she said. "I think I must look like someone."

"So this is where you girls ran off to – I thought you'd abandoned me," said a cheerful American voice. A guy with floppy brown hair had come up behind them. Mike. He caught sight of Seb and his face burst into a grin as he slapped his shoulder. "Seb! God, man, where have you been?"

"He has a girlfriend now," pouted Céline, tucking her arm through Mike's. "I am very sad at this. You'll have to comfort me later."

"Oh, hey, that's too bad," said Mike in a soothing voice. "Yeah, we'll have to have some serious comforting time when we get back."

They'd reached the bottom of the stairs; somehow the three girls and Mike had gotten ahead of them. Smiling widely, Mike turned and gave Seb a double thumbs up as the girls started filing through the metal detector.

Willow's expression was slightly dazed. "Friends of yours?"

Seb shrugged; he could hardly believe they'd all appeared. "I know them from the hostel I was staying in."

Something in Céline's handbag had set off the machine; the guard went through it as Mike and the girls clustered around. The other guard motioned for Seb and Willow to wait.

Willow watched as Céline laughed and flipped back her chocolate-brown hair. "The girls are all very pretty, aren't they?" she said in a neutral tone. "That one, Céline, really seems to like you."

Seb stared down at her profile. Was he imagining things, or had there been a glimmer almost like jealousy from her? Then Willow seemed to shake her head at herself and the sense faded. The guard motioned her through; she groped in her pocket for her ticket and moved forward, heels clicking on the marble floor.

They came out into the packed main cathedral. As Seb had seen before when he'd had a look around, the bones of the place had been altered somewhat since his boyhood – but its flesh was now completely different. Far away down the aisle, golden angels shone from the ornate floor-to-ceiling altar; smaller ones held candlesticks aloft from the corner of each pew. There were several real angels too, gliding through the high-domed space, wings flashing like mirrors. Reaching out with his mind, Seb found a throng of them sitting in the unseen office area – easily over a dozen.

"Look, here's a seat," said Céline, tugging at his arm. "There's room for all of us, if we squeeze."

"Thanks, but Maria and I will—"

Céline ignored him and reached across to take Willow's arm instead, laughing as she drew her into the pew. "Come, come! We haven't seen Seb in weeks – we want to meet his girlfriend!"

Behind them, people were waiting to get past; Mike shoved Seb good-naturedly into the pew ahead of him, beside Willow. "Nice wings, dude," he whispered. "You took my advice, didn't you – told her you're a devout."

Seb's eyes met Willow's as they both realized: it was either make a scene and perhaps draw attention to themselves, or stay where they were. "I think it'll be all right," murmured Willow to him as they sat down. "The service will be starting soon, anyway."

"We must play a game," announced Céline once they were settled. "What actress does Maria look like? Because she looks so familiar it's driving me insane. Seb, who do you think?"

He shrugged. His heart was suddenly pounding. "I don't know," he said, gazing at the converted cathedral and trying to sound uninterested. "She's more beautiful than any actress."

The three French girls all cooed in delight. Mike nodded. "Definitely the right answer." He offered his hand to Willow. "I'm Mike, by the way. I'm from Sacramento, what about you? I heard an American accent, right?"

"I'm from Maine," said Willow, shaking his hand. Seb could sense her anxiety. "Bangor."

"Yeah? What brought you down here?"

Her lavender wings moved as she shrugged. "The same as everyone else, I guess."

"How did you two meet?" asked Nicole, leaning forward. Her eyes had circles under them. She looked approvingly at Willow's angel wings. "Did the angels bring you together?"

"Um…" Willow swallowed and glanced up at Seb, her gaze searching his. "Yes, sort of."

Her hands were tense on her lap; he took one of them, and she gripped his fingers tightly. "It's a long story," he said. "But I'll tell it if you like. It's very romantic." He was already planning how he could spin it out; make it so boring that they'd completely lose interest in Willow.

"Wait, wait, I know the actress!" burst in Céline, bouncing slightly in her seat. "It's that girl with long blonde hair – what is her name? She's been in so many things!"

Seb froze. Long blonde hair. *Madre mía*, in another moment she'd have it.

"No, people usually say Keira Knightley," said Willow quickly. "Or…or Katie Holmes."

"Keira Knightley?" Céline frowned in surprise. "No… well, maybe a tiny bit…"

To Seb's immense relief the service started then with a rippling of harp music, and conversation stopped. The three French girls faced forward, eyes shining as the preacher made his way up the small spiral staircase to the angel-winged pulpit. Willow let out a breath. Seb stroked his thumb across her fingers, aware that he wasn't at all sorry to be posing as her boyfriend.

The preacher looked younger than Seb had imagined, with dark hair and a wide smile. He raised his hands to the sky, smiling out at the congregation as he spoke into a microphone. "*Bienvenido a la Catedral de los Ángeles.*"

An interminable sermon about the angels' love; how lucky Mexico was to now have its own personal angel; lots of standing and singing hymns and then sitting down again. Céline and the other girls knew the hymns by heart, though the lyrics were in Spanish. Willow pressed close to Seb as they shared a hymnal, her head down – obviously trying to keep her face away from their notice now.

Finally the moment came when the preacher asked if anyone wished to be blessed on behalf of the angels.

He came down from the pulpit to the balustrade, his questioning tone echoing through the speakers. Thankfully, the angels they'd seen when they first entered the cathedral were gone now, apparently sated. When Seb checked, he could sense they'd joined the others in the office area for the time being.

A few people started going hesitantly towards the front, footsteps echoing on the shining marble. Willow gave Seb's fingers a meaningful squeeze as she released them. He nodded. "Excuse us," he whispered to Mike. The American's eyebrows shot up; Seb could practically hear him thinking, *What – really?* But he didn't comment as Seb and Willow edged past.

Neither spoke as they went down the long centre aisle. They both knew more angels could appear at any time, and sense his and Willow's energy, if they got close enough. Willow's chin was up, her gaze steady on the balustrade where people were kneeling. The preacher was already blessing the second applicant, his lips moving in prayer as he held the man's hand. The woman he'd just blessed stayed kneeling, head down.

And from nowhere, the thought flashed through Seb's mind how right this would feel, if circumstances were different: to walk towards an altar like this with Willow someday. If she felt the same, he'd even do it now, despite both their ages. Because, as he glanced down at her beside him, he knew that this girl – this woman – was the only one he'd ever love. She'd had his heart for almost his entire life; she was woven into the very fabric of him.

They reached the balustrade with the great golden altar gleaming before them, and kneeled side by side on blue velvet cushions. Willow bowed her head; Seb could sense her complete focus on the job at hand. Pushing away his thoughts, he cleared his own mind, getting himself into the relaxed state that he used for his readings.

It seemed to take for ever. Finally the preacher reached Seb, his eyes gentle. "Do you wish to be blessed by the angels, my son?"

"Yes, father." Seb held out his hand; felt the priest take it.

A burst of sensation, images, knowledge. Seb's heart sank. This wasn't the usual preacher at all – the usual preacher was sick. This man was visiting from another state, and though ecstatic at the thought of meeting the Seraphic Council in a few days, he'd arrived only hours ago – had hardly even had a chance to speak to anyone before he'd been asked to do the evening service. Seb probed deeply, but his spirits were sinking. There was nothing here to get; this man didn't know the details of the reception yet.

The priest lightly touched Seb's bowed head and moved on to Willow. Seb stayed where he was. He could sense her discouragement after a moment, and knew she'd found out the same thing as him. At last the preacher moved on again, to a man wearing a grey business suit.

Seb turned his head on his clasped hands, gazing sidelong at Willow. Their eyes met; she bit her lip, and glanced at the arched door in the shadows that led to the offices. "Seb, we've got to go in there," she whispered.

He nodded reluctantly, eyeing the office doorway. Maybe he could leave Willow in the corridor, while he attempted to go past the angels himself.

She was regarding him with a small smile. "Think again," she murmured.

Seb blew out a breath and looked back towards the door. As he did, he saw the first woman the preacher had blessed, still kneeling with her head on her hands...and his eyes widened as he took in her aura. The other life energies at the balustrade were either grey and sickly, or soft pastel hues of devotion; hers was an ugly, furtive mustard-yellow, with angry red veins.

As he watched, one of the woman's hands left the top of the balustrade and pressed something underneath it. She rose and walked quickly away.

Seb's skin crawled with sudden apprehension. Turning, he saw at least ten people with similar auras, all of them now hurrying towards one of the side exits. The woman was running now. A man spun around as he reached the door and shouted, "El DF *is dying! Funds for doctors, not angels!*"

As the first explosion rocked the cathedral, Seb lunged for Willow, tackling her to the ground and shielding her with his body. He heard her cry out and closed his eyes tightly as another explosion came, and then another. Things were pattering to the floor around them; something small and hard bounced off Seb's back. The smell of smoke – Willow's body trembling under his. Shrieks of fear and pain, mixing with the thunder.

Finally the explosions stopped.

Screams echoed through the cathedral as the congregation started stampeding for the doors. Seb dared a glance up and saw pews and bodies lying twisted and tangled; debris; the golden altar blackened. The man in the business suit sat slumped against the splintered balustrade, covered in blood. The young preacher lay motionless, half his head blown away. Seb had barely taken it in when a flock of angels with furious faces streamed out through the wall from the office area. They circled once in the smoky air and then angled up and out, vanishing through the high ceiling.

Urgency pounded at him; they had to get out of here. He struggled to his feet, helping Willow up – she was pale and shaking. Looking back at the entrance, his gaze somehow found Mike sprawled across a pew, obviously dead. *Mike.* Seb stared, stunned, wondering fleetingly if Céline and the others were all right. He couldn't tell; the main entrance had turned into a seething mass of people, screaming and struggling to escape.

Suddenly a stained-glass window shattered inwards, the glass angels splintering as the crowd outside battered something through its panes. "El DF *is dying! Let the angels die too!*"

Willow stood staring at the preacher, tears running down her smoke-smudged face. Seb grabbed her hand, pulling her after him as he started running towards the back of the cathedral, to the exit he'd told Kara about. Willow was still crying but stopped short, tugging at him. "Seb, no! We've got to go back into the offices; this is our only chance!"

Forget about saving the world, I just want to save you! But she was right. Seb held back a curse; still gripping her hand, he turned and headed for the shadowy corner. They both had their arms to their mouths, coughing; as they passed the mangled altar again, Willow's face was pale but resolute – he could sense she was holding onto herself tightly, determined to do what had to be done. They reached the office door, where she jabbed in the security code unhesitatingly.

A green light glowed. Seb threw open the door and they ran down a narrow stone hallway lined with paintings of angels. As the door closed behind them, the sound of shouts cut off abruptly; an almost eerie silence descended. Around a bend were the new offices – a large reception area with sofas and chairs. The door just beyond stood open; Seb could hear the hum of computers.

They rushed in – there was another door to the right. Opening it, Seb saw a large mahogany desk. This computer was on too; he slid into the chair and tapped the mouse. The box requesting a password came up, and he swore. He glanced at the mouse again, rested his hand on it. He wasn't usually very good with objects, but he didn't need *details*, just some kind of hint; a clue—

Only jumbled images of angels came. *Ángeles*, he typed. Wrong password. *laiglesiadelosángeles*. Nothing.

Willow had gone for the filing cabinet, tugging at it fruitlessly. She ran over. "Keys, are there any keys?"

As she spoke, Seb's gaze fell on a carved wooden angel beside the monitor. A tickle of knowledge came, and he grabbed for it – small silver keys lay underneath. He snatched them up, gave them to Willow.

"Try the mouse for me – we need the password," he said tensely.

"Oh god, I'm not great at this…" She touched the mouse, frowning. "Um – something about the angels' glory, maybe?" She sprinted back to the files. "What's the Spanish for 'Seraphic Council'? And 'security'?"

Seb told her, furiously typing in *lagloriadelosángeles*. It worked, and he heaved a sigh of relief – but no sooner had he accessed the email account than the lights in the office flickered and died. The computer screen went black. Seb stared blankly at it. At the filing cabinet, Willow gave a surprised yelp; then her angel appeared overhead, casting light on the files.

Somewhere, a rhythmic banging noise had started.

Seb looked up, his skin prickling. He reached for his own angel self, sent it soaring down the hallway. As he burst out into the main cathedral, he saw that most of the congregation had now escaped, but the place was full of rioters – tipping over pews, smashing windows. Several of them were battering at the locked office door with an angel statue, their auras blood-red as they yelled obscenities. Wheeling on one wing, Seb saw the wooden door start to buckle. Someone else ran up – a man shouting at the others to move aside. He pulled a gun and began firing at the door.

Seb sped back to the offices; as he merged, his human self was already lunging towards the filing cabinet. "Willow, we've got to go!"

She shook her head anxiously. "Wait, this file might have something – it feels important—"

Seb heard the door crash open down the hallway, the echo of shouts. "*Now!*" He pulled Willow bodily from the filing cabinet; she resisted for a second, hanging back to yank the file out, and then they were both running, Willow with the file clutched to her chest.

They raced back out into the narrow hallway. Around the bend, it sounded as if the rioters were ripping the paintings down from the walls and smashing them. Then came running footsteps, heading their way. Seb and Willow were already tearing down the corridor in the opposite direction, her angel flying overhead to light their way down the dim, windowless passage.

As they turned another corner, Seb saw that the fire exit he'd remembered was still there, its sign looking blessedly ordinary as it beckoned to them. He threw himself against the door's metal bar and they spilled out into the cool twilight of a car-lined street behind the cathedral.

There was no time to be relieved – they'd burst out into another battle. Crusaders and Faithful were fighting each other in a seething mass, at least a hundred of them: fists swinging, the sticks from placards being used as weapons. Angels with enraged faces flew overhead, occasionally ducking down to rip away the life force of a Crusader. A man screamed, clutching his chest as he fell to the ground. The fighting continued around him like churning water.

Seb and Willow ran along the side of the cathedral. Her angel had returned to her, leaving them bathed in shadow. All at once, Seb stopped short, feeling both Willow's sudden, pulsing fear and a rushing sensation like a wind tunnel: a huge flock of angels was heading right towards them. Oh god, their half-angel energy – Seb didn't know if the angels would stop long enough to sense them; couldn't take the chance. Too hurried to be gentle, he shoved Willow up against the rough stone wall of the cathedral, his body hiding hers as he grabbed hold of both their auras with his thoughts – struggling through sheer force of will to bring them so close to their bodies that they couldn't even be seen, so that he and Willow were only shadows in the darkness.

Their auras seemed to scream in protest; Seb's muscles shook with the effort to hold them in the unnatural position. Energy roared over his senses as more than fifty angels sped past barely a wing's-length away, soaring over the cathedral.

The rushing faded. Mental silence, with only the physical sounds of fighting still going on. Abruptly, Seb became aware of how closely he was pressed up against Willow – the warmth of her body next to his. Letting go of their auras, he pulled away, feeling drained and trembling.

Willow's eyes looked huge as they stared at each other. He saw her swallow. "I – I didn't know you could do that," she said. Distantly, the wailing of sirens filled the air.

Seb shook his head. "No, me neither," he got out.

Behind them, the fighting was still going strong, though the angels who'd been joining in had departed, apparently joining the larger flock. There was the sound of breaking glass nearby; in the distance he saw a pack of dark figures running. A car on fire.

Suddenly Willow gasped. "Oh my god – Alex! I totally forgot—" She fumbled in her jacket pocket for the cellphone, then searched her other pocket, her expression turning frantic. "My phone's not here! It must have fallen out in the cathedral—"

Seb slapped at his trouser pocket, but knew already he didn't have his phone, either; he was so unused to carrying one that he always forgot it. The thought faded as he stared at the burning car. Without answering Willow, he reached for his angel self and flew upwards into the night, hovering above the cathedral as he scanned the streets around them.

The *centro* was on fire.

Or at least that's how it looked at first glance. Riots had broken out all around them – people were surging through the streets, breaking store windows, setting things alight. The sound of gunshots echoed from somewhere; more sirens. The Zócalo appeared to be a single heaving mass of people; Seb could hardly even see the Metro entrance. It was the same in almost every direction he looked. And the AKs' house lay over a mile to the south, just past the thick of it all – attempting to go back there now would be madness.

Willow's angel had joined him in the air; she swooped in a circle, her lovely features distraught. On the ground, Willow's human self was staring at him. "Where are Alex and the team?" she said in a strangled whisper. "I can't see them anywhere! Do you think—" She broke off.

Seb gripped her hand. "Can't you sense them?" He meant, *Can't you sense Alex?* He himself wasn't close enough to any of the team to bother trying. The only person to whom he'd ever been close enough to sense was Willow.

As their angels returned to their human bodies, Willow closed her eyes tightly. Finally she gave a small nod. "They're alive," she said. "I think…I think they're all okay. I can't really tell; I'm too upset to get much." Her expression was pained. Seb knew she was thinking about Alex, and dread kicked through him as he remembered what he still had to tell her.

The shouts behind them intensified; more people were throwing themselves into the fray. Glancing back, Seb could hardly even tell if it was still the Crusaders fighting the Faithful, or just herd mentality turned vicious. With a chill, he remembered the angel wings they were both wearing. "Come on, we'd better get these off," he said, yanking the elastic straps from his shoulders. A moment later both pairs of wings lay on the ground beside the cathedral.

"What now?" asked Willow in a tiny voice. She was still clutching the file to her chest, and Seb could sense she was barely holding onto her composure – that the deaths they'd witnessed were battering at her, threatening to take her down. She cleared her throat. "I…I don't think we're going to make it to the house anytime soon."

"No, it's not safe," agreed Seb. He felt bludgeoned by what they'd seen too; he ached to take Willow in his arms and just hold her for ever, comforting them both. But they needed a safe place to go until this was over – and given the way Céline and the others had almost recognized Willow, none of the city's devout-filled hostels or hotels would be it.

The only direction that had looked relatively clear was to the north.

As the answer came to him, Seb's jaw tightened with grim humour. He might have known that he wouldn't get out of going there – that somehow events would herd him to the place like a dog herding sheep. Only with the *centro* literally in flames would the neighbourhood of his childhood ever seem like a safe haven, so that he could even consider taking the girl he loved to it.

Willow touched his arm. "Seb, what is it? Where are you thinking of going?"

"Tepito," he said. He took her hand; barely resisted the urge to kiss it. "Come on — I know someplace there we can go."

CHAPTER *Twenty-three*

ALEX STOOD WITHOUT MOVING AS Willow and Seb headed across the square. Willow looked amazing in the short skirt, but he wouldn't have been able to take his eyes off her even if she'd been wearing her usual jeans and sneakers. He watched her figure grow smaller as she and Seb neared the cathedral, her legs striding briskly in the heeled sandals.

She didn't look back. He hadn't really expected her to. As the two of them disappeared into the line of waiting people, he let out a breath.

"You okay?" asked Kara.

"Yeah," said Alex shortly. For a second, he longed to go running after them; to draw Willow to one side and… what? She'd made it clear there was nothing more to say, that she cared more about her friendship with Seb than her relationship with him. Deep down, he knew it wasn't so simple – that there were shades of grey, among the stark blacks and whites that had kept him awake, staring into the darkness, these last two nights. He felt incapable of untangling them. All he could see was Willow's pink cheeks when he'd accused her of always thinking about Seb – the look on her face as she'd touched the sleeve of his sweater that night. He was still so in love with her that it hurt, but he had no idea where her head was any more.

Forget all of this – just forget it. He was sick of his own stupid thoughts.

"Come on," he said to the team finally. "Let's make a move."

Half an hour later they were standing in front of the cathedral, listening to an angelic hymn drifting out. Behind them, someone was yelling through a megaphone about the inequity of a city that would spend money on angels, and not beds for its dying. As the crowd roared in approval, the Faithful screamed their protests, trying to get past the security guards – who looked pitiably few in number now, shouting unheeded orders at Crusaders and Faithful alike.

"Man, they're going to lose that battle any second now," murmured Kara, watching the guards struggle. "And when they do, that's going to turn nasty."

Alex nodded; just being near the scene was making him jumpy. The AKs couldn't have chosen a worse time to be here if they'd tried. He took out his cellphone again and glanced at the screen. No call from Willow.

"Wait, what's happening now?" Brendan peered down the dark steps to the entrance. "The singing's stopped."

Alex couldn't make out the preacher's words, but it seemed about the right time for the blessings to be taking place. *Be careful, babe, please be careful.* He was helpless to stop the thought. Hands jammed in his pockets, he stood against the outside wall of the cathedral, resisting the urge to look at his phone again.

He jerked upright as an explosion rumbled, the force of it trembling the ground under his feet.

"What the hell—" Sam's eyes were wide; his voice drowned out by the thunder of several more explosions.

Oh Jesus, there *had* been an attack, and Willow was in there— Alex bolted for the entrance while the explosions were still going, hurled himself down the steps. He met a stampede head-on – thousands of shrieking, panicked people, all fighting to get out. The metal detector was trampled to the floor with a crash; people were pushing at him, shouting, forcing him back up the stairs in the swell of humanity.

"Let me through!" he yelled in Spanish. He propelled himself into the hysterical crowd. "Let me *through*!" Three crying girls shoved forward, shouting in French. Alex lunged past; found himself grappling a man with a frantic face. Howling obscenities, the man threw a punch that connected hard with his chin; Alex punched back without thinking and was past him in a second, battling his way against the tide. Willow was in there, Willow—

Others were fighting to get in too – there were shouts of "Kill the angels! Kill the angels!" as some of the Crusaders barrelled through in a group. A dark-haired woman clutching a baby stood crying in fear, battered from both directions; he saw her start to go down. Despite his own frenzy to get inside, Alex couldn't ignore her – she and her child were seconds from being trampled.

Gritting his teeth, he got over to the woman and put his arms around her, then fought his way across to the wall with her, shielding her. He could feel the woman shaking as he was pounded from side to side, rocked by the crowd. "It's okay, you'll be okay," he kept repeating in Spanish, and all he could think was, *Willow, please god, let her be alive.*

Finally the crowd thinned; an opening appeared on the stairs behind him. "You'll be all right now, *Señora*," he said quickly, stepping back. She threw herself at him, kissing his cheek.

"*Gracias, Señor, gracias*—" She turned and ran, holding her child tightly; she hadn't even made it to the first step before Alex was racing into the smoking cathedral. Several of the pews were crackling with flames; bodies lay scattered like abandoned toys, surrounded by hymn books and debris. The rioters were everywhere – pulling statues over, smashing paintings into splinters, shooting at the stone columns that marched down the centre aisle. With a cheer, a gang threw a pew through a stained-glass window; it crumpled into brightly-coloured fragments.

Alex drew his gun and made his way, coughing, to the front, checking out every body that he passed – terrified that one would be Willow, her green eyes empty and unseeing. *Oh god, Willow, I'm sorry, I didn't mean anything I said – please, just be alive, we'll work it out, I promise—*

In front of the altar, near the charred and crumpled balustrade, he found Willow's phone lying on the floor, its screen cracked. He gripped it hard as he looked wildly around him. Had she dropped the phone while escaping? Or had she been so close to this bomb that there was barely anything left of her? He shoved the thought away. The office; maybe they'd searched the office – he ran towards it, weaving past the sprawled, lifeless bodies.

The office door had been shot open by rioters. Suddenly

he was in a smoke-filled tunnel. He plunged forward, eyes streaming as he held his arm over his face.

"Willow!" he called in a strangled voice. "Willow, are you in here?" A bonfire crackled halfway down the corridor: oil paintings warping and twisting. He took a running jump and got past it somehow; half-fell as he landed and kept going. When he reached the office door more smoke was pouring out – the reception area and inner offices were all in flames, furniture lying on its side, files scattered.

"Willow!" he got out again. He searched the smoky den the best he could, crouching low and feeling his way around the floor. The heat was a solid wall; the smoke was in his throat, up his nose – fogging his brain, making it hard to think. A splintering crash came as the desk collapsed. Sparks flew, sizzling at his exposed hands and cheeks.

"Alex!" Kara had appeared, holding someone's jacket over her face as she tugged at his arm; her eyes looked like red, burning coals. Her shouts were muffled. "We've got to get out of here—"

"No!" he choked out. "Willow—"

"She's *not here!* Do you want to die, you idiot?"

He resisted, but the smoke had made him weak. Kara half dragged him from the office. In the corridor, smoke lay heavy in both directions; taking the slightly better way, they found the paintings on the stone floor had almost burned out. They got past the sputtering flames and burst back into the relative clarity of the cathedral. Police had arrived, struggling with the rioters – Alex saw someone go down as an officer clubbed him over the head.

"They won't like us any better," gasped Kara. "We've got to get to that side exit Seb told us about."

Alex was bent over coughing. He shook his head, wiping his streaming eyes. "No, I've got to keep looking – she could be in here—"

Kara gripped his arms, her nails gouging at him. "Listen to me!" she hissed. "There is an angel *war* going on outside, and your team's on their own! If she and Seb are alive, they'll take care of each other. If they're not, it's too late anyway, so come *on*!"

Even through his shirt, Kara was clutching him hard enough for her nails to break the skin. The pain cleared his head. She was right. He hated it, but she was right. With a last look at the bodies that lay scattered around them, Alex nodded. It felt like he was tearing his heart out and leaving it behind.

"Come on," he said shortly.

As they escaped out the side door, he thought to do a scan, cursing himself for not doing it sooner. He lifted above his chakra points while they pounded back towards the Zócalo, searching feverishly. Around them shouting gangs were smashing windows; looting from stores; rocking cars over. He couldn't feel Willow's distinctive half-angel energy anywhere. So either she'd gotten away and was somewhere on these riot-choked streets, or she was dead. Alex gritted his teeth. No, he refused to believe the latter. He refused.

Take care of her, Seb, he thought as they reached the Zócalo again. *Oh man, I beg you – take care of her.*

There was no time for further thought. The riot raged through the square as Crusaders and Faithful battled it out; the police were there but not enough of them. Overhead, dozens of angels swooped like fiercely beautiful birds. In a bizarre way, the scene was reminiscent of the Love the Angels concert he and Willow had watched their first night here.

"Where's the team?" Alex couldn't see them anywhere.

Kara stood staring, her beautiful face smudged with smoke; she held a pistol half-hidden under her bag. "I don't know! When I went in after you they were still near the cathedral, but—"

She broke off as a flying angel exploded into nothing near the Palacio Nacional.

"There!" said Alex. With his own gun drawn, they took off at a run, skirting the edges of the crowd. A ripple had passed through the angels at the death – they were now gliding in the same direction as he and Kara. Dozens of them, and he was still too far away to help the team.

Please don't all be sticking together in a group again, he prayed as they ran. Their only hope was to use guerrilla tactics and hide in the mob, picking off the angels one by one. They'd be massacred otherwise.

Almost as soon as Alex thought it, he spotted Sam's broad shoulders and blonde hair. He grabbed Kara's arm and they ducked into the throng. Reaching Sam, Alex found him gazing up at the sky, blue eyes narrowed.

"Where's the rest of the team?" he demanded, raising his voice above the shouts.

Sam leaned close, bellowing in his ear. "Don't worry! I've got 'em posted all over. We've got our phones on vibrate too, so you can call us in when you need to. The designated meeting spot is over by the Palacio, near the main doors."

Relief made Alex's muscles weak. "Good work," he called back. "Really good work, Sam; I mean it."

Sam was squinting up at the sky again. "Yeah, it's this asshole lead I'm stuck working under – guess maybe he taught me a few things."

Alex clapped him on the shoulder. "Come on, we'll fan out too," he said to Kara.

She nodded. Her eyes met his as she slipped away into the crowd, and he saw the same thought that was in his own mind: without the security information, their attack on the Council might now be doomed – but at least they could do something about what was happening here.

Alex's jaw tightened. More than that, taking some kind of action might stop him from going insane right now.

Hidden by the battling crowd, Alex chose his moments carefully – only firing when he had a clear shot and trying not to get sucked into the fray. Soon he'd brought down three angels; as he aimed at a fourth it burst into glittering leaves of light. *Nice one,* he thought to whoever had gotten it.

"Alex!" called a female voice.

Willow? His pulse thudded as he spun in place. But the woman struggling her way towards him was around thirty years old, with shoulder-length brown hair. For a confused second Alex couldn't place her; then his muscles stiffened. Christ, he'd never expected to see Sophie Kinney again – would have been just as happy not to, the way she'd left Willow to die in Denver. What was she doing *here?*

With a flash of radiance, an angel dove at someone right behind her. Alex quickly took aim, and felt dark amusement as Sophie stopped short, eyes wide – she apparently thought he was about to blow her head off. He pulled the trigger; the creature vanished into fragments. Sophie gave an alarmed cry as the rush of energy from the kill swept past. It affected you like that at first. Then you got so used to it you barely noticed any more.

"An angel," Alex explained as he closed the distance between them.

Sophie gulped, nodded. "Yes, of course." She glanced nervously at the boiling throng around them. "Alex, I need to talk to you."

Before he could reply, frenzied screams broke out, along with a pulsing, hissing noise. People shoved past, drenched and running. Alex grabbed Sophie's elbow, moving them hastily with the flow. More police had arrived, and they'd brought water cannons – jetting, merciless blasts that were knocking people off their feet, making them scramble away on all fours. In a matter of minutes, everyone still here was going to be arrested, and probably handed over to the angels. Jogging now, Alex veered towards the Palacio Nacional; through the dispersing crowd, he glimpsed Trish and Brendan, already heading that way. As he and Sophie ran, he pulled out his phone and punched a few buttons, calling the rest of the team in.

"I've rented a truck – it's parked nearby," panted Sophie.

He brought her aura into view, scanning it. No sign of angel burn. "Good," he said shortly. "We'll need it, to get through these streets." And under everything was the constant heartbeat of *Willow, please be okay – please, please...*

As the team gathered, Alex frowned to see Wesley clutching his left forearm. "What's wrong? Are you hurt?"

Wesley's face was an ashen grey. "An angel was reaching

for my life force. I shot it, but I think it tore away a little bit over my arm or something."

Alex's heart sank as he and Kara glanced at each other. He knew doctors could do nothing – Wesley would regain the use of his arm as his aura tried to heal, or he wouldn't. It was how Cully had lost a leg. He tried to quell the immediate voice that told him this was his fault; that he shouldn't have had the team out on their own yet.

Wesley's expression had gone hard, watching them. "What?" he demanded. "It'll be better in time for the attack, right?"

"If we're lucky," said Alex. Their late-night conversation in the range came rushing back; hiding his doubt, he clasped Wesley's good shoulder. "Seriously, it could be totally fine – we just need to get you back so you can rest."

"Alex, I have *got* to take part in the attack—"

He broke off as Trish drew closer, her face creased with concern. "Wes, are you okay?"

Wesley nodded, his expression softening a little. "Yeah, I'm fine." Like everyone, he got along well with Trish; Alex wouldn't be surprised if he'd even told her about his family having angel burn. She touched his arm, unconvinced.

"Man, that's gotta hurt," said Sam, wincing. Then he noticed Sophie, and scowled. "Who's this?"

Looking back, Alex saw the police had arrived in full

force now, and were sweeping through the square. "CIA," he said. "It's okay, we can trust her. Come on, we've got to get out of here."

Sophie's poise had returned, so that now she was as cool and businesslike as he remembered. "My truck's parked nearby – let's go." She led the way, hurrying across the square.

Liz glanced around as the team followed. "Wait, where are Willow and Seb?"

"I don't know," bit out Alex, walking in long strides. "Hopefully still alive."

Liz started to say something else and stopped, looking stricken. Kara cleared her throat. "Hey, is Miss CIA who I think she is?" she asked, obviously changing the subject.

Alex had told Kara what had happened the day of the Second Wave – how Sophie had left Willow at the cathedral with no escape plan. "Yeah, that's her," he said grimly.

Sam was still glowering with suspicion. As they reached the street, he hauled Alex to one side. "That's who? She's not another half-angel, is she?" he hissed.

And despite everything, Alex almost laughed. "No, Sam. She's not another half-angel."

It took us over half an hour to walk to Tepito by back streets. The sandals pinched at my feet; I ignored them and walked even faster. When I peered over my shoulder, I could still see a reddish glow in the sky over the *centro*; hear the incessant blaring of sirens. Once there was a distant explosion – a burning car, maybe. My breath clutched at the sound; for a second I almost went faint, seeing again the bodies in the cathedral. Seb glanced at me in concern, his fingers tightening around mine. We hadn't stopped holding hands since we'd started walking. Distantly, I supposed I should pull away, but there was no way I could have brought myself to, right then. If it hadn't been for the warmth of Seb's hand, I'd have gone crazy.

Swallowing hard, I searched mentally for Alex again. At first there was nothing, and then faintly, through the chaos of my mind, came the familiar feel of his energy. It was like getting a static-y radio station, but it was there. He was alive. That was pretty much all I could tell, and in a way it was enough – though remembering the cold look that had been in his eyes before Seb and I went into the cathedral, my heart ached even more than before.

Stop it, I ordered myself harshly. *It was over between the two of you anyway. If you doubted it, then that should have been your tip-off – because if he was still in love with you, there's no way he'd have let you go in there without telling you. None.*

The thought of it really being over between us – of Alex not being in love with me any more – hurt far too much to dwell on. I'd put the file that I'd stolen under my jean jacket, buttoning it into place, and now, as we walked, its stiff cardboard jabbed against my ribcage. Focus on that, I told myself, not Alex. And absolutely not on what happened in the cathedral. The file; the sandals hurting my feet. Seb's hand. Just focus on Seb's hand – the firm grip of it; how warm and caring it feels – and not bodies, sprawled helpless and bloody across the cathedral floor. Not the young preacher, with half his head blown away and one eye staring up at the painted angels on the ceiling.

Definitely do not think about these things.

The sidewalk had become trash-ridden and more crowded with people now; the buildings to either side looked run-down and grimy. I could sense from Seb's sudden reluctance that we were almost there, though his body language was as laid-back as ever. He let go of my hand and put his arm around my shoulders.

"You're my girlfriend again, okay?" he said. "Don't look around you too much, no matter what you see. They don't like outsiders here. They think of them as prey."

I nodded, my throat almost too dry to speak. "No matter what I see?"

We turned a corner and there was a marketplace ahead: a long, dingy street filled with lit stalls. I could see clothes for sale; jewellery and cellphones. Vendors were shouting at customers in Spanish, hawking their bargains. Seb's expression as he took it all in was twisted with more bitterness than I'd ever seen on it.

"This is the place where you can buy things," he explained shortly. "Drugs, weapons. The end of someone's life. Just ignore anything you see."

Entering Tepito was like ducking into a long, rustling tunnel, formed by the plastic awnings of the market stalls. They seemed to close in around us, just like the thudding rock music that was suddenly everywhere. There were stalls selling angel statues, angel key chains, angel T-shirts. DVDs of popular movies, lots with the titles misspelled. Racks of "designer" clothes with labels that were just as wrong. I glimpsed two men off to the side; one tucked something inside his jacket as money changed hands. White, flashing smiles.

I tore my gaze away and tried to pretend I was back in Pawntucket, scraping through the hangers of the town's single JC Penney, so bored that my eyes were glazing over. Even so, I couldn't help staring when we passed what looked like the entrance to a small chapel. There was a skeleton sitting on a throne inside, wearing a tiara and a frilly white wedding dress. Flowers and lit candles were spread in front of it. There was even a glass of wine sitting there, as if it might decide to have a drink.

"*Santa Muerte*," said Seb to my unspoken question. "Saint Death. Many people here worship her." He snorted slightly. "At least she's not wearing angel wings yet."

I knew how much Seb hated being back here; I kept getting flashes of memory from him that made me cringe. But as he walked, his lean body had an indifferent look – as if he belonged on these streets and still had his switchblade in his pocket. His arm, looped around my shoulders, seemed just as relaxed. A few people glanced speculatively at us, took him in, and then looked away again.

And even though it was only Seb, who'd probably had his arm around me half a dozen times…something in me had gone very still at the nearness of him. Remembering the weird moment of jealousy that had come over me when Céline had kissed him – how, for a second, I'd actually hated her for the attraction that had shone so clearly in her eyes – I shook my head in confusion. God, what was wrong with me? I was still so conscious of the pain over Alex that it was like a boulder pressing on my heart. I couldn't deal with whatever this was now; my emotions were tattered enough already.

Seb didn't falter as he led me through a gap I hadn't even noticed between two stalls. With a rustle of plastic, we were suddenly out on another street, just as crowded and tunnel-like as the first. No wonder the locals could tell who didn't belong so easily; only someone who'd been raised in Tepito could prowl it with no hesitation. Seb stayed quiet as we wove through the stalls – and I knew that the violence and death we'd witnessed at the cathedral made his memories at being back here even more raw. Scrounging food from a trash can because he hadn't eaten in days; hiding fearfully under a stall table, hoping his mother's boyfriend wouldn't find him. I swallowed. I'd seen images like this from him before, but never so loaded with emotion.

Suddenly I had that prickling feeling again, like I was being watched, just like I used to get so often back at the house – only this time when I looked, there was actually someone there. A stocky guy in his early twenties stood nearby, leering as he took in my short skirt. I held back a shudder; it felt like clammy hands running over me.

I realized my eyes had met his and looked hastily away, but it was too late – he came sauntering over, blocking our path. Though shorter than Seb, he was a lot broader, with beefy muscles. With a silky smile at me, he made a comment in Spanish. Seb answered tersely, trying to steer us past. The man grinned and sidestepped in front of us; my stomach turned at the smell of stale sweat and too much cologne. He looked lingeringly at my chest – and then with a smirk he reached out and stroked my cheek, saying something that sounded slimy no matter what the language.

I jerked away, but Seb was faster. He'd stiffened when the man spoke; now he grabbed his shirt and shoved him off me, low, furious Spanish spilling from his lips. With a lunge, the guy pushed Seb back, sending him staggering a few paces. They faced each other on the sidewalk, eyes locked.

"Seb, it's all right!" I clutched his arm. His muscles were rigid as he stared at the man; I could feel the hard swell of his bicep. "Whatever he said, it doesn't matter – please, just forget it."

The guy sneered and said something else. You didn't have to speak Spanish to get the gist: *Yeah, listen to your girlfriend. She knows I'd flatten you in a fight.*

I ignored him and took Seb's hand, squeezing it. "Come on, let's go." Trying to laugh, I added, "Look, I didn't even *understand* what he said. Really, just forget it. It's okay."

Seb's hand gripped mine as if it were a lifeline. Finally, he let out a long breath. "Yes, you're right," he said softly.

Without another word, he put his arm around me again and we walked away. The bustle of the marketplace around us continued without even a ripple; no one had paid any attention to the scene. The man called something after us, laughing.

Seb's jaw was still tense. I could feel how tightly he was holding himself together, and knew it was all caving in on him: what had happened at the cathedral, and now being back here. Of its own accord, my arm slipped around the lean warmth of his waist and I pressed close against him.

A shiver ran through me. Nothing made sense right then, especially whatever I was feeling – I just knew that I wanted so badly to comfort us both.

Seb looked quickly down at me. Neither of us spoke. I couldn't sense much from him; my own emotions were in too much turmoil. Everything seemed so surreal, like a dream I'd wake up from any second now: the plastic blue and yellow awnings around us; the bodies on the cathedral floor; the fight with Alex.

Alex. My mind flinched away like I'd jabbed a bruise.

Don't go there, I thought as we continued through the rustling tunnels of Tepito. *Just…don't.*

Somehow Sophie battled her rented 4 x 4 truck through the *centro* – almost a full square mile of riots, cars on fire, howling gangs. Alex scanned non-stop as they drove, searching for Willow's energy. There was no sign of it anywhere. None.

Finally they reached a street where everything was quiet, apart from a single car that sat smouldering. Sophie pulled over and killed the engine. "What are you doing?" demanded Alex. "We've got to get Wesley home."

"No, I don't want to know where you live," said Sophie. "It's safest, in case I get caught."

"I'm okay," said Wesley from the back. He sat stiffly

against the seat; his voice sounded tense. "It doesn't really hurt. It's just numb."

"Come on," said Sophie, opening the truck door. "This is for your ears only, Alex."

He started to protest, but she was already striding away up the dark street. He swore under his breath and followed, banging the truck door shut after him. She stood waiting in a nearby doorway. She'd just lit a cigarette; its tip glowed red in the darkness.

"What's going on?" he demanded, joining her. "How did you find us?"

Sophie blew out a stream of smoke. "Ever since the Second Wave arrived, I've been putting out feelers, trying to locate you. A rogue angel down here heard about it, and got in touch with me."

Alex leaned against the doorway, watching her. "A rogue? I haven't seen any signs at all of rogues in this city."

Sophie shook her head. "No, most of them have been assassinated by the angels – apparently there was a mass execution just after the Second Wave. But there's at least one left who they don't know about; she's working covertly with the Seraphic Council. Her suspicion was that you might be down here with a new team, because of all the recent angel deaths." She offered a tight smile. "Well done."

"Yeah, go me," said Alex shortly. "So why didn't this rogue get in touch with me herself?"

"She hasn't been able to find you yet; it's difficult for her to get away without raising suspicion. But I had a feeling you might be in the Zócalo tonight, with that demonstration going on."

That's not why we were there, he started to say, but Sophie was still talking, her tone urgent. "Alex, listen – it's vital that the Seraphic Council are killed. If they are—"

"Is this seriously what you came thousands of miles to tell me?" he broke in. "Look, we know all about it – the Council, the reception, everything. That's why we're in Mexico City in the first place."

Sophie didn't miss a beat. "Good, that makes things easier." She unzipped her bag and pulled out an envelope. "Here," she said, handing it to him. "There's a memory stick in there with all the details you need. You've also got ten VIP passes to the reception; they'll get you and your team onto the top floor of the Torre Mayor."

Slowly, Alex reached out and took the envelope. He could feel wallet-sized plastic cards inside. "Where did you get this?"

"From my contact. Her name is Charmeine and she used to know Nate; she worked with him back in the US until he joined the CIA. She'll help you any way she can." She nodded at the envelope. "Like I said, all the details you need are in there."

All the details they needed. Alex tapped the envelope against his palm, frowning. "So it sounds like *Charmeine* was pretty confident you'd find us in time," he said at last. "Was there a backup plan?"

"No one was confident about anything, believe me," said Sophie. "And no, there's no backup plan – she's the only rogue left; if she tried to act on her own she'd be killed before she even put a dent in the Council. A trained team of Angel Killers is our only chance."

Alex snorted. *Our* – yeah, just as if Sophie had been down here helping them out all along. "So what's the proof that Charmeine's definitely a rogue, and this isn't a trap?" he asked.

"She's legit, I'm sure of it." Sophie took another puff of her cigarette; the smoke looked ghostly in the dark. "She knows things about Project Angel that only Nate could have told her."

"Angels are psychic," he reminded her dryly.

"Not *that* psychic without touching you. Listen, I took some convincing too, but she was definitely friends with Nate – she has all the inside information on how we attacked the gate when the Second Wave arrived. Plans, details, everything. The only way she could know all of that is if Nate told her. And if she wasn't on our side, then they'd have tried to stop us at the time."

"Okay," said Alex finally, sticking the envelope into his

pocket. "We'll check it out – compare it with what we've already got." Which wasn't *that* much, but at least they had the classified blueprints to double-check things against.

"Yes, do that," said Sophie. "You'll find that it's all accurate."

Alex nodded without comment. But Jesus, if this was for real…then it was the answer to all their prayers. It also meant that if Willow hadn't survived, her death had been for nothing. He shoved the thought away before it could drown him.

"And I'll be there too, Sunday," added Sophie. She stubbed out her cigarette, grinding it against the concrete wall. "I'll meet you in the lobby of the Torre Mayor before you go up, and do whatever I can to help."

"Wow, really? You mean you're not going to get whisked off to a safe location this time?"

Sophie's expression didn't change. "No, not this time. Here." There was a jingling sound as she pulled the 4 x 4's keys from her bag and handed them to him. "My hotel's just a few blocks away – you can drop me off in the truck and get your team back home. Keep it until after the attack; I only rented it in case I found you all."

Alex accepted the keys; as his fingers closed over them, he thought of something else. "Where's Willow's mother? Have you got her someplace where she's protected?"

Sophie's brown eyebrows shot up. "Have I what? Alex, didn't you see on the news? Willow's mother and aunt were killed in an arson attack, the night of the Second Wave."

"But I thought…" Alex stared at her in the dim light. "You mean that wasn't staged?"

"Not by me," she replied, zipping her bag shut. "I've hardly had any resources since the Second Wave; I've been working on my own. To pull off something of that scale would be totally beyond me." She glanced at him. "Why? Is there reason to believe it *was* staged?"

"No, I guess not," said Alex after a pause. He had no idea what this meant, but wasn't about to go into the details of it with Sophie. At least Willow had been able to sense that her mother was okay, wherever she was.

They made the short journey in silence, with Alex driving this time. The team sat quietly, their expressions carefully neutral in the rear-view mirror, though he knew they must be dying to hear what had been said. When they pulled up in front of Sophie's hotel, she cleared her throat. "I added something else to that memory stick too," she said. "A sort of proposal for you. Hopefully we won't need it after the attack, but it's what I've been working on since the Second Wave. Anyway, see what you think."

"All right," said Alex, keeping his tone non-committal. "So we'll see you Sunday, I guess."

"Yes, you will." Sophie hesitated, gripping her bag with both hands; he could tell she wished they were speaking alone again. "And, Alex, look – I know we have our differences, but you're the finest AK I've ever seen, bar none. I'll be honoured to do whatever I can to help."

"Yeah, okay," he muttered, embarrassment battling with dislike. Sophie could say whatever she wanted; he was still never going to warm to her.

After Sophie had disappeared into her hotel, Alex got out too, leaving the 4 x 4 idling. "Drive them home, okay?" he said through the passenger window to Kara. "And start checking this stuff out." He gave her the envelope as she emerged from the back seat of the truck.

"What's in it?" she asked, gazing down at it in her hand.

"VIP passes, and all the security details we need for the attack. Don't ask me about it now," he added. "I'll tell you when I get home." Half-hidden by the truck, he checked his pistol. "Can you give me some of your cartridges? I'm running low."

Kara took out her gun and ejected the magazine; her eyes were worried as she handed it over. "Where are you going?"

He clicked her cartridges into his own magazine, his thumb working with a quick, steady rhythm. "To try to find Willow," he said tersely. He tucked his gun back in its holster. "If she and Seb are at the house, call me, okay? The second you get there."

"I will, but…Alex, those riots are still going strong—"

"Here," he broke in, handing her the empty magazine. "Get Wesley home."

"There's no use arguing with you about this, is there?" Kara's face looked pained with concern. He didn't reply, and she leaned forward and kissed his cheek. "All right. Please take care of yourself."

He nodded. As Kara climbed into the 4 x 4 with a flash of long legs, he turned and jogged down the shadowy street towards the *centro*, where he could still see orange blazes licking at the sky. He scanned non-stop as he went, searching for Willow's energy, praying with every second that passed that he'd suddenly feel it. Their fight seemed inconceivable now – something he'd done in another lifetime. Okay, she was close to Seb; maybe she was even attracted to him. So what? He himself was the one she was in love with, and he *knew* that. How could he have been so jealous, so stupid?

The city had taken on a nightmarish feel of flames and shouting; the sound of breaking glass and sirens came from somewhere nearby. *Oh god, Willow, please be alive,* thought Alex as he raced towards the chaos and the looting. If Willow had died, his heart would die, too. Though he knew he'd still try to save the world from the angels – for his family and Willow's family and everyone else who'd been hurt by them – for him, it would be too late.

The world would already have ended.

CHAPTER *Twenty-four*

FINALLY WE LEFT THE PLASTIC tunnels of the marketplace behind and came to a dark street full of warehouses and boarded-up buildings. I felt Seb scan; decide it was safe. "This is it," he said, heading down the side of one of the warehouses.

I stepped carefully, hardly able to see – there was only the distant gleam of street lights. A rustling noise came from some nearby weeds. A cat, maybe. A tall chain-link fence rose up alongside us, with razor glints of barbed wire curling over the top.

Seb went to a dim corner, where the barbed wire lay

flattened for a foot or two. "Can you get over?" he asked.

I eyed the fence. "You'd better go first," I said. "Then I can land on you if I fall." I wasn't totally kidding; high heels weren't ideal for things like this.

Seb nodded and grasped the fence; it rattled as he climbed up and swung himself over. He dropped the final few feet, landing nimbly on the cracked concrete. I took out the file from beneath my jacket and slid it under the fence. Then I followed, angling my sandalled feet awkwardly in the diamond-shaped holes. Manoeuvring myself over the top, I was hotly conscious of my short skirt, and just how much leg I was showing.

Finally my feet touched the ground again. Seb was barely visible – just his white shirt, and the slant of his cheekbones catching the faint light. "It's over here," he said. He led me to the back of the warehouse, where I could just make out a pile of trash lying against the corrugated metal wall: an old sofa; some broken office chairs, scraps of plywood.

He glanced at me. "I'm sorry – we have to crawl. There's a loose panel behind this we can get through."

I thought of the rustling noise from the weeds, but I nodded. "That's okay. How did you ever find this place?"

Seb was already on his hands and knees, edging behind the sofa. It lay at an angle against the warehouse, forming a sort of entrance. "Just poking around, after I escaped from the orphanage," he replied, his voice muffled. "I used to have lots of hiding places, all around the city. Most of the buildings are torn down now, though."

A metallic creaking noise, then a long pause.

"Seb?" I called, hugging the file to my chest.

The sound of a match striking. "Yes, it's all right," he called back. "Come on."

I buttoned the file into my jacket again, then kneeled down and started to crawl. The old velvet sofa smelled mouldy; gravel dug into my palms and knees. Ahead, a sliver of light beckoned from the warehouse wall, where a piece of corrugated metal didn't quite lie flush.

The panel lifted as I crawled towards it – Seb, holding it open for me. I squeezed through, past his arm. Once inside, I got to my feet and brushed myself off, looking around in amazement. The light came from a small cluster of lit candles that seemed to be growing from the concrete floor. A sleeping bag lay beside them, along with a stack of children's paperbacks with worn spines. I picked up the top one, surprised that I recognized the cover – *The Incredible Journey.* Our fourth-grade teacher had read that out loud to us. I placed it carefully back, straightening it so that it lined up with the others again.

Seb stood with his hands in his pockets, looking embarrassed. "When I was a boy, I stayed here often," he said with a shrug. "I stole all the books," he added.

I cleared my throat. "It's okay, I think you get a special pass for stealing books. From what I hear, it's something book lovers would understand." It felt like we were both treading water to stay above the surface, avoiding all the topics that might drag us under. I pulled out the file and laid it on the sleeping bag. "What *is* this place?" I gazed into the shadows beyond the candlelight. "Is it just abandoned?"

"No, someone owns it." Seb bent down and snapped a candle from the floor; it came away like a small tree, with waxy roots spreading out. "Come, I'll show you."

Our footsteps echoed on the concrete. I couldn't hold back a gasp as the first face appeared from the gloom. Statue after stone statue stood scattered throughout the warehouse, like some weird, silent cocktail party. Propped up against the walls were several huge stained-glass windows – the candlelight flickered across their panels, sending a rainbow of colours sparking around us.

"Is this all from a church?" I touched the cold stone face of the nearest statue: a man in robes, his expression kindly – as if he might have some answers to everything that was going on, if only he could speak.

Seb was beside me, holding up the candle. He nodded. "Even before the Church of Angels really got started here, a few smaller churches were taken over by angel-worshippers. I think someone must have stored these things here then, to keep them safe maybe. But they seem forgotten now." He lifted a shoulder. "Perhaps whoever stored them died, or got angel burn."

As I let my hand fall from the statue, I saw a small room built against the opposite wall. "What's in there?"

"Just an office," said Seb. "There's a bathroom, too," he added. "It used to have running water; maybe it still does."

"Really?" I could hear the relief in my voice. "Can I borrow the candle?"

The black shadows of the bathroom shrank away as I entered with the candle. By some miracle, there *was* still running water, and even a little toilet paper. A few minutes later, I stood washing my face in the tiny sink as I tried to get the worst of the grime and the smeared eye make-up off. Gazing at my candlelit image, for a second all I could think of was that slumber party game, Bloody Mary. A chill prickled over me. I tried to push it away, drying my hands as best I could on the jacket.

When I returned to the sleeping bag, I found Seb examining the file in the glow of the candlelight. I put my candle with the others, then kicked off my sandals and sat next to him, curling my legs under me as I looked down at the Spanish words. The document he was reading seemed to be an email printout.

"Is there anything there?" I asked.

Seb nodded, rubbing his jaw as he turned a page. "Yes, a lot. We've got what Alex wanted, and there's more too – floor plans, information about the reception. Even the code for the stairwell door." He closed the file and put it to one side. "Your instincts were very good, *querida*."

I held back a shiver as I remembered the church office – the banging noise that I'd completely disregarded. "So were yours, to get us out of there in time."

Seb looked down, and I knew he didn't want to think about the cathedral any more than I did. His hand tightened to a fist, tapping against the sleeping bag. "Willow, I'm sorry," he said after a moment. "When we met that man in the marketplace—" He broke off; I could sense his turmoil. "I haven't let anyone get to me like that in so long. I should have just gotten both of us away from there—"

"Seb, no, stop," I said, touching his arm. "I know how hard it is for you, being back here. I could feel it, every step of the way."

"It doesn't matter," he said shortly. "I should have better control than to almost get in a fight with some *cabrón* who means nothing – especially when I'm taking you through Tepito."

I shifted on the sleeping bag, watching him. "So…what did he say?"

Seb went silent. One of the candle flames flickered. "He

asked if I'd like to share you," he said finally. "And the way he looked at you…I don't think I've ever wanted to hurt someone so much in my life."

"I'm glad you didn't," I said softly. Not that I'd care if anything had happened to that pile of sleaze, but to Seb… I swallowed. "Anyway, don't blame yourself – we were both upset. After what happened—"

I stopped, my chest tightening as I saw it all again in gut-wrenching detail. I couldn't hold it back any longer. A trembling breath that was weirdly like a laugh escaped me. "Oh, god, Seb. They're supposed to want to *help* people…"

His throat moved; he took me in his arms without speaking. Burying my head against his shoulder, I clung to him and wished I could wipe out everything we'd seen. I knew I'd never be able to, never – even the tiniest details would be with me for ever. The preacher staring at the ceiling with his one eye flashed through my mind, and I wondered dully why I wasn't crying.

"Most of the Crusaders can't have known about it," said Seb roughly. "It had to be a – a smaller group who planned it, working on their own."

I knew he was probably right; it didn't help much. "What's the use of being psychic, if we can't stop something like that?" My voice sounded distant, as if it was coming from somewhere outside of myself.

"I know," whispered Seb against my hair. I could feel his pain; it was as helpless as my own. "But that's not how it works; you know it's not."

Inside of me, my angel was straining for his. I let her fly free, and Seb's angel was there almost immediately – radiant and powerful, his beautiful face etched with our shared sadness.

The light from our ethereal bodies cast a tender glow in the warehouse as we hovered, facing each other. Somehow, just seeing Seb's angel was a balm; it soothed the very core of me in a way that I didn't even understand.

His eyes on mine, Seb's angel reached out his hand. And this time I didn't hesitate – I stretched out my own angelic hand to him.

Our fingers touched in a burst of light. I caught my breath at the sensation, watching in wonder as our hands merged in a blue-white glow. The details of the cathedral attack mercifully receded, leaving just Seb and me, and this feeling that was like nothing on earth – having no boundaries at all between us; our energy turned into one.

This is way too intimate, I thought belatedly. But I couldn't have taken my hand away for anything. Seb's angel and I gazed at each other in awe; slowly, he stroked his hand up my arm and, without quite knowing how, I found myself doing the same to him – feeling the slight resistance against my fingers as they caressed their way through his energy; the warm shiver in me as he explored my own.

In our human forms below, Seb and I had both gone very still. He pulled away a little as his gaze searched mine, the golden flecks in his hazel eyes clear in the candlelight. I was trembling. I could feel the depth of his love for me; how much he longed to hold me in a way that wasn't brotherly at all. Somewhere far away where I couldn't face it was the pain over Alex – but right now there was only Seb, my friend Seb, who I cared about so much that it almost hurt, and whose angel-hands were making me feel things I'd never felt before in my life. In that moment I didn't know whether I loved him only as a friend or something more – I just knew that I never wanted him to stop touching me, never.

I'm not sure which of us moved first. I saw Seb swallow; one or maybe both of us leaned forward…and then somehow I was running my hands through his loose curls and his lips were on mine, so warm and gentle that I was falling.

Time faded to nothing as our mouths teased each other – tiny, sipping kisses that sent electricity pulsing through me. Seb's curls were so soft under my fingers, just as soft as I'd always imagined, and I could feel the prickle of stubble near his mouth; the strength of his hand as he lightly cupped it around the back of my neck. He murmured my name, pulling me to him. The kiss slowed, deepening into heat as our mouths opened together, exploring each other. Seb's arms were locked around me as I pressed tightly against him, stroking his firm back and feeling his heartbeat pounding with mine, and if I could have gotten even closer to him, I would have – and meanwhile our angels were still touching hands above, and there was nothing in the world but this kiss; this kiss that was the most amazing thing I'd ever felt.

The minutes passed. We sank down to the sleeping bag, our mouths still drinking hungrily at each other. Whispering something in Spanish, Seb kissed my neck, then my mouth again, his hand caressing its way up my side…and I wanted it to feel as wonderful as it had at first, but little by little, unease was growing in me. Seb's lips weren't the ones I was used to; his body against mine felt different. I shoved the thought away – I refused to think about Alex now; I didn't want to think about anything; I just wanted to keep losing myself in this warmth, this moment – but then slowly, slowly, the kiss ended.

Seb raised his head, looking down at me.

And it all felt so wrong suddenly that I wanted to cry.

The weight of what I had done came crashing down on me. I sat up shakily as our angels rushed back to us. "Seb, I – oh my god, I'm so sorry—"

He sat up too. His mouth looked bruised where I'd just

been kissing it. "Why are you sorry?" But from the expression in his eyes, he knew.

I hated saying the words; they tasted like bile. "I'm not in love with you. I shouldn't have done this – it was a mistake."

Seb hesitated. Almost in slow motion, he touched my hair, just like he'd done the first day that we'd met. "You are in love with me, a little," he said softly. "I can feel it."

I shook my head, hardly even aware I was doing it. "No. I love you as a friend. That's all." My words came out quiet and certain. Because no matter how wrong it had been, kissing Seb had done one thing at least: rid my mind of any confusion I might have had. Everything seemed so clear now, as if the world had just leaped into sharp focus.

His throat moved. The candles still burned around us, their warm golden light playing on the wall. "Maybe this was just too soon – maybe someday you'll feel different." He reached for my hand and gripped it tightly, his emotions raw on his face. "I've loved you for so long, Willow. It's always been you, my whole life."

My heart was breaking. I wished so much that I *was* in love with Seb; that it was possible for me to say that someday I might be. But it wasn't. Whatever strange alchemy it is that makes you fall in love with one person and not another just wasn't there for me, with him. Maybe

I'd been picking up on his feelings and mistaking them for my own, a little – but now, when I was really looking at it, I could see the truth.

Gently, I disentangled my fingers from his and cleared my throat. "You know, my dream was right," I said. "I hate the thought of ever being without you, Seb. You're one of the most important people in my life. And you deserve an amazing girl who's just…so completely in love with you. But I don't feel that way. I'm sorry."

A long pause spun out around us. "You don't have to apologize," said Seb at last. "You never have to apologize."

I pushed my hands through my hair, leaving it in wild spikes. "I do! I shouldn't have kissed you, not when I wasn't sure—"

"It was very nice, though," he said, trying to smile. "I think I'll manage to forgive you."

Maybe, but I'd never forgive myself. Oh god, why did everything have to be such a mess? Unconsciously, I touched my neck – it felt bare and wrong without the crystal pendant Alex had given me hanging from its slender chain. Remembering his coolness as Seb and I had gone into the cathedral, I wrapped my arms around my knees and rested my cheek on them, wishing so much that I'd seen a hint, just a hint, that he still felt the same way about me.

"Yes, he still feels the same," said Seb quietly.

My heart quickened with sudden hope. Seb sat gazing down at the sleeping bag; when he felt my eyes on him, he glanced up and shrugged. "I saw him, when you weren't watching. The look on his face—" His mouth twisted. "He's still in love with you, just too stubborn to back down yet."

I should have been relieved – instead, staring at Seb, dread started growing in me like a dark, tangled vine. "There's something else, isn't there?" I said. "Whatever it was that you said you'd tell me later, back at the cathedral."

Seb let out a ragged breath. Leaning back against the corrugated metal of the warehouse wall, he scraped his hands over his face. I could feel his reluctance like a weight on my throat.

"Seb?" I whispered.

"*Querida*, please, believe me," he said finally. "This is the last thing in the world I want to tell you."

CHAPTER *Twenty-five*

A LONG TIME LATER, I was lying on my back on the sleeping bag, staring up into the dark shadows. Seb still sat against the wall. The flickering light had drawn in around us as the cluster of candles burned lower. One of them had sputtered out altogether, dying with little hissing noises.

I still couldn't sense Alex very clearly, no matter how much I wanted to. I kept searching for him, and feeling that he was alive but getting nothing about his emotions. His energy was there though – his warm, familiar energy that I loved so much – and I ran my thoughts gently over it, wondering what he was thinking; whether he was still angry at me.

After what Seb had told me, I hoped that he was. That he never got over being angry, ever.

"I'm sorry," said Seb again, for about the tenth time. "I really didn't know. When you first asked me, I was sure that we didn't, but…" He trailed off.

"It's okay," I whispered. I could hardly even imagine how Alex would have reacted if I'd tried to break things off with him because Seb had told me that we cause angel burn – I think he might have tried to kill Seb.

Even though it all fitted. Oh god, it all fitted – his migraines, his headaches. The worst ones always seemed to happen just a few hours after the two of us had been close together. I had a flash of lying on his bed in his arms, and closed my eyes tightly against the sudden pain. I wiped my cheek with the heel of my hand and tried to marshal my thoughts.

"The Council attack is the most important thing, for all of us," I said. "So when we go back to the house, I can't touch Alex, not at all – I have to stay as far away from him as I can. If he got a migraine during the attack—" I broke off; the thought was too terrible to contemplate.

Seb's gaze on me was very still. "And if he tries to make up with you? What will you tell him is the reason for not touching him?"

"I don't know," I said softly. Alex had always refused to even consider the idea that I might cause angel burn. No matter what was happening with his aura, I knew he was unlikely to start believing it now. Even if he checked out his aura and saw the damage, I could just hear him saying that it didn't matter; that we couldn't be certain it was because of me.

"I don't know," I repeated – but really, there was only one option, wasn't there? My brain flinched away from the thought of it. "Hopefully…hopefully he'll still be angry at me, and it won't even be an issue. We can just keep avoiding each other."

And after the attack – if by some miracle we managed to succeed, and there was an "after" to think about – I could never be with Alex again. I just prayed that whatever damage I'd already done to him would get better in time; that it wasn't permanent. I felt cold even in my jean jacket as I stared up into the shadows. How ironic, though. I'd just told Seb that we could never be together, but if we hurt humans with our touch, then there was no one else in the world for either of us, was there? Literally, no one else in the world. And so perhaps we *would* end up getting together someday – years from now, maybe, once this pain had faded a little – but I knew it would never be anything like what I'd had with Alex. Nothing else would ever be like that. Not in my whole life.

"No," said Seb, his voice fierce.

I glanced over at him. He was staring at me angrily, his hand a tight fist on his thigh. "You were right, what happened was a mistake," he said. "If it happens again between us, it won't be because we're the only two half-angels. It will be because you're in love with me, as much as you are now with Alex. I don't want you any other way – I'd rather be your brother for ever."

"Seb..." I didn't know what to say. Oh god, now I'd hurt Seb, on top of everything else.

He shook his head. "This isn't the time," he said shortly. "But I know what we could have together, Willow. And I won't take anything less."

I let out a breath. "Look, I'm sorry. It was just a stupid, random thought, that's all. You weren't supposed to hear it." I didn't blame Seb for feeling the way he did, but knew it meant that nothing would ever happen between us again in that case, not even decades in the future. I covered my eyes with both arms, suddenly feeling beyond weary; battered by the past few days. "Can we just...not talk about this any more?" I asked in a small voice.

I sensed rather than saw his cool shrug. "We'll never talk about it again, if you don't want."

I didn't answer. If Seb was still hurt, I seriously couldn't deal with it right now.

We didn't speak for a long time. Another candle choked

out, casting us into a deeper gloom that seemed hideously symbolic. I could sense my angel inside of me, and had a flash of hatred for her so intense that it curled my stomach. How could I ever forgive myself for hurting Alex? How could I go through life, knowing my touch would damage anyone I got too close to?

Anyone I got too close to. The thought froze me so that I could hardly breathe, and I sat up with a gasp. No. *No.*

"Willow?" Seb moved quickly from the wall; the sleeping bag made a soft noise as he kneeled beside me.

"Mom," I whispered. "Seb, what if…what if I was making her angel burn worse all those years?" I covered my face with my hands as I began to shake – seeing her sitting in her chair, her dreamy smile. And all the hours I had spent sitting next to her: holding her hand, stroking her arm. Each memory was like being kicked in the stomach. I couldn't live with this; I just couldn't – if it was true, then I didn't even want to live any more.

"Stop, *querida*, stop—" I felt Seb start to take me into his arms.

Somehow what had happened between us made it impossible for me to touch Seb now – even though he was the only person I *could* touch. I pulled away. "Don't! I can't – I can't let you hold me any more—"

"Willow!" Cradling my face in his hands, he gently forced me to look at him, his expression distraught. "Listen to me. Tonight didn't happen – I'm still your brother. Please, let me help."

I hugged myself, struggling with everything I had to hang on. "Nothing can help," I got out finally. My voice sounded dead and buried. "Nothing, not ever again."

I could feel Seb's compassion, so tender that something inside of me gave way. He put his arms around me again as I started to cry, drawing me close against his chest. I didn't have the energy to resist this time – didn't even want to any more. I let him hold me, and I cried against his warm shoulder while the shadows played on the wall beside us.

Eventually I must have fallen into an exhausted sleep. When I woke up later, Seb and I were both lying down. My eyes felt bruised and puffy. The crying hadn't helped – my head throbbed with thoughts that hurt too much to dwell on. Only one candle was going now, its flame sputtering weakly.

Seb was still holding me; he'd fallen asleep too. In the dim light, I stared at his sleeping face – at the mouth that I'd kissed so passionately – and knew with a sinking heart that he was wrong. Tonight *had* happened. And because of it, the dearest friendship of my life had been soured. Seb could never really be my brother again.

I didn't have the boy I loved, and I didn't have my best friend, either.

The next morning, as Seb and I walked back to the house from the Metro station, I could hear the tinkling, glittery sound of glass being swept up. Storekeepers were out taping sheets of cardboard over broken windows; burned-out cars sat here and there like weird sculptures. But shoppers strode by as usual on the sidewalk, and in the street, cars and taxis swept past. Already, life was returning to what passed for normal, here in Mexico City in the wake of the Second Wave.

Though Seb and I tried to talk the same as always, awkwardness had settled between us like a thick fog from the moment we'd woken up that morning. As we reached the street where the house was, Seb stopped suddenly, touching my arm. "Willow, please – can't we just forget it happened, and be like we were before?" His hazel eyes were deep wells of worry. "We kissed; that's all. It doesn't have to change what we are to each other, not unless we let it."

I shivered, not looking at him. All I could think of was Alex. I hated my hands as they gripped my elbows, knowing that I'd hurt him with them. Except it wasn't just my *hands*, was it? No, it was all of me, like poisonous venom oozing through my veins. Every time I'd caressed Alex's body, kissed his lips, I'd caused him harm.

"I'll try," I said at last.

"*Querida—*"

"Don't—" I broke off and shut my eyes hard against the sudden pain; it was a fist gripping my heart. "Don't call me that," I said.

"All right," said Seb softly. And I knew that this time he meant it, and that the easy banter we'd once shared was gone. Though it made me feel ten times worse than before, in a weird way it also seemed like no more than I deserved.

Seb sighed and jammed his hands in his pockets as we started walking again. "Don't blame yourself," he said, sounding tired. "You're the kindest person I know – you would never have touched him if you'd realized."

Even now, he could read my thoughts so easily. *So what?* I wanted to say. *I've still been causing only god knows what damage to the boy I love more than anything.* I didn't bother saying the words out loud. And when it came to Mom, I couldn't think about it at all. I just…couldn't.

We neared the house; it looked as vacant as always. I hesitated outside for a moment, the cool Mexico City breeze stirring my hair. I had the file buttoned up under my jacket again, and I touched my chest, feeling its cardboard outline. I wanted to see Alex so badly, and at the same time I dreaded it more than anything in the world.

Please still be angry at me, I thought. *Please – that'll make it so much easier for us both.* Otherwise, I could hardly stand the thought of what I was going to have to do.

"Seb, will you help, if I need you to?" I asked finally, my voice faint.

"Yes, I'll help." But his face looked troubled; I could feel that he hated this almost as much as I did.

When we went inside, Kara was sitting at the kitchen table with her head slumped on one hand, an untouched cup of coffee in front of her. Her chin jerked up as she saw us, her brown eyes going wide.

"Hi," I said. "We, um...we ran into some trouble." Remembering the blasts that had trembled through the cathedral – the screams, the bodies – my voice came out sounding thin and unreal.

Kara slowly shook her head; she hadn't stopped staring at us. "Oh my god, you're really okay," she murmured. To my surprise, a broad smile grew across her face. "Listen, I know someone who is going to be *very* pleased to see you!" She leaped up, sending her chair skidding. "Alex!" she bellowed in the direction of the boys' dorm. "Alex, Willow's here!"

Apprehension and longing filled me. I swallowed and took the file out from under my jacket, setting it on the kitchen table. Though Seb was standing several feet away, I could sense his concern. Kara turned to me with a relieved grin. "He was out all night looking for you. He just got back about an hour ago – I've never been so worried about him, not even after Jake died. He was sure you'd been killed—"

"*Willow!*" Alex burst into the kitchen. His gorgeous face was bruised and burned; there were dark circles under his eyes – and his aura had exactly the damage in it that Seb had described. I had a heart-wrenching glimpse of tarnished blues and golds, and then Alex had scooped me up into his arms before I could stop him. "Oh, Jesus, you're alive—" I could feel him shaking as he held me, and for a helpless moment I couldn't stop myself from hugging him back. I pressed my head tightly against his warm neck; the hard strength of his shoulder. *Alex.*

"Willow, I'm sorry; I'm so sorry—" He buried his fingers in my hair as he kissed my cheeks, my eyes, my mouth. "I've been such an idiot. Please, please, forgive me."

Kara had tactfully melted away somewhere. Seb still stood near the table, his face expressionless – and I knew to my absolute dismay that I was going to need him there to make this believable.

It took every molecule of strength that I had to pull myself away from Alex. "Don't, um…don't do that, please," I said, taking a step back.

He froze as if I'd just cracked a slap across his face. I saw his throat move. "Willow, I…I know I've been acting like a controlling jerk. You're right to still be angry at me – if you never forgave me, I'd deserve it. But—" He glanced at Seb with a sudden frown, and gently put his hand on my shoulder. "Look, let's go someplace private, where we can talk— " He broke off as I shook away from his touch.

"No, don't. I mean…thanks, but there's no point."

"No point?" he echoed, staring at me.

I tried to make my voice sound normal, as if I wasn't dying inside. "No, there isn't," I said. "Alex, I'm really sorry, but…"

He looked from me to Seb. His eyes widened. "No," he breathed. "No way."

"I'm sorry," I said again. "It just happened." And the fact that something really *had* happened made my cheeks flush guiltily. I used it, hurrying on before I could weaken. "Last night we were hiding out, and…somehow we started kissing. One thing kind of led to another, and…" I trailed off; I couldn't finish. The frozen look on Alex's face – the stunned hurt, the anguished disbelief – was killing me.

"One thing led to another," he repeated.

"Yeah," I got out. "I still really care about you, but… I just can't help what I feel for him. I'm sorry."

He slowly shook his head, like a dazed animal. "What are you saying? Are you telling me you and he—" He moved so quickly I hardly saw it; suddenly he had Seb slammed up against the wall with a thud that echoed through the kitchen. He spat something in Spanish; the muscles in his arms were rock hard. Seb didn't move, didn't try to defend himself.

"Alex, no!" I tugged uselessly at his arm. "Please, stop – it's just the way I feel; I can't help it!"

He and Seb were inches apart; Alex's jaw was rigid as he stared at him. Finally he let go of Seb with a shove.

"So let me get this straight," he said. "While I was out all night in the middle of riots looking for you, going out of my mind, thinking maybe you were lying somewhere dead…you and Seb were—" He broke off as a muscle in his jaw leaped; turned away and raked a hand through his hair, breathing hard. When he spoke again his words were flat, dead. "Okay, got it. That's really good to know. Thanks for coming here to tell me what a fool I've been."

"Alex…" I was close to tears; Seb must have sensed I was wavering. He put his arms around me from behind, drawing me close. I leaned against his chest, and wrapped my arms around his to hide my trembling.

"It's all right, *chiquita*," he said, kissing my head. "Sorry, man," he added to Alex. "These things happen, you know?"

Chiquita. It was Spanish for "babe"; Alex's word for me. He stiffened, nostrils flaring, so that for a second I thought he was going to punch Seb even with me in front of him. "No," he said suddenly. "No, I am *not* just going to stand here and—"

He grabbed my shoulders and pulled me away from Seb, hands tight on my arms. "Look me in the eyes,

Willow," he demanded. "Look me in the eyes and tell me that you really don't love me as much as I love you. I don't believe it – I don't care *what* you did with him, I don't believe it—"

I loved him so totally that I knew he must see it written all over my face; must feel it even through my clothes, burning out of me like the sun. In another second I was going to blurt out the truth. Alex would argue with me; he'd tell me that his sick-looking aura had nothing to do with me at all – that his migraines were only a coincidence. I wouldn't be able to resist him a second time. I'd just curl up in his arms for the rest of my life, like I was a fraction away from doing now.

And then all of us, the whole world, might be lost.

From somewhere deep within, I found the strength to say words that would make him hate me for ever. "It's true," I said. "I never told you, but the dream I had about the Council – Seb was in it, too. I dreamed about him before I even met him. It's why I wanted to come here, because I knew it's where he would be."

Slowly, Alex's hands fell from my shoulders. "What?"

"I dreamed about him," I said levelly. "That's how he found us; he saw my dream in my shirt. And in my dream, I didn't want to leave you, but I knew that I never wanted to be without Seb. That...he was the one I really loved." Except for the most important words of all, everything I was saying was true – and I knew Alex heard it in my voice. He stared wordlessly at me.

My throat was sand. "I do care about you," I said again. "I'll never regret anything that happened between us. But Seb and I are both half-angel, and…I just can't fight that."

Seb put his arm around me. "Sorry, man," he repeated to Alex with a shrug. "She didn't want to hurt you, but I guess it's just fate, you know?" And even though I could sense how much he wasn't enjoying this, I had a stab of hatred for him, that he was playing his part so well.

The expression on Alex's face made me feel like I was being battered inside. To keep myself from throwing my arms around him and taking it all back, I reached up and gripped Seb's hand as hard as I could. "We…found the information about the Council's visit," I said shakily. "It's in that file." I nodded at the table.

Alex didn't look at it. He put his hand over his face, rubbing at his temples. "Get out, both of you," he said finally.

I licked dry lips. "But what about the Council? We still want to help; you'll need everyone you can get—"

Alex dropped his hand, and my chest clenched at the utter hatred in his eyes. "You have *got* to be kidding me," he hissed. "Do you think you're actually going to stay here in this house and still be part of the team? I've got news for you; the team doesn't trust you, neither of you. And you know what? I don't trust you now, either. Just get out – get your things and get the hell out. I never want to see you again, Willow." His gaze fell on Seb. "And if I ever see *you* again, I swear to god I'll kill you."

He turned and left the room. I stood motionless, staring after him, taking in his dark hair; the firm line of his shoulders. The way he moved. Alex. *Alex.*

Seb gave me a quick shake. "Hold yourself together," he ordered, letting go of me. "I'll get our things."

I shook my head, stunned. Somehow, I hadn't expected this. "But Seb, we can't actually *leave*," I said in a small voice. "What about the attack?"

"We've seen all the information," he said. "We can go there, we can still help them. But for now—" His mouth twisted grimly as he glanced in the direction Alex had gone. "I think he means what he says."

The world was crashing in my ears. "All right," I said after a pause. "I'll get my own things."

No one was in the girls' dorm; it was a relief. I changed out of Liz's clothes and sandals, leaving them neatly on her bed – she'd probably burn them or something, once she heard what had happened – and pulled on a pair of jeans, a T-shirt, my hooded sweatshirt. My purple Converse sneakers. I remembered buying them with Alex; the way he'd grinned and said, *This is a girl thing, isn't it?*

No. Don't think about it.

I didn't have a bag any more, but there was a plastic carryall in the closet that looked like it had been there for ever. I shoved the rest of my things into it. The necklace with the crystal pendant Alex had given me lay at the bottom of one of my drawers. I hesitated and then took it out, slipping it into my jeans pocket. Its chain felt cool against my fingers.

When I returned to the kitchen, Seb stood waiting for me with his knapsack over his shoulder, wearing jeans and his long-sleeved grey shirt. I was keenly aware of how silent the house was. Somehow I knew that everyone knew – I could just *feel* them all sitting back in the TV room, talking in low whispers. Alex was in his room; I could tell without even trying. And he thought Seb was the one I was in love with. That the two of us had... I swallowed; I could hardly even complete the thought.

Suddenly the only thing I wanted was to leave the house by myself and not have to be with anyone, not even Seb. No – especially not with Seb. The thought of being alone with him now, knowing what Alex believed – and knowing the grain of truth that had been our kiss – made me cringe.

All of this came and went in a second. Seb stiffened as he picked up on it; I sensed his pain in a quick stab. Responding to my unspoken thought, he said quietly, "I'm not leaving you on your own. Even if there were no angels, *el DF*'s a dangerous place for a white girl who doesn't speak Spanish. Once all this is over, I'll go away if that's what you want – you'll never have to see me again. But I'm not leaving you by yourself in this city."

I felt cold, locked away from myself. "Okay, you're right," I said finally, my voice dull. "And I didn't mean that I never wanted to see you again. It's just…everything's really complicated right now."

"With you and Alex, yes. With us, it's only as complicated as you're making it," said Seb shortly. He took the carryall from me and wrestled it into his knapsack. The material bulged as he zipped it shut. His face was expressionless as he swung the bag over this shoulder again. "Ready?"

I almost asked where we were going, then realized I didn't actually care that much. Slowly, I reached into my jeans pocket and drew out the necklace. I gripped it in my hand, feeling its facets against my palm and remembering the look that had been in Alex's eyes when he gave it to me. Then I lay it on the kitchen table beside the file. The teardrop crystal rolled a little as I put it down, sparkling like a diamond.

"Ready," I said softly.

CHAPTER *Twenty-six*

SOMEHOW THAT DAY PASSED — Alex wasn't really sure how. Once Willow and Seb had left, he went over the plans on the memory stick in detail; ran target practice with the team; ate a dinner that tasted like sawdust. From the forced conversation and concerned sideways glances, everyone knew that Willow had been busy spending the night with Seb while he, like a complete idiot, had risked his life looking for her on the riot-choked streets. He supposed Kara must have told them — he'd run into her as he'd headed to his bedroom, and told her what had happened. The look of shock on her face had been almost gratifying.

"Oh, Alex," she'd breathed. "I am so sorry—"

"Yeah, well don't be," he'd said. "I'm better off."

The muscles in Kara's slim arms were taut; she was as furious as he'd ever seen her. "God, I don't believe it! And I actually sat there and smiled at her! I'm going to—"

"Don't do anything, just let them go," he'd broken in coldly. "I just want them *gone*, okay? That's all."

And so they'd left without incident, though Willow's necklace on the kitchen table had provided an extra knife in the guts when Alex had found it later. Kara had been in the kitchen too; her eyes had flown to his. "Alex..." she'd started.

"Forget it." He picked up the necklace with its shining pendant – the pendant that had reminded him so much of Willow's angel self, with her wings glinting in the sun – and shoved it roughly into his pocket, wondering why, exactly, he wasn't just pitching it into the trash.

"Okay," he said. "Let's go over the plans."

And for a few hours he'd almost been able to lose himself in them, even though some little voice inside of him was still dazed, bleating over and over, *I don't believe it; Willow wouldn't do this. She just wouldn't.* Whenever he thought it, he mentally kicked the voice to death until it shut up. Because all he could see was Willow in her short black skirt, reaching up to hold Seb's hand; hear the calmness in her tone as she told him that, by the way, she'd forgotten to mention it until now, but all along her dream had included *Seb*, and he himself had apparently just been the chauffeur to get her to Mexico City. God, no wonder she'd looked so thrilled when she first met Seb, her green eyes shining with wonder – probably the only thing that had been on her mind from that point on had been how quickly she could dump Alex, now that she'd found another half-angel.

This thought came to him later that night in his bedroom; he only barely managed not to punch the wall. He couldn't just sit in here; he'd go insane – he pulled on a pair of sweatpants, yanked on a T-shirt, and headed out. Sam, Wesley and Brendan were in the dorm playing cards. They looked up as he passed through. Wesley's arm was in a home-made sling; it hadn't improved much since the day before.

"Hey bud, you okay?" said Sam, his voice casual.

"Great," said Alex shortly. He opened the cabinet where the towels were kept and grabbed one.

"You working out? Want me to join you?"

"No, thanks."

Down in the exercise room, he did fierce, pumping reps on the machines for almost an hour, then ran for miles on the treadmill, until the sweat was streaming and his muscles felt limp. Finally he stopped, panting. He'd pulled off his T-shirt as he ran, and now he used it to mop his face and chest. The house was quiet around him; he knew it must be after midnight.

His frenzied workout hadn't helped much. It hadn't even obliterated the fact that this was the night he'd been going to take Willow to the hotel, so that they could finally have the privacy they'd both been craving. He'd actually bought *flowers* to put in the room; chocolates, which now the maid or someone would eat. He'd wanted it to be so incredibly special for them both, but especially for Willow.

And instead, she had been with Seb.

Oh god, do *not* think about this. He wadded up his shirt and threw it across the room. Restlessly, he went upstairs to the TV room, where he sat on the sofa and opened up Brendan's laptop, studying the plans once more.

When he'd first looked at them, the relief had been almost indescribable. This was exactly what they'd needed: someone on the inside, getting them in as guests. The attack might actually succeed now – Charmeine the rogue angel had thought of every conceivable detail. Any doubts he might have had about the information's authenticity had vanished as he read through the notes; Charmeine clearly wanted the Council dead as much as they did. The VIP passes meant they could just walk right in through the main entryway without being stopped. There were also floor plans of the VIP area; a schedule for the afternoon's events; notes pointing out where the private audiences would take place and at what times. Best of all, the team now had a private audience with the Council themselves.

The first private audience will be for "Mexico City University". This is you, said a note. *Keep your minds as blank as possible and wait until they're talking to open fire, to catch them off-guard. Don't hesitate. The Twelve have extremely strong psychic abilities, though we don't know whether these extend to humans. It's essential that they're dispatched without ever letting them get the upper hand – or else your team will be summarily executed and humanity will not stand a chance.*

Alex tapped his thumb against his mouth as he read, frowning slightly as he pictured the scene. If Wesley's arm wasn't healed by then, there would be six of them against the Twelve. The target practice they'd done earlier had focused on that – all of them standing in a line, each going for their own particular two targets. The team was proficient enough by now that this slight variation on their skills hadn't fazed them; they'd all been performing at well over ninety per cent by the time he'd finally called a halt. Hopefully Wesley *would* be okay, though – they could really use a clean-up man standing over to the side, to shoot any angel that the others might have missed. If

Wesley was still injured, then Alex would have to fill that role himself, nailing his two angels quickly and then going after any others.

Earlier, he'd brought the paper file that Willow had given him in here too, and now he leaned forward to the coffee table and flipped it open again. Neither he nor Kara could read Spanish nearly as well as they spoke it, but he could make out enough to see that most of the details were the same as on the memory stick. The only discrepancy was to do with one of the hallways. The computer file said they should exit by that route to reach the elevators quickly – the paper file said there were renovations going on and the doorway at that end was blocked. But the computer file was clearly more up-to-date; the work must have been completed by now.

As he glanced at the laptop again, Alex suddenly remembered what Sophie had said about some kind of proposal for him. On the main menu screen, he found a file he hadn't noticed before: *Nevada*.

He clicked it open, and discovered plans showing an underground camp in the desert – a huge, sprawling bunker of a place, sleek and modern. As he read, he learned that it had been used for some kind of military training and was now in the hands of the CIA, who apparently had been considering moving his dad's camp up there.

It's fully stocked with survival gear and weaponry – with

the addition of holographs for training, it would be a perfect base for the AKs, read a note from Sophie. *There was limited knowledge of the facility even when Project Angel was running; I am reasonably certain that this information, along with the access codes contained here, are now known only by myself.*

Reasonably certain – great. *I've already got a base,* thought Alex as he moved the laptop to one side. Besides, they'd only need a place to operate from if they failed to kill the Council – and if that was the case, the odds of the AKs even being around afterwards seemed pretty slim.

In just a few days, he could die.

Alex sank back against the sofa, staring at the ceiling. Being raised as an Angel Killer meant that, deep down, he'd always expected to die young – and he wouldn't mind, not if it rid the world of the angels. The only time he'd ever wanted more had been these last few months with Willow, when the desire to actually be around long enough to have a life with her – seeing her smile as she woke up beside him every morning; hearing her laugh – had given his fight against the angels more of a purpose than ever before. Even now, he loved her so much that uppermost in his mind was gladness that she wouldn't be there for the Council attack. That no matter what happened, she'd at least be safe.

God, what a sap he was – when she was with Seb right this second. He closed his eyes against the sharp twist of pain.

"Hey," whispered a soft voice. The cushion sank down as someone sat beside him.

His eyes flew open. Kara was there, clad in the shorts and T-shirt she wore to bed. "I came down to the kitchen and saw the light on," she explained, tucking her long legs up under her. "You okay?"

"Fine." He stayed slumped where he was, not bothering to straighten up. Distantly, he was aware that the house felt cool now, the air prickling at his bare chest. "Couldn't be better."

Kara was silent for a long moment. Without make-up, the dramatic lines of her face looked softer, more vulnerable. "I know how you feel," she said finally. "I really do, Alex. I never told you, but do you remember David?"

At first Alex didn't. The camp in New Mexico had been home to hundreds of potential AKs over the years. A lot of them didn't have what it took and ended up being escorted out again – without ever having known exactly where the camp was, in case they later got angel burn and tried to confess everything. Then he vaguely remembered a good-looking guy with broad shoulders and red hair, like a Viking.

"Wasn't he a college football player, or something?" he asked.

"That's the one," said Kara with a humourless smile. "Mr. All-American. Anyway, we sort of had a thing going for a while. And what can I say? I fell in love with him – totally, completely in love with him. I thought he felt the same way, but…"

Alex didn't say anything – memories were starting to come back. David had ended up leaving the camp unexpectedly with a married AK named Susie; gossip had buzzed around the camp for days afterwards. "Did you know about Susie?" he asked after a pause.

Kara shook her head. "Nope. Didn't have a clue. I found out later that she hadn't even been the only one. I felt like such a…" Her voice faded, then she cleared her throat. "And you know what? The stupid thing is that part of me still loves him. I mean, I'd spit in his face if I saw him again, but I still love him. Almost as much as I hate him."

"Yeah," murmured Alex. That summed it up, pretty much. He'd die for Willow, even now, but he'd meant it when he said he never wanted to see her again.

Kara was sitting sideways on the sofa, her legs still curled under her. "Jake was so great, you know, after all that," she said. "He let me cry on his shoulder so many times. That was when I started to think that maybe someday…" She looked down. "Your brother was a really good guy," she said finally. "I miss him."

"I know," said Alex. "I miss him too." He wondered what Jake would have said about Willow. After he'd finished kicking Alex's ass for being involved with a half-angel in the first place, he had a feeling Jake would have taken him out to get drunk a few times. And brought lots of pretty girls over to their table, as if Willow could be replaced by anyone with two X chromosomes.

He became aware of the stillness of the house. He turned his head and looked at Kara. She was sitting very close, her brown eyes fixed on his; he could smell the gentle scent of body lotion.

She hesitated – and then in slow motion, she reached out and stroked her hand up his bare arm. When she came to his tattoo, she explored it as if she'd never seen it before, tracing its letters. The heat from her fingers was like little suns. "Remember the Christmas party that time?" she asked.

He knew immediately the party she meant – it had been just a few months after Kara had first come to the camp. She'd worn a Santa hat and carried around a sprig of mistletoe, giving everyone quick, laughing kisses. Including him – his first kiss ever. The other AKs had thought it was hilarious; he'd just wanted to grab the mistletoe from her and do it again.

Kara still had her hand on his arm, trailing her fingers back and forth. "Yeah, I remember." His voice was rough.

"Al, listen," she said quietly. "I know you're still in love with her. But you and I really care about each other, and in a few days we could both be dead. Maybe we could just…keep each other warm, for a little while."

Pain and longing mixed within him, so that all at once his heart was beating fast. He'd wondered ever since he was fourteen what it would be like with Kara. So why not, when the girl he loved was lying in someone else's arms right now? Why the hell not?

But for some reason the words *Yes, great idea* wouldn't come.

The room grew heavy with tension, like the air before a storm. Looking down at her hand, Kara slowly glided it across Alex's chest, inch by inch. It dipped up and down over his muscles, making him shiver. Finally her palm came to his other shoulder and stopped. For a long moment her eyes searched his…and then she leaned over and kissed him.

Alex sat very still. Her lips were so soft, so gentle, and this was Kara, *Kara* – who he used to lie awake at nights thinking about. He was enjoying this, he told himself – a gorgeous girl who he'd had a crush on for years was kissing him; of course he was enjoying it.

The image came from nowhere: Willow, sitting at the picnic table in Chihuahua. The smoothness of her neck under his palm as he kissed her; her laughter as she complained that his lips were too spicy.

He pulled away almost harshly. Kara sat back in surprise, her eyes wide.

"Sorry," he muttered. His throat was so tight he could hardly speak. "I can't. I just can't."

Lying in bed later, Alex stared unseeingly into the darkness and wondered what exactly was wrong with him, that he couldn't even bring himself to *kiss* someone else. As if he thought he'd be cheating on Willow or something, when she'd dumped him as thoroughly as it was possible to be dumped. When according to her, she'd been using him for weeks, just to get to Seb.

He couldn't believe it. He still just couldn't believe it.

Wake up, it happened, Alex told himself harshly. Anyway, to hell with this. He had a team to take care of. He had to be there for them these next few days; that was the only thing that mattered. Thinking of the upcoming attack, Alex was aware of the same dread Willow had sensed in him on that long-ago night in New Mexico. But everyone was going to be okay, he'd make sure of it. *He* could die; that was fine – but not his team. He'd do everything in his power to keep them safe.

And if he still had a life once this was over with, then he'd get on with it and forget about Willow.

He had a sudden flash of her lying beside him, so vivid he could almost smell her shampoo; feel the silky warmth of her skin. The memory gouged through him. Yeah, sure, he'd forget all about her. Nothing to it. Who was he kidding? The only way he'd ever get Willow out of his mind would be to have a brain transplant – and even then, he had a feeling she'd still be twined around his heart and soul for good.

CHAPTER *Twenty-seven*

RAZIEL COULD SEE THE TORRE Mayor from his hotel window: a curved green tower that caught the sun's rays like a promise. There was a minibar in the room; he poured himself a glass of cognac while he gazed out at the view, swirling the golden liquid in a cut-crystal glass. Angels couldn't get drunk, of course, but the taste of anything so vintage and expensive was pleasant. He took a slow, savouring sip, his eyes narrowing at the tower as he remembered how the Council had threatened him in his own cathedral; the slurs they'd been casting on his leadership ever since they'd arrived.

The Zócalo, with its converted cathedral, was also visible; the building's exterior looked placid and undisturbed even after the terrorist attack earlier that week. Raziel took in its solid, ancient form, thinking of how the Twelve had appointed Tyrel as head of the Church in Mexico just to insult him. Not to mention their televised "promise" of his demise. Oh, he was looking forward to this afternoon, all right. No matter what happened, he was looking forward to it very much indeed.

Luckily, the chaos caused by the terrorist attack hadn't kept Sophie Kinney from encountering Kylar; it was a relief to have the information safely in the Angel Killers' hands. Sophie had been surprised to find out that her role in the operation was now at an end though – Raziel had done the honours himself the day before, just hours after arriving in Mexico City. When he'd glided into her hotel room in his angel form, she'd been sitting curled up in an armchair, tensely watching TV. He'd latched onto her mind with a smooth shimmer.

"Hello, my dear – we meet at last," he'd said as he started towards her.

She'd known who he was immediately, but had been powerless to do more than gape at him. "You – but how—" she stammered, staring up at his radiant form.

"Yes, it's me," he said gently, reaching for her aura. "I have my ways. I'm an angel, you know."

Annoyingly, it turned out that Nate had marshalled her, making her energy so unpalatable that Raziel had only been able to feed for a second before breaking off in distaste. So instead he'd simply had to dispatch her – crude, but effective. He'd left Sophie still sitting in her chair, looking far more peaceful than when he'd found her. A heart attack. What a shame, in someone so young. Still, smokers were prone to them.

Raziel leaned against the window sill, one hand casually in his jacket pocket as he took another sip of his drink. The AKs must be getting ready; the attack was only a couple of hours away. It was irritating that he couldn't know for sure, now that Willow had split off from the others. She and the other half-angel had returned to his bolt-hole in Tepito – the boy was as resourceful as Kylar, in his way. Raziel hadn't been checking on his daughter as much since then; he'd found her heartbreak these last few days fairly tedious.

Even so, thinking of Willow's upcoming death, Raziel felt a twinge almost like regret. After the attack, if his gamble went as hoped, he'd be on hand to tidily do away with the Angel Killers, trapped like rats in their dead-end hallway. Kylar's death, of course, would be nearly as pleasurable as the Council's to witness, but in a strange way he knew he'd miss Willow – he'd become very used to the workings of her mind. He had little doubt that she'd be there for the attack, regardless of what had happened between her and Kylar. She was determined to take part in it, and like Raziel himself, things she was determined about tended to happen. He started to dip into her thoughts again, then restrained himself; it felt somewhat morbid, when he knew his daughter was about to die. He couldn't deny that he was curious to see her face-to-face again though, this girl he now knew so well.

Pity. But never mind.

Gazing at the sleek lines of the Torre Mayor, Raziel drained his drink and put the empty tumbler on the window sill. As he did so, it caught the sill's edge – the crystal shattered in his hand. He hissed as a dagger of glass sliced deep into the fleshy part of his palm. Swearing, he went into the bathroom and eased the glass out, his hand throbbing as ribbons of blood streamed down. His human body could feel pleasure; the annoying correlation was that it could also feel pain. At least he knew the blood would stop quickly.

By the time he left to go to the Torre Mayor, it would be just as if nothing had occurred at all.

Seb and I were on the Metro when it happened.

We'd been sitting on the rattling train car without saying very much, which wasn't unusual now. Sometimes over these last few days, it had been all I could do to make conversation with Seb at all, when before there hadn't been enough hours in the day for us to talk. As he sat beside me, I could sense the depth of his sadness over this; that he'd do anything in the world to have our friendship back the way it was. I couldn't help him. I knew it was me who had changed, but I felt too battered inside to try to figure out why, or how I might be able to fix it. All I could see was the look of stunned hurt that had been in Alex's blue-grey eyes. It made my heart feel like some small, wounded creature that had curled up, whimpering, in the corner.

The attack was in less than two hours.

We'd gone shopping earlier, with what was almost the last of our money, so that we could blend in with the others at the reception. I looked down at the clothes I had on: black trousers with a turquoise top. It was weirdly reminiscent of what Beth Hartley had been wearing a lifetime ago back in Pawntucket, when I'd given her a reading and seen an angel, its radiance reflected in the shimmering water of a stream. That was what had started all this, so it was sort of fitting I was wearing almost the same thing now.

Our plan, such as it was, was to go back to the house and join the team as they left for the attack; it was where we were going now. I had no idea how Alex would react when he saw us. But regardless of how agonizing all this was between him and me, he must know that he'd need every single person he could get to help in the attack; he was too good a leader not to. Imagining seeing him again made my veins turn to ice. If the hatred was still in his eyes, I thought it might kill me to see it.

Trying not to think about it, I stared at the grimy Metro map on the wall. Since leaving the AK house, Seb and I had been hanging out at the bridge in Chapultepec Park a lot, watching the Torre Mayor. I'm not really sure what we hoped to achieve by it; mostly it was just something to do that might be vaguely useful.

But whatever was going on in there felt…weird. Actually, so did the whole city. Just as I'd noticed a few days before, the energy felt different, calmer – more so than ever now. That sense of "New York on a caffeine jag" was gone. And when I looked up at the Torre Mayor, I kept getting an odd mental image: roots curling down; thick, gleaming coils of energy that twined deeply underground and then wove under the city in a dense tangle. Far away in the distance, I could just sense thinner shoots heading off here and there, in all directions.

"What do you think they are?" I'd said uneasily to Seb when we'd first noticed them. It was almost the only thing we'd said to each other in an hour. We were also standing in practically the exact same spot where Alex had caught us holding hands that first day; I'd shoved the thought away with a painful twinge.

Seb had shaken his head, staring upwards. "I don't know," he'd said finally. "But they feel…alive."

Neither of us had said anything else, but my scalp had chilled; it was exactly the right word. On the Metro now, I sat tensely on the hard plastic seat, wondering again what the Twelve were doing. The roots they'd put down felt practically pulsing with purpose, their energy a part of the earth. As if the Council's energy had been part of the earth all along.

A *mariachi* singer strumming a guitar was wandering through the train. His warbling voice pounded at my skull like a bad dream. Beside me, Seb had his knapsack with all our stuff in it – neither of us had really wanted to leave it behind; it would be too much like admitting we might not survive this. His switchblade was back in his pocket too; Kara had left it lying on his bed at the AK house, where he'd found it when he went to pack his things. I could feel how aware of it he was – his knowledge that soon he'd probably have to use it.

Glancing at Seb's profile, I was heavily conscious of the silence between us. I hated it, when we could both be dead so soon – but somehow I could still hardly think of anything to say to him. It was like there was a wall separating us now, and I was unable to break through, even though I'd put it up myself.

I started to rouse myself to say something anyway;

I don't even remember what. Before I could, I gasped and clutched my hand.

Pain – I'd cut myself. A shard of glass, a window sill. I stared down in confusion, expecting to see blood streaming down my palm.

"Willow?" said Seb, watching me with a frown.

I shook my head as I ran my fingers over my undamaged skin, half-sure I was going to encounter glass sticking out. I could *feel* it in there – no, it was being pulled out. I gritted my teeth at the sliding sensation, the warm rush of blood. A sink that was a stylish white slab. Pink water swirling down the drain. *Good thing it'll stop soon – wouldn't do to look less than perfect when the Council dies, now would it? After all, it might be my first moment as the new Seraphic Head.*

The images and the internal voice faded, leaving me reeling. Raziel.

"Willow, what's wrong? What are you seeing?" Seb's voice had turned urgent over the noise of the train; he started to reach for my arm and then pulled back.

"Wait," I murmured. "I just have to…" Jumbled thoughts were sweeping over me: the energy stream my first night in Mexico City, so strong and pulsing that I'd been afraid it might drown me – how it had trickled to nothing seconds later. That sense of being watched sometimes. My angel's distress, and the way whatever had been bothering her had just vanished, the moment both Seb and I went looking.

The train, the people, had all taken on a surreal edge. I closed my eyes and searched fervently once more, feeling my frustration mount with every second. There was *nothing there*. But I'd felt Raziel – what he was doing, what he was thinking. He was *in* there somehow, he had to be.

And then it came to me. If I couldn't find him inside of me...then maybe I was inside of him.

I flicked my consciousness from within to without and tried to sense my own energy, the same way I looked for Alex's – drifting, searching, letting it come. After a moment, a silver and lavender flutter appeared. I swallowed as I took in its gentle light, wondering if my hunch was true. Instinctively, I knew that I had to be very, very careful.

With only the tiniest nudge of my thoughts, I touched the grain of energy...and found myself in Raziel's mind. A world with tall towers and robed beings; an amphitheatre where lectures were given psychically, and it was all so boring, boring; the wall between worlds where he'd slipped through thousands of times to indulge himself on humanity.

Knowledge flowed into me like water pouring into a glass. I caught my breath, cold with shock. Oh my god, it wasn't just that there was a spark of me in Raziel; there was a spark of him in *me*, too. Nausea rose in my throat as I realized he'd been spying on me all along – taking in all my private thoughts, my feelings. Knowing all our plans. And now I could see his. Sophie, a memory stick. False directions for escape.

I felt dizzy as the details washed relentlessly over me. It was a trap. Destroying the Council might not kill all the angels after all; that was only one possibility. And as the others came, my blood went cold.

One of them showed the earth trembling – major cities all around the world collapsing into dust.

I sat stunned, hardly able to believe what I was getting. This couldn't be true, it just couldn't be. So many people might die. Raziel didn't even *care*. If it happened, he thought any surviving angels would still have plenty to feed on, especially with the way "the creatures" bred. And no matter what, Mexico City was certain to go if the Council was killed – those roots of their own energy that they'd woven deep below the city's surface would ensure it.

My stomach lurched. The second I had everything, I rushed out of Raziel's mind and back to my own. I had to get rid of it, get it out of me *now*.

He'd hidden it so, so well, nestled deep in my consciousness. I'd never have guessed that the tiny flame of his energy was there in a million years. Vibrant silver, with a purple tinge. I eased it from its hiding place, loathing its familial feel. With an urgent flutter, my angel appeared; cupped in her shining hands, the spark glowed brighter, and then vanished. Raziel couldn't spy on me any more – but it was a little late for that now.

My eyes flew open. Panic was crashing through me; I stared blindly at the crowded Metro train; the *mariachi* singer who was still strolling through. Seb sat half-twisted in his seat, his hands gripping mine. I didn't know how long he'd been holding them, but from the expression on his face, long enough. He looked just as sick and pale as I felt.

I could hardly get the words out. "Seb – did you see—"

"Yes, I saw," he said grimly, just as the car reached our station. He snatched up his knapsack from the floor by his feet. "*El DF* for certain, and maybe even more."

"We've got to get to the house in time! We've got to stop them—" I jumped from my seat and pushed through the crowded car, with Seb right behind me; we hit the platform running and pounded up the concrete stairs onto the street. Everything we passed, every car, every person, suddenly seemed as vulnerable as an eggshell. My lungs were burning as we raced towards the house, and in a weird way it was almost like that first day, when we'd run after the angels through the park.

Except that if we didn't manage to stop the attack now,

then Alex and the others were all going to die…and so might millions more.

"Okay, I think that's everything," said Alex.

He'd just finished putting Kara's bag in the back of Juan's white van along with the rest of their luggage. As he emerged, he glanced up at the house, trying to think if they'd forgotten anything. That morning, it had suddenly occurred to him that after the attack there'd be no reason for them to remain in Mexico City. Either they'd have succeeded, in which case they could all head home to the US, or else they'd be on the run for their lives, and need to get the hell out of the city anyway.

There was a third option, of course. He set his jaw and ignored it.

"Good. We're almost ready, then," said Kara. Her nails were red again today, with little flecks like diamonds; they matched her bright red top. Thankfully, things hadn't been too awkward between them since the other night, though Alex had the impression Kara thought he was kind of an idiot not to take what she'd been offering and just enjoy it. He couldn't really argue.

Sam appeared, carrying a cardboard box on his shoulder. "Have we got room for this?"

"What is it?" asked Alex.

"Just some of the food supplies. Munchies for the road."

The decision that they should pack up had been met with obvious relief by the rest of the team. Though Alex hadn't expected it to act as a morale boost, it obviously had – it gave the attack this afternoon a sense of *when* we succeed, instead of *if*.

"Yeah, I think there's room." Kara moved past him to delve into the van, shifting Alex's tent and sleeping bags to one side. Alex looked away, remembering lying in that tent with Willow. If he was still alive after the job today, he'd soon be putting hundreds of miles between them, with no idea where she even was any more. Frankly, it was part of the appeal of taking off. He wanted to get as far away from memories of Willow as possible.

"I still think we should just steal the 4 x 4," said Sam, passing the box to Kara. "Man, I have *travelled* in this van. It's like rolling around in a box of marbles."

"We'll be all right," said Alex. He had the 4 x 4's keys in his pocket; he was going to follow the others over to the Torre Mayor to return it to Sophie.

The others had drifted out and were standing in the drive. Now that the time was almost here, the mood was a pulsing mix of anticipation, fear, excitement. Everyone looked unusually polished, like a group about to go on job interviews. The girls all had on trousers this time instead of dresses; the need to draw their weapons with a complete lack of fumbling had trumped fashion. Alex himself was wearing grey trousers and a dark blue shirt. He'd considered a tie but decided against it – he'd never worn one in his life and wasn't going to start now, on what might be his last day ever.

Wesley was flexing his arm. "Are you sure you're okay?" asked Alex in an undertone. Though Wesley claimed his injury was healed now, Alex wasn't convinced.

"I'm fine," said Wesley. He glanced sideways at Alex; raised an arched eyebrow with a slight smile. "So don't go hassling me 'bout it, all right?"

Alex was painfully aware that Wesley was one of the best shots he had – but if he wasn't fully functioning yet, no way did he want to send him in there. "Wes, if you're not sure, you've got to tell me now."

Wesley's brown eyes flashed. "Listen to me. *I am sure.* Don't do this to me, man. You know why I've got to be there today. *You* understand better than anyone."

"Yeah, I understand," said Alex quietly. He felt the same way; what had happened to his own family was half the reason he was doing this. "But if your aim's off—"

"Then maybe I die," broke in Wesley. His voice was low, fierce. "And maybe I don't care much if I do, and maybe I'd rather be there *trying* than anything else in my whole sorry life – okay?"

Alex let out a breath. The harsh truth was that he wasn't

in a position to say no to someone who was willing; even injured, Wesley could be a tremendous asset. And more than that, he didn't think he really had the right to tell the guy he couldn't come, when it meant so much to him and he was aware of the risks.

"Yeah, okay," he said finally. Relief swept Wesley's face; he nodded wordlessly.

Trish cleared her throat. She was standing to one side; from her pained expression Alex could tell she'd heard some of their conversation. "So…are we almost ready?"

Alex glanced at his phone, checking the time. "Almost. I'll just look through the house again, make sure we haven't forgotten anything."

"I'm sure we haven't," said Kara, clambering out from the van.

He headed back inside anyway. As he wandered through the vacant rooms, the place felt like a ghost of itself; as if everything that had happened here had happened long ago, to other people. The kitchen table, where they'd talked and squabbled and even laughed occasionally. The firing range, where he'd made his first announcements as the lead and then spent hours training the team – saw them slowly come together, learning how to be actual AKs instead of just angel spotters with guns. *I can be proud of that,* he thought, gazing at the targets hanging motionless on their chains. *No matter what, I can really be proud of that.*

His bedroom.

Alex stood motionless against the doorway as he took it in. The room was full of Willow. He had a flash of her stealing in one morning: the look in her eyes as she'd slipped into bed with him; the smell of her as he'd brushed his lips against her neck. With a grimace, he shook the memory away. Okay, this had been a bad idea. He pushed himself off the door jamb – and then stopped, looking up at his shelf.

Willow's necklace was still there, where he'd tossed it after finding it on the kitchen table. He deliberately hadn't packed it today. Now he realized with grim certainty that this was what he'd come back for. Somehow, he couldn't just leave it behind. Feeling more idiotic than ever, he shoved it in his pocket, cursing the memories attached to the thing. The way he felt about Willow seemed like a sickness now. He never wanted to be this in love again – it wasn't worth it. But the necklace remained in his pocket.

He went back outside. "We're ready," he said tersely.

Kara nodded and reached for her keys; she was going to drive the van. As everyone started to climb in, Alex cleared his throat. "No, wait a second. Guys, listen…no matter what happens, I'm proud of you, okay? The way you've trained these last couple of months has just been amazing. You're all good AKs now – really good. We can do this thing; every one of you has got what it takes."

The group had gone very still as he spoke, varying expressions of shy pride on their faces. From the driver's seat, Kara's brown eyes met his. He had the sudden feeling she was thinking of his father, and the back of his neck warmed.

"Yeah, yeah, enough of the mushy stuff," said Sam finally. "We love you too, you jerk. Now come on, let's get the hell out of here and kill some angels."

"Kill *all* angels," corrected Liz firmly.

"Yup – kill 'em all. Yee-haw!" bellowed Sam to the van's ceiling.

Suddenly the mood was exuberant. Alex knew it wouldn't last, but it was good for now; exactly what they all needed. With a grin, he started back towards the 4 x 4. "Okay, I'll see you there," he said over his shoulder. "You've all got your passes, right? Meet me in the lobby if—" He broke off, shock stiffening his muscles.

Willow and Seb were running up the drive.

"Oh, what the hell is this?" muttered Kara, swinging herself quickly out of the van. Sam got out too, scowling. The rest of the team stayed put, watching warily as the two jogged to a stop, both breathing hard. Willow's eyes went straight to Alex's as if the others weren't even present.

"Alex, the attack can't go ahead," she gasped. "It's a trap – a *trap*."

"*What?*" He stared at her in distrust, hating the way his heart had leaped when he saw her.

"It's Raziel, he's using you! He was using all of us – he wants the Council dead, but—" She gulped, struggling to catch her breath.

"It's true," put in Seb. He stood near Willow, though not touching her. "You must listen to her."

"*Raziel?* The angel in charge of the Church in the US?" Kara's eyes narrowed. "And why would he want the Council dead, pray tell, when that means all angels will die, including him?"

Willow's bright hair moved as she shook her head impatiently. "Because it *doesn't* mean that! It might, but it might not! The Council's going to take his leadership away, and he's willing to take the chance—"

"How do you know this?" broke in Alex.

"Yeah, I'd sorta like to hear that too," said Sam in his low drawl. He was leaning against the van, one foot propped up behind him.

"I—" Looking at the other AKs, Willow seemed to really notice them for the first time. She swallowed. "Because I was able to read Raziel's thoughts," she said at last. "He's my father," she added before Kara could ask.

Seb moved closer, but still didn't touch her. A stunned silence; every face in the van was gaping at her. "You have got to be kidding me," breathed Kara. "Alex, did you—"

She cut off as she saw his face. "Oh my god, you did! You knew this."

"It didn't seem important," said Alex shortly.

Kara's voice rose. "Not *important*? Your girlfriend's father is like, Mr. Head Evil Angel, and that wasn't *important* enough to ever mention it to us?"

"She's not my girlfriend any more," snapped Alex. He turned to Willow. "Look, what do you mean, you were able to read his thoughts? What's going on?"

Willow glanced at the others again; her face was tense but determined. "Could you and I go inside maybe, and I'll explain?"

Alex blew out a breath. Part of him wanted to tell her that if she had something to say, she could say it right here – but her eyes were pleading with him. "Fine," he bit out.

"*Alex*—" protested Kara, straightening in alarm.

"I'll just be a minute." He turned and strode back to the house, heading for the front door; Willow and Seb followed. "You and I" had apparently meant "Seb too".

"This seriously *cannot* take long," Alex said from between gritted teeth as they went inside. "We've got to go."

"I know, we were coming to help you," said Willow. They were in the range; she stood against the wall near the basement door. "But then on the Metro…" She hesitated, visibly shaken. Alex ignored the concern he felt; Willow wasn't any of his business any more.

She collected herself and went on. "On the Metro, I found out that I have a sort of...link with Raziel."

Just the word made Alex's hackles rise. "Really? Is this like your link with Seb?"

Seb gave him a narrow look. The tips of Willow's ears turned red, but her voice was level. "No, not really," she said. "When Raziel and I fought in Denver, it's like we exchanged particles of energy, or something. He's had a spark of his energy in me, and I've had one in him. I didn't know anything about it until now, but he's been using it to spy on us. Alex, he's been manipulating everything all along."

"Manipulating how?" he demanded.

"Everything! It's why Luis suddenly trusted Kara; it's why Sophie suddenly appeared to give you security details and VIP passes—"

A chill went over Alex. "How did you know about that?"

"I just told you! I've been in Raziel's head!" Willow's voice rose in frustration. "Things are different in this world than in the angels' world. It's not definite that all angels will die if you take the Council out; that's only *one* option. What Raziel's hoping is that only the Twelve will die, and that he'll still be alive to take everything over, but...but there's other possibilities too..." She faltered to a stop.

"*El DF* will be destroyed, that's almost certain," put in Seb. "The Council have put down roots of energy here – if they die, they take the city with them."

"But not just Mexico City!" Willow's tone was anguished. "Alex, they've done the same thing all over the world, in every place that they think feels out of control. There are so many major cities that could be affected now, *everywhere* – there could be earthquakes, cities falling – millions dead—"

The hair on the back of Alex's neck rose as he stared at her. "This doesn't even make sense," he said in a low voice. "If the angels destroy so much of humanity, how will *they* live?"

"It's not the angels, it's just Raziel!" cried Willow. "He knows the Twelve will kill him anyway, so he's willing to take the gamble! And if it pays off for him, the AKs will all be executed – the information Sophie gave you is flawed. There's a…a hallway on the map that's not right, or something. You can't get out that way."

Remembering the plans, Alex suddenly felt cold with dread; his stomach clenched so tightly that he felt physically sick. Oh, Jesus. Was this really true?

"Please believe me," said Willow softly, her gaze fixed on his. She made a motion as if to take his hand and then pulled back, her face pained but imploring. "No matter what's happened between you and me, you know I wouldn't lie about this. Alex, the attack can't go ahead. It just can't."

"Okay, that is *enough*," hissed Kara's voice. "I don't know what she's been saying to you, but I hope you're not believing it."

Alex spun, and saw that she'd come in through the kitchen; Sam was behind her. Seb had straightened too, his eyes watchful as Kara strode over to them, her boots rapping against the floor.

"Let me deal with this, Kara," said Alex shortly.

"Alex, please," whispered Willow, ignoring everyone but him. Her hands were tight fists at her sides. "Please."

"She's Raziel's daughter!" cried Kara. "Of *course* she's trying to get you to stop the attack – she's trying to save the angels!"

Alex slowly shook his head, staring at Willow as he remembered her sobbing with relief in his arms to know that her mother was still alive. "She hates Raziel, she always has," he said. All he could think was…*millions dead*. Even if there was a chance that it wouldn't happen, if it was a possibility at all, they couldn't take the risk.

Watching him, Sam's expression had turned dumbstruck. "Alex, you can't really be listening to her, right? This is *saving the world*, man! We gotta do it, we don't have a choice!"

"Yes, tell me you're not listening to her," said Kara, her eyes hard. "She *lied* to you, remember?"

"I remember." Alex's gaze was still locked with Willow's; on some distant level his heart felt shredded just from being next to her. Yeah, she'd lied to him – but he couldn't doubt her, not about this. He let out a breath. "Look, guys, I think—"

Kara moved so quickly that he hardly saw it. Suddenly she'd jumped at Willow and grabbed her from behind – one arm tight around Willow's throat, the other holding a gun to her head. Willow gave a choked cry.

Alex's pulse jumped and he started forward; in a blur, he was aware of Seb lunging too – of Sam throwing himself at Seb in a flying tackle. The two of them crashed to the floor with a heavy thud, struggling.

Kara flicked the safety off her gun, stopping Alex in his tracks.

"Think again," she said. The muscles of her forearm were rigid against Willow's neck. "I am *not* letting you compromise this mission, Alex. Drop your gun. *Now.*"

"Alex, don't," gasped Willow, clutching Kara's arm. "I'm only one person; it doesn't matter about me—"

"You don't even know what she said!" burst out Alex at the same time. "Kara, *listen* to me! It's true; the attack can't go ahead—"

"Did you hear me?" she snapped. "Because I'll blow her brains out right now if you don't drop your gun."

Out of the corner of his vision, Alex saw that Seb was

making a decent showing for himself as he and Sam scuffled, but the Texan outweighed him by at least fifty pounds. There was the sharp crack of fist against skin – and then the next second Sam had him down, as Seb let spew with a string of Spanish that it was lucky Sam didn't understand.

Alex kept his eyes on Kara's, not letting his glance flicker to the weapons cabinet on the wall behind her. They'd packed most of the guns away into the truck, but a couple of small pistols were still in there – cheap .25s that none of them liked using. If he played along with Kara for now, he might be able to get to one.

Slowly, he reached for his gun and tossed it onto the floor.

Kara didn't stop watching him for a second. Her forearm still mercilessly tight around Willow's neck, she transferred her gun to the other hand, shoving the muzzle up under Willow's jaw. In a single motion, she bent and scooped up Alex's gun, tucking it away into her waistband.

"Good," she said as she rose again; Willow was gasping for breath. "Now your VIP pass and the keys for the truck."

Alex's muscles were clenched, watching. The cabinet was about ten feet away. If Kara's attention left him for even a heartbeat, he'd go for it. He dug into his pocket. His fingers hesitated as he touched what was in there; then keys and card followed with a clatter.

"You're making a mistake, Kara," he said. "Raziel *wants* the Council dead – and if they're killed, millions of people could die."

"Is that what she told you?" Kara's lip curled. "God, you're still so in love with this little liar that you can't even think straight." With no warning, she bundled Willow away through the basement door; he heard Willow cry out.

Alex dove for the weapons cabinet. Locked. Oh *Jesus*, since when did they ever lock it? He raced for the basement, dimly aware of the intensified struggle behind him, Seb's shouts. As he reached the open door, Kara burst out and shoved him hard at the stairway. He spun towards her, trying for her gun – but the next second Seb had slammed into him and they'd both gone tumbling down the stairs.

CHAPTER *Twenty-eight*

ALEX SCRAMBLED TO HIS FEET, barrelling back up the stairs just as the door slammed shut; he heard the bolt glide home and threw himself against the unyielding wood anyway. "You're *making a mistake!*" he yelled. He slammed the door with his fist. "Kara! Don't go ahead with the attack, *don't!*"

"I'm sorry, Alex," she called, her voice already fading. "But believe me, you'll thank me for this someday." The sound of the front door closing filtered down to him. Alex gave a wordless bellow of fury and frustration and shouldered the door again; it shuddered but stayed firm.

"Somehow, I don't think we're going to break the door down," said a dry voice. Seb was there, his cheek already looking bruised and swollen. Reaching into his trouser pocket, he pulled out his switchblade.

"What, you had a *knife* the whole time?" demanded Alex.

Seb flicked the knife open and angled the blade through the gap between door and wall, probing at the bolt and trying to slide it back across. "You had a gun – and you weren't even getting your face smashed," he pointed out. "At least I managed to hold onto my blade."

As the knife scratched and scraped, Alex glanced down the stairs at Willow. She stood at the bottom holding onto the railing, grimacing slightly as she rolled her ankle. Their eyes met. "Are you all right?" asked Alex after a pause.

She nodded and put her foot to the ground, testing it. "Fine. She just – pushed me really hard."

Even now, Alex's impulse was to go to her and hold her. It wasn't his place any more – it was Seb's. He looked away.

The minutes dragged by. Seb swore softly as the blade skittered across the bolt. Finally he shook his head and started on the hinges instead, twirling the knife's tip deftly in each screw head. "Oh, man, that's going to take for ever," muttered Alex, shoving his hair back. The reception would be starting soon; their private audience was the first one scheduled. They had maybe an hour, tops.

"I look forward to hearing your much better idea," said Seb without looking at him. One of the screws came out; he tossed it aside with a tiny clatter. After what seemed a hundred agonizing lifetimes, all the screws had been removed. Alex helped Seb lift the door off and they burst out into the range.

Alex raced to the weapons cabinet. A heavy wooden chair sat against the wall nearby; he picked it up and swung it at the cabinet in almost the same motion. There was a splintering crack as the door gave way. The .25s were there, just as he'd remembered. Alex shoved one into his holster and glanced at Seb and Willow, who had joined him.

Seb nodded at Willow. "Give it to her; I've got my blade."

Alex handed it over wordlessly. "Thanks," said Willow; her voice was a ghost of itself. She reached past and took a spare holster from the cupboard, turning away from both of them as she strapped it on under her trousers. *Why bother?* thought Alex bitterly. Both he and Seb had seen her undressed.

As they passed by the TV room, Alex ducked into it. The paper file was still on the coffee table; quickly he found the sheet with the code for the top of the Torre Mayor's stairwell. "Okay, come on," he said, tearing the code off and shoving it in his pocket. Though none of them had discussed where they were going, they all knew. Alex thought how ironic it was – he was now allied with Willow and Seb against the team he'd been ready to give his life to keep safe.

Willow swallowed. "How are we getting there? The Metro will take—"

"The truck," said Alex shortly. He led the way out the front door.

She blinked. "But you gave Kara the keys."

"No, I gave her the keys for the Shadow." Out on the drive, Alex saw that someone had thrown all his stuff out of the van before they'd taken off. *Thanks, guys,* he thought wryly. He grabbed up his things and dug into his pocket; his fingers briefly brushed Willow's necklace as he pulled out the keys to the truck.

Seb got into the back of the 4 x 4, tossing his knapsack on top of the sleeping bags; Willow sat up front with Alex, her face tense. They had less than half an hour now.

Spinning the wheel, Alex screeched them out of the drive. Soon they were speeding through the *centro*. The streets were relatively clear; he still found himself driving like a maniac, swerving in and out of traffic, with horns blaring in his wake.

What had Kara told the team? The last-minute mutiny must have stunned them. The thought made him inch the speedometer still higher. Their performance might be thrown now; if he didn't get there in time to stop this, they could all die when they faced the Council.

His hands tightened on the wheel. No. They would not die.

"Tell me everything," he ordered.

Willow did so, gripping the dashboard with a white-knuckled hand. As Alex listened, he became more certain than ever that this was true. Christ, of *course* Raziel had been spying on them; it was how Charmeine had known the details about their previous attack against the angels.

Though it wasn't a massive surprise, his jaw tensed at the news that both Luis and Sophie were dead. One had been devout to the angels, the other dedicated to stopping them. It didn't matter; they'd both gotten in the way and so they'd been discarded like used toys.

"Okay, do we *know* that killing the Twelve will cause damage to our world?" he asked as he steered them onto the Paseo de la Reforma. Up ahead, the empty plinth where the Mexico City angel had stood for decades was like a solitary sentinel, with traffic streaming past on both sides.

"It'll definitely cause damage to Mexico City," said Willow. "Apart from that – no, we don't know. It might be that killing the Council really *will* destroy all the angels. That's what most angels think will happen. Or it might be that it kills only some angels and not others, and the rest of the world will be fine. But—" She broke off, her face pale. "I just don't think so," she whispered. "They've put down roots like that under dozens of other major cities, too. There's a chance those may not have had time to take effect yet, but the Twelve's energy feels so entwined with our world now – I can't imagine that there aren't going to be serious consequences all over."

With just over ten minutes to go, they were nearing the Torre Mayor. It rose up above the other buildings in a graceful curve of green glass, its half-moon summit gleaming. As he turned onto the Rio Atoyac, Alex swore suddenly.

"What?" demanded Seb from the back.

Alex explained, his voice terse. His original plan for getting the team into the loading dock area had depended on them having the white van, which actually *looked* like a delivery van – he'd then announce a delivery for a company that always took for ever before sending someone down to let the guy into the elevator.

"Plus I was going to piggyback along with the afternoon FedEx delivery," he finished grimly. "So that we could get into the service elevator when someone let the FedEx guy in." He rapped the steering wheel, trying to think. They were going to have to force their way past the guard, except how could they? Somewhere overhead, security had their beady eyes on the video screens – they'd bring the service elevators to a screeching halt the second they saw guns being waved around.

Willow shot him a concerned glance; for a second, it was as if things between them were the same as always. "Go on to the gate and tell the guard you've got a delivery," she said suddenly. "I think I might have an idea."

Seb seemed to sense whatever it was; in the rear-view mirror, Alex saw his face slacken in surprise. "Willow, I'm not sure this is even *possible* – and besides, you've never tried it!" he burst out.

"Well, no time like the present," she muttered, shoving a hand through her red-gold spikes. "And since it happened to you once, it shouldn't be impossible for us to do it at will, right? In theory, anyway."

The conversation with half its words missing did nothing to reassure Alex. But they didn't have much to lose. They were almost at the service entrance by then, with the building looming up over them; he turned into the barricaded drive and stopped by the guard booth. Putting on a relaxed smile, he said, "*Buenos días, Señor*. I've got a delivery for Ortega Graphics."

The guard frowned, his gaze scanning over the blue 4 x 4. Just beyond the security barrier, a blocker rose out of the drive: a huge metal wedge that faced them like a solid wall. It would stay there until the guard lowered it into the ground.

"Oh?" said the guard. "What company are you with?"

Alex named a company that often made deliveries to

Ortega. In a white van, which this so totally wasn't. Not to mention that he looked like he was dressed to go to church or something.

Beside him, he was aware of Willow concentrating hard; shifting his consciousness, he saw her angel self soar out of the truck and hover unseen near the guard booth. Meanwhile, the man's expression had turned even more suspicious. "*Un momento*, I'll have to confirm this." He rarely confirmed deliveries for Ortega – just let the drivers through and then buzzed someone to come down.

Alex could feel Willow's human self straining with effort. And then slowly, her angel became more...*tangible*. There was no other way to describe it. Instead of an ethereal being of light, she shifted until she looked almost solid, as if Alex could reach his hand out the window and stroke one of her gleaming wings. It was what the angels of the Second Wave had done, he thought in a daze: slowed down their frequency so they could be seen.

Instead of reaching for the phone, the guard stood gaping, taking in the radiant creature that had suddenly appeared before him, emanating peace and kindness. The psychic blast Willow's angel sent towards him was so strong that Alex caught it too: *Let them in. It's all right. Let them in.*

Alex had seen hundreds of people encountering angels; the expression on the guard's face now was as awestruck as any of them. Staring at the angel with a wondering smile, he slowly pressed a button. The security barrier swung open; beyond it, the blocker sank into the drive.

"*Gracias,*" said Alex hurriedly, and gunned them through before the guy came back to his senses.

The loading dock was a dimly lit cave. With Willow's angel still flying above, they parked with a shriek of wheels and ran up the short concrete ramp that led to the service elevator. Someone was just wheeling an empty cart off it, and they plunged in.

They stayed tensely silent as the elevator hummed its way to the fifty-fourth floor. With an effort, Alex kept his eyes off the security camera. Glancing sideways, he could tell how drained Willow was from the effort with her angel, and felt a stab of anger towards Seb, who gave her a concerned glance but then just stood there without even putting his arm around her.

Though Willow looked nervous, her chin was lifted firmly. *She's determined to be there. She loves you very much, you know.*

As the words came back to him, Alex went still, taking in Willow's face. He realized he was staring and looked away. *Get a grip*, he thought, irritated with himself. He had nothing to do with why Willow was here any more; she was in love with Seb.

"Is there a plan?" asked Seb as the elevator neared the

top. He looked almost relaxed, his eyes coolly determined.

Alex shook his head. Glancing at his phone, he was agonizingly conscious that their private audience was due to start in less than a minute. "I wish. Just follow me, as fast as you can – I know where the team will be heading. We've got to get to them before they go in."

The elevator stopped; the doors glided open. A few seconds later, they were in the stairwell, rushing up the concrete stairs. Time slowed; Alex was hyper-aware of everything: Willow ahead of him, her short spikes bouncing as she ran; the thin scar on Seb's arm catching the fluorescent light; the adrenalin pumping through his own veins.

They reached the door at the top. Alex punched in the code; the light turned green and he flung it open. High glass ceilings, a glimpse of blue sky and clouds – and then they were hurtling their way down a carpeted corridor towards the lavish reception ahead.

At promptly five past three, Raziel shifted to his angel form with a smooth ripple; wings spread, he glided out into the Mexico City afternoon. The metropolis of over twenty million people stretched out to the horizon in every direction, ringed by low purple mountains in the far distance. Raziel could feel the unnatural calmness here since the Council had been interfering, as if a soothing blanket had been draped over everything. It irked him, so that he was almost glad the place was about to be levelled.

A shame about the cathedral though. He circled it once on his way to the Torre Mayor, taking in its ornate, ancient lines and the golden angel newly gleaming at its peak. Once the interior damage caused by the rioters had been repaired, it would have been a fitting place of worship indeed. Still, it was satisfying to know that Tyrel was about to have such a prize snatched away from him.

Why Raziel, that's rather dog-in-the-mangerish of you, he thought, and chuckled as he flew on to the Torre Mayor. It rose up over the city, its green glass curves reflecting the clouds.

At exactly three-fifteen, Raziel landed on the building's helipad, touching down at its precise centre. The view from here was no better than when flying, but it was still pleasant to change to his human form and survey the city with his hands behind his back, feeling the wind lick at his hair and suit jacket. He'd pondered for some time before deciding what to wear. Even a gatecrasher wanted to look his best – especially if the clothes he put on might be either the last thing he ever wore, or the outfit in which he'd finally take leadership. At last he'd decided on a dark grey, almost black suit, with a rich purple shirt, open at the neck.

When Raziel finally received the psychic call from Charmeine, he'd long since become bored with the view and started to pace about the helipad. He stopped in his tracks, pulse quickening as he felt the unmistakable pull of her energy. "About time," he murmured.

He shifted to his angel form and glided into the glass portion of the building. The plan was for him and Charmeine to be in an adjacent room when the shootings took place, so that they could properly savour it. Feeling the Twelve's deaths would no doubt be painful if he survived, but Raziel was looking forward to it anyway, with a dark anticipation. Every death-pain would mean that another of the Twelve was gone.

He cruised over the VIP floor, taking in the lavish afternoon reception: waiters gliding about with silver trays; a high, slanted glass ceiling overhead; a crowd of excited-looking humans. Some of the Twelve's angelic entourage were there too, feeding from starry-eyed victims, and Raziel smiled to himself. *Don't look like you're having too much fun; you'll get into trouble.*

Letting the tug guide him, he flew through a tall white wall.

A slam of energy, a binding, as if several invisible nets had been thrown on him at once. Instantly he felt like a cartoon cat, frantically trying to back-pedal in mid-air. Because Charmeine wasn't alone in the room: the Council were there, seated at a long conference table.

"Raziel," said Isda mildly. "How good of you to join us. We were looking forward to seeing you in your cathedral again, but this is even better."

He struggled to free himself, but the psychic bindings drew tighter with every wing-stroke. Down below, a broken-looking Charmeine stood slumped against the wall, wearing a short black dress, her face wet with tears. The Twelve sat in a row down one side of the long table, male and female angels alternating, with Isda at the centre. They all stared up at him dispassionately, as if he was of no more interest than a trapped moth.

As their energy slowly reeled him in, Baglis, another of the Twelve, spoke, his resonant voice echoing through the high room. "We were most surprised to hear of your plans for us, Raziel. However, your friend Charmeine doesn't seem quite certain of all the details. Perhaps you can help."

They kept him a foot or so off the floor, making him hover though every movement of his wings was agony now. Raziel's eyes met Charmeine's; she gave an almost imperceptible shake of her head. So the Council knew there was a plot – but *what* exactly might still be hidden.

"I don't know what you mean," he said aloud, then cried out as a dozen mental whips scorched his mind.

"Oh, we think you do," said Isda. "Charmeine, as it turns out, is very good at hiding things – but I rather imagine you'll be easier to delve."

There was a knock at the door. It opened a cautious crack, and a human attendant stuck her head in. "Excuse me, *Señora* Isda – but it's time for the private audiences. Shall I send the first group in? It's the one from Mexico City University." She didn't even glance at Raziel; in his angel form, he was as invisible to her as air. Remembering that this first group was the AKs, Raziel shoved the knowledge away as hard as he could.

"Just give us a few minutes, and then send them in," directed Isda.

Once the attendant had withdrawn, Isda sat back in her seat, her gaze fixed on the mentally-trussed Raziel as he hung suspended before them. The faces of the Twelve were bland. "*You don't seem to have taken our warnings about moderation and angelic dignity to heart, Raziel,*" she said on the psychic level. "*Such a shame.*"

He cried out again as he felt himself shifted by force into his human body. The sensation was exceedingly unpleasant. "*Conspiring to assassinate us is treason,*" continued Isda as a chorus of psychic voices joined hers. "*And we* will *get all the details out of you before your execution. For now, watch and learn while we show you that it's possible to feed without getting carried away with gluttony.*"

Trapped in his human form, Raziel felt just as ensnared as before, as if he'd been bound from head to toe. He stood weakly against the wall, keeping the surface of his mind as impassive as possible. Underneath, he was fuming. At least he had a ringside seat for what was about to occur – and oh, was he going to enjoy it. He watched the door, thankful that he was out of direct view. He only prayed that neither Kylar nor Willow would see him until it was too late.

The Twelve shifted to their angel forms and lifted up in a fiercely-burning row, glowing even brighter as they lowered their frequency so they could be seen by humans. And like a tiny, apologetic tendril, Charmeine's thought came creeping into his mind: *I'm sorry, Raz. They delved me when I wasn't expecting it. I just couldn't hold them off any more.*

Raziel shrugged mentally; it was too late to do anything about it now. Then the door opened, and a group of six young adults filed in – three males and three females.

Where was Kylar? Raziel only just managed to restrain the leaping thought. Were these the assassins, or not? He reached quickly for his connection to Willow. It was gone.

She knew. His pulse rate doubled, and Isda gave him a sharp look. He writhed under the sudden pain of her psychic probe – and knew that, this time, he hadn't managed to hide the group's identity. The awareness of the humans' intentions rippled ominously through the Twelve, their expressions never changing.

Looking nervous, the team faced them, blinking from the glow. A tall black woman with exquisite features and masses of long braids nodded to the Twelve. In Spanish, she said, "Good afternoon; we're from Mexico City University. It's an honour to—"

She broke off, startled, as the Twelve swooped forward in a rush. "Now!" she cried, ducking back.

A few AKs fumbled; others grabbed their weapons smoothly and started firing. The room erupted into flapping wings and exploding light as the first bullets found their targets. Raziel could feel the Council's stunned fury that their move hadn't caught the AKs more off guard; that they were actually being destroyed by *humans*, of all creatures. Standing so close meant the pain juddered at Raziel like machine-gun fire as some of the silenced bullets hit their targets. Yet it was his mind, more than his body, that was under assault. He'd always assumed it was the physical connection with the First Formed that was the vital one – but as one after another of the Council members erupted into nothingness, Raziel knew it was the mental connection that would destroy him. He could feel his mind starting to buckle. The Twelve were leaving the world. It couldn't be. The angels would be adrift without them, for ever adrift.

Only seconds had passed. Seven of them were gone now. The guns' muffled thuds kept on. Awash with numb despair, Raziel slid down the wall to the floor, watching the shards of radiance floating all around him. What had he done? He could sense the other angels in the building, still in their divine forms – dazed and in pain, some of them dying already from the shock.

Fight this! he screamed at himself. *It's a delusion, a momentary weakness. Once the Twelve are gone, I'll have exactly what I've always wanted!*

He gritted his teeth, focusing on that – only on that. Somehow he managed to wrest his mind back, though his body was still held captive. Overhead, the remaining five First Formed angels rallied as one and flew at their assailants. And as they reached out psychically towards the AKs, Raziel knew with a dark twist of joy that their power was already greatly depleted – because the bonds on him had just weakened.

Alex pounded down the corridor, with Willow and Seb right behind him. Up ahead was the soaring room where the reception was taking place. Music from a string quartet floated through the air, competing with the noisy buzz of the guests' conversation. Alex glimpsed a few angels in there too, feeding but weirdly motionless; their victims stood gazing with adoring awe.

The AKs were nowhere in sight – their audience with the Council must have already started. He drew his gun as they reached the meeting room; and flung the door open.

Five angels, brighter than any he'd ever seen, were in combat with his team – blurs of burning white light that dove, snarling, at the human attackers. Only four AKs were shooting. Alex stopped in his tracks, blood chilling as he saw that Trish's face was damp with tears; she was pulling frantically at Wesley's arm as he struggled with her. "*Don't shoot!*" she sobbed. "We can't do this; we can't hurt the angels!"

Oh god, no. Trish.

Kara and the others looked dazed but were still battling. Somehow Alex shoved aside his feelings – but having drawn his gun, he saw suddenly there was nothing to fire on, unless he was going to start shooting at his team. He wouldn't, not even to save the world.

With every instinct screaming to aim his gun at the angels, he instead hurled himself at Kara and wrested the pistol from her hands. "Stop the attack!" he yelled. "Everyone, stop firing *now!*"

"No!" Kara's face contorted with desperate fury as she fought him. Meanwhile Willow and Seb's angels had appeared and were darting around the room – blocking shots from the AKs at the same time they were protecting the team from the Council. Alex saw Willow's angel swoop between a Council angel and Liz, spreading her wings over Liz for a second time.

Across the room, another Council angel vanished in a spray of light; Alex couldn't tell who'd gotten it. The human Willow stood pressed against the wall beside Seb; she'd drawn her gun but obviously realized, like him, that there was nothing she could do. Wesley was still trying to fend off the crying Trish. As Wes shot again, Seb's angel flinched in the air; the human Seb staggered.

Fleetingly, Alex noticed a woman with pale blonde hair struggle to her feet. She surveyed the room with a small, satisfied smile and slipped out; then one of Kara's punches almost connected and he forgot about the blonde woman. He got Kara's arms pinned behind her. She was gasping, almost crying. "Alex, she's got you under a spell! Don't do this!"

He ignored her. "Stop the attack!" he shouted again. "This is what Raziel *wants*, it could destroy our world!"

Most of the team were panicked now; no one even seemed to have heard him. Another Council angel dove straight at Sam, who froze wide-eyed – then shook himself with a roar as he aimed and shot. Willow's angel darted in front; the bullet went through her as the Council member twisted away.

Alex heard the human Willow gasp in pain and had to

force himself not to go running to see if she was all right. Instead, he shoved Kara hard to one side and flung himself at Sam as the Texan fired again. They crashed to the carpeted floor. Sam squirmed out from under Alex and kept firing; another Council member, a male, went down in a spray of radiance.

Only three angels remained. They grew brighter, glowing with a painful light that throbbed at the air. Brendan was running back and forth as he dodged Willow's angel; in a blur, Alex saw Willow herself sitting on the floor with her eyes closed. Seb had his switchblade out, but hardly looked capable of using it. Another bullet hit his angel and he stumbled, catching himself against the wall.

"Stop! We can't do this!" Trish was pulling frantically on Wesley's injured arm. Alex saw him cry out and clutch at it, dropping his gun.

"Wes, look out!" he shouted. But a Council angel had already taken the chance to fly right at him; Wesley froze as he stared into its eyes. The next moment he was theirs.

"No – we can't hurt the angels – what are we *doing*?" he gasped. He lunged at Brendan, sending them both sprawling. "Stop! Don't hurt them!"

Sam took aim at another angel; Alex threw himself at his arm and his shot went wild. Suddenly Alex noticed the man in the dark suit who sat slumped against the far wall. Oh Christ, it couldn't be. *Raziel.*

Willow's father shook his head briefly, as if shackles were falling from him. Gazing at the scene, his handsome jaw hardened. Wesley's dropped gun lay nearby on the carpet and he reached for it, fingers closing around the weapon.

Still on top of the struggling Sam, Alex aimed his own gun and started firing, even though he *knew* it would do no good; angels couldn't be killed in their human forms. Raziel gave a hiss, recoiling as the bullets rained into him – but still he lifted the gun, aiming at a Council member who was darting at Liz.

Sam saw him too. Abruptly, the fight went out of him; his startled eyes met Alex's. "Stop!" he bellowed. "You guys, *stop!* He's right!"

It all happened in seconds: Brendan shoved Wesley off and fired at the same time as Raziel; the Council member went down in a fountain of light. Another angel swooped at Brendan, tearing at his life energy; he staggered with a cry and went down, clutching his leg. At the same time, Kara had grabbed a fallen gun and was struggling with the hysterical Trish – she battled away Trish's flailing hands and nailed the angel who'd given Wesley angel burn, sending it flying into fragments.

Then Kara saw Raziel. Her eyes went wide; she gave Alex a startled look. Flying unsteadily, Willow and Seb's angels both started towards Willow's father – who stood aiming the pistol at the last of the Twelve.

No! The hyper-awareness came back to Alex. In slow motion, he and Sam scrambled to their feet, lunging across the room in unison; dimly, he was aware of Wesley still on the floor, and Trish grappling with Kara again. A muscle in Raziel's jaw tightened as he took aim. His wounds were bleeding slightly, staining his expensive-looking suit.

Alex had the blurred impression that the last Council angel was trying to do something – wield some kind of power over Raziel. Though she was now burning so brightly that he could barely look at her, whatever it was wasn't successful. Raziel's lip lifted in a sneer.

"My world, my rules, Isda," he said softly.

Willow's angel was a little ahead of Seb's; she darted in front of the final Council member just as Raziel shot. In the same moment, Alex and Sam tackled him, bringing him down with a crash. It was too late. Alex looked over his arm and saw that the bullet had passed through Willow's angel and hit its mark: the final Council member was shuddering in the air, her scorching wings flapping helplessly. Willow's angel was now nowhere in sight.

The explosion as the last of the First Formed died was silent, but Alex felt it through every inch of him, and ducked his head against the blast. It roared past, a vortex of gut-wrenching sensation that tore at his skin and hair. A shudder seemed to pass through the world – and then calmness fell. When he finally looked up, only twinkling lights remained, glinting around the room like fireflies on a summer night.

Alex lay, breathing hard, aware that the others had been thrown to the floor, too. Bizarrely, only minutes had passed since they'd entered the room. In the sudden silence, he could still hear the string quartet playing Mozart.

Willow – was Willow okay? He scrambled to his feet. Against the wall, he could see a weak-looking Seb sitting up now, gripping her hands and talking softly to her; her eyelids fluttered. Alex's shoulders sagged. His relief was matched only by the longing to go to her himself.

Sam had risen also, his broad face bruised and swollen. "Alex…look," he said, staring at the floor.

Raziel had gone still.

Alex's heart started beating painfully fast as he stared down at Raziel's body – the moist blooms of darkness on his purple shirt; the crisp black hair with its widow's peak. He heard Willow's voice again: *It might be that killing the Council really does kill all the angels – that's what most of them think will happen.*

"I…I think maybe we've done it," whispered Sam in a choked voice. "I think maybe we've really done it."

Kara was just getting up, looking shaken. Suddenly Alex did a double take around the room, his skin prickling with alarm. Wait a minute, where were Trish and Wesley? No, he wasn't imagining things – they were both gone.

The moment he registered it, their shouts drifted in from the reception: "*They've just killed the Council! They've killed all the angels!*"

Oh, *Christ.* He and Kara moved at the same time, leaping for the door and banging it shut. There was another exit from the room; hopefully they'd get a chance to use it. Sam joined them. "Grab the table!" ordered Alex. Gripping the heavy wooden table, they dragged it in front of the door as the sound of shouts started heading their way. He and Sam threw a few of the chairs on top for good measure; it would hold them for a few minutes, at least.

A faint rumble shook the building.

It came and went in a second. Kara breathed in between her teeth, and Alex knew she'd felt it too: the sense of something having come loose in the world. "Oh my god," she whispered, staring at him. He saw the fear in her eyes. "You were right, weren't you?"

There was no time. Brendan was struggling to his feet, wincing on his injured leg; Liz stood still, apparently dazed. Seb staggered as he rose, his arms around a sagging Willow.

"Okay, you guys, *move*," barked Alex as a pounding started up on the door. "Go out the other door but don't turn left; it's a dead end. We're taking the stairwell. Kara, you help Brendan; Sam, help Liz but make sure she doesn't have angel burn first. If anyone gets separated, don't hang around – just *get out of here. Now!*"

As the others leaped into action, Alex rushed over to Seb and Willow. "Is she okay?" Seb had lifted her into his arms; she lay slumped against his shoulder with her arms around his neck, her cheeks white.

Seb nodded. "She's just passed out, I think." He still looked pale himself. As he shifted his grip on Willow, Alex saw how unsteady he was.

"Give her to me, you can hardly stand," he said. The table shuddered as people banged on the door, shouting. The others were all gone now – Liz must be okay.

"I'm fine," said Seb with obvious effort. He stumbled slightly as he started for the door.

"You are *not* fine," snapped Alex. "Do you want her to die?" He took Willow from him just as Seb's knees buckled. She clung to Alex with a small moan, not seeming to notice it was him. Alex held her tightly and put his other arm around Seb; he seemed ready to pass out now too. "Come on, *hurry*—"

"Must you really go so soon?" enquired a low, silky voice.

Alex whirled. Raziel was on his feet, wan but very much alive as he pointed a pistol towards them. "You know, I'm rather going to enjoy this," he confided. "Isn't it nice when the tables are turned?"

Alex stared at him dumbly as the shouting outside the

door intensified. *Or maybe only the Council will die.* No. *No.*

The sense of déjà vu from the cathedral in Denver was almost overwhelming. Though he knew it wouldn't do any good with Raziel in his human form, Alex took his arm from around Seb and shot anyway. It didn't even slow Raziel down this time. With a sneer, he levelled the gun at Alex's head and pulled the trigger. There was an empty click.

The angel stared down at the gun in furious disbelief …and then shifted to his ethereal form and soared from the room.

Alex cursed, but couldn't get him now. Clutching Willow to him, he grabbed hold of the drooping Seb again, hauling him into the back hallway. The shouts sounded louder out here – part of the mob must be coming around from the other direction. "Come *on*," he ground out to Seb, half-carrying him down the corridor. "I am not going to die because of you. You don't get to die either – I promised to kill you, remember? *Move.*"

Seb seemed to rouse himself by sheer force of will. "Yes, I remember," he murmured. He pulled from Alex's grip, managing to break into an exhausted run.

Willow had her arms weakly around Alex's neck; her hair smelled just like it always had. *I'm getting you out of here, babe; I won't let anything else hurt you,* thought Alex as they ran down the corridor. Frenzied shouts sounded behind him; doors banging open as people searched for them.

Sam and Liz came rushing back from the other direction. "They've cut us off; the stairwell's blocked," gasped Liz. "There's a whole crowd there, waiting for us."

"Where are Kara and Brendan?" demanded Alex.

"I don't know; they were ahead of us! They must have gotten through." Sam scraped a nervous hand over his blond spikes. "The elevators are blocked, too. Oh, man, what now? Do we try to shoot our way through?"

There was a door directly to his left; Alex cast frantically through his mind, but couldn't remember where it led. Just then there was another rumble – overhead, the light fixtures swayed. It decided him, somehow.

"In here," he said, throwing the door open. Stairs, leading up. *Up?* thought Alex as they barrelled up them. *We're already on the highest floor.*

A locked door waited at the top of the stairs. "Stand back," said Sam, taking aim. He shot; there was the whine of bullet hitting metal as the bolt gave way. He threw the door open and they poured through.

Open sky. Wind, whipping at their clothes. "Oh, Christ," whispered Alex, still clutching Willow to his chest.

"Yeah, that about sums it up," said Sam tightly. Liz stared around them helplessly; her mouth opened and then closed again. Seb let out a curse in Spanish, glancing back at the stairs – where Alex could now hear the sound of shouts coming up. The crowd had found them.

And they were up on the helipad.

CHAPTER *Twenty-nine*

ALEX AND I HAD ALWAYS wondered what would happen if my angel self was injured. As it turned out, it felt like being smashed over the head with a hammer. With every bullet my angel took, the force of it slammed through my skull until I thought it was going to splinter. During the attack, I sat slumped against the wall, fists tight as I somehow clung to consciousness, focusing all my attention on my angel as she flew. The Council saw who I was, of course, but were too distracted to react to either me or Seb. I could sense their utter shock over what had happened; their impotent rage. In over three millennia, no one had ever dared to attack them.

Raziel was there too. Naturally – where else would he be? This was his glorious hour.

He didn't hesitate for an instant when my angel self swooped in front of the final Council member. I saw his face gazing coolly upwards as he aimed. The force of the bullet slammed through me, and I felt myself drifting, barely able to make it back to my human form. Against the wall, my fists slowly unclenched as a dark tide washed me away.

Then there was Seb, picking me up in his arms. *Seb, I'm sorry, I want things to be the same between us again,* I thought. I couldn't get the words out. I clung to him as the world swam and slipped away from me once more. Vaguely, I had a dream that it was Alex holding me instead; the feel of his embrace was so real that I wanted to stay wrapped up in it for ever.

When I came to, I was looking up at the sky. Distant shouts; a scraping noise. I sat up, my head still groggy – and saw the view from my dream. All of Mexico City was spread out below, stretching into infinity. There was a weird hush in the air, as if the very world was holding its breath. My scalp prickled. The roots the Council had put down felt loose now, dangerous – like the bodies of headless snakes moving restlessly about, causing ripples in the earth.

I struggled to my feet – I was on a helipad. There was

a door nearby; Alex, Seb, Sam and Liz had just dragged some sort of metal unit in front of it. The door shuddered rhythmically as the sound of shouts came through.

"Hold on, everyone!" called Alex. Even through his shirt, I could see his muscles flexing as they all strained to hold the barricade in place.

Still feeling dizzy, I ran to add my weight to theirs. The metal unit looked like part of a giant air conditioner. I shoved myself against it and pushed. Seb was beside me – head down, hands propped on the metal edge as he groped for purchase with his feet. "Are you okay?" he gasped, glancing at me.

"I think so," I said faintly. Alex's eyes met mine and I could see the deep flicker of thankfulness in them; then he turned away without speaking as the metal unit scraped across the cement. The door burst open a few inches, then banged shut again as we all heaved. Incoherent shouts, a glimpse of angry faces.

"Oh god, they're going to get through!" Liz's cheeks were red with effort. "Alex, what are we going to do? There's no place to hide up here!"

"Start pickin' 'em off one by one as they come through," grunted Sam on the other side of me. His broad shoulders looked like they had softballs in them as he pushed.

"Yes, that will work for about two minutes maybe," said Seb, raising his voice over the shouts. The door was shuddering, shaking. "How many cartridges do you have?"

"Enough to make them sorry they ever followed us up here," said Sam grimly. "I'm going down fighting, that's all *I* know."

"But we'll still go down," said Liz, sounding agonized. "There's just too many of them! And Trish and Wesley—" She broke off with a sob. I felt like crying myself. Trish, who everyone had loved so much; Wesley, who'd wanted only to avenge his family. Were we supposed to open fire on them now?

The screams intensified as the door shoved open by almost a foot; we struggled to close it again.

"Okay, don't panic," said Alex. "We'll have the advantage as they come through the door. We're going to have to let go of the unit and position ourselves over to the side. When the crowd bursts through, start firing. Try a couple of warning shots first, but don't waste too many cartridges if it doesn't work."

Though his tone stayed matter-of-fact, I knew how much he must hate this; he loathed the thought of using a gun against another human being. He wasn't the only one. I imagined pulling the trigger; seeing someone crumple in front of me. My lips went dry. I didn't think I could do it.

"Give me your gun and get behind me when we let go," said Seb to me.

I swallowed. "Seb, no – I can't let you shield me—"

His voice was strained. "Please, just *do* it. You don't think you can shoot, and I can."

"Seb's right," said Alex shortly. "Stay behind both of us."

And as our eyes met again, I saw what I already knew in his: Liz was right, too. There were just too many of them for us to fight – and from the sound of their shouts, they weren't going to be slowed down much by warning shots. Unless we could think of something else, fast, we were going to die.

"Okay, on the count of three," said Alex, loudly to make himself heard. The shouts were almost deafening now, the door thudding open and shut like a heartbeat. "*One.*"

I looked wildly around us, frantic to find something that maybe the others had missed. Like an elevator, that would be a good thing to find. My gaze came to the edge of the building, and stopped. I stared at it, my thoughts tumbling.

The unit almost hopped as it scraped forward six inches. "*Two,*" said Alex, his jaw tight.

My dream. The tower that I'd flown from; the way my wings had felt so heavy. Seb turned his head and stared at me as he picked up what I was thinking – and it was so completely insane that I knew it was our only chance.

"*Th—*"

"No, wait!" I burst out. "I've got an idea!"

It took an agonizing minute or so for Seb and me to prepare ourselves, while I tried not to focus on the metal unit sliding steadily backwards – the door inching open. As I concentrated, I heard the others' grunts of effort to keep holding the door shut; beside me, Seb was straining as both our angels hovered overhead. He obviously found this just as hard as I did.

Finally I reached up and touched my angel's foot as she looked down at me. Her face was my own, as white as a statue; her wings gently stirred the air. The foot felt cool and firm. It was a very weird sensation, to literally touch another you.

I glanced at Seb; his angel looked just as solid. He nodded. "We're ready," I said, lifting my voice. I managed to keep the fear out of it. If I was wrong, then we were about to plummet to our deaths.

Alex's brow was damp as he struggled against the unit. "On the count of three, then – a good shove, and then run. One – two – *three.*"

We heaved hard; howls came from the door as people were shoved back. Then we raced for the edge of the building, with the two angels gliding overhead. There was a loud scraping noise as the air conditioning unit was shoved aside; then I could hear people stampeding through.

We'd already decided who should go with who. The human Seb was stronger than me, so he was going to have to hang onto two of them, and he couldn't support both Alex *and* Sam – and I definitely couldn't support the burly Sam.

So it was only common sense that I took Alex. Even so, my heart thudded as we reached the edge, and I knew what we were about to do was only part of it. For a second, Alex's blue-grey eyes were unguarded as we glanced at each other; my pulse skipped at the expression in them. Oh god, if I knew for certain we were about to die, I'd tell him everything.

The crowd of almost a hundred people had seen our angels now, and stopped uncertainly. Some carried makeshift weapons – jagged pieces of wood that looked like they'd been torn from picture frames. Raziel appeared from their midst in his human form, his poet's face contorted as he yelled at them. I didn't have to speak Spanish to get what he was saying: *See, they have no halos! They're not real angels, it's a trick! They killed the Council, don't let them get away!*

Trish and Wesley burst up from the stairwell. "They're Angel Killers! Stop them!" Feeling sick, I tore my gaze from their familiar faces. This was *not* the time to think about it.

"Okay, let's do it," said Alex grimly. He wrapped his arms around me and I held onto him, feeling his heart beating against mine. Beside me, Sam was lifting Liz up into his arms as Seb stood behind him, supporting him across the chest. My eyes met Seb's as both of us silently urged the other on. Our angels hovered overhead, centring themselves, getting ready.

The crowd charged. Trish and Wesley were gaining on the others, still shouting. At the head of them all was Raziel, his suit jacket flapping – and as I glanced back, for a dizzying second I was catapulted into his head again. I caught my breath in shock at what I found there, my arms tightening around Alex.

Half the angels in the world were dead.

Raziel knew it instinctively, just like he knew his own heartbeat. Half the angels were really gone. *Gone.* I felt a rush of dazed relief...then stiffened as other knowledge came. Raziel was intrigued by me, sorry that I had to die. He'd enjoyed wandering around in my thoughts.

Suddenly it was like a gate had been slammed shut, severing the connection. "You don't actually think you'll get away, do you?" called my father, the wind whipping at his words as he ran towards us.

I shivered as I stared at him. I hated that he'd been in

my mind; if I could dip my brain in bleach, I'd do it.

"One way to find out," I said softly. And as my angel put her arms around us, Alex and I stepped over the edge.

Wind rushing past – the blur of angry faces staring down at us. The street below spiralled, growing larger; I could see our falling reflections in the curved green glass. In my angel form, my wings beat frantically as I struggled with the unused-to weight. A little away from me, Seb was having the same trouble, only worse – his angel was carrying three people.

I was *not* going to let us crash; somehow managed to get the fall under control. It was like a parachute had opened, snapping us into buoyancy. Below us, I saw to my relief that Seb's powerful wings were in control now, too.

"Are you okay?" asked Alex over the wind.

"Fine," I got out, my arms still tight around him. I could smell his warm Alex-smell. We were so close, just like we'd been a thousand times before; all I wanted was to lift my face to his and kiss him. I looked away, but not before I saw his throat move.

"Willow…" he started – and then broke off as a sound like thunder rumbled. That ominous sense of the Council's roots, moving on their own now. The Twelve's absence had unbalanced everything, like a boulder teetering on the edge of a cliff.

"It's not good, is it?" said Alex, watching my face.

Before I could answer, my angel self stiffened in alarm – and in a bright blur, Raziel swooped down out of the sky, his angel-image reflected in the glass.

"You know, I think this whole scenario would go better if there was more *falling* involved," he said, and he beat at my angel with wings of light that jolted her, threw her off kilter. My human hands went icy as our fall accelerated again – we were still about thirty storeys above the ground.

"Hang on," shouted Alex in my ear, and he let go of me with one arm to reach for his gun. Raziel saw the motion; with a snarl, he reached for Alex's life energy, his long fingers stretching towards it.

No! In my angel form, I let my wings go completely still, plummeting us downwards like a rock. My human self clung to Alex as we started to tumble, earth and sky and wings flashing past. I almost lost my grip; his arms tightened. "I won't let you fall; I'll never let you fall," he murmured, and I knew he wasn't even aware he'd said it out loud. The wind was tearing at me; my angel self could barely move her wings. No, we were *not* going to die this way. Panting, I beat frantically.

I righted us just as Raziel appeared again; his wings flashed through the blue sky as he dove at Alex from behind.

"Alex!" I cried. He turned sharply, but my angel's wings were in his way; she was too exhausted now to manoeuvre. He swore as Raziel drew closer. My pulse was racing. No. This was not going to happen. I took a deep breath; drew my gun and aimed at his halo.

"Oh, I don't think you'll do that," sneered Raziel as he craned towards us. "I know you very well now, my daughter."

Without answering, I pulled the trigger.

I missed, but it was enough to startle him; he jerked backwards, flapping. I could see Seb above us with Sam and Liz; sense his distress that he could do nothing to help. Sam was firing on Raziel though, and the angel hissed as he realized it, darting away. Alex finally got a clear shot and aimed, holding onto me tightly with his other arm. "Oh, man, he is *so* going to die this time," he muttered.

The world met us with a crash as we landed on a stretch of grass beside a parking lot. My angel self had slowed us down as much as she could, but it still felt like we'd slammed into a brick wall. I cried out as Alex and I rolled together; there was a shout of pain from someone as Seb and the others landed nearby. My angel merged with me again, limp and exhausted – I could feel her relief that she'd gotten us down safely.

I lay on the grass for a moment, shaking. Feeling Alex's arms around me. "Are you okay?" he whispered.

My face was against his neck; I closed my eyes tightly, savouring the warmth of his skin against my lips. "Fine." Somehow my voice sounded steady. I pulled away and sat up, my heart beating hard.

And then I stared at the sky above us.

Raziel was high overhead now, out of reach of our bullets – but he wasn't alone. Charmeine, the female angel I'd seen in his thoughts, was speeding towards him, her long hair whipping in the wind. Several dozen angels were following her. "There's the traitor who assassinated the Twelve!" she called. "Don't let him get away!"

Of course, I thought dazedly, remembering what I'd glimpsed of the power-hungry Charmeine from Raziel's mind. He only thought he'd totally delved her; she'd fooled him and the Council both. Her gamble had paid off – and now that he'd helped her do away with the Twelve, she didn't need him any more.

The angels' wings glinted like knife points as they descended; somehow I knew this was all that remained of the Council's hundred-strong entourage. With a snarl of fury, Raziel shot straight up in the air, twisting away from the small army. I watched, sickly fascinated; I knew that I was about to see my father's death.

I cried out as the ground bucked like a living thing. The sound of breaking glass came from somewhere. Car alarms going off.

The ground shook again…and all at once a thick strand of energy burst out of it.

It snapped through the air, whipping wildly – almost invisible, an *intensity* more than something you could see. It mowed through the battling angels overhead, sending them scattering; lashed back again, so that some of them erupted into bursts of light. My arms went cold. I couldn't tell who was who any more – what was happening?

Alex had been watching too. "Come on, let's get the hell out of here," he said, scrambling to his feet. He offered his hand to me. I started to take it and then remembered, drawing back just in time. I couldn't touch him again, not for any reason – already, I might have damaged him even more.

"Sorry," I muttered, standing up.

Hurt flashed across Alex's face; his jaw hardened. He glanced over to where Seb and the others were. It looked like Sam had twisted his ankle – he was scowling as Seb helped him to his feet, leaning heavily on him.

"Here," said Alex shortly, handing me the keys. "Go get the truck; we'll be there as fast as we can."

I nodded, longing to be able to explain. Instead I turned and ran. The Torre Mayor was right beside us; overhead, the remaining angels were just a few bright, struggling blurs. Running footsteps caught up with me as Liz appeared.

"This is so not good," she panted as another rumble

shook the ground. Trash cans clattered nearby. I couldn't answer; suddenly urgency was hammering through me, making me run faster than I'd ever run before.

We rounded the corner onto the Rio Atoyac. The guard had abandoned his booth; we ducked under the barrier and scrambled over the metal blocker, skidding our way down the other side. In the loading dock, the 4 x 4 was just where we'd left it, looking weirdly ordinary as it sat there.

Liz got into the front next to me as I started the engine. I spun the wheel, screeching us into reverse – and then stared at the blocker at the top of the drive. From this angle, it was a steep ramp jutting off into space. As another tremor hit, I sent my angel speeding to check the guard booth. The buttons on the display panel needed a key to operate them – there was no key in sight.

Only seconds had passed. "What…what are you going to do?" asked Liz as my angel returned in a flurry.

The Dukes of Hazzard flashed grimly into my mind. "Um – I think seat belts might be an idea," I said, buckling mine on. My mouth felt dry; the ramp was looking steeper by the second. I gripped the steering wheel and took a deep breath, keeping my gaze fixed on it.

Liz clicked on her own seat belt, her pale cheeks growing paler as she glanced at me. "Willow, you're not really going to—"

"Hang on," I said – and floored it.

We hit the ramp going about thirty miles an hour and, for a heart-stopping second, catapulted through the air, clearing the barrier. We slammed to the ground, front wheels first; the truck rocked like a bucking bronco, wrenching us forward and then back. Somehow I kept control; I pumped the accelerator and threw the wheel hard, lurching us out onto the road and then back towards where we'd landed.

"Oh my god, we actually made it!" gasped Liz. I let out a shaky breath. I was sort of surprised myself.

Alex and the others were half a block away. When I pulled up beside them, Alex threw the car door open and he and Seb helped Sam in. "Christ, I swear I've broken it," muttered Sam, dropping his head back on the seat. His face was white.

Alex slammed the door shut once they were all inside. "I think it's just a sprain – but you got off lucky, okay? We all did."

I could feel Seb's anxiety prickling at my skin, and knew he could sense the same thing I could: the giant roots were completely out of control now, lashing through the earth. We had to get out of this city, *now*.

As I roared away from the kerb, I saw that there were only two angels fighting up above now. Two. Did that mean Raziel was still alive? The road trembled and I accelerated, trying to keep ahead of the tremor as another whip of energy slashed through the air. As it swiped past the two angels there was a burst of radiance, like sun sparkling on water.

And then nothing at all.

My heart felt ready to burst in my chest. Was Raziel really gone now? Briefly, my eyes met Alex's in the rear-view mirror. I could tell he didn't know either – but I knew the answer he was hoping for. Then I swerved the truck onto the Paseo de la Reforma, and we couldn't see the place where they'd been any more.

I swerved us in and out of traffic, completely ignoring the honking horns. The road got clearer as I went on – as the tremors continued, people were pulling over to the side. Mexico City got a lot of earthquakes. In an ordinary one, not driving was probably the sensible option. I had no intention of taking it, not with the way the energy of this place suddenly felt. A truck was in my way; Sam howled in pain as I hurtled us up onto the grassy divide and then back onto the road again. And as we continued north down the Paseo de la Reforma, I saw with a chill how right I was to want to get us out of here as quickly as possible.

Up ahead was the empty column where the Mexico City angel had once stood, holding her golden garland up to the sky. It was swaying back and forth like a too-tall Jenga tower.

"*Dios mío*," whispered Seb from the back.

There was no way around; I gritted my teeth and sped towards it. As it started to fall across the road, Liz screamed, scrabbling backwards in her seat – then we'd shot underneath it and were safely out the other side.

Sam laughed weakly. "Oh, man – where can I nominate you for driver of the year?"

My hands were clenched so hard it felt like they'd been glued to the steering wheel. "Don't push our luck," I said, keeping my eyes on the lurching road. "Maybe you should hold off until I actually get us out of the city."

"You will," said Alex, his voice firm. "You will."

And somehow I did.

By sunset, we were wending our way up a mountain road. The quake didn't seem to have been so bad here, though we still had to manoeuvre around fallen trees sometimes. It felt peaceful though: the way the mountains reached towards the sky like they'd always been there and always would be.

Peaceful was good. Peaceful was very good.

Alex had taken over driving; I was in the back beside Seb. He sat without talking, his gaze distant, and I could feel his pain over what had happened to the city of his birth. Because as I'd finally reached the outskirts of Mexico City, I'd seen something in the rear-view mirror that had stolen the breath from my lungs: the earth had reared up from the *centro* and was literally rolling. Buildings shuddered and fell as the concrete tidal wave passed; cars slipped into crevasses. I'd pulled over to the side of the road, trembling too hard to drive as we all stared.

Finally the wave had juddered out into nothing. And then there'd been the most complete silence I'd ever heard, with dust rising up in a great plume.

That's when Alex had taken over, getting out from the back and opening the driver's door. "Get in the back, you've had enough," he said, his face like stone from what we'd just seen. I didn't argue.

Hardly any of us had spoken after that. Hardly any of us were speaking now, several hours later. The expression on Seb's face wrung my heart. He'd always hated Mexico City because of all he'd been through there, but for him to see it flattened that way...I swallowed, my temples throbbing. Though I ached to hold him and be held, somehow I still couldn't break through the awkwardness between us, no matter how much I wanted to.

From the front, Liz cleared her throat. "I wonder if Kara and Brendan are okay," she said in a small voice. She didn't mention Wesley and Trish. I didn't blame her. Just thinking about them hurt too much.

"Hope so," said Alex shortly, shifting gears. We'd tried to call them, but nobody's cellphones were working. And what we all knew hung in the air, unspoken: they could easily have been attacked by a mob on their way down the stairwell, especially if they were slowed down by Brendan's injured leg.

I pressed my forehead against the cool window as I stared out at the passing trees. I'd told the others what I'd sensed from Raziel, about half the angels in the world being dead. It should have felt like a victory, I guess… but right now it didn't seem like much of one.

As we drove around a bend, a view of the city was spread out below us in the dying rays of the sunset. Alex stopped and we all got out, even Sam, supporting himself with a hand on Alex's shoulder. We gazed down at the ruined city in silence. True to its status as the most earthquake-resistant building in the world, the Torre Mayor was still standing, its green glass walls curved against the sky.

It was almost the only thing that was. All around it in a rough circle that must have spanned several miles, the city had been virtually wiped out: a few other buildings were half-standing; most had collapsed into rubble. Though I could make out the flat rectangle of the Zócalo, I couldn't see the cathedral at all.

Liz shivered, hugging herself. "Do you think this really happened all around the world?" she whispered. "Or just here?"

None of us had an answer for her.

Finally Alex let out a breath. "Okay, come on. Let's find a place to stop for the night."

Seb stood motionless, still staring at the city as the others started walking back to the truck. Glancing up at him, I saw the dampness on his cheeks. It unlocked something inside of me, and I wrapped my arms around him with a sob. He hugged me hard, clutching me to him; we stood trembling, holding each other tightly. And oh god, I'd been so stupid; so completely wrapped up in my heartbreak over Alex. Seb was right. We'd kissed, that was all. It didn't have to change things between us unless we let it.

"I'm sorry," I whispered against his neck. "Seb, I'm so sorry. I want things to be like they were between us again."

"I want that too," he said raggedly. "I want that more than anything."

Closing my eyes, I let out a shaky breath as I pressed against him. I could feel the prickle of his stubble against my hair; the strong warmth of his arms around me. Nothing had changed; everything had changed. I had my friend back. I knew Seb was still in love with me, and he knew that I wasn't in love with him, but somehow it didn't matter, not to either of us – we needed to be in each other's lives anyway. And oh god, after everything we'd just been through...knowing that our friendship was still intact felt more important than words can even explain.

Finally I pulled away, kissed his cheek. "Come on," I said, wiping my eyes. "Would my brother walk me to the truck?"

"Anytime, *querida*," said Seb with a small smile. And he put his arm around my shoulders and we headed back.

The moon was just rising by the time they stopped, high in the southern Sierra Madre. Up here, with the stars and trees, it was as if nothing had happened at all. It was a relief, thought Alex. Never – not for as long as he lived – would he forget the sight of that concrete wave as it took down the city.

His team was now tattered into shreds.

Somehow he shoved it all aside and did what he had to do in order to hold what was left of his team together. Seb produced a lighter from his jeans pocket and they built a campfire. Alex put up the tent for Willow and Liz to sleep in; he and the other guys could crash in the back of the truck. He tore one of his shirts into long strips and bandaged Sam's ankle; the minute he got it snugly bound, Sam's broad face relaxed. Which in turn relieved Alex – it probably wasn't broken, in that case. And that was good, since god knew when they'd manage to find a doctor, if other places in the world had been affected the same way as Mexico City. The idea was too catastrophic to take in, like trying to imagine what was beyond the edges of space – so he didn't think about it, and thought about food instead.

He found a few energy bars in his bag. That was dinner for them all. There were also a couple of bottles of water in the truck, plus a stream nearby. Sam took a swig of water and grimaced as they sat around the campfire. "I sure wish this was something stronger," he said glumly. "A few shots of Jack would go down good right about now."

No one responded, but from everyone's faces, they were all thinking *Join the club*. Liz stared bleakly into the fire; Willow and Seb sat close together, though not touching. Alex tossed a stick onto the snapping flames. Remaining in charge was the last thing on the planet he wanted to do after today – but he knew he had even less choice now than before.

"Okay, guys, here's the deal," he said finally. "We're not going to let this destroy us. We all did what we thought was right – and if we had to do it over, we'd all act the same way. So there's no point in wallowing. The important thing is that half the angels in this world have been killed. We wouldn't have chosen to do it this way, but it's a victory, so we'll take it."

Everyone was watching him; Sam nodded slightly. Willow's gaze was gentle on his, then she looked down, playing with the cuff of her shirt. He saw her throat move.

"What now?" said Liz finally.

Alex shrugged. "Personally, I plan to keep fighting." He told them about the base in Nevada that Sophie had been offering; the memory stick with the details was safe in his bag. "So we've got a place to go," he finished. "It's fully stocked, and I have the access code."

"We?" echoed Willow. Her face in the firelight looked very still.

Alex nodded. "Yeah. You're all welcome to join me, if you want." He kept his voice neutral. For a while there, in the aftermath of the attack, things had actually felt the same as always between him and Willow – a delusion that had been forcibly dispelled when she wouldn't even take his hand to let him help her up. Having her around all the time when she was with Seb would be more painful than he really wanted to imagine. But he needed every person he could get now – and besides, they were part of his team. Even Seb. Bizarrely, something had shifted between the two of them today; Alex thought he could actually work with the guy without killing him now.

Willow looked worried as she and Seb glanced at each other; he seemed to be trying to read an answer from her eyes.

"Don't tell me now, any of you," said Alex. "And don't feel obligated to come." He scraped a hand over his face, trying not to see the city falling again. Or Wesley and Trish as they'd run after them with the mob, shouting. He felt weary down to his bones. "Today was…the worst," he said finally. "But it still may not be as bad as it ever gets. So think about it. Think about what it means, to keep on with this. I wouldn't blame any of you if you just wanted to hide out in the mountains somewhere and try to build a life for yourself."

Sam snorted. "Who the hell would do that? Yeah, I'm in; I can tell you right now." He was sitting against a fallen log; he shifted, keeping his injured leg straight out in front of him. "No way am I gonna just hide away and do nothing, after today."

"Me too," said Liz softly.

Willow cleared her throat, not meeting his gaze. "We'll think about it, okay? And tell you tomorrow."

We. Alex tried not to feel the sting. "Yeah, sure," he said, tossing another stick onto the fire. "It'll take us a few days to get back to the US anyway – if that's where you're going," he added.

Seb looked at Willow again, searching her face with a slight frown. "I don't think we know yet," he said.

No one said much for a while after that. Though the fire burned down some, it still kept the coolness of the night away; Sam crossed his arms over his chest and closed his eyes, looking half-asleep where he sat. Eventually Liz got up to go get the other bottle of water from the truck. When she didn't come back, Alex went after her and found her curled up asleep in the front seat, looking beyond exhausted. He started to wake her up so she could have the tent, but decided against disturbing her. She'd be okay out here; he and Sam would sleep in the back. Thinking of Willow and Seb in the same tent that he'd shared with her was a further kick in the guts, but he supposed he'd survive it. After today, he could survive anything.

When he got back to the campfire, Sam's snores were filling the air. Willow and Seb were obviously deep in conversation. They broke off when he reappeared; the tension on Willow's face made Alex feel like an intruder. It also made him want to put his arms around her and hold her for ever – an emotion he seriously didn't need right now.

"I'll get some more firewood," he said shortly, and walked off without waiting for a response.

There was a clearing not far away, awash with moonlight. Alex sat down against a rock and stared up at the sky. All the familiar constellations were still there – the same as they'd been after his father's death, and then his brother's. The night sky's patterns always remained predictable, no matter how much your world had just been rocked. At times in his life he'd found this soothing, and at other times infuriating. Now he just felt numb, cold as starlight.

Wesley and Trish, rabid with angel burn. God, he'd *known* Wesley's arm wasn't better yet; he should never have let him take part. Okay, so maybe neither of them had actually died, but angel burn had always seemed almost worse than death to Alex; it took away a person's choices. If he'd just managed to do things better – get there faster, stop the attack after all – then maybe it wouldn't have happened. And he didn't even know if Kara and Brendan were still alive or not. Even if they'd somehow managed to make it out of the Torre Mayor, what were the odds that they'd actually left the city in time? Or that Juan's old van had made it through those lurching streets?

Alex pinched the bridge of his nose as the thoughts pummelled him. He didn't have any answers. None. And now the world would never be the same again and he had to keep on being a leader somehow – just because there was no one else around to do it.

"Hi," said a soft voice.

He looked up. Willow stood in the moonlight. "Hi," he said after a pause.

She swallowed. "Can I, um…sit with you for a while? I think we should probably talk."

Standing there in the silvery light, she was so beautiful that it made him hurt inside. He shrugged wearily. "If you want."

Willow sat near him, keeping a careful distance. Tracing

at the ground with her finger, she cleared her throat. "Alex, I just wanted to say that…I'm really sorry I hurt you."

He sighed. Yeah, this was exactly what he felt like talking about right now. "Can we skip this conversation?" he asked, rubbing his forehead. "Seriously, I'd rather not have it. I don't need to hear how sorry you are."

She sat watching the motion of his fingers anxiously; then seemed to catch herself doing it, and glanced away. "All right." Her voice was thin, strained. "But Alex, I don't think Seb and I will be going with you to Nevada. I just don't think it's a good idea for – for me to be so close to you. So I don't know if I'll see you again after tomorrow, and I wanted to tell you—" Her voice broke; Alex froze, his heart aching as he saw she was close to tears. "…to tell you that I still love you," she got out. "I really do, Alex, and – and I'm sorry for everything."

Wiping her eyes, she jumped to her feet. Alex leaped up too, pained bewilderment clutching at his throat. "Willow, wait! What—" He touched her arm; she pulled away, hugging herself.

"Please don't," she said in a small voice.

She looked miserable, almost frightened. Alex stared at her. "Don't what? Don't touch your arm?"

Willow almost said something and stopped, shaking her head. "I…I'd better get back." She started to walk away.

"No, *wait*." He dodged in front of her; a sudden suspicion had taken root and was growing by the second. "Willow, why can't I touch your arm? Why wouldn't you take my hand when we fell on the grass?"

She gripped her elbows, not meeting his eyes. "I just didn't want to, that's all. Sorry. I didn't mean to hurt your feelings, or anything." She was a terrible liar. And now Alex recalled that same flat tone had been in her voice when she'd stood there with Seb in the kitchen, and even earlier, back in the storeroom before their first hunt, when he'd asked her what was wrong. She'd had that same look on her face then too – complete agony as she started to tell him something but didn't.

Oh god.

The truth slammed into him. He reached for her arms again without thinking; she jerked away. "*Don't!* Don't touch me!"

"You think you're giving me angel burn," he said urgently. "That's it, isn't it? That's why you broke up with me." She didn't answer; she didn't need to. She covered her face with one hand, her shoulders shaking.

He could barely hear his own words over the pounding of his pulse. "Are you really in love with Seb? Did you two really—"

"*No*," she broke in. "We kissed, that's all. And it was totally wrong, and it just made me realize how...how much I—" She broke down then; Alex wrapped his arms around her and held her tightly, his heart racing with sudden hope.

"Tell me again that you're not in love with Seb," he whispered into her hair. "Please, please, tell me again."

She shook her head against his chest; her voice was muffled. "I'm not in love with Seb; I never was. I do love him, but not like that. Alex, I shouldn't be touching you—"

He ignored her. "What about your dream?"

"It was true – all except the part about being in love with him." She looked up, her eyes wet. "I didn't mention it to you at the time because I didn't even believe it; I didn't see how I could ever feel so strongly about a boy who isn't you. But now I see that I can, only it's just friendship; it's like he's my brother – Alex, I *can't* touch you! Let me go; I'm hurting you—"

"You're not hurting me! Willow—" He pulled away, gripping both her hands. "I'm still in love with you," he said fervently. "I love you more than anything. Do you still feel the same about me?"

She went very still, the moonlight glinting on her face. For a moment the look in her eyes was salvation – and then her face went dull. "Of course I do," she whispered. She pulled her hands away from his. "And that's why I can't be with you. I knew you'd do this; it's why I didn't tell you before. You think I'm not hurting you, but I *am*. I can see it in your aura right this second."

"My aura?"

"Yes! It looks—" Her face crumpled slightly; she regained herself with visible effort. "It looks sick," she said. "And it's because of me. It's something about my energy, being half-angel – the effect must be cumulative, but it's *there*, it happens."

"What effect? Willow, what are you talking about?"

Her spiked hair looked darker than usual in the moonlight; her elfin face lined with sadness. "Your migraines and your headaches are because of me," she said. "I know they haven't always been, but the ones you're having now are. Alex, your aura looks—" Her gaze went to the outline of his body, scanning it. "Dull," she finished. "Not healthy. And there are these dark spots…" She trailed off.

"But—" He stared at her as images came and went in a flash: his father, back at the camp; Cully, after an extended hunt. Himself, sitting on the Metro, wondering how much damage he'd been taking lately. "Willow, did you think that was because of you? Oh, babe…" He tried to put his arms around her again; she sidestepped out of his reach.

"Of course I think it's because of me! What else am I supposed to think?"

"It's because I'm an AK! It's something that happens

if you're exposed to a lot of angel fallout; the aura takes damage. Willow, my dad used to get the same thing!"

She went very still, on her face he saw doubt battling with a longing to believe. "So how come you didn't have this when we first met?"

"Because the aura usually restores itself! I only killed about an angel a week back then. But I've been going on hunts every day for weeks now – go and check out Sam's aura; it'll be just the same!" His words spilled out quickly; he felt desperate to make her see the truth.

She gave a short, humourless laugh, wiping her eyes. "Sam's aura is *not* just the same. Sam's aura looks fine, actually."

He pushed his hair back in frustration. "Okay, well I don't know – maybe it *is* cumulative then; I've been doing this for years. But, Willow, it is *not you*. I swear to you, when I looked at my dad's aura once, it was just the same. And there were no half-angels at the camp, all right?"

The moment stood poised on a knife blade. Willow slowly shook her head. "I could still have something to do with it. You don't know for a fact that I'm not hurting you, and neither do I. Haven't you noticed that every migraine you got was less than a day after…after we got really physical together?"

"Fine, and what about all the times we got really physical, and *nothing happened* – except we both enjoyed it a whole lot? Willow, it's just a coincidence!"

Her expression was the same as when she'd told him she was going to try to stop the Second Wave – sad but determined, unaffected by any argument he might make. "You can't know that, and I won't take the chance," she said. "I won't hurt you, Alex. I refuse."

He stared at her in disbelief; the statement was so ludicrous that he barked out a short, bitter laugh. "You think breaking up with me *didn't hurt* me? I've been in hell these last few days. Complete hell."

Pain creased her face. "Me too," she whispered. "But—"

"And even if you *are* causing it, even if you're making me sick in some terrible way we don't know about – Jesus, Willow, I could be killed tomorrow anyway! I don't expect a *long life* doing what I do, okay? And for however long I've got left…I want to spend it with you." He took her hands; held them between his and kissed them. "Please," he said. "I want to spend it with you."

Her eyes were damp; her face filled with longing. For a moment he thought she was going to relent – then she gently pulled away. "And what if being with me makes your life even shorter than it would have been?" she asked. "What if you die a year sooner than you would have anyway, and that year would have made all the difference in fighting the angels?"

"Yeah, and what if being with you makes me so happy that I get a few *more* years, because I've actually got something to live for?" he said hotly. "We can't know! You don't get to just decide this for both of us!"

"But it's not only about *us*, don't you see?" Her eyes were agonized. "I already have to live with knowing that... that I played a part in what happened today. A whole city – all those people..." She trailed off helplessly, and shook her head. "Do you think I'd do anything, anything at all, that might hurt the world even more?"

"None of it was your fault," he said in a low voice. "It was Raziel – he used you; he used all of us. Don't you think *I'm* scared? Two of my team have got angel burn now; two of them are missing – I couldn't stop any of it! But I've got to keep on, and so do you. Don't let him tear us apart, on top of everything else."

She let out a breath that was almost a sob. Hugging herself, she stared at a nearby tree, as if she was taking in its every detail in the moonlight. "Alex...I just can't. I'd be terrified every day that I was hurting you; I'd be worried sick every time we touched."

The thought that this was the only thing keeping them apart was torture. "Willow, you're *not hurting me*. And if you really break us up over this, when you love me as much as I love you – it'll be the biggest mistake ever." He took her hands again, gripping them hard. "How do I convince you that you're wrong – Christ, what do I say, what do I do? Please, help me out here—"

She stood motionless. Finally she let out a long breath. "There's nothing you can say, and there's nothing you can do. Because neither of us can know for sure. And I won't take the chance." She gazed down at her hands in his – squeezed his fingers, and then softly drew away. Her voice was thick with unshed tears. "I'm sorry. Please don't touch me again."

No. *No.* He couldn't let her do this to them; he had to get her to see the truth somehow. The ridiculous thing was how psychic she was – with anyone else, she could just touch their hand and see the truth for herself. But her emotions were so entangled when it came to him that Alex knew she'd get nothing.

The answer came to him all at once, along with a rush of hope so intense it was almost painful. "Wait!" he said as she started to turn away. "Willow, what if Seb reads me? What if he sees in my hand that I'm right – what then?"

Her face went blank with surprise as she stared at him, statue-still in the silvery light. Then her throat moved as she swallowed. "That...would be the most wonderful thing in the world," she said in a tiny voice.

* * *

When they got back to the campfire, they found Seb still there; he'd built the fire up again, and was gazing into its flames. Sam lay snoring softly against the log, out to the world. They sat beside Seb as Alex quickly explained.

"So do you think you can help?" he finished. His muscles were tense; he was suddenly all too aware of what a gift on a silver platter he was offering to Seb – all the guy had to do was tell Willow that yes, she was causing him angel burn, and that would be the end of their relationship for ever.

Seb hadn't commented while Alex spoke; now he shook his head, his stubble glinting in the firelight. "Willow can't read you because her feelings are too involved – but you don't think mine are too?" he pointed out dryly.

"Not as much as mine, not when it comes to reading Alex," said Willow. She touched his arm. "Please, Seb, just try. I've got to know the truth."

Seb glanced back at Alex. Finally he gave a shrug. "Yes, all right. I'll try." He closed his eyes for a moment, seeming to centre himself with a few slow breaths. Then he opened his eyes and held out his hand; his gaze met Alex's impassively.

Alex put his hand in Seb's. It felt warm and dry, slightly rough; fleetingly, he thought how weird it was to be sitting here holding another guy's hand. No one spoke as Seb concentrated; the only sound was the low crackle of the fire, and Sam's steady snores. Alex watched Seb's face, hoping for some hint of what he was picking up – what he was going to say.

At last Seb let go of his hand. He gave Alex a considering look, as if he was thinking how to choose his words, and Alex felt his heart drop. "So…what did you get?"

Seb rested his forearm over his knee. "Your father had migraines too," he said. "So did his father. The men in your family, they've all been leaders and they all care very much – it makes them too tense."

Alex remembered now his father telling him that his grandfather had had migraines, though he'd forgotten this. "Yeah, okay, but—"

"I tried to look at your future, and see what might happen to you," went on Seb. "I didn't get very much, because I think I'm there too." Alex's pulse beat faster: surely Seb wouldn't be there if Willow wasn't? He glanced at Willow; she sat watching Seb, her expression taut. Seb went on, "But I saw your aura looking healthy again, then looking sick after a hunt. And you keep getting migraines. You should take better care of yourself," he added mildly. "Look for ways to not be so tense – long walks, meditation, these things would help."

Alex suddenly felt like Seb was his therapist; he had to resist the urge to shake him. Before he could say anything, Willow cleared her throat. "What does all that mean, exactly?"

Seb's expression was gentle. "I don't think his migraines are anything to do with you, *querida*. And his aura looks bad, but his father's often looked worse. It got better – his will too. I don't think you're causing him angel burn."

I don't think. Alex winced; he knew Willow wouldn't be convinced by this. Sure enough, she bit her lip as she stared at Seb. "You don't know for sure though?"

Seb reached for her hand and squeezed it. "I am maybe ninety-nine per cent certain," he said. "If I could have gotten more, then I think I'd be a hundred per cent certain. For only one per cent, you should take the chance and be happy with him." He lifted a shoulder with a small smile. "If you were one of my customers, this is what I'd say to you."

As the fire crackled gently, Willow sat staring at Seb as if she hadn't understood the words – then all at once she lunged forward, throwing her arms around his neck. "Thank you," she whispered. "Oh, thank you."

"I'm glad I was wrong," Seb murmured back.

The relief was indescribable. Alex let out a breath, his shoulders sagging.

Willow detached herself from Seb and looked at Alex. Her expression was wondering, almost shy. In slow motion, she reached out and stroked back a strand of his hair; the feel of her touch shivered through him. "So, um… I guess—"

Alex stopped her with his mouth, cradling her head in his hands and kissing her almost fiercely, and then they were in each other's arms, holding on as hard as they could. Willow. *Willow.* He felt her shaking and realized she was crying; he kissed her hair as he clutched her to him, then buried his head against her neck and savoured just having her in his arms again. Dimly, he was aware that Seb had slipped away.

"Come be with me in the tent," he whispered against her smooth skin. "I want to hold you all night – I want to feel you next to me."

Willow nodded vehemently; she pulled away to wipe her face and then simply gazed at him for a moment. She swallowed. "You really, really can't imagine how good that sounds."

She went to the truck to get her things. Alex's own bag was on the ground nearby, where he'd left it after rummaging for the energy bars. As he started towards it, he caught sight of Seb – he was standing in the clearing with his hands in his jeans pockets, looking upwards.

Alex hesitated, and then went over to him. For a few seconds neither of them spoke as they studied the night sky with its piercing stars.

"So why did you do it?" asked Alex in Spanish. He glanced over at Seb, studying his profile. "You didn't have to tell her the truth. Maybe she thinks she only loves you as a brother now, but that could change, if you'd told her something different."

Seb gave him a dry look. "We're both psychic, *amigo*. I can't lie to her."

"When she was already so worried about it anyway?" Alex shook his head. "No, I bet you could have managed to lie, if you'd wanted."

Seb didn't respond at first, and then he shrugged. "I want her to be happy," he said. The moonlight played on his high cheekbones as he looked up at the stars again. "You make her happy. It wasn't exactly a complicated decision."

Alex's throat tightened, and he thought how ridiculous it was that after everything that had happened today – the mental ruin of friends and teammates; the sight of the destroyed city – it was this unexpected decency from Seb that was making him choke up.

"Thank you," he said finally.

"You're welcome." Seb's mouth lifted slightly. "I didn't do it for you, though."

"Yeah, I know you didn't." They regarded each other; Alex was almost painfully aware of how much he'd misjudged the guy. "So, you're coming to Nevada, right?" he said.

Seb went quiet, rubbing his jaw with the back of a finger. "I'd like to," he said finally. "I never had a way before to fight what the angels are doing here – I guess I never even really knew I wanted to. But now, after what's happened to my city…" His face tightened. "Yeah, I'd like to come. Even if it wasn't for Willow, I'd like to come."

"Good," said Alex.

Then Seb raised an eyebrow. "But are you sure you really want me to? I'm still in love with her, *hombre*. If I can take her away from you, I will."

Alex tilted his head up. The stars were so incredibly clear up here; even clearer than in New Mexico. "If I'm not keeping her happy enough to hold onto her, then I'll deserve it," he said. "Yeah, I want you to come. You're part of my team."

The tent was lit with a soft glow from the campfire. For a long time, Alex and I just lay in the sleeping bags with our arms around each other, listening to the sound of our heartbeats; the crackle of the fire. I closed my eyes as I ran my hand over the familiar warmth of Alex's chest; felt him stroke my bare back; gently kiss my neck. I knew the vision of the levelled city would never leave either of us – that it would visit us in nightmares for years to come – but for now, just having this together again felt like sanity. Blessed, healing sanity.

Neither of us spoke, just then. Neither of us needed to. Later, of course, we would. In the days that followed, we talked about everything – how Alex's deepest fear, right from the start, had been that something would happen to his team; how I'd been so scared of my angel's actions, but somehow couldn't talk to him about it. How Sophie hadn't been the one who'd protected my mother after all – which panicked me when I heard, so that I had to check her again and again to reassure myself that she really was all right, even if we had no idea where she was or who with. Alex's old crush on Kara, and the way she'd kissed him in the AK house; my own kiss with Seb. My friendship with Seb, which was never going to go away, ever – and which Alex really was fine with now. It turned out that he had been ever since the night of the terrorist attack, when he thought I'd died and had spent hours searching for me – it "kind of put things in perspective" for him, he said.

We'd talk about all of these things later; we'd hash them out and look at them from every angle and make them all okay…but for now, the only thing that mattered was the two of us in the tent together. The softness of the sleeping bags, and the warmth of our bodies.

At last the glow from the campfire was almost gone, leaving the tent cast in shadow. We'd heard Seb and Sam go to bed in the truck a long time ago; the world was quiet. Alex rolled over onto his side and lay looking down at me in the dim light, propped up on his elbow. The expression in his eyes was as serious as the first time he'd told me he loved me. He took my hand and kissed its palm, his lips pressing against my skin…and my heart quickened. I knew before he said it.

"Willow, listen…" He stroked a strand of my hair back. "I know we said we wanted to wait until it could be perfect, but—"

"This *is* perfect," I interrupted. I touched his face. "We're here together. It couldn't possibly be more perfect."

Alex didn't say anything, but I caught a wave of his emotions as he bent down and kissed me, and my breath caught with their intensity. Then he pulled away, stretching down to the bottom of the tent. I raised myself up, admiring the beautiful lines of his body as he reached into his bag and pulled something out.

He came back up and put the small box he was holding to one side – and the expression in his eyes as he turned to me made my heart twist. Alex. Oh, Alex. I wrapped my arms around his neck, pulling him down to me; his heart was beating as hard as mine was.

"No, wait," he murmured suddenly. Straightening up, he reached across me for our pile of clothes, fumbled in the pocket of the grey trousers he'd been wearing.

"Here, sit up," he said softly. I did, the sleeping bag slipping off me with a rustle. I saw a flash of silver in his hand, and my eyes widened.

"You kept it," I whispered. I reached up to touch the cool facets of my pendant as he fastened the chain around my neck. My fingers clasped around it tightly. "I thought you'd – throw it away, or—"

"I tried to. I couldn't leave it behind." He kept his hands on my neck for a moment, his forehead resting against mine. "Willow, things feel more uncertain than ever now," he said finally. "But I love you. For as long as I live – if that's fifty years from now, or just next week – I'll love you."

I could hardly get the words out. "I love you too," I said. I kissed him, our lips lingering together. Then I swallowed, my hand on the back of his neck and my crystal gleaming between us. "And…let's stop talking for a while, okay?"

When I woke up, it felt like early morning; the blue nylon sides of the tent had a faint glow to them. I was lying in Alex's arms, our bare limbs entwined. I lay without moving for a few minutes, gazing at the rise and fall of his chest; the curve of his dark eyebrows. I kissed his tattoo gently, loving the feel of his warm skin. The pain of the ruined city was still there, like a heavy weight inside of me – but now there was this new joy too. The night before had been…well, let's just say it was worth waiting for. Very,

very worth waiting for. And it showed every sign of being something that would get even better.

I stretched across Alex and found my clothes, squirming in the sleeping bag as I put them on. Drowsily, he opened his eyes and stroked my arm. "Where are you going?"

"Just outside for a minute," I kissed his cheek. "I'll be right back."

The morning air hit me coolly as I crawled out of the tent, zipping it shut behind me. The truck sat a little way off – no one else was awake yet. I started down to the stream…but then I saw a break in the trees and stopped. Though I hadn't noticed it the night before, you could see Mexico City from here too.

I walked over, drawn helplessly by the shattered view, and stood staring down at the remains of the city for a long time. And as I did, a chill ran over me. There were no helicopters flying over it, no sign of relief aid. What did that mean? Even if no one else in Mexico could help, what were things like in the United States, if they hadn't sent aid after such a major catastrophe? The only answers that came to mind weren't really ones that I wanted to dwell on.

I thought I saw a few angels circling over the ruins, though – bright, moving glimmers that somehow I knew weren't just a trick of the light. A shiver went over me as I watched them.

Footsteps on the grass, and then Alex was there; he had

on jeans and a T-shirt, his dark hair still rumpled from sleep. Without speaking, he put his arms around me from behind and drew me back against him as we both stared down at what used to be the largest city in the world. I knew from the tightening of his muscles that he'd noticed the lack of helicopters too, but he didn't comment. My chest felt empty as I watched the tiny angels glinting over the devastation. The sorrow I felt was too great for tears now – too deep for anything that could be verbalized.

"Okay, enough," said Alex finally. He turned us both around so that we were facing the mountains to the north. "Look that way instead," he said, his voice firm. "That's the way we're going."

The view was clear, uncluttered, and something in me eased. Somehow, looking at the soaring mountains with the sunrise on them made me able to breathe again. Alex was right. We couldn't live our lives looking back – no matter what, we had to move forward to whatever waited for us. Alex and me, Seb, Sam, Liz, whoever else we managed to recruit – we all had to keep moving forward, or else we were lost.

After a long time, I cleared my throat. "So anyway, when we get to Nevada…I think we should rethink your dad's rule."

Alex glanced down at me and smiled – the first real smile I'd seen on his face in a long time. "You know what?

It's already been rethought and completely ditched," he said. And he wrapped his arms around me and we stood looking up at the mountains, with the rising rays of the sun lighting them from the east.

GET READY
FOR THE FINAL STUNNING BOOK IN
L.A. WEATHERLY'S ANGEL TRILOGY

ANGEL
FEVER

OUT 1ST OCTOBER 2012

ISBN: 9781409522393

EPUB: 9781409541776

KINDLE: 9781409541783

ACKNOWLEDGEMENTS

Angel Fire was a book that, at times, I really didn't think was going to get written.

During the writing of the first book in the trilogy, *Angel*, the fictional world I'd envisaged grew and changed; so did my perceptions of the characters. This meant that although books two and three had been planned out in some detail, by the time I reached the end of *Angel* I realized that a lot of my ideas about those books weren't really valid any more.

So, even though he's fictional, my first and most heartfelt thanks must go to Seb. When he suddenly appeared out of nowhere – this former street kid and thief who's so in love with Willow, and who, not incidentally, is another half-angel – I knew I'd found the spark that would propel not only this story, but the next one too. The sheer relief of that day is something any writer will understand. Thank you, *querido*.

Thanks are also due to:

Linda Chapman and Julie Sykes, for emails, coffee, shared spa days, and being the first people on the planet to read and offer comments on *Angel Fire* – not to mention their patience in listening to me talk about it non-stop for almost a year now! Love and thanks to you both. My brilliant agent Caroline

Sheldon, as always, for being such a stalwart, constant support. My former editor Megan Larkin, whose solid instincts were such a great help during the early stages of *Angel Fire*. My UK editors Rebecca Hill and Stephanie King, who ensured that the transition to having a new editor was completely painless, and whose excited response to the finished manuscript was really everything an author could hope for. Huge thanks to both of you for all your insightful suggestions. (And a special thank you to Stephanie, who, for her sins, often gets to deal with me on the phone, and is unfailingly a calm voice of reason!) My US editor Deborah Wayshak, who received the manuscript at the same time, and whose enthusiasm and perceptive comments were again all I could have wished for – between her, Rebecca and Stephanie, I really feel that I have a dream team of editors. Amy Dobson and Anna Howorth, of Usborne Publicity and Marketing respectively, whose efforts in promoting the series simply couldn't be bettered. They're also to be thanked for putting together the incredible *Angel* soundtrack (a link can be found at www.angelfever.com), which I've listened to more times than I can count. My brother and sister, Chuck Benson and Susan Lawrence, for being so thrilled over their little sister's career. Love you both! All of the friendly and helpful people my husband and I met in Mexico City when I went there for research, particularly our driver Fernando (I wish I'd gotten your surname!), who cheerfully answered all my nosy questions about life in the amazing Mexican capital. Neil Chowney, for his much-appreciated advice on motorcycle repair – if I got something wrong, it's not Neil's fault! Helen Corner, who told me one night in a London pub that Willow absolutely could NOT have shoulder-length brown hair, and that I had to give her a short, funky cut of a startling colour instead. You were totally right, hon. My fab friend Julie Cohen, for her spot-on story instincts and all the lame carbonite jokes. Composer Bear McCreary, whose music has been playing in the background almost every day that I've written this story. All of the wonderful bloggers who've taken the time to review *Angel* – thank you; it's enthusiastic readers like you who make it all worthwhile! Everyone who contributes to the *Angel* Facebook pages on both sides of the Atlantic (www.facebook.com/angel.trilogy and www.facebook.com/AngelBookTrilogy) – I love reading your comments, and also seeing your picks for the stars in a fantasy movie version of *Angel.* (Some of the picks for Alex have been SO hot; I can hardly wait to see who you suggest to play Seb!) A huge thank you as well to my followers on Twitter, for having such a passion for the series and being so eager for *Angel Fire* to come out. I can't tell you how many times a tweet from one of you has made me smile. Particular thanks goes to @MarDixon, @DarkReaders, and @EmpireofBooks. And on the subject of Twitter (my addiction to which is the fault of @Usborne, by the way!), thanks to fellow authors and Twitter-holics Zoë Marriott and Cat Clarke – both of whom have unknowingly saved my sanity at times, just by being there to tweet back and forth with for a few minutes during the day. And, to all of my readers who've loved the story and wanted more – thank you, more than I can say.

Last but absolutely not least, my husband Peter, who really could not be blamed if he wished he hadn't married a writer, but is in fact an endless source of support, encouragement, and love. Thank you, Pete. I love you. x

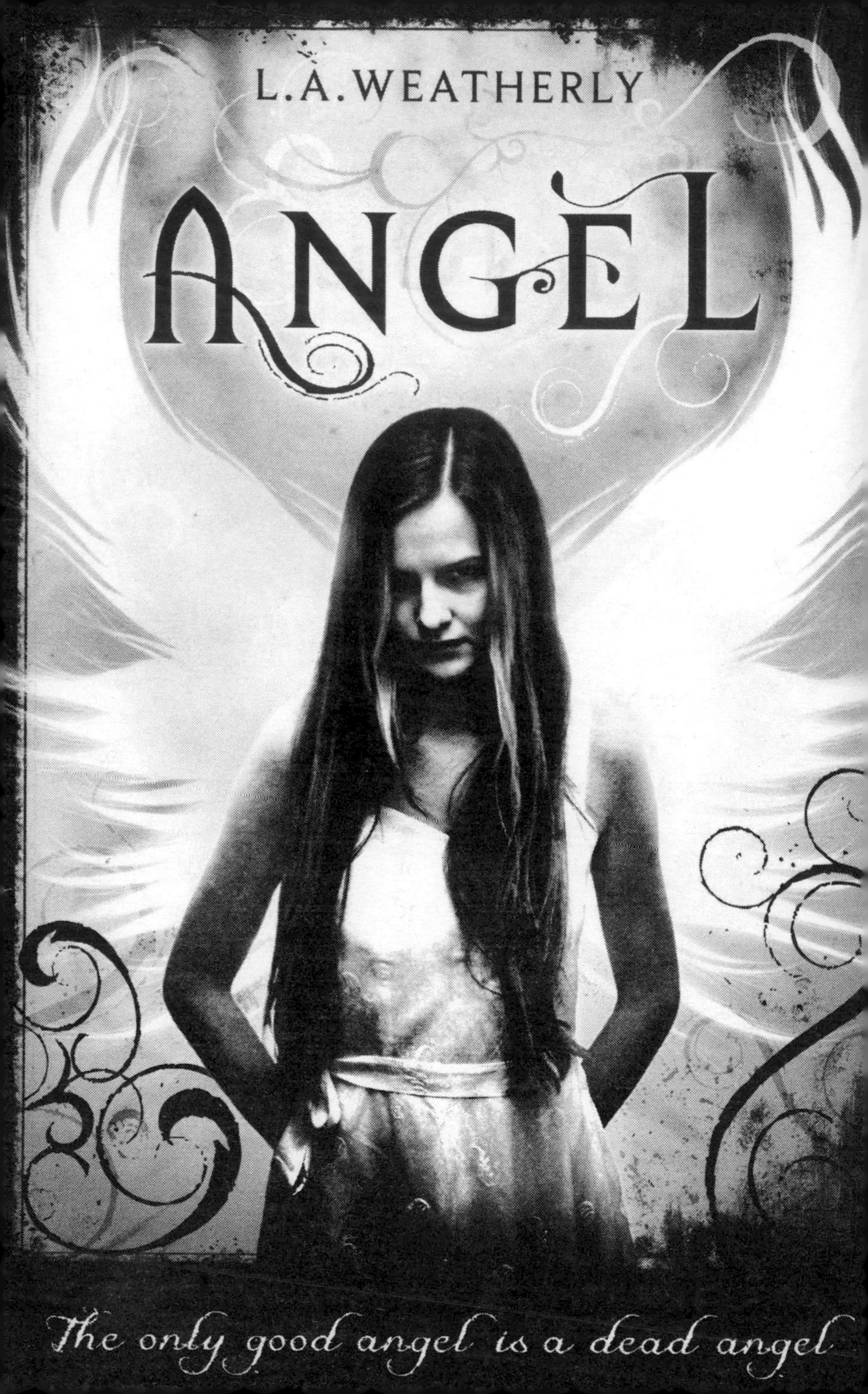
L.A. WEATHERLY
ANGEL
The only good angel is a dead angel

ANGEL

THE FIRST CAPTIVATING TALE IN
L.A. WEATHERLY'S ANGEL TRILOGY

Willow knows she's different from other girls.
And not just because she loves tinkering around with cars.
Willow has a gift. She can look into people's futures, know
their dreams, their hopes and their regrets, just by touching
them. She has no idea where she gets this power from...

But Alex does. Gorgeous, mysterious Alex knows Willow's
secret and is on a mission to stop her. The dark forces within
Willow make her dangerous – and irresistible.
In spite of himself, Alex finds he is falling in love
with his sworn enemy.

ISBN: 9781409521969

EPUB: 9781409530930

KINDLE: 9781409530947

www.angelfever.com

For more breathtaking reads, go to
www.fiction.usborne.com